PRAISE FOR DONNA GRANT'S BEST-SELLING ROMANCE NOVELS

"Grant's ability to quickly convey complicated backstory makes this jam-packed love story accessible even to new or periodic readers." *–Publishers' Weekly*

"Donna Grant has given the paranormal genre a burst of fresh air…" *–San Francisco Book Review*

"The premise is dramatic and heartbreaking; the characters are colorful and engaging; the romance is spirited and seductive." *–The Reading Cafe*

"The central romance, fueled by a hostage drama, plays out in glorious detail against a backdrop of multiple ongoing issues in the "Dark Kings" books. This seemingly penultimate installment creates a nice segue to a climactic end." *–Library Journal*

"…intense romance amid the growing war between the Dragons and the Dark Fae is scorching hot." *–Booklist*

WICKED TREASURES

Seized by Passion ~ Enticed by Ecstasy ~ Captured by Desire

Books 1-3: Wicked Treasures Box Set

HISTORICAL PARANORMAL

THE KINDRED SERIES

Everkin ~ Eversong ~ Everwylde ~ Everbound

Evernight ~ Everspell

KINDRED: THE FATED SERIES

Rage ~ Ruin ~ Reign

DARK SWORD SERIES

Dangerous Highlander ~ Forbidden Highlander

Wicked Highlander ~ Untamed Highlander

Shadow Highlander ~ Darkest Highlander

ROGUES OF SCOTLAND SERIES

The Craving ~ The Hunger ~ The Tempted ~ The Seduced

Books 1-4: Rogues of Scotland Box Set

THE SHIELDS SERIES

A Dark Guardian ~ A Kind of Magic ~ A Dark Seduction

A Forbidden Temptation ~ A Warrior's Heart

Mystic Trinity (a series connecting novel)

DRUIDS GLEN SERIES

Highland Mist ~ Highland Nights ~ Highland Dawn
Highland Fires ~ Highland Magic
Mystic Trinity (a series connecting novel)

SISTERS OF MAGIC TRILOGY

Shadow Magic ~ Echoes of Magic ~ Dangerous Magic
Books 1-3: Sisters of Magic Box Set

THE ROYAL CHRONICLES NOVELLA SERIES

Prince of Desire ~ Prince of Seduction
Prince of Love ~ Prince of Passion
Books 1-4: The Royal Chronicles Box Set
Mystic Trinity (a series connecting novel)

DARK BEGINNINGS: A FIRST IN SERIES BOXSET

Chiasson Series, Book 1: Wild Fever
LaRue Series, Book 1: Moon Kissed
The Royal Chronicles Series, Book 1: Prince of Desire

MILITARY ROMANCE / ROMANTIC SUSPENSE

SONS OF TEXAS SERIES

The Hero ~ The Protector ~ The Legend
The Defender ~ The Guardian

STILL OF THE NIGHT

SKYE DRUIDS

FIVE

NEW YORK TIMES & USA TODAY BESTSELLING AUTHOR

DONNA GRANT

CHAPTER ONE

SKYE DRUIDS

Isle of Skye

"*Come*," the forest beckoned.

Ariah ran the last few feet to the refuge of the woods, an unspeakable, unnamable fear chasing her. Only then did she pause. Only then did it seem as if she might finally shake off the dark image that had invaded her dreams.

She only truly felt peace among the towering trees. Nature was a balm for her soul. She came to the forest to meditate, cry, laugh, and just be. It had always called to her—and she had always answered. Not once had it turned its back on her. It'd never shunned her, never told her she needed to be more than she was. The woods gave unfailingly to all those in need. It was her shelter, her sanctuary.

Ariah drew in a breath and slowly released it. Gradually, the fear twisting her gut released the last of its hold. Things were off. She had known it for some time. All Druids on Skye did. There was no getting around it. The problem was that no one had figured out how to deal with the growing malevolence yet.

Or even determine where it had originated.

She walked deeper into the forest, her footsteps softened by the decaying leaves. The last vestiges of winter clung to the early morning air. Spring had arrived, but it would be weeks yet before it shook the chill completely. The sun-dappled ground marked the path before her.

Her thoughts shifted to her restless night. It had begun normally, but it wasn't long before obscure dreams with an underlying, menacing threat disturbed her sleep and woke her repeatedly. Each nightmare became progressively worse until she gave up on sleep altogether and rose. Though she had yet to shake loose the gloom that had hung over her like a pall since the first dream.

Ariah tried desperately to recall something about the nightmares, but the only thing she could say with any certainty was that something had meant her harm.

Her home was warded but that didn't mean something hadn't gotten in. She searched the house with a spell at the ready to force whatever might be there to leave. But she didn't find anything. Still, Ariah cleansed the house with sage—twice—just in case.

The forest helped to center her, but it couldn't completely dispel the gloom.

Or the knowledge that something was coming for her.

Ariah paused beside one of the tall pines and rested her hand on the rough bark. She closed her eyes and sought the calm usually within easy grasp. It was elusive this morning, remaining just out of reach.

Something brushed her leg. She looked down to find Moon at

her feet, staring up at her with big yellow eyes. The small gray cat issued a soft meow before dashing off, tail in the air. Ariah watched but didn't follow. It had been a long time since she had felt so out of sorts, and it wasn't a good experience.

She headed to the small mound amid a cluster of trees that had been her meditation spot since she was a small child. From the beginning, Druids recognized the power of nature and how being in tune with it was a harmony all should seek—though few did.

Ariah settled cross-legged atop the mound. Her eyes closed as she focused on her breath. Normally, she went easily into her meditation practice, but it took several tries before she could clear her mind. The moment she gave herself up completely, something dark and dangerous loomed over her. Hastily, she moved away, her gaze scanning the area as she shielded herself.

But nothing was there.

Just like at her house.

Birds chirped excitedly, and a squirrel barked angrily at something. A hare darted off to the side. All of it should have calmed her, but it didn't. Something had been there. It had been in her dreams, and it remained near.

Ariah swallowed and tried to rein in her pounding heart. She looked away and spotted Moon sitting on a fallen tree, her long tail swishing side to side in agitation. The cat's gaze was locked on the spot where Ariah had been sitting.

"Do you see it?" she asked.

The feline's gaze slid to her. A moment later, her tail stopped moving.

Ariah shook her head, not sure what to make of any of it. She turned and started back toward her house. Moon ran ahead of her, pausing to wait for Ariah to catch up, only to rush ahead again and repeat the process all the way home.

She opened the door, and Moon darted inside. Ariah watched the cat carefully to see how she reacted since animals saw more things than humans did. But all she wanted was food. Ariah got them both some breakfast before tying up her long hair in a scarf. Moon sat on the counter cleaning her face with a paw while Ariah gathered her things for the day. She paused and kissed the top of the cat's head.

"Stay out of trouble. I'll be back this evening," Ariah said on her way out the door.

It was a routine that had begun the first day Moon arrived on her doorstep three years before. Ariah locked the door and walked to her car. The call of a bird had her gaze searching the sky. She found the magnificent golden eagle soaring over her toward the forest. It was almost enough to dispel the events of the morning.

However, plenty lingered that made her wonder if she should share what'd happened with someone, specifically the head of the Skye Druids and her friend, Rhona. Ariah debated whether to bother the Druid leader. She had her hands full with trying to determine the evil that had invaded the isle and how to get rid of it. The last thing she needed was Ariah bothering her about some nightmares. If things got worse, she would go to Rhona. Besides, everyone had bad dreams.

When Ariah reached the road that would take her to Rhona's, she continued on. The nightmares were probably nothing more than her subconscious working things out while she slept. Ariah was worried about the state of things, just like every Druid on Skye. First, there was the mist that had killed Druids.

Thankfully, Rhona and a group of Druid warriors had caught

the one who controlled the mist. Kerry, a well-known and prominent member of the Druid community, had been the culprit. She now spent her days in prison. Though it wasn't a normal jail. This one was deep in the mountains created by Druids *for* Druids.

The few who had balked at Kerry not being given to the police to stand trial were quickly silenced when the full story of her misdeeds and the number of people she'd killed spread. Kerry was where she needed to be so as not to hurt any more people.

If only things had settled with Kerry's removal. Yet the isle was still beset by…something. Some Druids were losing their magic for seemingly no apparent reason. The Ancients were also silent. Though the Ancients—long-dead Druids—were particular about who they talked to. Even when they did deign to talk, they spoke in riddles that made things difficult to comprehend.

Ariah parked at the side of the stone building and climbed out of her car. A sea breeze brushed her cheeks, making her smile. She paused and looked around. Boats left the harbor, shops readied for the day, and people went about their lives as if nothing was afoot. Skye was a mecca for tourists, and while the busy season wasn't until summer, there were always visitors. She adjusted her purse strap on her shoulder before heading toward the entrance.

The black-and-white-striped canopy over the door read *Tea Talker*. She had painted the door a forest green. The glass panels and deep green color stood out against the gray stone construction. The shop was Ariah's pride and joy. It was everything she had dreamed about having. And while some of her blends were infused with magic for the Druid community, those without magic sold just as well. She had been approached to sell her recipes to bigger corporations for millions, but it had never been about the money.

Blending the different teas wasn't just her passion. It was also her magical gift.

She touched a leaf of one of the climbing rose plants that ran up the sides and across the top of the building. There were no blooms yet. They would come with the warmer weather. Ariah unlocked the door and entered. Her soft-soled shoes made nary a sound on the wooden floor. After she'd put her purse away in the back, she began taking down the chairs from the six tables. Nothing matched, but that was how she wanted it. A mishmash of chairs and different-sized tables, because wasn't that how life was? Few things were ever concentric and orderly. At least, not for her.

Then, she moved on to watering the plants scattered throughout the store. Some were hanging, others on shelves, still more in pots. There was also the ivy that grew along the rafters. The plants thrived in the location, mainly because the ceiling was paned glass that allowed filtered sunlight.

Ariah didn't just water the plants. She spent a few moments with each, stroking their leaves and telling them how beautiful they were. Few knew that she'd named them. Even fewer realized that each had its own personality. That was because while people saw the plant, they didn't *see* it. She did.

She was putting the cash in the register when the bell over the door chimed. Her gaze met Ruby's. Blond, blue-eyed, bubbly, and beautiful, Ruby was a favorite among the regulars. She was also a good friend.

"Morning," Ruby called happily as she sauntered in, ponytail swinging.

"Good morning," Ariah replied. If she said it enough, maybe she could will it into being.

Ruby returned a moment later, tying a short apron around her waist. "Rain is coming."

No sooner were the words out than Ariah heard the ping on the glass above. She looked up to watch the fat raindrops splatter on the roof. Ruby flipped the sign on the door to let customers know the store was open and began cleaning the wooden shelving units that displayed the hand-painted teacups, saucers, and teapots.

Ariah almost asked if Ruby had had any nightmares but decided against it at the last minute. She wasn't quite ready to talk about her night or what had occurred in the forest. So, she turned her attention to filling the customer orders that had come in during the night.

She printed the receipts for the non-magical teas and turned to the wall of jars behind her. With each she opened, she took a moment to smell the ingredients. It was a ritual of sorts, and it wasn't long before she was immersed in the work. Each order was then tied with a bright green ribbon and placed on top of their printout.

Only then did she work on the requests from the Druid community. Ariah checked the front to see Ruby filling an order for a regular while a couple of tourists shopped the teacups. Ariah slipped into the back to gather the magical ingredients.

She was in the middle of it when she saw something dark rushing toward her out of the corner of her eye. It caused her to jump back, a jar slipping from her fingers and crashing to the floor. But when Ariah looked, nothing was there.

"Are you all right?"

Her head swung to the doorway where Ruby stood staring, concern lining her face. Ariah wasn't sure she could answer. "The jar slipped," she lied.

Ruby's blue gaze dropped to the shattered glass, then moved back to Ariah. "I'll get the broom."

"It's fine. I'll take care of it."

Ruby hesitated as if she were about to say something else. Then she nodded and returned to the front.

Ariah braced her hand on the shelves next to her. Something had been there. She had seen it charge her. There hadn't been a sound, but every time she closed her eyes, she saw a mouth open in a snarl.

CHAPTER TWO

Killian adjusted his grip on the steering wheel as he drove slowly off the ferry onto Skye just as it began to rain. He swallowed hard and followed the vehicle in front of him. After merging onto the road, Killian took the curves around the isle with trepidation and anticipation. An odd mix, to be sure.

Nothing had changed.

And yet, so much had.

It felt like a lifetime since he had last been on the isle. In many ways, it had been exactly that. When he last drove the roads, he had been on top of the world. It had been the best summer of his life. He hadn't a care. No worries, no doubts. No fears. How naïve they had been—*he* had been.

The windscreen wipers diligently kept the glass clear as the drops beat fiercely upon his SUV. It kept him from catching a glimpse of buildings and the landscape, but he knew from his memories how deep a blue the water was, and how vibrant the green grass could be.

Killian kept to the roads along the coast instead of heading straight to his destination. Mainly because he was a coward. His nose wrinkled at that. His father would've denied such a thing, but it was true. He was scared. More frightened than he had ever been about anything, including standing in court in defense of his clients' livelihoods.

He found an area to pull off the road to stare through the rain-drenched windscreen to the brooding Cuillin Mountains. Locals called this range the Black Cuillins because of the dark color of the rock. Killian dropped his gaze. His mood matched the weather. Maybe it was a sign that it had begun to rain the moment he drove onto Skye. Or perhaps he was being superstitious. There was no way the weather cared about mood, much less one person in billions. Killian shook his head and pulled back onto the road.

His drive took him through one village and then another. He passed cottages dotting the landscape. Some near the coast, some higher up in the hills. He drove around lochs and past waterfalls. It was the same, yet different. Each time he attempted to head toward his destination, something held him back. Finally, he gave up and made his way to the B&B where he had rented a room.

His mobile rang from its place in the cupholder. Killian ignored it, not even bothering to look down. He knew it was his father. Killian kept his focus on the road. The problem was, Killian wanted something he couldn't have. Yet a last teensy bit of hope had sent him toward Skye the night before. One way or another, he would find the answer to the question he didn't dare speak aloud—not even to himself.

The ringing finally stopped, only to start again a moment later. Killian reached over and silenced it. He would talk to his father eventually, but not yet. Brian Flanagan had a very narrow view of the world, and few things could alter it. Killian didn't want to waste his time explaining—for a third time—only for the conversation to end in another argument. His father could wait.

Everyone could wait.

For the first time, Killian was doing what *he* wanted.

That thought brought a flood of memories from that long-ago summer, and with them, the soft, Scottish words, *"It's your life. You get to make your own decisions."*

He had brushed off her words then. If only he had listened. How different the last nine years would've been... The only time he had done what he wanted was that summer. For as long as he could remember, his life had been planned for him. Where he went to school, university, his job, and even when he was expected to marry, along with *who* he was to take as his bride.

The tires of his vehicle crunched over the B&B's pebble-lined drive. The house was as charming as one would expect from such a location, but he didn't care about that. It was the first one that'd come up on his search, and he had booked it without looking at any others. Plus, it was close to the location where he would head next.

Killian climbed out, pulling the collar of his coat up in a vain attempt to keep the rain away, then got his luggage from the back of the vehicle and walked to the door. He shook himself off under the awning before entering. A friendly woman and her wife greeted him. He spent a few moments exchanging pleasantries while being checked in, but once he had the key, he promptly made his way up the stairs to the second floor.

He barely noticed the floral wallpaper, the light green bedspread, or the throw pillows when he dropped his luggage near the bed and walked to the large window. Trails of water mixed with drops on the glass, giving him a rain-soaked view of Skye. Melancholic gray clouds covered the expanse in every direction and hid the sun and blue skies. Killian quite liked the weather. He'd always had an affinity for storms, especially those involving thunder and lightning. But any storm would do.

He sank onto the chair next to the window and continued his perusal of the landscape. There was a small sliver of blue from one of the lochs he had driven past. Had he swum in those waters? It seemed they had always been swimming that summer. Swimming and loving, laughing and talking.

The sun had never been brighter. The storms never so fierce. Life had never been so vibrant and beautiful.

Love never so abundant.

Killian blew out a breath as he stood and pulled out his laptop. He set it aside on the bed, searching for the stack of papers he had put with it. He found them and carefully folded them to stuff into the inside pocket of his coat. He paused, trying to decide whether to remain in the room with his memories or dare to face the past.

He swiped his keys from the bed and strode out of the room, the B&B, and into the storm. Once he was behind the wheel, he started the engine, only to hesitate again. Rain pelted the windscreen with fat drops. He'd left his mobile in the cupholder of the vehicle. The screen lit up with another call. Killian flipped the phone around and put the SUV in reverse.

His stomach didn't churn as it had when he'd first driven onto the isle. After pulling onto the road, he took the long route to town. Funny how he still knew where everything was after so many years. Truth be told, he hadn't wanted to leave that summer. Who would? No matter where he went, who he was with, or how much money he spent, no holiday had ever compared to his summer on Skye.

But it hadn't been the location or his travel companion. It had been *her*.

It had always been her.

The fast *whoop-whomp* of the wipers matched the pounding of his heart the closer he came to town. He stopped to allow someone to dash across the road to their car, then stopped again when it looked as if a family were thinking of making a run from the cover of a shop to their vehicle. They decided against it, which meant Killian had to keep driving.

He saw the black-and-white-striped awning before he reached it. Like a giant, flashing arrow pointing to the building from above. Killian parked but didn't get out. The Tea Talker was busy, even with the weather. He rested his hand on the Audi's door handle, ready to open it as his gaze locked on the entrance. Whenever it opened, he sought a glimpse inside in the hopes he might see her. Killian thought he spotted someone with dark hair at the same instant the wipers swiped across his view. Then the shop door closed.

If he wanted to see Ariah, he would have to go inside. But to do so would be to face her and the terrible words he had spoken so long ago. It was the reason he had come to the isle, but it proved a lot easier said than done. He should've spent time thinking about what he wanted to say during his eleven-hour drive. Instead, all he had been able to do was think about their summer together and how he wished to turn back time and change his decisions. Take back his words.

Ariah would listen to what he had to say. That was the kind of person she was. She wasn't one to lash out or retaliate. Ever. Her grace and compassion weren't weaknesses nor limitations as he had once thought. They were her strength and power.

His hand fell from the door. What would he say to her? What *could* he say that might allow her to forgive him besides: *I'm sorry.* That didn't seem like enough. It wasn't.

He was sure she would forgive him for the simple reason that she knew he wanted it. But would it heal what he had done? She might not even want him anymore. Ariah had never been one to follow others. She didn't stay on a path. She wandered and rambled, creating her own course.

His father called her a free spirit. Brian couldn't understand anyone who didn't follow guidelines. Maybe that was why Killian had found Ariah so appealing. Their chemistry had been undeniable—like magnets unable to stay apart. They had met his first day on Skye and were inseparable afterward.

Killian wanted to be a part of Ariah's life. He'd had the chance once. Would she give him another? He didn't deserve it, but maybe if he proved that he wasn't the same man he was then, she might open her heart to him again. He would do whatever he had to, try for however long it took.

But first, he had to see her.

He looked at his mobile. He could call her. He had nearly done just that so many times over the years. On several occasions, he had punched in her number but hadn't been able to hit *call*. Fear of being rebuffed kept him from doing it. It was the same anxiety that'd brought him to Skye. Nothing like being rejected face-to-face.

Killian chuckled to himself, shut off the engine, then climbed out of the Audi and forced his legs to move. He was soaked before he reached the awning. His hand pushed open the dark green door before he changed his mind. He stopped short the moment his feet touched the narrow-planked wood floor that ran in diagonals.

If any place was the epitome of Ariah, it was the Tea Talker. The store *was* Ariah, from the soothing, eclectic décor to the numerous plants.

"Welcome," said a blonde in a green apron as she walked past.

Killian let the door close behind him and scanned the interior while searching for Ariah.

"You look soaked through. I can take your coat and hang it up if you'd like."

He belatedly realized the blonde was speaking to him. He shrugged out of his coat and handed it to her. "Thanks."

"Take any table. The best is over in that corner."

He followed her finger to see a two-seat table tucked between a wall of glass and a wall of plants. It did look inviting. Now that he was here, he never wanted to leave. Everything about the shop was inviting and alluring.

"First time?"

"Aye."

Her smile widened. "It won't be your last. I'm Ruby. I'll be by in a moment to get your order. You can see a list of teas near the register."

Ruby walked away while Killian headed to the table. His gaze was drawn again and again to the wall of glass jars behind the wooden counter and the old-fashioned cash register. But where was Ariah?

As if his thoughts had made her materialize, she came from the back, holding a bag. He stood frozen, afraid to move or speak. Ariah was unchanged from when he had last seen her, as if time had stood still for her. But he knew every inch of her heart-shaped face and delicate features, particularly the dusting of freckles across her nose and cheeks. He knew the suppleness of her lips, the way her golden-brown eyes could ensnare him with a single look. He knew the softness of her creamy complexion.

He knew the wild abandon with which she loved.

His fingers itched to tug away the scarf holding the lengths of her dark locks to see it cascade down her back. Was it as long as it used to be? Longer? Gold earrings with stars and a crescent moon dangled from her lobes. The swells of her breasts were outlined by the maroon shirt she wore with its long bell sleeves and low neckline. He spotted bracelets on her wrists. A leather belt revealed her narrow waist as her vibrant Bohemian skirt flared and hung nearly to the floor, giving just a glimpse of brown boots.

The mere sight of her took his breath away. Just as it had the day he'd met her. Just as she always would.

He had one chance to make things right, one opportunity to have the future he had so recklessly and thoughtlessly thrown away.

CHAPTER THREE

SKYE DRUIDS

Ariah had no time to think about the episode in the back. She was happy to have her mind forced onto something else since she had been consumed by thoughts of whatever had been happening to her since the wee hours of the morning.

After she'd cleaned up the broken glass and spilled contents, she finished the order. She had just tied the ribbon when the computer screen in the back showed a last-minute rush order. She saw it was from Theo's account, and by the order, someone wasn't feeling well.

Ariah grabbed a jar and scooped the loose-leaf ginger blend into a packet, adding an extra serving. She included a package of peppermint and a few other blends that would help to calm an upset stomach, all with magic. She walked from the back just as Theo came through the shop door, looking haggard and sleep deprived. Out of the corner of her eye, Ariah saw someone sitting at the back table.

"Thank you," Theo said with a relieved smile as he approached.

"I've been up all night with Ferne. We think it was something she ate, but if this doesna ease her suffering, I'm forcing her to seek help."

By *help*, Theo meant the Healers. They were the last resort for some Druids, and cases where a Druid didn't want to—or couldn't—explain how they'd been injured to the authorities. Skye might be home to the largest segment of Druids in the world, but they still hid much of themselves.

Ariah handed Theo the bag of teas. "I added a few extras. The ginger can be a bit much for some, so if that doesn't work, one of the others should."

"Anything so Ferne gets better." He held out a small white paper bag. "I was ordered no' to come without this."

Ariah smelled the delicious strawberry scone through the bag. "You didn't need to do that."

"You know Ferne."

"I do." Ariah accepted the bag with a smile. "Don't hesitate to call if you need something more. I can run it by if need be."

Theo ran a hand through his dark brown hair. "Want to tell me what's wrong?"

"Nothing."

His brown eyes studied her. "You sure? You doona seem quite yourself."

Ariah glanced to the side and quickly shook her head, still not ready to share anything. "I'm fine."

Theo's gaze grew intense. "You know my job as a detective inspector is to read people and determine when they're lying, right?"

"Of course."

"You're a bad liar, Ariah."

She turned to look at the register over her shoulder and make sure no one was waiting to check out. Then she met Theo's unwavering gaze.

"Look, if you doona want to talk to me, that's fine."

It was on the tip of her tongue to tell him, but Theo didn't have time to listen. He needed to return home to Ferne. "I'm just a little off. I'll get it sorted."

"You're never off," he said, his brow furrowed. "Did something happen? Something with…?" He waved his hand to indicate Skye and the issues that had been occurring.

"Nay. Maybe. I don't know," she said with an irritated sigh. "It's nothing."

"I'm here if you wish to talk. I'm sure Ferne will be feeling better soon after your teas. I'll have her call you. At the verra least, contact Rhona. Let her determine if it's nothing or no'."

Ariah didn't like the idea of being a burden. "I'm sure it's nothing."

"You're probably right. But we can no' take any chances. No' with how things have…progressed," he said in a tight voice.

She gave him a smile and squeezed his arm. "Always thinking of others. It's what makes you such a good friend. Now, get to Ferne with those teas. The sooner she can get it into her stomach, the sooner she'll begin to feel better."

"Aye. Doona think I will forget our conversation. I'll be back," Theo said with a grin. He shoved some money into her hand and walked out.

Ariah watched him for a moment, his words lingering in her head. She turned on her heel and put the money in the register. As soon as she was there, it seemed every customer was lined up to be checked out.

Carefully, she wrapped a teapot with four cups and saucers for a tourist and placed it in one of the brown bags with a green bow. Once the transaction was completed, she was able to take a breath. She took that moment to walk around the shop and check on customers. Ruby kept everyone happy with her cheery smile and prompt attention.

Ariah finished with table five and turned to the customer in the corner when her gaze collided with olive-green eyes. Her heart skipped a beat, and shock ran through her, rendering her immobile when she realized she was staring at none other than Killian Flanagan. The man who had obliterated her heart.

There was no doubt it was him. He had filled out, replacing the handsome face with rugged, sculpted lines that made her traitorous body ache with longing.

He wore his blond waves longer on top now with the sides neatly trimmed. There was the start of lines around his deep-set eyes. She didn't need to get close to know the color of his eyes was a pale olive with a deep green circling the iris. She had stared into those eyes for so long that the memory of them would never be shaken loose. A shadow of a beard graced the hard line of his jaw and chin. She didn't allow her eyes to linger on his wide lips for too long lest she remember how easily he had once wrung orgasms from her with his mouth. A sky-blue Henley hugged wide, muscular shoulders while his arms stretched the material, showcasing thick sinew.

Nine years ago, he had been handsome, a young man just coming into his own. Now, he was all male. Utterly commanding. Wholly masculine.

Unreservedly confident.

And she hated that he could still cause such feelings within her.

She wanted to walk away and pretend that she hadn't seen him. But he was a customer. So, she swallowed what little pride she had left and walked to him on legs that threatened to give out at any moment.

"Hi," he said, his tempting lips curving into the crooked smile that used to make her melt. Damn, if it didn't still have some power over her. "It's good to see you."

The polite thing to do would be to at least say *hello*, but she couldn't muster even that. The sound of his Irish accent flooded her with emotions that threatened to choke her. The memory of their very first meeting flashed in her mind, him wearing that same charming smile. It had won her over then. It wouldn't now.

His thick-lashed gaze darted around. "This place is amazing. It's everything you once described. You did it, Ariah. I'm happy for you."

Her mouth was dry, leaving her unable to even swallow. What was he doing here? Why had he returned to Skye? He should've given her some warning.

Killian cleared his throat and glanced nervously at his mug. "You didn't expect to see me again. I shouldn't have just shown up. I, ah, I have no right to ask, but can I talk to you?"

"Isn't that what you're doing now?"

He swallowed, his Adam's apple bobbing. "I am. Will you sit?" he asked, motioning to the chair across from him.

Ariah didn't look away. It was all she could do to remain standing. Her blood rushed in her ears, and her stomach churned with worry—and, aye, even a smidge of elation that Killian was back. He was the only man she had ever loved. The one she had thought to spend her life with.

A man who had cleaved her heart in two.

She couldn't go down that road again. Being near him was a reminder of how deeply she had loved him, only to be found lacking. She had barely survived last time. It had taken everything she had to pick up the pieces and get on with her life. "I'm working."

"Tell me a time. I'll be here. Or wherever you wish," he said, anticipation filling his expression.

"I don't think that's a good idea."

His lips compressed as he wound his hands around the stoneware mug. "I don't blame you for being cautious. I deserve that and more. But there are some things I'd like to say. Please."

"I don't think so."

"I want to apologize."

"Do it in an email. It's on my website. I might read it," she said and walked away.

She made it to the back room and the sofa before her legs gave out. She collapsed onto the cushions, her heart thudding against her ribs. It wasn't her way to intentionally hurt anyone, but Killian still held sway over her. That could be perilous. Her only course of action was to set firm boundaries. Once he realized she wouldn't talk, he'd return to Ireland and his family and let her get back to her life.

Ariah leaned forward and put her head in her hands. One look. That was all it had taken to be transported to that summer when she had fallen head over heels for a man she'd believed loved her in return.

Her head snapped up when something touched her arm. She found Ruby beside her.

"He's gone," she said as she squatted before Ariah.

She nodded and looked away. "Good."

"Do you want me to keep him out?"

She smiled as she met Ruby's blue eyes. "He won't be back."

"I'm not so sure. You didn't see the way he watched you leave."

"I have no idea what brought Killian to Skye, but if there's one thing I know for sure, it's that he'll return to his family."

Ruby nodded slowly. "Why don't you head home? I can handle things here."

"Thanks, but I'm fine."

"You've been saying that a lot this morning. Somehow, I don't believe you." Ruby straightened. "The offer stands."

Ariah leaned back on the cushions. "I'm really glad you applied to work here."

"I'm really glad you hired me." She gave Ariah a wink before going back to the customers.

Ariah rose and walked to the long wooden table and the white bowls on it. She had to get her mind off Killian and the past. Only sadness and regret lay there. It didn't do her any good to return to it.

She picked up one jar and then another. Ariah began a new blend for the Druid community. Doing this was usually a source of joy and excitement, but now, she kept seeing olive-green eyes. No matter how many times she shook her head to dislodge Killian's face, he kept reappearing in her mind's eye.

And with his image came the memories.

The laughter, the love. And the heartache. She had grieved for their lost relationship, for what would never be, and had done so for years until she finally—carefully and purposefully—released him. That was the only way she could move on and continue living. Something would remind her of that summer or him a few times a year. She never shied away when that happened. She let herself remember the good times with fondness and a smile before letting it go once more.

Killian was more than just a memory now. He was a flesh-and-blood body looking more handsome than he had any right to.

And she had no intention of letting him close again.

CHAPTER FOUR

Killian gripped his coat tightly as he stepped out of the building. Water dripped from the awning onto the pavement while a fine mist of rain blanketed everything else. He clenched his jaw and paused. Nothing had gone as planned.

After he had made his way to the table and Ruby took his order, he hadn't been able to tear his gaze away from Ariah and the man she spoke with. One look at her long, slim fingers transported him back to that summer when she had threaded her hand with his as they strolled along the beach beneath the full moon, the waves crashing against their feet. Her eyes had sparkled as brightly as the stars, and as beautiful as she had been, it was the love he saw in her face that he remembered.

Killian had been lost in the memory when Ariah turned to him. Dread churned in his stomach when her smile melted away. The moment she stood before him, his mind had gone blank. All he'd wanted to do was hold her, feel her body against his.

He had said the first thing that'd come to mind. Everything

after that was wrong. He knew it yet couldn't stop himself. Desperation kept him talking, which only pushed her further away.

Now, here he was.

"Great work, Killian," he muttered to himself as he walked to the Audi.

He tossed his coat onto the passenger seat and climbed inside. Calmly, he started the engine and adjusted the heater to remove the chill. Then his gaze lifted to the store. He relived every achingly awful exchange of words.

"Goddammit!" he bellowed, slamming his hand on the steering wheel.

Killian closed his eyes and took a deep breath. Getting angry wouldn't help. Nor was he ready to give up. He would think of another way to talk to Ariah. He wanted to say his piece in person because he felt he owed her that. Sure, a letter or email would've been easier, but there was also the chance that she would never read it. He needed to know that she heard him. It was more than just an apology, though he owed her that in spades.

He put the SUV into drive before he did something stupid like go back inside. Ariah needed time. So did he. The next time he saw her, he would have a better plan. He would have his words ready instead of a blank head and an open heart.

Killian drove slowly through town. He spotted a co-op and pulled into the lot. He wasn't sure what he was looking for, but it wasn't as if he had any clients. And he didn't want to return to the B&B and his empty room. He entered the building and meandered through the aisles.

He found paper and envelopes, but he didn't pick them up. Would it be better to write her a letter? He could get his words out succinctly instead of rambling. Her facial expressions wouldn't alter his words, either. It would allow him to write several drafts before creating the final document. Then again, he could do that on his computer. But an email seemed so impersonal. So did printing out a typed letter. If he was going to explain his return to Skye in any type of written communication, it would be in his own handwriting.

Yet he still didn't pick up the items.

"Having trouble?"

His head turned to the side to find a woman with shoulder-length light-brown hair with hints of red. Pale-green eyes looked up at him, waiting. "Uh…just thinking."

"Unfortunately, we don't have a large selection of any particular item. We make up for it by having a bit of everything," she said with a warm smile.

Killian forced a grin. "Sometimes, there are too many choices."

"I've never heard anyone say that. Especially here. Are you visiting our beautiful isle?"

"Aye."

"Your first time?"

Killian shook his head and looked back at the paper. "It's been a few years, though."

"There's another Irishman around. You might run into Finn while you're here."

He nodded, unsure what to say.

"I'll leave you to it, then. I'm Kirsi if you need anything. And if you're looking for just a few sheets of paper, don't buy that. I'll give you what you need."

Killian looked at her and smiled. "Thanks. I'll think about it."

Once he was alone again, he continued perusing the shelves.

Kirsi was right. They did have just about everything. He ended up back in front of the paper as the door opened, and someone entered. Killian was thankful that Kirsi would be focused on someone else instead of seeing him standing in the same place as before, still undecided.

The door opened several more times, proving the co-op was a busy place. He heard voices but tuned everyone out. He had no idea how long he stood there before he sensed a presence. Somehow, he wasn't surprised to find Kirsi standing there again.

"Take this," she said, holding out a notebook and pen.

Killian found himself reaching for it before realizing what he was doing.

"This way, you aren't committing to a purchase. If you need to write something, you have it. Maybe then you'll decide you need the stationery set. Or you won't. But I think you need this."

He blinked down at the beige cover with a black-and-white moth. Was he that obvious? "Thanks."

"It's no big deal. I buy entirely too many notebooks. Trust me, I won't miss one."

He tucked the notebook and attached pen against him. "I appreciate it." He held out his hand. "I'm Killian."

"Nice to meet you," she said and shook with him.

Killian tapped the pad. "I'll return it."

"It's yours for however long you need it." With that, she turned and walked back to the counter.

He left the store and started toward his vehicle. Still, he didn't wish to return to the B&B. Killian slowly moved his gaze around. The moment he spotted the sign for the pub, he headed there. It wasn't until he sat in a booth that he realized he still had the notebook in his hand. After ordering a pint, he laid the pad on the table in front of him.

Killian opened it to the first page and started writing. He poured his heart out, crossing out words and scribbling notes in the margins when he thought of something else. When he finished, he had five pages, front and back.

He ordered another drink and turned the page. This time, when he began writing, he realized it was in journal form. And he had a lot to say. Pages and pages. His hand cramped several times, forcing him to pause. The writing was illegible, but he knew the words. He knew the hurt, anger, and frustration he poured onto the pages. It was a lifetime's worth, but it wasn't just the pain focused on his father and family. It was at himself, too. Ultimately, the decisions had been his.

He'd had the power to refuse or take another path. He hadn't.

Not until now.

When there were no more words, he closed the notebook and tucked the pen into its place. He looked outside to see that night had fallen. His stomach growled in hunger. Killian ordered some food. As he ate, he tried to organize the haphazard thoughts he'd originally written to Ariah. He still wished to speak to her, but if he could only reach her through a letter, then he would do it.

He finished and paid his tab, swiping up the notebook as he got to his feet. The night sky was clear, and the air chilly as he walked to his vehicle. He had just dropped the notebook inside when the sound of crashing waves caught his attention. A stroll was just what he needed. Killian put on his coat and locked the SUV before making his way to the water.

The stars winked above him as he got as close to the waves as he dared without getting wet. He hadn't gone far when he spotted someone sitting on some rocks. Killian continued toward him, but the man didn't seem to notice until Killian was nearly upon him. The guy nodded in greeting. Killian did the same and kept walking.

It wasn't until he turned around and retraced his steps that Killian saw the man duck out of sight as two women shouted for someone named Callum. Killian decided to take pity on the guy.

"There's no one out here but me," he told the women.

They huffed and walked away.

"They're gone," he said when he drew closer to the rocks.

Who Killian presumed was Callum peered over the boulder before taking his seat once more. "Appreciate that."

"It's rare for a man to turn down two women."

"You wouldna say that if you knew them."

Killian chuckled. "We've all had an ex who wouldn't take a hint."

"I didna date either of them. They're…well, it's a long story."

"I have one of those, too. It's the reason I'm here."

Callum motioned to the rocks with his head. "This is a good place to sit and think, if you've a mind to."

"It's direction I need." Killian sat, leaving distance between them. He glanced at Callum to find his long, pale-brown hair tied back and a visible wound on the side of his face. "Tell me that isn't from those girls."

"It isna."

Killian took the hint when Callum didn't elaborate. Killian looked out at the dark water as it ebbed and flowed.

"There is a lass."

Killian looked at Callum, surprised he had spoken. "Is she the reason you're out here thinking?"

"We're no' together."

"Is she not interested?"

"If you were from the isle, you'd understand why there can never be anything between us. I wouldna do that to her."

Killian frowned at that. "Then leave. Go somewhere no one knows you."

"If only I could."

"Trust me when I say not to let family make your decisions. It'll ruin any happiness you might have."

Callum's gaze lowered to his hands as he leaned his forearms on his knees. "I'm tied to this place in ways you can no' understand. If I could leave, I'd do it in a heartbeat and never look back."

"I let the ties to my family dictate my life. It's why I'm back. Though my attempt to make up for past mistakes has gone very badly so far. But I'm hoping to repair what I destroyed. She's worth it. She was worth it then, but I foolishly believed she needed to leave Skye and see the world in order to achieve anything. I fell in love with this place years ago. But it wasn't just the isle that stole my heart. She did, too."

"What happened?"

He scratched his forehead as he felt Callum's gaze on him. "I came with a friend from uni for the summer. He spoke about Skye so often that I had to see it. Those months were…" Killian paused, trying to find a word that would encompass the happiness, joy, laughter, and perfection of it all. "They were bliss. But, like all things, it came to an end. I wasn't ready for things to end, but I couldn't stay. I had to return to uni. Stupidly, I assumed she would come with me. After all, I planned to be the man who showed her the world and opened her eyes to all the possibilities she'd never find on Skye."

"Did you convince her to go?"

Killian turned his head and met Callum's eyes. "I did not. She refused to leave. We spent the next semester in a long-distance relationship. But I hated it. It took me the entirety of that semester to even get her to agree to visit England. I was shocked to learn she had never been out of Scotland."

Callum grunted. "I'm no'. You obviously doona know this community."

"Obviously." Killian drew in a deep breath and released it as he looked at the waves. "When she arrived, I was sure things would go my way. We were good together. The kind of good you know you'll never find again. She stayed for almost two weeks, and I knew I wouldn't be able to part with her again. We were meant to be together."

"On your terms."

He slowly nodded. "I hate to admit it, but aye. My father had already planned out my future. Get my degree and return to Dublin to work at the family law firm. It was what they expected the moment I was conceived. Even though it wasn't what I wanted, I didn't dream of going my own way. So, I laid out my plans. I even said she would never have to return to Skye again. That I could have someone box up all her things so she could remain with me from then on out."

Killian looked up. "We stood under a sky just like this. Clear and cool. She didn't yell or scream or tell me I was a wanker or controlling or any number of other insults she could have. She simply said she had no intention of ever leaving her home." He swallowed past the regret. "It kills me to know I acted like my father that night when I refused to hear what she had to say. I told her that was a stupid idea. That the only chance she had to make something of herself was to get away. I told her she had no idea what existed out in the world because she had never dared to see it. Do you know what she said?"

"What?"

"That she wasn't the one who didn't see the world. I was. Yet I still didn't hear her. I told her she could either come with me to Ireland or we were done because my life was there. I was losing her, and I knew it, so I held on tighter, my voice rising with every word. She stood there crying, taking everything I said. Then, she wished me well in life and walked away."

Callum blew out a breath. "Bloody hell."

"Aye."

"I hope y—"

His words cut off. Killian looked over to see Callum's gaze behind him on the road. Killian turned to see what had gotten his attention.

"Is that…?" Callum began.

"Ariah," Killian finished as he jumped up and rushed toward her, where she walked down the middle of the road.

Callum was right on his heels, but Killian held out his hands to halt him when they caught up with her. She stared straight ahead, seemingly seeing nothing. Callum looked at her feet to see them bare and covered in wet grass and dirt.

"What the shite?" Callum whispered.

Killian shrugged and continued to follow Ariah. Callum came up on her other side. The road was deserted, but Killian kept an eye out just in case.

"Has she done this before?" he asked softly.

Callum shrugged helplessly. "No' that I know of."

Ariah suddenly turned and headed to the co-op.

"Shite," Callum murmured under his breath.

Ariah stopped at the door and grabbed the handle, jerking it so hard the door rattled loudly. A light above flicked on.

"Stay with her. I'll be back," Callum said.

Killian had no intention of leaving Ariah. He thought she might be sleepwalking, and he knew never to wake someone in such a state, but that didn't leave him many options. Callum returned with Kirsi a moment later, keys rattling in the woman's hand. She was attempting to get one in the lock to open it when Ariah gave a final shove, pushing the door open.

"That isna good," Callum said.

Ariah went inside, and Killian followed with Kirsi and Callum directly behind him. Ariah stopped in the middle of the store. Killian moved to stand before her. She looked right through him. Then she turned to the right and went to one of the cold units in the back, pulling out milk and drinking from the carton.

Killian watched her blink slowly. Through the light from the cooler, he saw her gradually come back to herself. It wasn't long before her gaze slid to him.

"What are you doing in my house?" she demanded.

Killian fisted his hands so he wouldn't touch her. "We're not at your place."

CHAPTER FIVE

Ariah's brow furrowed as she looked at Killian, her confusion intensifying. What did Killian mean, she wasn't at home? Where else would she be? Her gaze moved past him to the aisle of merchandise, then to the cooler before her. Recognition slammed into her. She wasn't standing at her fridge, she was in the co-op. She looked down at her hand with the opened carton. She hated milk. Her stomach turned when she realized she could still taste it on her tongue.

She turned and spotted Callum and Kirsi standing together, wearing matching expressions of concern. Ariah shook her head, panic setting in when she couldn't draw up memories of leaving her home. "I don't remember driving here."

"You didna," Callum said, looking pointedly down.

Ariah dropped her gaze and saw the state of her feet. Immediately, pain exploded up her legs from the briars lodged in the soles. Callum caught the milk when it slipped from her fingers as she doubled over.

"It's okay," Killian said in a soothing voice, lifting her into his arms. "I've got you."

Ariah didn't want to be in Killian's arms, but she welcomed his warmth and strong, steady hold. Her mind was a whirlwind of puzzlement and pain that made it impossible to think straight.

Kirsi motioned for them to follow her and headed to the counter, flipping on some lights as she went. "Callum, grab some antiseptic wash and one of the towels."

Ariah shivered so violently that her teeth knocked together. Killian gently set her on the counter and shrugged out of his coat before draping it around her shoulders. She stuck her arms into the sleeves and hugged them against her, his scent and warmth cocooning her. And if it gave her a measure of relief, no one needed to know but her.

Killian knelt, one knee on the floor, carefully taking one of her feet in his hands. Ariah hissed at the contact. Olive eyes briefly lifted to meet her gaze before he returned his attention to her wounds. Kirsi held a torch so the guys could see Ariah's feet better.

She looked at the top of Killian's head bent over her foot, noticing the windblown blond locks. She braced herself for the pain, but he was gentle. So very gentle. It reminded her of how much she had missed being in his arms. How much she had missed *him.*

She didn't want to think about Killian or why he had returned now. With so many other things to analyze, she shifted her thoughts. Why had she come into town? Why didn't she have any memories after climbing into bed? Why had she walked? Had it been the dark figure she'd seen in her nightmares, the one that had plagued her during the day?

There were no answers. And that scared her.

Even with Killian's coat, Ariah couldn't seem to get warm. She had stopped shaking, at least. The co-op was quiet, the silence broken only by the sounds of Killian and Callum working on her feet.

Ariah pulled her attention from Killian's head and looked around. Her gaze halted on the sight of the forcibly opened door. Who had done that? Had it been her? It couldn't have been. Could it?

Questions would be asked. Things Ariah wished she could answer. She replayed her evening in her head, searching for anything that might give her pause. She had fought rest for as long as she could, hoping to be so exhausted that she'd sleep through the night. That and some tea to help her drift off had given her exactly what she wanted.

Or had it?

Ariah gasped in pain as Killian pulled a long sticker from the ball of her foot. Her gaze met his. His brow was furrowed, his expression filled with worry and unease. No doubt, he wondered how she had walked with something like that embedded in her foot. She pondered the same question.

It seemed like an eternity before both feet were finally cleaned and bandaged. The adrenaline had subsided long ago, leaving her dazed and antsy. She immediately turned to Kirsi. "I'm so sorry. I don't know what happened, but I'll pay for any damage."

"Don't worry about it," Kirsi said, rubbing a hand on Ariah's arm. "I'm just glad you aren't seriously hurt."

"I'll take you home," Killian said.

Ariah found herself looking into his olive-green eyes.

"No' alone," Callum said. "You seem like a decent fella, but we doona know you, mate."

"Fair enough." Killian pulled keys from his pocket and tossed them to Callum. "Drive my vehicle. It's the black Audi Q3 on the street."

Callum was out the door a moment later. Killian went to the door and did his best to fix it so it would close and lock. He managed to get it done, but the door would still need to be replaced. Ariah had an uncomfortable feeling that she was somehow responsible for that. Yet it didn't make sense. She didn't have the strength to force open a door like that.

Headlights approached. As soon as Killian saw it was his vehicle, he gathered Ariah against him. She wound her arm around his shoulder on instinct and then regretted it immediately. It was too easy to be around him. How could it not be when she still carried so much love for him? But she knew how it would end. She didn't want him here tending to her, but she also couldn't send him away. Even she wasn't too proud to admit that she was glad for his cool head and quick thinking.

Callum was getting out of the driver's seat when they approached. Killian motioned for him to remain, then set her in the back seat and pressed a button that turned on the seat heaters. She sank into the warmth while her gaze watched Killian walk around the SUV and climb into the seat next to her. Callum shot a glance at Kirsi over his shoulder before driving off.

"Are you okay?" Killian asked.

Ariah shrugged and looked out the window. She was far from all right. "Hard to say."

"Have you ever sleepwalked before?"

Callum watched her in the rearview mirror, seemingly waiting for her reply. She glanced at Killian and shook her head. "Never."

"Something made you walk over three miles from your home

to the co-op. Do you remember anything from earlier this evening?"

Though she had anticipated these questions, they still irritated her. Mostly because she didn't have clear answers. "I got home, fixed dinner, watched the telly, and went to bed."

"You're leaving something out."

She swung her head to Killian, ready to deny it, but he wasn't looking at her. Callum, however, met her gaze in the rearview mirror. It was clear that he agreed with Killian. She couldn't even be angry at them because she had, indeed, left something out. Ariah looked at Killian once more. He wasn't one of them. He had no idea who she really was. She had kept it from him that summer, and when she had been ready to share everything, their relationship had ended.

He was an outsider. Magicless. Sharing her secrets or things about the Druid community wouldn't do any good. Not when a struggle for Skye was ongoing. Then there was the fact that Killian's family held sway over him. He would return to them.

"It's nothing," she finally answered. "I didn't sleep well last night and wanted to be sure I slept through the night this time."

"Did you take something?" Killian asked.

Callum slowed the Audi to take the turn to her home. "Did you have tea?"

She gazed out the window at the dark shapes the few porchlights and headlights didn't reach. "Nay, I didn't take anything. I did drink some tea. A blend to help with ni—" She stopped before she finished the word, but it was too late.

"Nightmares? Is that what you were about to say?" Killian probed.

She felt his eyes on her and met his gaze. "Aye."

CHAPTER SIX

Killian sensed Ariah and Callum knew some secret they weren't sharing. He didn't like it, but he was an outsider. The way Ariah had stopped short of saying "*nightmares*" troubled him. Why not say the word? Everyone had bad dreams.

The SUV drew to a halt. Callum had it in park, the engine off, and was out the door to Ariah's cottage in a blink. Killian walked around the vehicle to get Ariah. She had the door open and was about to step out when he reached her. It might be the last chance he ever got to hold her. To feel her softness against his. To believe, even for a second, that he could mend what he had so callously destroyed.

"Please," he said. "Let me."

She hesitated before giving him a reluctant nod.

It cut Killian to know she would rather walk on injured feet than have him touch her. It was a reminder of the damage he had done. Maybe the hurt was too deep for him to atone. He still intended to make up for past mistakes. If she didn't want to hear him, then perhaps he could show her. Actions always spoke louder than words.

He gathered Ariah against him. Her arms went around him once more, and a pang of longing and shame scored his already battered soul.

"House is clear," Callum announced as he stood in the open doorway.

Killian met his gaze as he approached. The man moved out of the way as Killian turned to the side to enter the cottage with Ariah. Just like her shop, Ariah's touch radiated from every nook and cranny. The moment he stepped inside, the eclectic mix of accent colors, the array of plants, and the neutral-colored furniture created an atmosphere of peace.

"To the right," Ariah said.

He took the doorway on his right and carefully set her on the off-white sofa. When he would've shoved aside the assortment of pillows, she shifted completely out of his arms. He didn't need words to know that she wanted to be away from him. The hurt went deep, twisting in his heart. But he only had himself to blame. Killian straightened, hoping she met his gaze.

Instead, she shrugged out of his coat and held it out to him. He took it and draped it over his arm. When she couldn't quite reach the brightly knitted throw, he got it for her, unfolding it to lay it over her legs.

"Thank you," Ariah said and briefly met his gaze.

A noise from the front of the house drew his attention. Killian looked to the hallway where Callum stood in the doorway, looking toward the front door. He must have recognized whoever it was because he nodded in greeting. A moment later, two women walked in. One had chin-length black hair, and the other was a redhead. It took him a minute to recognize Rhona.

Rhona eyed him as she walked closer. "Never expected to see you back on Skye. Thank you for helping."

"Killian," Callum called.

He looked over to find Callum motioning him away with his head. Killian glanced at the two women sitting on either side of Ariah, talking in low voices and ignoring the men. His chance at finding out more about the nightmares was gone. Killian glanced at Ariah once more and then backed away before pivoting and following Callum out of the house.

"Rhona and Sabryn will take care of Ariah. You doona need to worry."

But Killian was concerned.

"I'll see you around," Callum said and started walking away.

That yanked Killian out of his thoughts. "Where are you going?"

Callum stopped and turned back to him with a shrug. "Back to the co-op to see if I can fix the door."

"I'm not exactly in the right headspace to get behind the wheel. Not after…" Killian sighed and ran a hand through his hair. "Drive us back. I'll help with the door, and if it can't be fixed, I'll replace it."

Callum stared at him for a moment without saying anything. Killian held his gaze. He had been surrounded by colleagues, family, and clients for years, but at that moment, he realized he hadn't had a true friend since he'd left uni. And right now, he really needed a mate. Or at least not to be alone.

He hadn't lied about not being fit to get behind the wheel. If

Callum wouldn't drive, Killian would walk. Because to get behind the wheel now was a recipe for disaster.

Callum nodded in agreement.

Killian blew out a breath, more relieved than he expected to be. They continued toward the SUV.

"Ariah will be all right," Callum insisted as he slid into the driver's seat. "Rhona is always the one to call in a crisis. She and her husband are who we turn to. Though you probably willna see Balladyn unless things go to shite. That's when he usually arrives."

Killian waited until his seat belt was buckled before he asked, "Balladyn? That's an unusual name."

"He's Irish."

Killian grinned. Callum's tone made it seem as if that were all the answer needed, and he supposed it was. Ariah's house grew smaller as Callum backed up before turning around and driving off. It was all Killian could do not to turn around and take another look at the cottage.

"Ariah is the reason you returned," Callum stated.

Killian stared out the passenger window, watching the shadowed landscape. "Aye."

"You've got your work cut out for you there, mate."

"Don't I know it?"

They drove the rest of the way in silence.

Callum parked and grunted. "I knew she'd be working on it. She never bloody listens."

Killian looked from Kirsi to Callum, putting things together. "She's the lass you were speaking of earlier."

"Aye."

"At least she's talking to you."

They shared a grin and made their way to Kirsi.

She looked up as they approached, her gaze briefly skimming over Killian before landing on Callum. "How is Ariah?"

"Rhona and Sabryn arrived soon after we did. I take it you called Rhona?" Callum said.

"I figured that was the best solution," she answered, shooting another quick look at Killian.

He'd thought they were keeping something from him earlier. Now, he was sure of it. "We came to see what we could do with the door."

"I don't think much can be done," Kirsi replied as she studied the object in question.

Killian stepped closer and used the light from his mobile to get a better look at the damage. There were three deadbolts. How had Ariah managed to push open the door? "I know little about sleepwalking, but is it normal for someone to have superhuman strength while in its clutches?" He looked between the couple. Then, he offered them a chance to fill him in on their secret. "That's the only explanation I can think of unless you know something I don't."

"It must be the sleepwalking," Kirsi said.

Callum sidestepped the question by examining the hinges. "Shite. These are bent. It'll make opening and closing nearly impossible until they're fixed. I had hoped they wouldna be damaged." He turned his head to Kirsi. "No such luck, I'm afraid."

"Who do I need to call to get a replacement?" Killian asked.

Kirsi folded her arms over her middle. "I'll take care of it. It takes about a week."

"Leave it to me," Killian said. "I'll stay here and make sure no one gets inside until you open. Perhaps then, I could just prop the door ajar so no one has to handle it."

"That could work, but I can't let you help with the door. You were just a bystander in all of this," Kirsi said.

Killian reached for his mobile, only to remember it was in the Audi. "You didn't ask for help. I offered. I'll be right back."

Once he had his phone, it didn't take Killian long to find a door company in Inverness. He left a message for them to return his call the moment they opened. With the right sum of money, any number of things could be achieved.

"We've got it," Callum told Kirsi. "Go get some sleep."

Killian put away his mobile. "He's right. Get whatever rest you can."

It took a little more nudging, but Kirsi finally went up the stairs to the flat above the store. Callum stared at her windows until the lights went out.

"What?" he asked when he noticed Killian staring at him.

"She doesn't seem to care about your family. You could have something with her."

Callum grunted and leaned back against the building. "It's *because* she doesna care that I willna do anything."

"That makes no sense."

"You'll find out soon enough when locals begin to move about. You'll get odd stares for being with me. The Kilmuir name isna a good one."

"Then make it one."

Callum glanced at him and shook his head. "I doona think a hundred generations of good Kilmuirs would wipe away the stain."

"I know what it's like to want something, only to let it go because of family. I know the pain of not following your dreams. I know the heartache of letting the love of your life get away. I'm a prime example of what will become of you if you continue on your current course. Heed my advice."

"I can no'."

The words were spoken so softly that Killian almost didn't hear them. He decided on another approach. "If you could go anywhere, where would it be? I'm sure you have a long list of places you'd like to visit."

"The only reason I want to leave is because of my dad."

Skye was beautiful. Beauty and splendor greeted a person in every direction. Pictures never did the isle justice. Despite that, Killian couldn't figure out what it was that made those like Callum and Ariah want to stay.

"Your dad won't live forever," Killian said. "Maybe leave until he dies. Then you can return."

"My family is cursed."

Killian leaned a shoulder against the stone edifice, not sure he'd heard that right. "Excuse me?"

"It goes back generations. Ask anyone. They'll tell you about the Kilmuirs. We're all drunk arseholes."

"You're not drunk, and you're not an arsehole. Not that I've seen so far."

"No' yet. It'll come. It always does."

"When?" Killian pressed.

Callum shrugged. "Good question."

Killian looked at the injury on Callum's brow. From what little he had seen of him, Callum didn't seem the violent type. But he had gotten that wound somewhere. Killian was afraid he knew exactly where, too.

For the first time, Killian took a hard look at Callum. At first glance, he looked like a typical bad boy, but Killian didn't believe that was who Callum really was. His light-brown hair was pulled back in a queue. His coat was tattered, the jumper beneath threadbare, and the sole of his left boot was coming apart from the shoe.

"How did you know about the hinges on the door?" Killian asked.

Callum lowered himself to the sidewalk and shrugged as he settled against the building once more. "I like mechanical things. People may hate my family, but if there's a problem with an engine, specifically a boat, I'm the first one they come see."

"If you're that good, you could work on any coast and bring in good money."

"Aye."

"No one deserves to be treated as you are. Not by your family or your community."

Callum grasped the thick silver band on his right ring finger and idly turned it. "Maybe. I'm going to break the curse, though."

"How are you going to do that?"

"The only way I know how. No' to pass it on. It will end with me, one way or another."

Killian dropped to the ground. "That would do it, but whoever you end up with might not agree to forgo children."

"That willna be a problem."

"Ah. I see. You intend to be alone."

"That's right."

Killian looked to the side at Callum. "Everyone has needs, mate. All it takes is one slipup for a woman to get with child."

"There willna be any slipups. Even if there are, there are ways to ensure there are no pregnancies." Callum finally met his gaze. "Do you have kids?"

"Nay," he replied with a shake of his head. "Not for lack of my mother hounding me, though. I did everything as expected. Except getting to the wedding ceremony."

"You walked out?" Callum asked in shock.

Killian propped his feet on the ground and rested his arms on his knees. "I ended the engagement a few weeks ago. She was intelligent, beautiful, and kind. And we got on great. Her family had groomed her to be the perfect wife to someone like me. We both followed family expectations. The difference was she wanted to marry me. I couldn't go through with it. Because she wasn't Ariah."

CHAPTER SEVEN

The click of the door closing behind Killian sounded final. Like a big dot at the end of a sentence. She should be glad he was gone. It was what she wanted. Why then did she want to cry? To call him back and beg him not to leave?

Ariah was bombarded with a slew of emotions that threatened to suffocate her. Astonishment at learning she had walked miles from her home to the co-op. Alarm at not recalling anything about the trek. Delight that Killian had been there. Then, irritation for being glad he was. Add in the pain from her feet, and she was all twisted up inside.

"Ariah?"

She jerked her gaze to Rhona, who sat on the coffee table across from her. "Aye?"

"I asked how you felt."

Ariah glanced at Sabryn, who sat beside her on the sofa and found the American's blue eyes studying her as intently as Rhona was. Ariah drew in a deep breath and released it. "Confused. Embarrassed. Scared."

"What happened?"

That was the question of the night, wasn't it? She put her chilled hands over her eyes and pressed. A moment later, she dropped them into her lap. "I don't know. Callum, Kirsi, and Killian might. They were there."

Rhona nodded thoughtfully, her green eyes never leaving Ariah's. "I'll talk to them. Right now, I'm more concerned about you."

"Your feet are bandaged. Do we need to call the Healers?" Sabryn asked.

Ariah shook her head. Being fussed over made her uncomfortable. "I'll soak them in some herbs."

"Let's do that now," Rhona said.

Sabryn stood, looking expectantly at Ariah. "Tell me what to get."

Ariah licked her lips. "I'll manage later."

"I'm good at following directions, you know," Sabryn said with a smile. "There's nothing wrong with accepting help. I understand it can be difficult since I struggle, too, but you can't walk."

She had a point. Ariah reached for a pad of paper and a pen on the table next to her. She jotted down the herbs and their measurements before handing it to Sabryn. "The bowl is in the cupboard next to the stove. The water needs to be warm but not boiling."

"Got it," Sabryn stated and then left the room.

Rhona silently waited.

Ariah leaned back against the cushions and put her hands under the blanket. "Apparently, I was sleepwalking."

"That's what Kirsi thought. Is that something new?"

"Aye. I guess. I've never done it before, at least not that I'm aware of."

Rhona refused to let her look away. "Did anything happen yesterday or in the days leading up to this that might have brought it on?"

"It was nothing."

"Obviously, it was something." Rhona's frown deepened. "You know the issues Skye has had. I can't figure out our next move and determine what might be striking next if I don't know what's happening."

Ariah glanced away as sounds from the kitchen reached them. "I wasn't sure it was even something to bother you with."

"It might not be, but we can't know that if Druids don't alert me or my deputies. What is it you don't want to tell me?"

Her feelings of foolishness had kept Ariah from going to Rhona, but now she felt like an idiot for *not* going to her friend. She let out a weary sigh. "I had bad dreams the night before. Each time I fell asleep, I was yanked awake. I don't recall what they were about, though," she added when Rhona's lips parted to speak. "The only thing I remember is a dark, shadowy shape."

Rhona's lips twisted. "Have you reinforced your wards recently?"

"Aye. Yours and Balladyn's mark is still with the others."

"Nothing should be getting in."

"Dreams aren't the same as a structure."

Rhona rubbed her palms on her thighs. "Good point. Is it just the nightmares?"

"Not exactly," Ariah grudgingly admitted. "I went into the forest yesterday for my morning walk. Once I began to meditate, I felt something over me. I sensed that it was huge and black. I couldn't determine a shape but felt its fury as it charged me."

Rhona's eyes widened. "Charged you? You battled it?"

"Nay. Nothing like that. I opened my eyes and jumped up, but it was gone. I almost doubted myself until I saw Moon staring at the spot, whipping her tail in agitation."

"Something was there."

Ariah shrugged and continued. "The last episode occurred at my shop. I was filling orders when I caught something big and dark out of the corner of my eye. It rushed me, teeth bared. I was startled and jumped back, but again, nothing was there."

"Bloody hell," Rhona said as she stood and began pacing the small area. "You should've come to me with this."

"I wanted to be sure there was something to worry about."

"I would damn sure say there is," Rhona snapped.

Sabryn stopped at the doorway with the large bowl in her hands. She glanced at Rhona before walking to Ariah and setting the bowl on the floor. "You should've told someone. Especially after what happened while you were working. However, Rhona… she didn't intentionally put herself in danger. She wanted to make sure there was an issue before notifying you."

"You already have so much going on," Ariah added.

Rhona stopped and faced them. "I'm supposed to keep everyone safe. I can't do that if I'm in the dark. But you're right, Sabryn." Rhona looked at Ariah. "I can't remember a time when you ever went to Corann for anything. Nor me after I took over leadership. You always do for others, but this time, you need to let us do for you."

"Be right back," Sabryn murmured.

She returned and poured the warm water into the bowl of

herbs. While Sabryn gently removed the bandages, Ariah added her magic to the mixture.

"Tell me what you remember about tonight," Rhona said as she sat on the coffee table again.

Ariah waited until she had both feet in the bowl. Only once the initial pain had subsided did she look at Rhona.

"There isn't much to tell. I stayed up for fear of having more nightmares. I wanted to be exhausted when I went to bed. So, I drank some tea to help ensure I slept peacefully. And no, before you ask, there was nothing it in that would have kept me asleep. It was a tea to calm and relax. Nothing more. It was after one in the morning when I climbed into bed. The next thing I knew, I woke up in the co-op surrounded by Killian, Callum, and Kirsi, with a container of milk I had apparently drunk from in my hand." She paused. "There is also the door. It looked…forced. I don't know who did that."

Rhona gave her a sympathetic look. "You."

"Me?" Ariah looked at the ceiling and sighed.

"You don't remember walking?" Sabryn asked.

Ariah shook her head and looked between the women. "I fell right to sleep. That's all." A memory made her pause. "Except…"

"What?" Rhona pressed.

Ariah wrinkled her nose. "I probably dreamed it, but…as I drifted off, I thought I heard a very distant drum."

"A drum? Are you sure?" Rhona asked, leaning forward excitedly.

Ariah shrugged helplessly. "I can't be sure."

"Right. Okay." Rhona bit her lip and sat straight.

Sabryn shifted to get more comfortable and crossed one long, dark-jean-clad leg over the other. "Who exactly is this Killian?"

"Killian Flanagan," Rhona answered, then slid her gaze to Ariah. "I didn't know the two of you had started up again."

Ariah glanced at the door where she had last seen him. "We haven't. He arrived today."

"And just happened to be near when you went for a barefoot walk tonight? I'm not fond of coincidences," Sabryn said. "Who is he? More importantly, is he a Druid?"

Ariah shook her head. "He doesn't have magic. He's a lawyer from a very wealthy and powerful family in Ireland."

"He's back. After nine years," Rhona said softly.

Ariah stared at her friend. "Don't. It doesn't matter what he says. He made his decision."

"People change," Rhona insisted.

Sabryn's voice was strangely cold when she said, "Not everyone. Some people never do."

There was a story there. Then again, everyone had history and baggage they carried around.

Rhona shoved her red hair over her shoulder. "Something got you out of bed, then made you leave the house and walk across land barefoot. All while unconscious. Could it be the Ancients?"

"Since when do the Ancients take control of people?" Ariah asked. The moment the words left her mouth, she grimaced. "Well, I mean, before Ferne."

Sabryn bounced her foot and asked Rhona, "Ferne was a conduit, though. Could Ariah be one, too?"

"Nay," Ariah answered.

At the same time, Rhona said, "I don't know. Maybe."

"I want to know if Ariah went into any other places," Sabryn said.

Rhona nodded. "Or what made her go into the co-op. I need

to speak to Killian, Kirsi, and Callum." She got to her feet and gave Ariah a pointed look. "Meanwhile, I don't want you alone. If anything else happens, someone needs to be here to witness it and help, if need be."

Ariah wanted to argue, but she knew it was no use. Rhona had made her decision.

"I'll take the first shift. I'll text the boys to head over next." Sabryn's gaze jerked to Ariah. "Unless you'd feel better having women only."

Ariah shrugged. She didn't have a problem with the rest of the members of Sabryn's group, the Knights. Carlyle and Finn were good people, and she had known Elias MacLean since she was very young. She and his sister, Elodie, were the same age. "It's fine."

"Good. I'll be back soon," Rhona said.

Ariah leaned forward to look over her legs into the bowl. She moved her feet slowly. The contact of the herbal water on her abraded skin made her grit her teeth.

"Anything else you need?" Sabryn asked. "Food? Tea?"

Ariah hesitated.

Sabryn chuckled as she pushed off the sofa. "I don't like being in a position where I need others to get me what I need, either. But sometimes we don't have a choice. Take advantage while you can. You might even enjoy being waited on."

"I doubt that. It's odd to ask for things I should be able to get myself. I feel fine."

"Except for your feet. You know, the things you need to stand and walk." Sabryn flashed a bright smile, her deep blue eyes crinkling at the corners. "Tell me what you want. Otherwise, I'll just start bringing things to you."

For the first time since she'd woken in the co-op, Ariah grinned. "You're very stubborn."

"You don't know the half of it."

"Tea would be great. Anything. I believe there are some strawberry scones left."

Sabryn rubbed her hands together gleefully. "I love those."

Ariah dropped her head back onto the cushion when she was alone. No matter how she tried, she couldn't recall anything about her stroll during the night, shoving open a locked door, or drinking the milk. Had she done anything else? Not knowing should worry her more, but she kept returning to the drumbeat. She wished she knew for certain if it had been real or not.

Sabryn returned with a tray of tea and scones and jerked her out of her thoughts. It was only after she'd taken the first sip of the black tea blend that Ariah turned to the American, who hid a yawn behind her teacup. "You and Rhona arrived quickly. Is something happening on Skye that we don't know about yet?"

"Besides your stuff?" Sabryn shook her head. "We were handling another situation involving Carlyle. He got a cryptic call from Mason, Ferne's brother, about his father."

"That's right. I keep forgetting Ferne and Carlyle know each other from the London Druids."

Sabryn's lips twisted. "Don't get me started on those assholes. Anyway, Carlyle can't reach his dad now, and he's frantic."

"You think it involves the London Druids?"

"Hard not to think so since Carlyle's family has been part of that group for generations."

"Do they know Carlyle is here?"

Sabryn shrugged one shoulder. "Maybe. Someone got to Mason. That much is clear. He was on board with Ferne coming to

Skye to help, but that has changed. He could have told the London chapter." Anger rolled off her. "Who are these bastards to think they can dictate where others go? And to banish someone from a family and London simply because they came to Skye? How utterly ridiculous. God, I hate them," she bit out.

"Surely, they wouldn't harm Carlyle's dad simply because he's here."

Sabryn lifted her cup in a salute. "Your guess is as good as mine, but that's why Carlyle wants to head to England."

"It could be a trap."

"It most likely is."

Ariah studied the American's all-black attire, taking in the slim sweater, skinny jeans, and boots. The Knights were among the warriors who had helped Rhona keep Skye safe. They needed to stay. Skye needed them because Ariah wasn't a fighter. "Are you going to take the Knights to England?"

"That's the discussion. I want to know if all of this is connected. Carlyle's dad, Killian's arrival, and whatever is happening to you. As I said earlier, I don't believe in coincidences."

Ariah had begun to wonder the same.

CHAPTER EIGHT

"Killian!"

He startled awake, heart pounding and the scream echoing ominously in his mind. Killian blinked at the fuzzy face before him. Slowly, it came into focus. Kirsi stood in front of him with a paper cup in hand. He glanced to the side where Callum had been to find him gone.

"He left," Kirsi said, holding out the cup. "I thought you might need this."

Killian cleared his throat and accepted the beverage, inhaling the scent of coffee as he sat up. His arse and legs were numb, but it was the lingering yell from his dream that unsettled him. He could've sworn it had been Ariah's voice. She had been on his mind for days now. It stood to reason he would dream about her.

He groaned and stretched his back. As he took a drink of the hot coffee, he glanced at the sky to see that dawn had arrived. "When did Callum leave?"

"About ten minutes ago. I couldn't sleep, so I came down a wee bit ago."

He looked up to see her gazing down the street. Killian gingerly got to his feet and stretched his back more. Then he removed the lid on the cup and drew in another deep breath of the rich brew.

"There's milk and sugar if you need it," Kirsi said as she faced him.

"This is fine. Thank you, by the way."

"Neither of you needed to stay, but I appreciate it all the same." Her gaze once more went down the road.

If Killian had to guess, that was the direction Callum had gone. He wondered if either of them knew the other fancied them. However, after what Callum had told him, Killian wasn't sure he would act on it even if he knew how Kirsi felt.

Kirsi realized he was staring and flashed him a nervous smile. Then, she held out a set of keys. "These are for you."

Killian slipped them into his pocket. "Callum seems like a good guy."

"He is. Others would know that if they gave him a chance." She quickly looked at him and crossed her arms over her chest. "Some people have a difficult time separating the father from the son."

"But not you?"

"Callum has always kept to himself. Always apart from everyone. I don't blame him. I'd do the same in his shoes."

Killian sipped his coffee, studying her. "He doesn't keep away from you."

Kirsi faced him. "Callum has been there for me when I needed it. Even when I didn't know I needed someone. I will do the same for him if he allows it. He isn't his father or his grandfather. Or anyone else in that family."

"You don't need to convince me he's a decent bloke. I've seen it for myself. Tell me about the Kilmuirs. What is it about the family that everyone disdains?"

"It goes back generations. If you talk to the superstitious, they'll tell you the family is cursed."

Killian grunted as he remembered Callum saying the same. "You believe in that?"

"Stay here long enough, and you'll believe it, too."

He took another drink and leaned his shoulder against the building. She faced the street and watched cars driving past as the isle started to wake.

"The Kilmuirs used to have one of the nicest places on the isle. It's gone to shite now. Joe, Callum's father, spends most days too drunk to remember his own name. Callum is the one who keeps the business running." Kirsi shook her head ruefully. "I've asked my parents about the family since they're around the same age as Joe. They said he constantly got himself into trouble. My dad thinks he did it because everyone expected it."

"Giving them what they wanted."

She glanced at him. "Exactly. My parents said he wasn't a drunk back then. He drank at the pub like everyone, but not in excess like he does now. Mum said that's how it is for every Kilmuir. And that it'll happen to Callum, too."

"What about Callum's mum?"

Kirsi swallowed and dropped her arms to face him. "Callum doesn't speak of her or his brother. Not since they left twelve years ago."

"Left?" Killian repeated with a frown. "Why didn't he go with them?"

Kirsi shrugged, her lips twisting. "I don't know. I've not had the nerve to ask."

Killian's mobile rang, interrupting the conversation. Kirsi walked away as he dug it out of his pocket and saw the number for the door company. He promptly took the call, explaining again what he needed. It took some talking and a rush fee, but they'd get the new door, including installation, that afternoon.

He returned his phone to his pocket and peered inside the co-op at Kirsi. She motioned for him to enter. He shoved his shoulder into the door and used his strength to get it open.

"The new door will be here by five," he told her.

She paused in distributing the money in the cash register. "How did you manage that?"

"I negotiate with high-powered lawyers for a living. A door company is nothing," he said with a grin. "Have you heard anything about Ariah?"

"Sorry, no." Kirsi finished with the money and closed the drawer with her hip. "How do you know her?"

Killian set the cup on the counter. "We were close a long time ago."

His mobile rang again, cutting off any questions she might have had. Killian looked at the screen to see his father's number. He shoved the phone away, then scraped a palm over his jaw to feel the whiskers. "I'll be back this afternoon before the door arrives."

"You've done enough already."

He raised the cup to her. "Thanks again for the coffee. I'll be around if you need anything."

Killian drove to the B&B and took a long shower. He was tired, but he knew it would be pointless for him to attempt to sleep. His mind was too full of questions and worry for it to shut off long enough to let him rest. He dressed and headed downstairs, where breakfast was being served. He filled his plate and drank two more cups of coffee while exchanging small talk with the owners. They were nice people, but his mind kept shifting to Ariah. Eventually, the hosts left him to finish eating on his own. Killian hurriedly polished off the meal but was then left wondering what to do. He wanted to check on Ariah but was fairly certain she wouldn't appreciate him showing up at her place. His safest bet was to go to her shop. They might have an update.

As Killian drove to the Tea Talker, he looked for any place along the shore that could be Callum's. He didn't locate anything, and before he knew it, he was once more in the village. Killian parked and walked into the building to find the tables filled and a line at the register. Ruby stood behind the counter, hurrying to check customers out.

There was no sign of Ariah, and frankly, he would've been surprised if she had been there with the state of her feet. It didn't take him long to realize that Ruby was alone. Killian walked to the counter.

Ruby glanced his way. "I'll be with you in just a moment."

"Let me help."

She snorted and greeted the next customer checking out.

Killian waited until she looked his away again. "I'm serious. You need the assistance, and I'm the only one offering."

Ruby stared at him for a long second before nodding. He jerked off his coat and tossed it aside before moving behind the register.

"I hope you learn quick," she murmured.

He watched as she checked out the next two guests. Then he nudged her aside. "I got it."

Ruby didn't leave until she had seen for herself that he could handle things. It didn't take him long to get into a groove. He remained at the register while Ruby saw to the customers on the floor. The rush went on for some time. It seemed everyone wanted Ariah's teas. He couldn't believe the number of blends she had created. Most were out front, but he learned there were some in the back, which weren't meant for everyone. When someone asked for those, he was to let Ruby know so she could get them.

Killian shut the till and readied for the next customer. Only there wasn't one. He placed his hands on the counter and sighed. He had been going nonstop for the two hours since he had walked into the building.

"You did a great job. Thanks," Ruby said as she walked past him with a tray of cups brimming with tea.

He gave her a nod and surveyed the shop. There was only one empty table, and no one seemed to be in a hurry to leave. A few patrons had laptops open and were working, while one bloke read, and others sat around chatting.

"You survived the morning rush," Ruby said as she came to stand beside him.

He met her blue eyes. "Is it always like this?"

"Most days. Then we'll have easy mornings like yesterday, but that usually means it'll pick up in the afternoon."

"I can't believe Ariah hasn't been approached by others to sell. I imagine she'd get an incredible price."

"Oh, she has. Several times."

He jerked his head to Ruby. "You're kidding."

"Nope. Ariah refuses every time. Doesn't matter how much money they offer. She's never interested."

"But she could be set for life."

Ruby laughed softly and wiped her hands on her short green apron. "That's the thing the companies don't understand. She *is* set for life. This is her life, her dream."

"Aye." Killian felt Ruby's stare and turned his head to her. "How is she doing?"

Ruby's eyes narrowed. "How do you know she's hurt?"

"I was there last night with Callum and Kirsi when it happened."

"You know what happened?" Ruby asked in a low, urgent voice as she stepped closer.

He nodded.

"Tell me."

Killian took the advantage he had. "Not until you tell me how she is."

She debated it for a long moment before leaning a hip against the counter. "She's resting. That's all I know. It was all she would tell me after letting me know she wasn't coming in. So, what happened?"

Killian kept his voice low and gave Ruby a quick rundown.

"She'll need to stay off her feet for a few days." Ruby absently looked off to the side, talking more to herself than him.

"I can come back."

Her gaze swung to him. "Why would you do that?"

"To help Ariah. And you, of course."

"Who is she to you?"

Killian realized that anyone close to Ariah would ask that

question because they were protective of her. "Someone she once knew."

"Someone who hurt her, you mean."

He bowed his head. "Guilty."

"Helping out here won't make up for that."

"I never believed it would. She's in a bind, and, as it seems, I have some free time."

Ruby smoothed her hand down the side of her blond hair and then along her ponytail. "Be here at five tomorrow morning."

"I'll see you then."

She started to walk away, then paused and turned back to him. "I promised Ariah I wouldn't let you back in."

"Then this will be our secret."

"Did you come to Skye for her?"

"I did, but I think it might be too late."

Ruby's lips softened into a smile. "Depends on how badly you want her."

"She's everything. I knew it before, but I…was stupid."

"Men usually are," she muttered before walking away.

CHAPTER NINE

Killian bit back a yawn as he waited outside the co-op for the door company. A brisk wind whipped from the water and penetrated straight to his bones. He held the cardboard cup of the tea Ruby had insisted he try with one hand to warm his fingers, stuffing the other in his coat pocket.

Kirsi waved at him from inside as she helped customers. He nodded in reply and turned back to the idyllic scene before him: quick-moving clouds across a brilliant blue sky, white-capped waves, and tourists and locals alike going about their days. While at the Tea Talker, his mind had been focused on getting through the rush. Now, he couldn't stop thinking about Ariah and the oddness of the night before.

He fought the need to check on her. She had friends to take care of her, but that didn't make it any easier for him to stay away. He had so many questions. Did she have any more nightmares? Was someone watching her so she didn't sleepwalk again? How had she been strong enough to break through the co-op door?

Ruby hadn't known anything more by the time Killian had left the shop. He planned to ask Kirsi, but he didn't count on her having any more information than Ruby had. The only one who *would* have his answers was Ariah. Well, her and maybe Rhona. And he knew neither would talk to him. Particularly Ariah.

Killian squeezed his arms against himself to ward off the chill. Fek, Scotland was cold. So much colder than Dublin. He sipped the tea, happy Ruby had put it in his hand as he walked out. He didn't even know what kind it was, but he liked the mild, nutty taste. It wasn't too sweet, either. He'd find out tomorrow what the flavor was. He hadn't had much time to look at the array of blends Ariah had concocted because there were so many.

That didn't surprise him. She had depth to her. It was one of the qualities that drew him to her. That and the serenity that seemed to emanate from her, encompassing all those near her.

His thoughts halted when a van with a door-company logo on the side pulled up. After a quick greeting, Killian was happy to see them getting to work immediately. He chatted amicably with the three men as they removed the busted door. One of them asked if the person who had rammed their car into the door was okay. Killian didn't disabuse them of their thinking. He smiled and nodded.

All in all, it took about an hour for them to finish the job.

"Wow," Kirsi said as she came outside through the new door, grinning. "The old squeak is even gone." Her gaze slid to his. "You aren't going to let me pay you back, are you?"

"Nope."

"Thank you."

He gave her a nod and a half-smile. "You're welcome. Have you heard anything about Ariah?"

"Nothing, sorry. I was hoping you knew."

He shook his head. "I only know she's resting."

"That's more than I've been told. If I hear anything, I'll let you know."

"I'd appreciate that." He looked down the street, suddenly not wanting to be alone. "Callum about?"

Kirsi wound her arms around her middle as a strong wind buffeted them. "Not that I've seen. I've learned not to look for him."

"What does that mean?"

"He does his own thing. Some people you know will be at the pub every day after work. Others go home. Callum rarely does the same thing two days in a row."

Killian finished the last of his tea as he mulled that over.

"Do you need him for something?"

He heard the suspicion in her voice, a reminder that he was an outsider. "Just seeing if he was about."

"If I see him, I'll let him know you're looking for him."

He gave her a nod, tossing the empty cup into the recycling bin before walking to his vehicle. Once inside, he turned on the heated steering wheel and seats. His hands were frozen solid, and he gave himself time to thaw before driving away. He had no destination in mind. No, that wasn't exactly true. He wanted to see Ariah but didn't allow himself that option. The way she had hurriedly pulled out of his arms when he'd set her on the sofa twisted his gut.

It wasn't as if he'd expected her to throw her arms around him and say that the past didn't matter. But he had anticipated at least getting to talk to her and explain. And perhaps, in doing that, build a bridge to help them both get past what had occurred nine years earlier.

Maybe he had expected too much. Ariah was a kind soul. However, that didn't mean she was a pushover. She set boundaries and didn't let anyone bust through them. In many ways, he was the same. He was used to talking his way around people and finding loopholes or bargaining chips he could use to get what he needed for his clients.

This wasn't for his clients, though. This was for him. For him *and* Ariah.

He had taken her being single as a sign that the timing was right for them. Yet the longer he considered things, the more he began to think she might have gotten over her love for him. And that was no one's fault but his. He had been the one to let her go, to bend to his father's will instead of holding on to the love and happiness he had found with Ariah on Skye.

A great wave of sadness and regret washed over him. What kind of man had something that precious and rare and let it go?

He shook his head in disgust, hating the twisting, gnawing, dark center of shame and guilt inside him. He was far from the man he wanted to be—or the man he should've been. If only he could stop time, rewind, and go back to that summer with what he knew now. But life didn't work that way.

His mobile vibrated, announcing another call. He pulled it out and saw that it was yet another call from his father. Fourteen missed calls today alone, and over two dozen texts. He wouldn't be able to ignore Brian Flanagan forever. Killian dropped the phone into the cup holder.

As he rounded a corner, a dramatic view of the sun sinking behind the clouds met him. A sign about Neist Point caught his attention. It was the most westerly location on Skye and the best place to see the sunset. Ariah had shown him that on his third day on the isle all those years ago. It was a popular destination, which meant he wasn't the only one with the idea this evening.

He parked the Audi in one of the last spots and climbed out. He passed the old shed, surprised it still stood since gales battered it relentlessly in the winter. After the shed, he found the concrete path. Flashes from the past and this same walk bombarded him: Ariah's bright smile as she turned her head to look at him over her shoulder, her glorious dark mane fanning out around her, excitement making her golden-brown eyes glitter.

Killian took the left on the path that eventually turned right to the steep steps that would bring him down the cliff face. He heard someone's laughter ahead of him. Or maybe it was from the past. It was becoming more and more difficult to differentiate between his memories and the present.

At one point, he looked down to see a hand clasped in his. He blinked, and the recollection faded.

Finally, he reached the bottom of the stairs and saw the second shed and its wire system. They had paused here that day as Ariah enthusiastically explained that the building and wires were used to get equipment down the cliff. If he listened closely, he could still hear her voice and see how her eyes glittered with happiness when she talked about her beloved Skye.

Killian slowly walked past the shed. His feet stopped when he spotted the grass path that broke away to the right. If he continued down the concrete section, it would take him toward the lighthouse where most everyone went. On his last night on Skye, Ariah had brought him here and tugged him along the grass path.

Everywhere he went, the memories of their time together

returned in vivid technicolor. How could he ignore this one? He diverted to the right and spotted the white spots of sheep dotting the landscape. They ignored him as he meandered until he came to the location he sought. Killian sank onto the rocky ground and looked out over the horizon. The scene took his breath away, a dazzling, majestic spectacle of nature's canvas at work.

The sky was lit up and pale yellow and looked like the sun had sunk into the ocean. The heavens faded to a salmon color with maroon clouds that stretched across the horizon. Lavender took over then, giving the clouds a deep purple hue. Then it was blue. A navy sky and nearly black clouds as night swept in with imposing force.

His fingers tightened onto themselves instead of linking with the only ones he wanted to share such events with, the very person who had shown him that such beauty existed.

Killian stayed, watching the last light of the glowing orb vanish so darkness blanketed the land in its shadowy embrace. Waves crashed against rocks, sheep *baaed,* and voices from those making the return walk to their vehicles intruded upon his privacy.

He usually preferred to experience things with others. But not this time. This sunset was just his. There was no exchange of words with any others, no photos snapped in an attempt to capture the essence. Just him and nature. Her showing off, and him drinking it in.

And a fractured part of him was somehow healed by it.

He would never be able to explain it. He wouldn't even try. But he knew it. Felt it.

"It's the magic of Skye," Ariah would say when something strange and unique happened. He used to chalk it up to her

obsession with the isle, but he was beginning to think she was right. There was something unique and extraordinary about Skye.

The temperature had dropped significantly, so Killian finally climbed to his feet and made the journey back. The path was light, fending off the shadows. His thoughts lingered on the past, but he knew he couldn't remain there. If he wanted a future, he had to fight for it. No matter how long it took.

Once he was at his SUV, he paused and took one last look at the water. The deep blue of the undulating waves was even more beautiful beneath the rising moon. Funny, he couldn't remember anything about the place after the sunset when he and Ariah had been here. He had been too immersed in trying to convince her to leave with him.

He was finally beginning to understand the isle's sway over everyone, not just the locals. It was too bad he hadn't seen it back then. Though he wasn't sure he would've cared. All he had wanted was Ariah, and he'd intended to have her at any cost. Killian had been so determined not to be his father that he hadn't realized he'd acted just *like* Brian Flanagan.

"Not anymore," Killian said before climbing behind the wheel and driving away.

He followed the winding, rolling roads back to the B&B. However, when he got there, he found it was the last place he wanted to be. So, he drove to the village and walked the shoreline as he had the night before. He searched for Callum, but he was nowhere to be found. Just as Kirsi had predicted.

That was too bad because he really needed a friend. Callum was the closest thing he had to that. Killian wasn't sure he liked what that said about him.

His last true friends had been at uni.

And Ariah.

He'd known that, felt it, but he had shoved it aside to be the best solicitor he could be—as his family expected. But he'd been searching for the kind of connection he'd had with Ariah since the day things had ended between them. He'd never even gotten close.

Killian never opened himself up to anyone as he had with Ariah. Losing her had hurt too much. He hadn't wanted to subject himself to that kind of pain again, so he'd cut himself off. He was the reason his friendships with those at uni had faded. He was the one who had severed the ties. His friends reminded him of Ariah, and as long as he wallowed in the pain—and aye, the guilt—of losing her, he couldn't achieve the things expected of him.

He didn't want to be that man anymore. He'd never wanted to be him, but he hadn't believed he had a choice.

"Liar," he whispered. "There was always a choice."

He hadn't wanted to make it. Not then, at least. He finally had. The fallout with his family had been breathtaking. Killian had spent years going through his days like a robot. Then, one day, he woke up and decided.

His ex-fiancée had demanded to know what had brought him to the decision. Killian couldn't answer because he didn't know. It was like a flip had been switched on—or maybe off. All he knew was that he had to get to Skye and, maybe, with a bit of luck and a lot of thought, win Ariah back.

CHAPTER TEN

Edie angrily glared at the bright morning sun coming through her car windscreen, preventing her from seeing the Tea Talker clearly. She had been up since four that morning, awakened by the ever-present voice in her head. The Ancients. A powerful group of dead Druids who communicated with a select few of their community.

And they had chosen *her*.

She rotated her hands where she had them closed around the steering wheel and stared at the store. Edie was special. So distinctive, in fact, that while a few Druids heard the Ancients in multiple voices at once, they spoke to her in only one voice.

And they wanted her inside that shop.

"*Your target is within,*" the Ancients told her.

But who could it be? Ariah? Ruby? They were the most likely candidates. The Ancients didn't answer. Or it could be any number of other Druids who went in and out of the building. Was she meant to stay all day?

"*Go.*"

A tapping on the passenger window made her jump and jerk her head to the side. The sight of her sister peering through the glass with a smile caused a surge of anger, but Edie managed to keep it in check. Elodie tried the handle to open the door but found it locked. However, there was no ignoring her.

Edie begrudgingly unlocked the doors, and Elodie climbed inside, acting as if nothing was amiss, as if she and their brother, Elias, hadn't been lying to Edie for years. They thought they had fooled her, but she knew the truth. She had always known the truth.

With blue eyes a shade lighter than Edie's, long, blond hair gathered atop her head in a bun, no makeup, gold stud earrings, faded jeans, and a trench coat, Elodie was effortlessly chic. She didn't even try. Unlike Edie, who spent hours with the latest makeup and hair tutorials, not to mention working constantly with her wardrobe to pull off the look her sister didn't think twice about.

"Hey," Elodie said as she shifted in the seat to face her. "Is everything okay? You've not returned my messages."

"There's a lot going on."

"Anything I can help with?"

Edie swallowed a biting retort. "I'm fine."

"It's just…you seem agitated. Is it something to do with one of the mothers from school?"

"It's always something." It was so easy to lie to her sibling. At one time, Edie would've died for them. But that was before they'd decided to keep the secret from her and leave her out of everything.

The eldest and the youngest were as thick as thieves, while Edie, the middle sibling, had been left to fend for herself.

"Let me know if I can help. You know you can always call me or Elias to pick up the kids if you need a break. Scott and I love when they stay overnight," Elodie said with a laugh.

Edie rotated her hands on the wheel again. "Too bad you weren't here when the kids were young. When I could have really used the help."

"I…uh…I know," Elodie said, her features pinching with guilt. "I'm sorry we lost all those years."

How many times would she give Elodie the chance to tell her the truth? How many more times would Elodie gloss over the fact that she had run away from Skye for killing their father and allowing their mother to take the blame for it, thus rotting in prison for fifteen years? Edie was flushed with righteous fury. It was on the tip of her tongue to let it all out and finally tell her siblings that she had been on to them from the beginning.

Elodie shifted in her seat. "Um…I wanted to talk to you about something. Want to get some tea with me?"

Edie had to go inside anyway. At least with Elodie sitting with her, it might not look so obvious that she was searching for whoever the Ancients wanted her to find. She shrugged. "I guess."

"You know you can talk to me about anything. *If* something's wrong," Elodie hastened to add.

This wasn't the first time her sister had made such an offer. "You mean like you talk to me?"

Elodie sighed. "I have many years to make up for, but we're sisters. I want us to be close. All of us. Don't you want that?"

It had been all Edie had dreamed of for years. "Aye."

"Come. Let me buy you some of Ariah's amazing tea."

Edie watched her sister exit the vehicle and walk around the front to wait for her. It wouldn't be tea that made her feel better, but her siblings weren't the only ones with a secret. Edie had one of her own.

"That's right. I'm always with you."

Edie walked with Elodie into the Tea Talker. It was crowded, and Elodie made a beeline for the one empty table before anyone else could grab it. Edie's gaze, however, was locked on someone she hadn't seen in years. Killian Flanagan was hard to miss. His blond hair looked almost like a halo around his head as he smiled at customers from behind the counter. Edie heard the giggles— giggles, for fuck's sake!—from grown women as they shamelessly flirted.

Young or old, single or married, it didn't matter. Women took one look at him and lost their senses. Edie wasn't immune, either. It was impossible not to notice someone as gorgeous as Killian.

Fingers snapping startled Edie. She swiveled her head to find Elodie sitting at the table, staring at her.

"You looked a bit starstruck there," Elodie said with a conspiratorial grin.

Edie said nothing as she sat down across from her sister.

"Do you know him?" Elodie asked, her gaze sliding to Killian.

"From a long time ago."

Elodie's smile widened as she leaned low over the table and whispered, "Were the two of you a thing?"

"His sights were set on someone else."

Elodie's brow furrowed as she sat up. She looked at Killian again. "Really? Who is he?"

"Killian Flanagan."

"Interesting," Elodie murmured.

Ruby walked up to get their orders, which gave Edie time to study Killian again. He seemed at ease behind the counter, as if he had always worked here. If Killian was back, he was here for one reason. Ariah. The fact that he was working at the Tea Talker all but confirmed it. Edie looked around but had yet to see Ariah.

The mention of Ariah's name caught Edie's attention. "What's wrong with her?" she asked.

"She injured herself and has to stay off her feet for a few days," Elodie answered.

Ruby jerked her chin to Killian, grinning. "His mere presence is doubling our usual morning rush. You'd think he was some footballer or actor, given the way everyone fawns over him. And he doesn't bat an eye at any of their scandalous and inappropriate comments. Just keeps smiling and greeting everyone."

"I hear he's returned to Skye," Elodie said with a waggle of her brows at Edie.

Ruby waved at some new customers who walked in. "He has. A blast from Ariah's past, apparently."

"Which explains why he's here." Elodie and Ruby shared a knowing smile.

Edie quickly forced her lips into a grin when they looked her way.

Ruby went to fill their order. Edie looked around at the customers, nodding hello to those she knew.

"So," Elodie said, scooting her chair closer to the table, "I wanted to talk to you about Mum. She'll be released soon."

Released. Edie wanted to bark in laughter. She never should've been sent to prison in the first place. She'd confessed to save Elodie and Elias. Edie might not have *seen* exactly what happened because she had been outside, but she had heard every horrifying second of it.

"I thought it would be great if we could all be together the first night she's back," Elodie went on, unaware of Edie's thoughts. "Let's have a big meal to celebrate all of us returning to Skye. You, Trevor, the kids, Elias, Bronwyn, Scott, and me. I thought we could have it at your place, but Bronwyn offered up the manor if you don't want the hassle. My house is way too small, or I'd host."

Sixteen years. That was how long Edie had been on her own after Elias, and then Elodie, moved away from the isle, leaving her all alone. She was rarely able to get her brother on the phone, but at least she spoke to him. During those years, Elodie had been like a ghost. Until her life was upended, and she had nowhere to go *but* home.

Edie was the only one who had visited their mother every month. The two of them had made plans. Edie would sign over one of her and Trevor's rentals for her mother to live in. It had been their agreement for years. Until Elodie—and soon after, Elias—returned to Skye. Now, apparently, they would be the ones setting their mum up somewhere, despite Edie telling them their plans.

Sure, her siblings had said it was better for Edie and Trevor since they wouldn't have to give up one of their revenue streams, but that wasn't the point. Whenever Elodie and Elias were involved, Edie became invisible.

But no longer.

Ruby arrived, set their cups on the table, and left. A frown puckered Elodie's brow as the silence lengthened. "It was just a thought. We don't have to do anything. I know Mum is excited for us all to be together again, but maybe we should wait until it's convenient for everyone."

"A family dinner sounds good. It'll make Mum happy, and she

deserves that after all this time." Edie wouldn't be the one to ruin such a night.

Elodie's smile returned, though it wasn't as bright as before. "That she does. I can't wait for her to get home."

"You could've gone to see her at any time."

Her sister froze with her cup halfway to her mouth. Elodie slowly lowered it back to the saucer. "I could have. I *should* have. I regret that more than you could possibly know."

"Explain it to me, then." Edie was pushing things, and now wasn't the time, but she couldn't seem to help herself.

"I buried things that happened here."

She had buried things, all right. Edie's anger became a living, breathing thing inside her, pushing her to say all the things she had kept to herself for years. "You mean Dad being killed."

Elodie glanced around nervously to see if anyone heard before pinning her with a dark look. "Aye, that. I shoved all of that aside and pretended it didn't happen. It wasn't the right thing to do, or even the healthy thing for me mentally, but I did it. I can't change that. I can only do things differently going forward. Repairing family ties that I destroyed is at the top of my list."

"You left me. You and Elias both."

Elodie lowered her gaze to the table and took a deep breath. As she released it, she reached across and covered Edie's hand with hers. "You were always the strongest of the three of us. You were the one who had her head on straight. You were the one who didn't need anyone."

"I needed my family. I needed you." God, how she had needed them, but they hadn't given her a second thought.

"I wish I could've stayed for you, but I left for me. Trust me, it was better that way." Elodie squeezed her hand.

The sounds of the business rushed into her ears all of a sudden, reminding Edie that this wasn't the place for them to air their family business. Besides, Elias wasn't there. She wanted both her siblings to face her wrath. They owed her that, at the very least.

Edie forced a smile she didn't feel. "Of course, I'll host the dinner. She is my mother, after all. No need for Bronwyn to put herself out."

"Great." Elodie shot her a bright smile and leaned back in the chair. "Don't worry that you'll be doing everything. Elias and I will pull our loads. Just tell us what you need, and we'll make sure it gets done. I'm so glad that's settled. I'll start a group chat between the three of us. We probably should've done that sooner. We can even do a family one with our significant others, children, and Mum when she gets back. How fun will that be?"

Edie wrapped her fingers around the teacup and looked at Killian when she heard him laugh. He had no idea what was coming. Neither did her siblings. Or Rhona, for that matter.

But they would soon enough.

"What do you think about taking Mum to Inverness for a weekend getaway?" Elodie asked. "We could do a spa day and a bunch of shopping, just the three of us. Later, we can do another shopping trip with Bronwyn since Mum will need new everything. I figure the lads won't want any part of such things." Elodie paused long enough to sip her tea. "This is going to be good, Edie, for all of us. Your children will get to know their grandmother, and we'll be a family again. The past is just that. The past. It's dead and buried. We all deserve a fresh start. I've gotten one. So has Elias. It's Mum's turn."

Edie was left out again. "And what about me?"

Her sister laughed as if it were some joke. When Edie didn't join her, Elodie sobered. "You're the only one of us who has had a stable life. You married the love of your life and had two beautiful children. Not to mention your successful rental business. You have it all."

It looked like that from the outside. But the truth was something vastly different.

"You're going to get everything you've ever wanted. We chose you."

CHAPTER ELEVEN

When she woke, raised voices from the kitchen came through Ariah's bedroom door. She rolled onto her back to check her mobile for the time. She grimaced to see it was nearly nine in the morning. She couldn't remember the last time she had slept past dawn.

Cautiously, she moved her legs beneath the covers. She had thought her wounds had healed enough to go without the bandages. It had been a mistake. Every time she moved, the sheets brushed against her feet and sent pain shooting through her legs. It had made for a fitful night of sleep. At least she hadn't sleepwalked again. And she'd had two nights without nightmares.

The voices continued, though they had quieted. Ariah understood and appreciated her friends' steps to protect her, but she was chafing at having her privacy invaded. She liked her quiet house and her time alone, and she hadn't had that in a day and a half. There had been no walks in the forest, either, and she felt the loss of her regular connection dimming.

She sat up and shoved the covers away to slowly slide her legs over the side of the bed. There, she took the time to inspect her feet. The swelling was gone, and most of the abrasions were now pink, signaling the healing process. Though a few nicks and punctures to the soles were taking longer. Those also happened to be on the balls of her feet, which made walking unbelievably painful.

"I can't wait. Not anymore."

Ariah was shocked to hear Carlyle's proper British voice since he had been guarding her since dinner the night before. He should've been relieved hours ago. Ariah tried not to listen to the conversation, but it was impossible as the voices rose again. Her cottage was small, and the walls were thin.

"I understand your frustration." This came from Sabryn.

Ariah tentatively pushed to her feet. The throbbing began almost immediately, but she wouldn't call for help. Especially not with the current conversation going on. She rolled to the outsides of her feet and leaned heavily on anything she could get her hands on until she finally made it to her dresser.

"I have to go," Carlyle stated.

Ariah quietly changed out of her nightclothes.

Sabryn spoke, but Ariah couldn't make out her words with the noise she made moving from each piece of furniture to her door. There, she paused and listened, but only silence met her. Quietly, she opened the door and glanced down the hall toward the kitchen.

There was no sign of Carlyle or Sabryn, and Ariah used the opportunity to start toward the kitchen. She hobbled, wincing when she overcompensated, and had to flatten her foot so she didn't fall over. She bit back a yelp of pain and grabbed hold of the wall. Suddenly, Sabryn and Carlyle were there.

"Why didn't you call for us?" Carlyle asked as he wound an arm around her, taking most of her weight.

Sabryn moved to her other side and did the same. "Because she's stubborn. Also, because she's uncomfortable accepting help."

Carlyle seated her at the table and straightened, his striking turquoise eyes moving from her feet to her face. His auburn hair was mussed as if he had spent the night raking his fingers through it. "I know what you need. The last of the scones, a cup of tea, and some herbal water for your feet."

"Already ahead of you," Sabryn said from behind Ariah.

A plate with a warm scone was soon set in front of her. Sabryn started the tea while Carlyle readied the herbal water. Ariah watched them move about her kitchen with ease, the tension from their conversation gone. They both smiled easily at each other and her, but Ariah wasn't fooled.

"I am grateful for everyone. In case I haven't said it," Ariah said.

Carlyle looked at her over his shoulder and grinned. "We Knights know all about stubborn women." He lifted his gaze to Sabryn.

"Oh, you're funny," Sabryn said as she placed three cups on the table. "If you want to hear about obstinate, pigheaded men, let me tell you about Carlyle. How about I tell the story of the pub in Paris two years ago?"

Carlyle shot her a look of horror. "Don't you dare."

"Oh, I would," Sabryn replied with a wicked grin.

Ariah chuckled as she looked between the two. "The bond you have is tight."

"All the Knights are close. It's what makes us so formidable against our enemies." Sabryn poured tea into each cup.

Carlyle carried the bowl of herbs and set it at Ariah's feet. "We're a family. We bicker, sometimes heatedly, but that's bound to happen when you spend as much time together as we do."

"But we work it out. I don't agree with allowing things to fester," Sabryn added.

Carlyle moved to the stove to heat the water, his arms crossed over his chest as he faced Ariah. "You have a good community here. There isn't anything like it in London. The Druid sect there is…"

"Abusive? Cruel? Sadistic? Violent?" Sabryn offered.

His lips twisted ruefully as he nodded. "All of that and more. You're lucky to have Skye."

"Aye," Ariah said, tearing off a piece of the scone to pop into her mouth. "Skye is amazing, and we are a close-knit community. In some respects. It isn't anything like what the Knights have. Though that's probably because you aren't contending with an isle full of Druids."

Carlyle chuckled. "That's the truth."

Sabryn leaned back in the chair and crossed one long leg over the other. "I haven't been back to the States in six years. We move constantly, fighting one battle after another to stop rogue Druids."

"Don't forget the Druid Others," Carlyle said.

Sabryn grunted. "Every time we think we've stopped Druids attempting to dominate in order to grow their ranks and take over more of our kind, more show up. I don't understand how Druids can be brainwashed into allowing others to siphon their magic to make themselves stronger. It's never-ending."

"Then we followed Elias to Skye." Carlyle carried the warmed water to the bowl and poured it. He stood with a shrug. "That's when we realized the things we had been fighting paled in comparison to what was going on here."

Ariah said the spell over the water before putting her feet into the bowl. There was an instant of pain before the herbs and magic began their healing. "I think I can speak for every Druid on Skye when I say we appreciate all the Knights have done."

"We didn't do it alone," Sabryn reminded her. "We had a strong group standing alongside us. It was a team effort."

And what had Ariah done during those battles? Made tea. It had been her choice, but now she felt as if she had somehow let Skye down. As if she had let *herself* down. Which made no sense.

Carlyle sank onto a chair and sipped his tea. He nodded at Sabryn before turning his gaze to Ariah. "We all have our parts to play and reasons we do what we do."

"I very much doubt tea will best the evil plaguing Skye." Ariah didn't like the note of bitterness in her voice.

Sabryn shrugged. "It might. I don't think you realize how integral you are to the isle and the community. Your teas are delicious, yes. Both the regular and the magical kinds. But it's more than that. You have a—" She paused, frowning as if searching for the right word.

"Poise," Carlyle said.

Sabryn nodded. "Yes, exactly that. You have a bearing, a self-confidence about you that instantly changes the atmosphere."

Carlyle lifted his cup in salute. "Well said. You're a child of the forest, Ariah. The only one on Skye. That is powerful."

"Aye." Ariah wrapped her hands around her cup to warm them. She couldn't understand how being a forest child would help, though. She got peace and tranquility from it. Never violence. But that was better left unsaid when those sitting at her table were warriors.

"Now," Sabryn said, leaning forward with her arms on the table, "any nightmares or dark shapes coming at you?"

Carlyle added, "Or sleepwalking?"

"Nothing." Ariah took a drink of tea and placed the cup on the table. "It's odd, though. That it would happen so suddenly and then leave?"

Sabryn's arms slid on the table as she leaned back in her chair again. "There are too many strange happenings on Skye to dismiss anything carelessly."

A soft meow filled the quiet. Moon trotted into the room and wound around Carlyle's legs before jumping onto Ariah's lap.

"Carlyle made Moon a special meal of chopped fish and some broth," Sabryn said.

Carlyle shrugged, offended. "What? I like to cook. You two were asleep, and she was hungry."

"I thought you were more of a dog person," Sabryn teased.

Carlyle ignored her by drinking his tea.

Ariah and Sabryn laughed. When a knock sounded on the front door, Carlyle jumped up to answer it. He returned a short time later with Rhona.

"You look rested. I hope that means there were no more nightmares," Rhona said to Ariah.

Sabryn got another cup for Rhona. "She was just telling us that nothing else has happened since the sleepwalking incident."

"I think she's trying to tell us she's ready to be on her own," Carlyle said with a wink.

Rhona's brows rose on her forehead. She took the empty seat, and silence stretched as she sipped her tea. "What if it returns when you're alone?"

"I won't know that until we test it," Ariah replied.

"And you want to test it?"

"Do I want more nightmares? Do I want to see that dark shape rush me or sleepwalk again? Nay. But I can't spend the rest of my life having someone watching over me."

Sabryn met Rhona's gaze. "She has a point."

"We could be nearby," Carlyle offered. "If anything happens, she could alert us."

Rhona ran the tip of her finger along the handle of the cup. "That's a possibility."

"It's what will happen," Ariah said. "I'd like my life back. I've spoken to Ruby, but I need to check on the shop."

Rhona held her gaze. "Ruby has things handled."

"I need to get to the co-op. At the very least, I need to get Kirsi and her family money for the door."

Rhona sipped the tea. "It's been taken care of."

Ariah looked around the table. No one had mentioned Killian. Had he left? It was what she wanted. Wasn't it? She almost asked if they had seen him, but that would open the way for a slew of questions, particularly from Rhona, who had witnessed the aftermath of their breakup.

"All right. We'll go," Rhona said. "I don't think you should be alone. If for no other reason than to have help with moving around."

"I'll manage."

"Please, change your mind about the Healers."

Ariah firmly shook her head. "If magic is waning, then there will be those who need Healers. I don't. I'll be fine. And I promise, if anything strange happens, I'll let you know immediately."

"I'm going to hold you to that."

Ariah smiled. "I know."

Rhona slid into the driver's seat and closed her car door. On the passenger side, Balladyn lowered the veil that made him invisible to others.

"Well?" her mate asked.

"You heard her. Ariah thinks the threat has passed."

"Perhaps it has."

"Nay."

"Nay?" he repeated.

She turned her head to him, meeting his red-ringed silver eyes that were a testament to his long life and all he had endured as a Fae. "Ariah was singled out. No one else on Skye experienced anything remotely like the nightmares or sleepwalking. My deputies are keeping on top of that."

"You know as well as I do that people keep things from others. Even important stuff. You can't be sure the Druids are telling the deputies everything."

He had a point. Rhona shook her head and looked at Ariah's cottage, which would soon be overflowing with flowers. "*Something* is here. I think it has set its sights on Ariah."

"We've known for weeks that something is here. The problem is sorting out *what* it is. And just how long its reach is. But Ariah? She's not a threat."

Rhona looked at him, suddenly irritated on her friend's behalf. "Why? Because she didn't join in the battles? You could say that about nearly all the Druids here."

"That isn't what I'm saying," Balladyn said, meeting her gaze.

"What are you saying, then?"

He drew in a breath and then released it, his lips flattening as he glanced at the stone structure of the old cottage. "I think the forces we're working against would go after more powerful Druids."

"Unless it knows something we don't." Rhona dropped her head back to look at the roof of her car. "We're constantly a step behind it, always on the defensive. I don't like it."

"Nor I. We're sorting it out. It may be slower than either of us is comfortable with, but it'll happen."

Rhona looked at the house and propped her elbow on the door to lean her head against her hand. "I hate coincidences."

"I may be a Reaper, my love, but I can't read your mind."

"Killian returned to the isle the same day Ariah woke with the nightmares."

Balladyn grunted. "You told me he wasn't a Druid. How can he be involved?"

"Maybe he isn't, but we need to find out one way or the other."

"Ariah didn't ask about him when you spoke to her. Don't you think she would have if he meant anything to her as he once did?"

Rhona twisted her lips. "I'm not so sure. Ariah fell hard for him." She looked at Balladyn. "*Hard.* She returned destroyed."

"All right. I'll check him out."

In the next blink, Balladyn was gone, teleporting out to find Killian.

CHAPTER TWELVE

Killian yawned and blinked several times to focus as he drove along the roads after his shift at the Tea Talker. The sky was bright and clear, proclaiming a new day. Two nights of little to no sleep, combined with two days of working flat-out on his feet, had worn him into exhaustion. If only that meant he could actually rest. But he knew better.

The moment he lay down, his thoughts were consumed by Ariah. From the moment he had decided to end the charade of following the path laid out by his family and return to Skye in hopes of reuniting with her, she was all he had been able to think about. Between memories of the past and wishes for the future, she dominated every millisecond of every hour.

The hairs on his nape rose, sending unease through him. He rubbed his hand on the back of his neck in a vain attempt to dislodge the feeling, but it was pointless. This was the third time since he'd woken this morning that it had felt like someone was watching him. No one was in the vehicle with him, and he saw no one on the road. Nothing explained the sensation.

He tried to ignore it. It was probably fatigue. Nothing a few hours of uninterrupted sleep couldn't fix. Killian followed the bend in the road and spotted someone walking along the side with their back to him. The moment he passed and saw it was Callum, he slowed and pulled over, rolling down the window.

Killian leaned out the window, looking back with a smile as Callum approached. It dimmed slightly when he caught sight of Callum's somber look. "Need a lift?"

"I'm good." Callum briefly met his gaze but kept walking.

Killian watched him for another second before shouting, "This isn't a handout, mate. This is about me. I…I could use a friend."

Callum halted. After a long pause, he turned and stared at Killian for an interminable minute. Then he walked to the SUV and climbed inside. Only to sit stiffly.

"Thanks," Killian said.

Callum raked a hand through his light-brown waves. "You'd be better off finding another friend."

"I don't want a handout, either. If you're here because you feel guilty, you can get out."

Callum fastened the seat belt in response. Killian checked for cars and pulled back onto the road. He glanced at Callum's profile. Something was bothering him. Or something had happened.

Or both.

Killian was reminded of the prickle before he'd come upon Callum. "Do me a favor. Look in the back seat."

"For?"

"Just tell me if you see anything." Killian felt Callum's gaze boring into him.

Eventually, Callum turned to look in the back. "There's nothing here."

"Are you sure?"

Callum looked a second time, twisting to check the floorboards. "Nothing."

Killian rubbed his neck again. It had felt as if someone were right there. He clearly needed rest.

They traveled in silence for a short time, and Killian felt his passenger's discomfort. Maybe he'd been wrong about Callum.

To his surprise, the other man said, "I have a hard time believing you doona have any mates."

"I've gone years without any true friends. Years. Who does that? Me, that's who. What do you see you when you look at me?" Killian glanced at him, their eyes meeting briefly.

Callum shrugged. "Success."

"You're not wrong. I have had an amazing career, but I'm not sure I can take all the credit. I work for my family, and they've made a name for themselves over the years. Money and power. That's what most associate with the Flanagan name in Dublin."

"I doona know many who would object to that."

Killian chuckled. "I certainly didn't for a long time. I told myself it was enough. I made myself believe."

"What changed?" Callum asked.

"I'm not sure. I never forgot about Ariah. She was always there, but like a distant, far-off ideal that couldn't be mine. One morning, I woke up and realized I didn't like my life. I saw clearly for the first time. True clarity. I wanted friends, the kind you can count on for anything. And I also want Ariah. Though I may not be able to win back her love. If I can't, I'll have to live with that— at least, I hope I can."

Callum's voice was filled with surprise when he asked, "You left everything behind?"

"I gave up my career, ended my engagement to a beautiful woman who deserved someone who actually loved her, and told the family I was done doing what they wanted. I gave up everything without a backward glance. Even the family money. I had to return to the last place I knew happiness, to be with a woman I love beyond reason."

"Is your family okay with that?"

At that moment, Killian's mobile rang, his father's name flashing on the screen. "Not exactly." Neither said anything until the phone stopped ringing. Killian glanced over at Callum to find him looking out the passenger window. "Maybe you could use a friend, too."

"You'll regret it."

"My father is a first-rate arsehole. People have always assumed I'm the same. So, I know a little about what you're dealing with. My point is, I don't give a shite what others think."

Callum was quiet for a long time. Then he said, "All right."

Killian took that to mean he wanted to be friends. "I'm hungry. How about you?"

"I could eat."

"Know of a good place?"

Callum directed him to a spot near the coast. They walked up the stairs and inside. That was when he first saw the view overlooking the sea. It was a prime location with an unbelievable panorama. As they were led to their seats, Killian noticed how the hostess tried to flirt with Callum, who appeared oblivious.

"Do you come here often?" Killian asked once they were alone.

Callum glanced at him over the menu. "Nay."

Killian kept quiet until after their order had been placed. Then he folded his arms on the table and caught Callum's gaze. "Can I give you some unsolicited advice?"

"I doona think I could stop you."

"Fair enough. If you've chosen to remain on Skye, then do it with your head held high. You've not done anything to deserve people's treatment of you. It's everyone else's shameful, small-minded prejudice that causes them to act so callously."

The server walking past tripped at his words. She glanced at them before hurrying away.

Callum ducked his head to hide his grin. "Did you know she was near?"

"If I had, I would've said more," Killian replied with a smile. "From what I've seen, you're a good man. And from what Kirsi told me, a good friend. You can't help what family you were born into or how they act."

Callum's lips curved into a wide smile. "Unsolicited or no', it's good advice."

"Good. I hope you have some for me."

"Advice about Ariah?" Callum's eyes widened in alarm.

Killian nodded. "I've not heard much since dropping her at home. All Ruby could tell me was that she was resting."

"If anyone knows, it's Ruby since she works at the shop. I'm surprised she told you anything. Ruby isna known for sharing things easily. Especially with strangers."

"The morning after we found Ariah, I went to the Tea Talker and helped her. The place was jam-packed. She wasn't thrilled to see me since she had been there to witness my encounter with Ariah, but she needed the help, and I was the only one offering. That's what I've been doing every morning since."

Callum chuckled. "Clever."

"I figure I have a few more days of earning Ruby's trust. Maybe then, I'll run into Ariah again."

"I expect Ariah to be back to work sooner than that."

The prickle on the back of Killian's neck started again. He glanced behind him.

"Everything all right?" Callum asked with a small frown.

Killian shook his head. "It feels like someone is watching me."

Instead of laughing it off, Callum's gaze slowly moved around the restaurant. "When did this start?"

"This morning."

"Was that why you asked me to look in the back seat?"

"Aye. It's probably just that I'm tired. Or," he said as another thought came to him, "my father sent someone to retrieve me."

Callum sat back as the server delivered their food. The moment they were alone, he said, "Would they take you by force?"

Killian met his gaze. "They could try."

"I'd like to see that," Callum said.

They shared a smile.

After Callum swallowed his first bite, he said, "The next time you think someone is watching, let me know."

Killian nodded, though he wasn't sure what Callum had in mind to do about it.

After the meal, they sat in the Audi as Killian tried to talk himself out of turning left, the direction that would take him to Ariah's.

"Stop in and check on her. Is that no' what people do for those they care about?" Callum asked.

"She told me to leave."

"You did."

"Nay," Killian said as he looked at Callum. "She told me to leave Skye."

"But you have no'."

"I have not." He shook his head. "I shouldn't push my luck yet."

"I thought you were going to win her back. You can no' do that by sitting here."

Killian grinned. "Is that your advice?"

"It is."

He thought about it but turned right instead. "Not yet. What are your plans for the day?"

"You mean besides convincing you to go see Ariah? Nothing."

"You don't need to work?"

There was a long beat of silence. "We're talking about you. Now, turn around and go see Ariah."

Killian had wanted a friend, which meant listening—and usually following—advice from said friend. He could argue that Callum didn't know what he was talking about, but Callum also saw things from a different perspective. Killian's view was colored by the past, regret, and his hopes for the future.

He found the first place to turn around and started the drive back to Ariah's.

"Good," Callum murmured.

Killian's heart began thudding louder and louder the closer he got to Ariah's. His hands grew clammy, and his stomach churned violently when he turned down her drive. He pulled to a stop behind her SUV and put the Audi into park.

"I don't know," Killian said. "This might be pushing things too quickly."

"If you want to win her back, you have to actually be around her," Callum said. "You can no' do it by talking to me about your plans and wishing them into action."

Killian glanced at him. "Manifestation works."

"I'll be happy to shove you out if you need it."

Killian's face broke into a smile, and his heart rate settled back into some semblance of normalcy. He opened the door and started to climb out when he looked back at Callum. "You coming?"

"This is all you."

Killian locked his gaze on the stone cottage with its lavender-colored door. His feet crunched on the gravel as he made his way to the entrance. He paused when he reached it, his hand lifted and ready to knock. It wasn't too late. He could drive away without Ariah being any the wiser.

CHAPTER THIRTEEN

SKYE DRUIDS

Ariah had just gotten to the kitchen when there was a rap on the door. It had only been a handful of hours since she had been left on her own. She looked toward the front of the house and plopped down in the chair. She had taken a few tentative steps, and while her feet hurt, it wasn't as debilitating as before. She didn't want to push it, though.

"Who is it?" she called out.

"Killian."

She stilled as a tremor of shock ran through her.

"I, uh…I know I'm not welcome." His muffled voice reached her through the door. "You don't need to let me in. I just wanted to make sure you were okay. See if you needed anything. If you do, you can let me know. I'll make sure you get it. Whatever it might be."

Ariah stared at the door, her body frozen. Killian was here. At her house. He hadn't left Skye. Not yet, at least.

"I understand," he said dejectedly.

Her heart jumped into her throat at the thought of him leaving. Then, words tumbled out of her mouth before she could consider the consequences. "Come in."

The door didn't open. Panic set in. Had she waited too long? Had he already walked away? She didn't want him to go. Ariah pressed her palms onto the table and pushed herself to her feet. The twist of the door handle drew her gaze. When the door swung open, her knees gave out.

She plopped back into the chair, her eyes glued to the opening where Killian stood in denim and a navy coat. Wind ruffled his hair. Their eyes met. She hated that the sight of him still made her stomach flutter with excitement and her body heat with awareness. And need.

Their attraction had been passionate and sizzling. All-consuming. Unbidden, a memory of Killian pressing her against the wall as he kissed his way down her naked body filled her mind. It was the kind of magnetism few ever experienced. The type of hold he still had over her, even after everything.

Her broken heart didn't stand a chance against him. It never had. Killian was gorgeous, brilliant, and extraordinary. He went through life with a fierceness and intensity that awed her. He could do anything. Unless it went against what his family wished. She'd found that out the hard way.

And still bore the scars to prove it.

Killian hesitantly entered and closed the door behind him. He never took his gaze from her while crossing the short distance that separated them. He stopped near the counter. "You look well."

"I've done nothing but rest." Her heart had yet to slow since he had announced himself. She even sounded breathless.

He shot her one of his crooked grins. "I'm glad to hear you've been taking it easy. How are your feet?" he asked as he moved to get a better look at them.

Ariah had to force herself to keep her legs still and not tuck her feet under the chair and turn away.

"The swelling is gone," he noted. "Some of the abrasions look almost healed. What about the soles?"

She straightened her legs and lifted her feet. He went down on his haunches, close enough to touch her if he wanted. It reminded her of how he had tenderly doctored her feet. She watched him look over first one foot and then the other.

His gaze shifted to her before he stood. "I'm impressed with whatever medicine the doctor gave you."

"I used my herbs." She lowered her legs, careful not to slam her feet against the floor.

Killian lifted his head to the plants hanging around the kitchen in various stages of drying. "You always did have a way with them."

His gaze eventually returned to her. A strained, awkward silence filled the space. It hadn't always been this way. At one time, they had been able to talk for hours. She had bared her soul to him, and, beneath the summer sky, discovered her soulmate.

"Any more nightmares?"

Ariah shook her head. "Not a one. No other sleepwalking incidents, either."

"You could've walked off a cliff. You could have..." He ran a hand down his face and sighed.

She swallowed and brought her hands to her lap. "But I didn't."

"Is there anything you need? I'll get whatever it is."

"I'm good. But thank you."

He stuffed his hands into his coat pockets, remorse lining his face. "I've missed you. I never stopped thinking about you. Never."

A knock sounded a second before the door opened. Ariah watched as Theo walked in with something under his left arm. He smiled warmly at her before his gaze landed on Killian. Both men looked each other over, and she was conscious of Killian's demeanor changing.

"How are you feeling?" Theo asked, his dark brown gaze returning to her.

Ariah made herself smile. "Better. Theo, this is Killian Flanagan, an old friend. Killian, this is DI Theo Frasier."

"Detective Inspector," Killian said and held out a hand.

Theo clasped it, and they shook briefly. "Flanagan. Do I detect an Irish accent?"

"Guilty as charged," Killian answered. But his easygoing nature was stilted.

"I willna hold it against you," Theo replied, his tone light and teasing. He scratched his temple and jerked his thumb over his shoulder. "Why is Callum sitting outside?"

Killian lifted one shoulder. "It's where he said he wanted to be."

"You know Callum," Ariah said to Theo.

"Aye, but…" Theo began.

He was interrupted by the door opening again, this time to admit his significant other, Ferne. Her green eyes were crinkled at the corners as she hurried inside carrying a large paper bag, not sparing the two men a glance as she made straight for Ariah.

Ferne set the bag on the table and smoothed a black curl away from her face. "First, you saved me with the teas," Ferne said in her refined British accent. "You are a genius. As a thank you, I brought…well,"—she shot Theo a sheepish look—"I brought everything."

Theo grunted. "She's no' kidding."

Ferne took out various boxes from restaurants to set on the table. There were also items from the co-op, which made Ariah grimace at the reminder of the door. Finally, Ferne held out her hands to Theo, who passed her two books.

Ferne handed them to her. "I thought of you when I saw these."

"She went hunting for them last night," Theo corrected. "At midnight."

Ferne shushed him with a stern look before giving him a wink.

Ariah smoothed her hands over the worn leather.

"Don't even think about refusing," Ferne said. "Besides, I have entirely too many books. They won't all fit in the store."

That made Ariah remember. "I've some plants ready for you. There are still a few others that would be good to use."

"Bring them all when you're healed. I won't be opening the bookstore for another few weeks yet. The sorting is taking up all our spare time." Ferne finally spotted Killian. "I apologize. I didn't see you there. I'm Ferne."

"Killian," he said with a smile and a head dip.

Ferne clasped her hands together and turned back to Ariah. "Have you eaten? Which would you like to keep out? I'll put the rest away in the fridge for you."

Ariah shifted her attention to the various boxes of food, considering each before deciding on the fish and chips. When she looked up, Killian was gone. She thought he might have moved to a different room, but it soon became apparent that he had slipped out without saying anything.

"You all right?" Ferne asked softly.

Ariah pulled her gaze from the door and smiled. "Aye."

"Is it time for another herbal mix?" Theo asked.

Ferne motioned for him to start it. "I saw Rhona and told her we were going to stop by. She made sure to mention that you might need another mixture for your feet."

"That would be nice. Thanks," Ariah agreed absently, her thoughts on Killian and his words before he'd been interrupted.

Ferne and Theo kept their banter going, and Ariah was grateful. Maybe she should be thankful that Theo had interrupted them. She had been so taken aback by Killian's confession that she hadn't been able to think of a response. She certainly couldn't tell him that a day hadn't gone by where he didn't cross her mind. Nor would she admit that she compared every man to him—and found them all lacking.

She had been given a taste of bliss once, only to have it yanked away. Bitterness had briefly seeped into her life afterward, but she hadn't liked the person she'd turned into. She'd had no choice but to release the anger and resentment. And it hadn't been easy. There were days, particularly beautiful, sunny days, where she revisited her memories and imagined how things might have been if they'd turned out differently.

Without a doubt, love was real. She had seen it, touched it. Experienced it. She'd also come to terms with the idea that she would only have a brief glimpse of it in this life. That she was meant to spend her days without such a partner. The simple truth was that not everyone found their mates, no matter how hard they looked.

"Ariah."

She blinked and turned her head to find Theo kneeling at her feet. His expectant expression caused her to look down and see the bowl of herbs already filled with water. "Sorry. My mind drifted."

"Killian is a handsome one," Ferne said, sinking into a chair.

Ariah felt both of their gazes on her as she lowered first one foot and then the other into the water. "Aye."

"I knew he looked familiar," Theo said, getting to his feet. He leaned his hands on the back of the chair. "He's the one from that summer, right? And he's back? That's good news." When Ariah didn't immediately reply, Theo glanced at Ferne. "Or maybe no'."

Ariah licked her lips. "I don't know."

"We interrupted them, I think," Ferne told Theo in a soft voice.

Theo pulled the chair out and lowered himself onto it. "I doona remember much about that summer. I dove feetfirst into my career and put every moment I had into it. But I do recall seeing the two of you together. I remember you going to Oxford, too." He paused. "And then you returning. Alone."

Ariah shoved back her long hair. "He wanted me to leave Skye. It was the only way we could be together."

"But...why?" Ferne's brow was puckered in confusion. "Why did you have to leave?"

"He's from a very wealthy, very powerful family. They run a law firm with offices in several countries. Killian's family had plans for him that were laid out since before his birth. He had no option to refuse."

Theo's brow puckered with sorrow. "I always wondered why I never saw him again. I'm sorry."

Ariah waved away his words. "These things happen. I couldn't give up Skye, and he couldn't refuse his family."

"Yet he returned. That means something," Ferne pointed out.

Theo's dark gaze swung to Ariah. "Only if you want it to."

That was the problem. She wanted Killian. She always had. That would never change. But she also wasn't sure she could put her heart out there again, knowing there was a good chance Killian would toss it away like last time.

CHAPTER FOURTEEN

"Well?" Callum asked after they had driven in silence for about ten minutes.

Killian shrugged. "She allowed me inside."

"That's an improvement."

"Aye."

Callum grunted. "I take that to mean things didna go well?"

"I don't know. I told her I missed her and thought of her every day."

"That took some balls. What did she say?"

"Nothing." Killian kept his gaze on the road. "Theo came in."

Callum winced. "Shite. That wasna good timing."

"When does pursuing someone to show them you've changed turn into something more sinister?"

"You're a long way from that, mate."

Killian shook his head. "It doesn't feel like it. Every second I'm here, I have to force myself not to go to her. I've spent too many years not seeing her in the flesh, and being this close means I can.

If only I could tell her everything. I thought…" He shook his head again. "Fek. I don't know what I thought."

"Aye, you do."

Killian glanced at Callum to find his friend staring at him. "You're right. I do. I believed if I could just talk to her and explain, she would give me a second chance, and we could start over. How could I have been so bloody stupid?"

"What do you do when you have a client in trouble?"

Killian frowned, unsure where the question had come from. "I figure out the problem and then determine how to solve it or work around it."

"Seems to me your problem is no' being with Ariah. You had a plan to solve it."

That was precisely what he had done. "Bloody hell."

"And that means you have a new problem."

"I have more than one."

Callum grinned. "That's usually the case."

Killian exchanged a smile with him. He was glad he had run into Callum that first night. He'd needed a friend more than he realized. "I guess that means I have several problems to solve. Want to help?"

"I have little experience with women and even less with relationships."

"That doesn't matter. You know Ariah. And you have a unique way of seeing to the root of an issue."

Callum laughed out loud at that. "Do I?"

"Aye, and I could use more of that."

"Then I suppose we should get to it."

They went to the B&B and sat in the garden, which was just beginning to sprout, heralding the coming of spring. The weather was mild enough that he and Callum ate outside with the owners, who were kind and welcoming to Callum. Killian was pleased when his friend relaxed and seemed to have a good time.

When they finished the meal, the owners returned inside while Killian finished off a bottle of wine and Callum drank some water.

"I wanted to sit down and talk to Ariah," Killian said into the silence. "I wanted it to be personal, but she isn't interested in that. However, I have things I need to say."

"Then tell her," Callum urged.

Killian tilted back his glass, only to find he had already drained it. He set it on the table and crossed an ankle over his opposite knee. "I intend to. I just don't like my options."

"Ah. Another problem to solve." Callum stretched out his legs, crossing them at the ankles. "This one seems easier. What are your choices?"

"Let's see…there's text."

Callum shook his head. "Pass. Next?"

"Email."

"Better, I suppose. I'm beginning to see your dilemma."

Killian raised his brows and nodded. "And my last option is to write a letter."

"That seems the most personal."

"There's an argument that typing out an email or text is also personal."

Callum wrinkled his nose. "Maybe for some, but Ariah isna like others. She notices the small things that others overlook. If you can no' speak to her, then I think you should write her a letter."

"What if she doesn't read it?"

"You wouldn't ever know if she read a text or email either."

Killian pinched the bridge of his nose with his thumb and forefinger. "True enough. I just…"

"Aye. I know," Callum said in a low voice filled with understanding. "Who's to say she willna want to talk to you after you write her?"

"Shite. I hadn't thought of that. I'd been too troubled by the problem at hand."

Callum stood. "I guess you'd better get to writing."

"Where are you going?"

"Wherever the night leads."

Killian pushed to his feet. "You're welcome to stay. That is if…" He stopped at the emptiness he saw on his friend's face. "I'm just saying if you don't have anywhere to go, stay. It's better than going home if you'd rather not. I escaped to uni after boarding school. I had time away. Sometimes, that's what's needed."

Callum said nothing.

Killian cleared his throat and briefly looked away. "All I'm saying is that you have a place to crash if you need it."

"Thanks."

"But look, you've listened to me moan about my troubles for hours. I'm sure you have somewhere better to be."

Callum turned away, silent for a long time. "You know, don't you?"

Killian squeezed his eyes closed for a heartbeat. He could lie and say he didn't know what Callum was talking about, which was probably exactly what Callum was hoping for. But Killian couldn't do that. But would it do more harm than good to let his new friend know he *had* figured out his secret?

He opted for something in the middle. "We all have things we don't like about our families."

Callum turned to pin him with a hard glare.

Killian blew out a breath. "Aye. I know."

"How?"

One word, but there was so much emotion in it that Killian wanted to find Callum's father and beat him until he couldn't stand. Instead, Killian said, "A mate at uni endured years of abuse. He was a close friend but kept it hidden until he got drunk one night and told me how it sometimes still happened when he went home. I looked at the world differently after that night."

"No one else can know."

"I won't say anything. Though I think you should tell someone. DI Frasier seems like a decent guy. Ariah trusts him."

Callum firmly shook his head. "This is my burden."

"And mine. As your friend."

"He'll kill you if you get involved."

Anger surged through Killian. "Who? Your father? I've dealt with men like him before."

"Nay, you have no'. Trust me on this. If you are the friend you say you are, I want your word that you willna say or do anything."

"You want me to stand aside and do nothing if you're hurt?" Killian jerked his chin to the wound still healing on the side of Callum's head. "Like that."

"That's exactly what I'm asking."

Killian stared at him in disbelief. "Why?"

"It's how it has to be."

"Fine," Killian bit out. "I'll agree, but I'm asking for something in return."

A muscle in Callum's cheek jumped. "If I can agree to it, I will."

"I want your promise that you'll come to me if you need help.

For anything. I don't care if it's money, to get away, or to find a flat in a city across the world."

"We just met. Why would you do that?"

Killian pressed his lips together. "That mate I told you about? He went home for winter break and his father killed him. I should've done more. I'm not going to make that mistake again."

"All right," Callum said with a nod after a long pause. "I give you my word."

Killian's neck prickled with awareness. He looked over his shoulder, searching for anyone who might be near.

"You feel it again?" Callum asked, moving beside him.

"Aye."

The word was barely past his lips before Callum strode into the night. Killian followed, lengthening his strides to catch up. He noted Callum's hands were lifted, palms out. Their feet crunched in the grass and over stones. Killian could hardly see anything, but Callum was surefooted as he quickly covered ground. Suddenly, he halted and turned in a circle, his head bent slightly to one side.

"What is it?" Killian asked in a low voice.

Callum turned toward him. "Do you hear that?"

"Nay." Killian couldn't see his friend's face in the shadows. "What is it?"

"I'm no' sure."

"That doesn't fill me with confidence."

"It's probably nothing."

Killian moved in front of Callum before he could walk back to the B&B. "The truth, if you please?"

"I'm not sure what I heard."

"But?" Killian pressed.

Callum signed. "There have been some strange happenings on the isle."

"Strange how?"

"Strange-strange."

Headlights bounced across the land before swinging over them. Killian caught the worry on Callum's face. "Do I need to be concerned about Ariah?"

"Skye might have a more sedate pace than Dublin, but it can be more dangerous," Callum warned as he walked around Killian and started for the B&B. "We should all stay alert."

"All right."

"I'll be back. I have somewhere I need to go."

"Then you'll need these." He tossed the Audi keys to Callum, who grasped them out of the air.

He nodded in thanks. Killian watched him walk around the side of the house and pause, his hand on the structure. He stood there for a long moment with his head turned away. Just as Killian was about to ask what he was doing, Callum left.

Killian glanced out into the darkness one last time, then gathered his empty wineglass and bottle and returned inside.

Worry churned through Callum as he drove to the other side of Skye. The sleek Audi handled the curves beautifully. He tested the vehicle's limits, as well as his when he pressed the accelerator and sped along the roads until he finally reached his destination.

Callum turned and maneuvered down the winding drive until Carwood Manor came into view. He pulled to a stop beside a black Range Rover and threw the SUV into park. Then he was out and striding toward the door. It opened before he got there. That drew Callum up short. He had witnessed things with the sentient house on a couple of occasions, but it still startled him.

"Thank you," he said, crossing the threshold.

He halted immediately. Dark wood graced the floors and walls. A rug spanned the entire width of the enormous foyer. A matching runner ran down the length of the hall that led into the house. Along the walls were portraits of long-dead relatives with judging gazes.

Bronwyn came out of the kitchen with a welcoming smile, her straight, dark hair in a braid. "Callum. What a nice surprise."

"I need to talk to…everyone," he stated.

Her grin faded, and apprehension took root in her hazel eyes. "Are you all right?"

"It isna me. It's Killian. I think he's in trouble."

"What kind of trouble?" Rhona asked as she came through the kitchen door, followed by Elias and Filip.

Callum threw up his hands. "I doona know, but it's something."

"All right. Start at the beginning," Elias urged.

Callum looked at the four faces around him. "Killian Flanagan. He's become a friend."

Rhona took Callum by the arm and led him to the library across the hall. She sat him in one of the chairs and took a seat on the sofa. "Friends are good."

"He found me walking today and offered me a ride. It wasna long after I got in that he rubbed the back of his neck and asked me to look in the back seat to see if anything was there. I didna see or sense anyone or anything, but when I questioned him, he said it had happened a few times this morning," Callum explained. "It happened again while we were having lunch and before I came here."

Elias leaned against the mantel. "And you saw nothing any of those times?"

"I didna see anything, but I *heard* something this last time."

Filip came to stand beside Elias. "What?"

"Breathing." Just thinking about it sent chills down Callum's back. He swallowed the fear lodged in his throat. "The same breathing I heard in The Grey."

Bronwyn stood in the doorway to the library, shaking her head. "I've not opened that portal since the last time. We closed it. You sealed the tear yourself, Callum. That thing couldn't have gotten out."

Elias walked to her and pulled her into his arms. Rhona's face was tight with concern, while Filip looked as if he might be ill.

"It's getting out," Callum said. "I thought it was just memories. I even told Kirsi that when I caught her tumbling down the mountain. She said that thing was after her. That it was there, beside her."

Rhona jerked her head to him. "I can't do my job if I'm not aware of what's happening. I need every detail about Kirsi and Killian."

Callum nodded. "That's why I'm here."

CHAPTER FIFTEEN

Rhona trudged up the Red Cuillin mountain, bundled up tightly against the wind whipping around her as if trying to dislodge her from the stones. It nearly succeeded a couple of times. It would've been easier to have Balladyn teleport her inside the prison crafted by the Druids long ago. But she had needed the walk to sort through everything.

She'd gotten a deluge of information over the past few days. At least she was learning what others had kept secret now, but she didn't like *why* they hadn't shared. Fear was a powerful emotion. It had the ability to change everything—and not necessarily for the better.

She placed her foot on a rock and stepped up, her thoughts shifting to Killian Flanagan and the conversation she'd had with her mate.

"I like him."

It was the first thing Balladyn had said after spying on the Irishman. Which was high praise because her mate didn't give that kind of endorsement easily. He had lived for thousands of years as a Fae, before Erith, aka Death, offered him a position as a Reaper. Balladyn had seen and experienced more in his long life than most could comprehend. If he approved of Killian, then so would she. "I wasn't expecting that."

"Neither was I. I found him working at Ariah's shop. He left and found Callum along the road."

Callum had also been a surprise recently. His family was known to cause trouble, but he had kept to himself. Until he was there during one of their darkest battles to not only save Kirsi, but also several others of their group from The Grey, a place between worlds that held nothing but terror and doom. "That's a pairing I wouldn't have imagined."

"Me, neither," Balladyn admitted. "Killian said he needed a friend, and we both know Callum could use one. They get along well."

"Interesting."

Balladyn nodded. "I wish that was all I had to report."

"Tell me," she urged.

"Someone is watching him."

Rhona frowned, taken aback by his words. "Someone besides you?"

"Aye. I thought Killian was referring to me when he said he thought someone was watching, but he looked in a different direction. Callum inspected both the vehicle and the restaurant. He didn't see anything."

"And you?"

Balladyn's lips compressed into a thin line as he slowly shook his head.

Rhona's breathing was labored as she continued the trek up the mountain. It didn't bode well for them if a Reaper couldn't see what watched Killian. More troubling was the fact that Killian, who was magicless, was being watched at all. It had been in the back of her mind until Callum showed up at the manor. That changed everything.

The entrance to the prison wasn't easy to find. It had been designed that way to keep those without magic away. However, that had been during a time when Druids inhabited most of Skye. That had gradually shifted through the centuries until those without magic outnumbered the Druids. With more tourists hiking the isle, she couldn't take the chance of anyone stumbling upon the prison, so she'd created a barrier using her magic mixed with Balladyn's Reaper magic to ensure that only she and a few select others could get inside.

A long strand of hair tugged free of its binding and slapped painfully against her cheek. She pulled it away and glanced up to see how much farther she had to go. With Balladyn's approval of Killian, she shifted her attention to who or what could be watching him. The truth of the matter was that it could be anyone or anything. Despite a couple of wins, they were no closer to determining what the evil surrounding Skye was or what it was after. And that made for some sleepless nights.

Thankfully, she wasn't in it alone. Because there was no way Rhona *could* do it on her own. The Knights played a big role. There were five in the group, though one was never seen. It was their hacker—Sabertooth. No one knew if Saber was a man or a woman or even their nationality. Saber monitored the Druid chatrooms online for anything about Skye, The Grey, or the monster inside The Grey. So far, there had been nothing much of interest.

Saber also kept tabs on Georgina Miller, aka George, the leader of the Edinburgh Druids, who had made it her mission to put Elias MacLean into prison. She had recently tried to frame him for murder, though she and a small crew from Edinburgh were caught.

That didn't stop George, though. She set up an elaborate plan to infiltrate Rhona's group, sending a spy into their midst to take down Elias, Rhona, and the others. It might have worked had Jasper not fallen in love with his target, Willa.

Still, George's plans didn't stop there. She had her eyes on an ancient Druid book.

It was now in the hands of Bronwyn's cousin, Beth Stewart, which made her alarmingly powerful and frighteningly dangerous. The book held long-forgotten Druid secrets. Whoever had the book was nearly unstoppable.

Beth and Bronwyn, once very close, were now enemies. Beth blamed Bronwyn for preventing her from being with her lover, Sydney—a man who had abused Bronwyn when they were together, killed her father, and had also been with George when she set up Elias. Bronwyn had tried to save Beth from herself, and set about a chain reaction that couldn't be stopped in the process.

Sydney now resided in a mental institution, which only fueled Beth's hatred more. But Beth was smart. She had the book and kept off the radar. Saber had a difficult time tracking her. It was only by facial recognition that he had been able to find Beth at all.

Rhona wished that was all she had to worry about, but someone had also managed to corral the souls of dead Druids, creating a mist that had been controlled by the person imprisoned within the mountain. Kerry didn't have enough magic to create the mist that'd ended up taking several Druid's lives. Which was the reason she had been imprisoned. As for who'd produced the mist, that was still a mystery. Rhona suspected it had something to do with the evil that hung over the isle. What she didn't know was if it was connected to The Grey and the monster within.

Or if it was who watched Killian.

But why him? He wasn't a Druid. Though he did have a connection to one. Rhona climbed the last hurdle and paused for a moment. She walked to the concealed entrance and shouldered her way past the doorway to make the walk down the long, dark tunnel. She never left a fire burning. The cold and darkness were part of Kerry's punishment.

Rhona whispered a few words when she reached the cavern. In the middle, flames soared upward from the hollowed-out circular stone. There were six units in total cut into the mountain from one side of the cavern to the other. The only openings were metal bars along the front. Those, as well as the stones themselves, had been infused with a spell, preventing anyone locked inside from using their magic.

Kerry sat in a corner of her prison with her back against one wall and her head leaning on another. Without the spell she used to color her hair, it had returned to its gray-streaked brown, hanging limply along her jawline.

"You have no idea what's going on, do you?" Kerry asked, her voice carrying through the cavern.

Sometimes, Kerry spoke. Other times, she didn't. Rhona had suspected Kerry might have something to say this morning. It was one of the reasons she'd come. "And I suppose you want to tell me what it is."

Kerry snorted a laugh and rolled her head toward Rhona. "I'm sure that's what you'd like. Instead, I'll sit here waiting for you to make a mess of things as I know you will."

"Your time here hasn't changed you at all."

"Did you honestly expect that it would?"

"I'd *hoped* it would," Rhona admitted.

Kerry moved slowly, her face pinched in pain as she moved her aging body onto her hands and knees. She gripped the stone wall to pull her stout frame to her feet. Rhona waited until Kerry came to the bars.

Her hate-filled glare raked over Rhona. "You aren't prepared. You'll be ripped apart. Everything you know, every*one* you know, will be annihilated. You're a bairn! Skye needed someone with a backbone to lead our ever-shrinking group of Druids, someone who understands the way of things."

"You." They'd had this conversation before. Nothing Kerry said hurt Rhona.

Kerry grinned. "I was chosen!"

"And yet, here you are. If you're so special, why didn't you win the battle? Why isn't it me in there instead of you?"

"There's a plan. There has always been a plan. You just can't see it."

This was more than Kerry had said since they'd brought her to the mountain. Rhona needed to keep her talking. Maybe she would impart something without realizing it. She was careful with her words, but Rhona could be, too. "You saw it, though, didn't you?"

"Aye." Kerry's gaze went distant. "I saw it all. I was at the center of it."

"Of what?" Rhona asked softly, not wanting to push too hard.

"A fresh beginning for the Druids."

Shock ran through her, but she carefully hid it. "Why?"

Kerry blinked, her glower returning as she raked her eyes over Rhona. "The fact that you don't know says it all."

"Then educate me."

Kerry began to laugh as she walked back to her corner, the sound growing with every second until the mountain rang with it.

Rhona knew she wouldn't get any more out of her today. She walked to the cell and removed the bag of food from inside her coat and the bottles of water from her pockets to place through the bars.

Kerry suddenly rushed her, causing Rhona to fall backward onto her butt in surprise.

"You'll never see it coming," Kerry foretold gleefully.

Her laughter filled the area once more. Rhona got to her feet and walked out. The fire died at her exit. She didn't stop until she was standing outside. Then, she paused to look over her beautiful isle and the water beyond, dread churning in her stomach.

CHAPTER SIXTEEN

Killian snapped awake. He didn't move from his side as his senses came fully awake. He looked around the darkened area before him, certain someone was in the room. Was it Callum? Killian had stayed awake until after midnight drafting his letter to Ariah, editing it multiple times before writing out the final copy and stuffing it into an envelope he'd gotten from the owners. But Callum hadn't been back by then. Exhaustion finally took Killian.

The hairs on his neck prickled, sending warnings through his body. Killian quickly rolled onto his back, ready for an attack. Except no one was there. He sat up and flipped on the bedside light, proving he was alone.

He scrubbed a hand down his face. It must have been one of those dreams that felt real but wasn't, the kind that made someone think they heard something like the clicking of a camera when they only imagined it. He couldn't recall the name of what that was, but there was no other explanation.

Killian rose from the bed and looked at his mobile. His alarm was set to go off in thirty seconds. He stopped it and saw a text from Callum.

LATE NIGHT. DIDN'T WANT TO WAKE YOU. KEYS ARE UNDER THE FLOWERPOT NEXT TO THE THIRD COLUMN ON THE RIGHT.

Killian set aside his mobile and padded into the connecting bathroom to ready himself for the day. Callum had been right. Ariah would be back earlier than he expected. This could be his last day at the tea shop. His mother would say the work was beneath him, but frankly, he enjoyed it. It was a refreshing change of pace, instead of trying to get clients out of seemingly endless troubles they continually got themselves into.

He showered but decided against shaving for another day. He was quite happy giving up the suit and tie for more relaxed wear. The owners of the B&B and other guests were still asleep when Killian tugged on his coat, grabbed the letter to Ariah, which he stuffed into the inside pocket, and headed downstairs.

After quietly letting himself out, he followed Callum's instructions and found the keys to the Audi right where he'd said they would be. Killian started the vehicle, wondering if his friend had returned home. That kind of physical—and likely emotional, mental, and verbal—abuse usually had a regrettable outcome for one or all involved.

He wanted better for Callum, but Killian couldn't force him to do something Callum didn't wish to do. All he could do was be there for his friend. And Killian intended to do just that.

The drive into town was uneventful. The roads were empty, with small, dark puffs of clouds scattered throughout the pre-dawn sky. It was a cool morning, but the weather predicted a warm afternoon. Killian hadn't yet decided how to give Ariah the letter. It might be better to just put it in her mail slot.

As he drove, he realized how excited he was to start the day. Even as early as it was. He'd had a fast-paced life in Dublin and had filled every second with something, be it work, social engagements, working out, family, or learning a new hobby. He hadn't allowed himself any downtime. When he did, his mind had always drifted to Ariah.

The problem, though, was that it didn't matter how busy he kept himself, she was always there.

Not having her with him had gotten easier over time, but he had keenly felt the loss through the years. It was like missing an arm or a leg. It had once been there, and there were still phantom feelings. Some mornings, he'd wake up and roll over to pull a body against his that he thought was Ariah. Except he'd open his eyes to find his ex-fiancée instead.

The pain that followed was terrible.

He pulled into his spot and reached the Tea Talker at the same time Ruby did, keys out to unlock the door.

"Ready for another morning?" she asked cheerfully.

He grinned. "How are you so jovial at this time of day?"

"Mornings are my jam. I get so much done in the quiet before the world wakes up. You should try it."

They entered the building, locking the door behind them, and walked to the back, where they hung up their coats. Ruby set aside her purse and began heating water for the day while he went to the front and took down the chairs from the tables.

The walk among the trees did wonders for Ariah. Her feet were still tender in places, but she had added extra padding to the bandages to cushion those areas. She likely wouldn't be able to stay on her feet all day, but it was a start.

The sky was a soft gray, proclaiming the pending arrival of the sunrise. It felt as if things were back to normal. Moon followed her into the forest and lay curled beside Ariah during her meditation. Now, the feline trotted in front of her on the way back to the house.

She gave the cat breakfast and added water to the fountain. Ariah then gave Moon one final pet before locking the door behind her. There was a smile on her face as she drove to work. The events that'd led to her injury still troubled her, but there'd been no more strange occurrences.

Skye was under attack by something sinister. Rhona and the group of warrior Druids at her side had been assaulted by other Druids looking to take them down. That had never happened before. Every group of Druids in the world knew that the strongest of their kind was from the Isle of Skye.

Druids were drawn to the magic of the isle. Some came for holiday. Some decided to call it home. Skye had once only been inhabited by Druids, but those without magic outnumbered them now. Some Druids believed their kind was dying out because their blood had been diluted too much by magicless individuals.

Those Druids had once been a small, insignificant group. However, their numbers had grown drastically over the last year. Many of those same groups had begun to shift from individual communities to joining larger Druid Others. It made them more powerful, but only those at the top of the organization since everyone fed their magic into them.

Ariah wasn't a fighter. She believed in peace. Violence begat violence. And while she considered herself a pacifist, she wouldn't stand by and allow anyone to murder more of her people. The mist had slaughtered too many Druids. And George and her henchmen were far from done with the isle.

Then there was Beth.

Ariah passed the co-op and saw Sabryn and Elias walking up the stairs on the side of the building to Kirsi's flat above. They could be there for any number of reasons, but her guess was that it was about the evil. Everyone called it that. Evil.

There really was no other word that encapsulated it so completely. It was a wrongness that penetrated deep into the ground, even through the water. It hung over the isle. It wafted from below. Simply put, it was everywhere.

Rhona worked diligently with her team to figure it out while also fielding questions from community members. Everyone had been on high alert for months. Ariah parked and shut off the vehicle. Her home had been ravaged by an unknown assailant. She could've been the latest victim. If so, she had gotten off nearly unscathed. Was it time she took a stand?

She opened the door and stepped out, only to pause by her car. Her gaze slowly scanned the town, waking up to greet the day. Everything appeared normal. But it wasn't. She couldn't put her finger on why. But something wasn't right.

The first streaks of color crept into the sky. Unease slithered down Ariah's back. She needed to warn Rhona. She hurried to the door, her mobile in hand to call the Druid leader. She spotted Ruby through the window next to the door. Ariah slipped inside and parted her lips to speak. Ruby's face went slack when she saw her. Ariah frowned at that, even as she lifted the mobile to her ear when the line began to ring.

"I've already watered the plants. And, nay, I didn't water all of them. I wrote down the ones that needed it daily," someone said from the back.

Ariah knew that voice. Killian. Her gaze slid to the back entrance as he came around the corner, wearing jeans and a white tee, the long sleeves pushed up to his elbows. The moment he saw her, he froze, his smile slipping. It hurt, knowing that her presence caused such a change in someone. She had made it clear that she didn't want him around, so what did she expect?

"I can explain," Ruby stated.

At the same time, Killian said, "I was just helping out until you were better. I'll leave."

"Hello?" Rhona said across the line.

Ariah's mind was locked on the scene before her. She couldn't tear her gaze from Killian, hearing his words from the day before in her head.

"*I miss you.*"

"Ariah?" Rhona said. "Are you all right?"

Killian rubbed the back of his neck with a hand, a frown creasing his brow. His gaze swung to a window, and anger flashed across his face.

"What is it?" Ruby asked while Rhona hollered in Ariah's ear.

Words lodged in her throat. She lowered the phone and took another step toward Killian.

He shook his head, the fury replaced by apprehension. His attention swung to Ariah. "Get out!"

His words rang through the building as the windows shattered, shards flying inward. Ariah dove under the nearest table and dropped to her haunches, covering her head with her hands as she hid her face against her knees. More glass breaking and falling from the ceiling cut off any other sounds. She felt the sting as tiny slivers of the windows embedded in her skin. The tinkling of glass hitting the floor seemed to go on forever.

Finally, it subsided. Ariah looked up to find Ruby in a ball on her side under a table, beads of red dotting her clothing and exposed skin. Ariah jerked her head to Killian. The sight of the large piece of glass lodged in his side had her heart dropping to her feet.

"Killian!" she cried as she slipped on glass, nearly going down a couple of times as she rushed to him.

He lifted his head, and their gazes met. Blood soaked through his shirt in various places, including his arms. "Don't," he warned.

Ariah ignored him as she fought to stay on her feet. She was nearly to him when his face drained of color. A moment later, he was thrown sideways, crashing into a table and chairs before sliding into a potted plant with such force that it cracked the ceramic planter, spilling soil atop Killian a moment before the tree toppled over.

"What is happening?" Ruby asked in bewilderment.

Ariah didn't have an answer. All she knew was that she had to reach Killian. Blood dripped from Ariah's fingers, dropping to the floor. Glass crunched loudly underfoot as she made her way to Killian, who hadn't moved.

"Please, please," she whispered.

He had to be alive.

"Ariah!" Ruby shouted.

She felt it then, the presence. Ariah whirled around, her magic up to shield herself and, hopefully, Killian. She couldn't see anything, but she knew it was there. Something pressed against her magic. She called for more of it. It slid through her body, rushing to her palms and then outward. The atmosphere was heavy with evil, but it became incensed at the push of her magic.

Killian let out a cry of pain behind her. Ariah backed up and dropped to the floor, trying to get close enough so her shield protected him, too. The air around her started to condense. Glass was embedded in her knees, but she refused to drop her shield.

Then, whatever had been there vanished. Ariah spun around to Killian. The sight of his bloody and battered body was almost too much. Sirens wailed in the distance as dozens of voices called out.

"Killian. Oh, God," she said and reached for him.

CHAPTER SEVENTEEN

Killian clawed through the darkness as the imperative to remain conscious hounded him. He needed to make sure Ariah was safe. Pain crashed into him, each breath agonizing and torturous. Oblivion waited just at the edges, promising him ease if he just let go.

A murmur of voices tried to break through his fog of pain. He needed to do something but couldn't remember what it was. It was important, but his body hurt too much for him to think properly.

"Killian? Oh, God," a voice said, cracking at the end.

Ariah. He latched onto her voice and somehow managed to open his eyes. It was only a blink, but in that second, he saw her face, glass stuck in her hair, and beads of red dotting her cheek. Her fingers found his hand. He gripped her tightly, needing to feel her. He couldn't move more than that.

"It's okay," she told him. "You're going to be okay."

He wasn't, and they both knew it. Killian succeeded in taking another quick look. Tears ran down her face. He hadn't gotten to give her the note. He didn't want to die without her knowing what a fool he had been and how much he loved her. He tried to form the words, but his lips wouldn't obey his command.

"Balladyn!" Ariah yelled.

Cold seeped over him. He wanted another look at Ariah. One more before he was gone.

"Balladynnnnnn!"

"I'm here," said a deep Irish voice near them. "Fek."

Killian could no longer feel Ariah's hand in his. He tried to hold on tighter, not wanting to let go. But it was too late.

Balladyn met Ariah's gaze. "You need to stay. This is too public. I will see to him."

How dare Balladyn say she couldn't go with Killian? What if the Healers couldn't save him? What if this was the last time she saw him? Balladyn didn't give her a choice. He gently removed her hand from Killian's, and then they were gone.

A cry of denial, one born of terror and rage, bubbled up. Ariah bit it back and dropped her head as she squeezed her hands into fists. The salt of her tears fell into the cuts and left a trail of stinging pain, but she barely noticed. She kept picturing the chunk of glass sticking out of Killian's side.

When she opened her eyes, her gaze locked on the pool of blood where he had lain. It puddled thick and dark. It had saturated his shirt and jeans, his life force pouring from him, thick and fast. She realized that it had soaked into her skirt at the knees, too.

The wail of sirens broke into her thoughts. Balladyn would get Killian to the Healers, and they would work their magic and save him. She refused to think of any other outcome.

Glass crunched behind her. "Ariah?"

She lifted her head at the sound of Theo's voice. It was then that she remembered Ruby. Her gaze scanned the shop for her friend and found Ruby being taken out by the paramedics.

"Ariah."

She swung her head around and looked into Theo's brown eyes. "Killian. I need to go to Killian."

"I'll take you, but you can no' leave yet. This was a public attack with many witnesses. I have to handle this with care, which means I need you to stay and give a statement," he told her.

Ariah reluctantly nodded, knowing he was right. "I understand."

"Rhona is en route. Sabryn and Elias were with Kirsi when the explosion happened. They didna see anyone. Did you? Do you know who did this?"

She lifted a hand to wipe her face, but Theo quickly grabbed it before she could.

"Shite. There's glass all over you," he muttered as he looked her over.

"I saw no one," Ariah murmured. She thought back to when she'd entered the building. How shocked she had been to find Killian here. He had been just as surprised by her appearance. Then he had looked outside and told her and Ruby to get out. Her heart lurched. "Killian saw something. He shouted a warning before the glass shattered."

Theo pursed his lips and nodded quickly. "I'll have a look. Right now, we need to get you cleaned up."

Theo shouted at someone. Seconds later, paramedics surrounded her. Only then did he release her arm. Ariah let them guide her from the building. She got her first look at the destruction when she glanced back, but she didn't really see it. She only saw Killian bleeding as he looked at her.

Ariah stood in a daze as three paramedics gently began removing glass from her body. She had no idea how long she stood there before she heard someone speak. She focused to find a female.

"…of those clothes and into clean ones."

Ariah looked down to see some clothing in the woman's hand.

The paramedic placed the items aside. "One of your friends brought them. When you remove your outfit, do so slowly and try to keep them inside out to trap any glass we may have missed. We'll dispose of them safely. Once you're dressed, give us a shout."

Ariah could only manage a nod.

"You're in shock," the woman said softly, kindness in her brown eyes.

Then, Ariah was finally alone. She followed the paramedic's instructions. A shiver went through her as she balled up her clothes and set them on the floor of the ambulance. She reached for her shirt and drew up at the sight of the bandages on her arms. She took stock of her body then, from all the white gauze to the dark stains on her knees. Killian's blood. She felt bandages on her neck when she turned her head.

There was hardly any pain. Most likely because of the shock. Ariah dressed quickly. A scarf held up her hair, but there was likely still glass there. She'd need to see to that soon.

"All right," she called after a slight hesitation.

The door opened, and the paramedic smiled as she entered.

"None of the wounds were too deep. Both you and your coworker were very fortunate."

Ariah felt guilty at not thinking about Ruby. "Where is Ruby?"

"She's already been sent home. Same as you soon."

"How is she?" Theo asked as he walked up.

The paramedic turned to him. "Not bad, all things considered. The most severe wounds were on her arms, but nothing that needed stitches." She turned her head to Ariah. "Which is fortunate."

"I dove under a table," Ariah explained.

Theo gave the woman a nod. "Thanks. I need to get a statement from her."

"She's in shock, so go easy," the paramedic warned.

"I will," Theo promised.

Ariah accepted his help getting out of the ambulance. Her gaze lingered on her ruined clothes for a long moment until he put a hand gently on her back and steered her away. Ariah wound her arms around herself, chilled from more than the spring morning.

Theo shrugged out of his suit jacket and placed it around her shoulders. He caught her gaze and held it. "I've no' found anything. Nor have I gotten word from Balladyn. Sabryn and Elias are with Rhona, searching the area. Saber is checking the CCTV cameras. Scott and Elodie are with Ruby to make sure her home is secure, and she's settled." He paused. "Rhona said you called her, but she couldn't hear you."

"Aye," Ariah said as she stared at the broken windows, still seeing Killian hurt. She closed her eyes and turned her head away. She looked at Theo. "Aye, I called her. I wanted to tell her that something felt off here."

"You saw something?"

She shook her head. "No. But then I walked into the shop and saw Killian." Her gaze returned to what was left of her business. "I was shocked to find him here."

Theo cleared his throat and glanced away. "Did you know Killian believed he was being watched?"

"What?" Her head snapped to Theo. "That's...nay. I didn't know that." She hadn't known because she refused to speak to him. "Callum might."

"It was Callum who told us last night."

Ariah wished she had known. She wished she had spoken to Killian instead of keeping him at arm's length to protect her heart. Fat lot of good that did since it was being squeezed mercilessly now as she waited to hear about his condition.

"I didn't know anything," she confirmed. "Do you know who it was?"

Theo shook his head. "Callum saw nothing. Balladyn was near a few times but didna see anything either. But both felt something."

Balladyn hadn't just happened to be *near* Killian. The Reaper had been spying. She might have been furious a day before, but now she was thankful that Balladyn had been there. On the heels of that was the knowledge that if Callum and Balladyn hadn't seen anything, then no one had any idea where to start until Killian regained consciousness.

"I need to go to Killian," Ariah stated.

Theo shifted his feet. "In a moment. Tell me what happened. Every detail."

She blew out a frustrated breath and had to remind herself that Theo was just doing his job. "I decided to come in today for a few hours."

"Did anything seem out of the ordinary?"

Her gaze slid to her car. "When I got out, I felt uneasy. I couldn't put my finger on why, exactly."

"Did you see anyone?"

"I saw a lot of people, but no one who stuck out. I stood by my vehicle for a few minutes, looking around."

Theo nodded as she spoke. "That's when you decided to call Rhona?"

"Aye. I walked into the building as I dialed her."

"And then what?"

Ariah pulled his jacket tighter around her. "I saw Ruby first. Then Killian came out of the back. I was so surprised to find him here."

"Where were you?"

"Near the door," she said, pulling up the memory. "Ruby was near the far wall, and Killian was just past the register."

Theo grunted.

She looked at him to see him writing in a small notebook.

"So, no' quite in the middle of the store?" Theo asked.

Ariah shook her head. "He rubbed the back of his neck."

Theo's gaze snapped up. "Are you sure?"

"Aye," she said with a nod. "Why, is that important?"

"Callum said that's what Killian did right before he mentioned something about being watched."

The guilt of not knowing about Killian's troubles weighed heavily on her.

"Tell me what happened next," Theo urged.

Ariah licked her lips. "He, ah, looked outside. Then he shouted for us to get out. I didn't have time to react because the windows exploded, followed by the ceiling. I dove under a table and waited for it to end. When I looked up..." She had to pause at the memory of seeing Killian in such obvious pain, his eyes beseeching her.

Theo gently touched her arm. "Take your time."

"There was a huge piece of glass sticking from his side. He looked at me. I went to him, but before I could reach him, something threw him."

"Threw him?" Theo repeated, his brow furrowed deeply.

"It looked like something came up and kicked him. He crashed into a table and chairs, then a plant. The force of the collision was enough to break the wooden table and my ceramic pot."

"And you didna see anyone?"

"No one."

Theo snapped the notebook closed and tucked it into his pants pocket. "Ruby gave the same statement."

"How is she?"

"A wee bit battered and in shock, same as you. She'll be fine."

Ariah stared at her ruined store. "How do I explain the windows shattering inside?"

"Let me worry about that."

Theo gently turned her and led her through the crowd to his vehicle. Ariah was aware of people milling about to get a look. She glanced up, allowing her gaze to move over the crowd as she slid into the passenger seat.

"See anyone who looks guilty?" Theo asked after he got behind the wheel.

"I see too many familiar faces. That's the problem."

CHAPTER EIGHTEEN

Kirsi watched the flashing lights near the Tea Talker, the sirens now silenced. Curious onlookers dashed toward the disaster to get a glimpse. Her ears still rang from the explosion that had sent Elias and Sabryn running from her flat. A sick feeling settled in her stomach as she wrapped her arms around herself and stared at the scene of the accident. Or was it a tragedy?

There had already been too much of that on the isle already. But more was coming. She could pretend otherwise, but the truth had been laid bare the moment Ferne reached out to her through her mind. Even then, it had felt like something far off in the future. Until Kirsi walked into The Grey.

There was no coming back from something like that.

No way she could ignore what was already here.

A figure came up behind her. She stiffened until she saw it was her father. He moved to stand beside her, his arm around her shoulders to offer comfort. She laid her head on his shoulder. Her plans to sleep late and organize her closet on her day off had been interrupted by Elias and Sabryn knocking on her door.

"Want to talk about it?" her father asked in the soft voice he used when he knew she was upset.

There was no way she would burden him with what she knew—or what she suspected. "Not really."

"Are you in trouble, pet?"

She hesitated. It wasn't the kind of trouble he thought it was, and she didn't want to tell him. He had enough to worry about with her mum's muscular dystrophy and the loss of his magic.

"It's just that I saw Elias and Sabryn at your door this morning," he said and turned his head toward her. His beard brushed her forehead.

Kirsi missed the days when all she had to worry about was getting the latest fashion and passing her courses. "They just wanted to talk." It wasn't a complete lie. She just omitted a few things.

"I might be getting up in years, pet, but I can handle anything you need to tell me."

She lifted her head and looked into her father's brown eyes. Kirsi wanted to tell him everything. About The Grey and the monster, about how that same fiend lurked in her dreams sometimes, how it had even tried to reach her while she was awake. She wanted to tell him how scared she was and that she didn't think she was strong enough to handle whatever was coming—because she wasn't.

Instead, she forced her lips into a believable smile and watched the wind moving his bushy brown eyebrows about. "If it was anything you and Mum needed to know, I'd tell you. You know that."

"Good. That's good." His gaze slid back down the street to the commotion. "I heard someone say it was Ariah's place. I want to know what happened, but I doona think the police need more spectators. I'm sure Rhona will alert us if its serious."

Kirsi wrapped her arm around her father. He hadn't said anything in days about his waning magic. It caused him great concern, as it would any Druid. "How are you feeling?"

"Oh, I'm great," he replied with a quick smile that didn't quite reach his eyes. "Your mum isna having the best day, but she refuses to go home. Stubborn woman."

It didn't matter how many times Kirsi begged, neither of her parents would ask the Healers if they could do anything about her mother's disease. Her mum was convinced it would be a waste of magic, but Kirsi wanted to know for sure. The time when they could've gotten answers had probably passed. Her father wasn't the only Druid feeling a change in his magic. It was happening all over Skye. It seemed to be random, but no one could say for certain. Her father's magic was dimming, but neither hers nor her mum's had been affected. Yet.

"I really am good," he promised, pulling her closer.

She stared into his eyes and nodded, accepting his answer for now. The thing was, her father was always fine. He had been from the moment of her mum's diagnosis. He was their rock, the pillar that stood as the storms of life battered their small family. He kept her and her mum protected, sheltered, and loved like no one else could.

"I need to get back in there and check on your mother. Stay close, eh?" he urged.

Kirsi nodded. He gave her a quick kiss on the cheek and returned to the store. She glanced down to see that she was still in her pajamas. After a quick look at the door leading into the store, she hurried up to her flat, changed into the first clothes she found, and wound her hair up into a bun. Then she debated on going to see Callum.

There was a chance his father would be around, and that never turned out well. But she needed to talk to him. She deserved an explanation for why he had gone to Rhona with her secret. She decided to try texting him first.

WHERE ARE YOU?

She waited, staring at the screen for the three little dots telling her he was replying. But there was nothing. She waited fifteen minutes before sending a second text.

WE NEED TO TALK. IT'S IMPORTANT.

Minutes ticked by without anything. Then she began to worry that he might have been at Ariah's. Callum had been seen with Killian. If they had been at the Tea Talker during the explosion, one or both of them could be hurt. Kirsi decided to call Callum.

She listened as the line rang, tapping her toes as if that would somehow make him answer faster. It went to voicemail. She let out a curse and ended the call before sending a third text.

PLEASE TELL ME YOU WEREN'T AT THE TEA SHOP. THERE WAS AN ACCIDENT.

Kirsi hesitated, her fingers hovering over the keys as she wondered if she should say more. Instead, she hit send and waited. Her stomach was in knots. She began to pace, her thoughts moving from one horrible thought of what might have happened to Callum to another. The longer it went without him answering, the worse those thoughts became. Until she couldn't take it anymore.

She grabbed her purse and keys and hurried out the door. Her feet moved so fast down the stairs that the heel of her trainers caught on a riser and tripped her. She grabbed the handrail before she landed on her back. After a beat to calm her racing heart, she took the rest of the steps at a reasonable pace and ran the short distance to her car.

Her hand shook as she attempted to stick the keys in the ignition. It reminded her of another time she had been shaky and Callum had been there to drive her. She finally got the key in and started the engine. Kirsi was about to pull out when she saw Edie walking to her vehicle away from the crowd at Ariah's. But it was the elation on Edie's face that gave Kirsi pause. No one else was smiling. No one else looked pleased. Why did Edie?

Kirsi kept her foot on the brake and watched Edie drive past. As she did, Edie looked right at her. A chill of apprehension slid down Kirsi's back. There was something not quite right about anything this morning. She remained until Edie was out of sight before pulling onto the road. A glance in her rearview mirror showed the edge of the Tea Talker building through the throng of people and the first-responder vehicles.

It was early. The tea shop hadn't yet opened. Maybe nobody had been inside. But as soon as that thought went through her mind, Kirsi knew it was wishful thinking. All she could do was hope that whoever was inside hadn't been injured.

Kirsi pressed her foot on the accelerator and headed to Callum's. She quickly looked at her phone in the cupholder. It sat still and silent.

Callum had the volume up loud on the speaker sitting on the table next to him as he worked. He had been waiting weeks for the part to arrive. He set aside the wrench and wiped his hands on a towel. All he had to do now was install it, and the customer could pick up the boat. After handing over payment, of course.

Callum carried the wrench and the part to the dry-docked vessel. He climbed aboard and walked to one of the rear seats that was lifted to allow access to the components. This was the trickiest part. He had to place it just right. If it slipped from his fingers and struck anything, it could do damage to several components.

Joe hadn't bothered to teach him that. Callum had to learn that on his own, which had cost him a hefty sum to repair the other parts. But that was Joseph Kilmuir. Father of the year.

There were times, like now, when Callum could pretend he lived alone. Days would go by without him seeing his father, and each time, he'd wonder if Joe had finally died. Unfortunately, his hope would be dashed soon after.

Things were always better when Joe stayed out of sight, too sotted to stand. Callum rarely went inside the house. He had moved his meager belongings to the boat shed years ago. Winter was harsh and barely tolerable, but anything was better than enduring Joe Kilmuir and the stench of the house.

It hadn't always been like that. Callum still had memories of when the smell of his mother's bread filled the house. She'd had flower boxes at the windows, overflowing with vibrant blooms from spring until fall. Sometimes, he could still hear the clothes she once hung on the line snapping in the wind.

Callum laid the component into place. He used the wrench to tighten everything and double-checked that all the lines were hooked back up properly. The only thing damaged was the skin near his knuckle. It was ready for him to put the boat in the water and take her for a quick spin to confirm that everything was in working order.

He straightened and reached up to pull the seat down as a few drops of rain scattered over him. He caught a glimpse of one of his tools as he did. Callum grabbed it, stuffing it into his back pocket as he pushed the bench closed with his other hand. The click confirmed it was locked into place. He used the towel he always kept on him to wipe off the grease he'd left behind, then turned around, only to jump back startled at the sight of Kirsi.

Her pale-green eyes glowed with fury as the wind dragged strands of hair from its fastening to dance about her face. Her mismatched clothes alerted him that something was wrong. The bright pink sweatpants had paint stains on them, and the yellow sweatshirt was oversized with tattered edges. She repeatedly shoved the sleeves up her forearms, but the cuffs were stretched out and kept falling to hang past her hands.

"You can't answer your bloody mobile?" she demanded in a raised, angry tone.

Callum glanced behind her to see if Joe had heard her arrival. There was no sign of his father, but he didn't want to take any chances that would change. The last thing Callum wanted was for Joe to accost Kirsi either by word or action. Callum just might kill him if he did.

"Well?"

His gaze slid to her face. Every time he dared to gaze into her stunning eyes, he became lost. It had been that way since he was seven, and she'd smiled at him at the co-op.

But she wasn't smiling now.

Rhona had warned him she would speak to Kirsi. He just hadn't expected it to be so soon. "Listen," he began.

She walked to him and grabbed his shoulders, turning him so he faced the water. Then she turned him once more. "You aren't hurt."

"Of course, no'. Why would I be?" he asked in confusion.

"You didn't answer my texts or my call."

Callum glanced toward the workshop where his mobile sat. "I had music on, and I doona keep my mobile on me. I've lost too many in the water that way."

She nodded, crossing her arms over her chest and taking a step back.

"What's going on?" he asked.

"There was an explosion at the Tea Talker this morning."

Blood rushed in Callum's ears. "What?"

"There was an explosion. I heard it. When you didn't answer, I thought…"

She didn't finish the sentence. Of all the people on the isle, she was probably the only one who had been concerned about him. "I'm okay. Killian was there, though. He's been covering Ariah's shifts."

"I didn't get close enough to see if anyone was injured."

"Then let's go find out."

She motioned to the boat. "What about this?"

"It can wait." Confirmation about his friend couldn't. "Come on."

They hurried to Kirsi's car. Callum kept his eyes locked on the house, willing Joe to remain unaware until they had pulled out and were headed toward the manor.

They didn't get far before Kirsi asked, "Why did you tell them?"

Callum didn't pretend not to know what she meant. "Killian has felt someone watching him. I was there a few times when it happened. I didna see anything, but the last time, I detected that something wasna right. Too many people have died already. I wasna going to be responsible for another because I kept my mouth shut."

"And I'm guessing Rhona asked if you knew if anyone else had experienced anything?" Kirsi asked, glancing at him.

"Aye. I'm sorry."

She moved hair from her face. "Don't be. I should've told Rhona about my…whatever it is that's happening."

"Are we good?" Because it was important to him that they were. More important than anyone would ever know.

Her smile was easy, even if it wasn't quite as bright as usual. "We're good."

CHAPTER NINETEEN

Even before Killian opened his eyes, Ariah filled his thoughts. The devastating fear that she would be hurt rushed to the forefront of his mind. His gaze cleared, and he found himself looking up at a wooden canopy. He started to get up to determine where he was, belatedly recalling that he had been hurt. Killian froze, waiting for the onslaught of pain, but none came.

He frowned, his confusion growing. Covers were pulled up under his arms, but he was naked beneath. He scanned the green tartan bedcoverings until his eyes locked on Ariah sitting beside the bed, asleep. One arm cradled her head on the mattress while her other hand gripped his. Her hair was loose, the long length falling like a curtain over her far shoulder. Her face was turned toward him. He longed to stroke her cheek but was loath to move and disturb her.

Small red marks from the accident dotted her cheek. There were more on her hand and arms, and a few deeper ones covered with bandages.

Was this a dream? Or worse, was he dead? Both were logical choices since he didn't recognize the place or have any pain. And he should have lots of it. He hadn't been able to breathe. Not to mention, there had been a rather significant-sized piece of glass sticking out of him.

Killian didn't want to think about what had happened, but there was no getting away from it. Even now, his stomach soured with the same fear that had gripped him right before the glass exploded. He could've tried to reach one of the tables, but all he had been able to think about was getting to Ariah and protecting her. Then he hadn't been able to move at all. He had been useless. Thankfully, someone had saved her.

Something wet and cold pressed against his cheek. He rolled his head away from Ariah and found himself staring into the blue eyes of a rather large feline with a cream coat and a dark-colored tail and ears. The cat sat beside his shoulder, looking as if the very sight of Killian bored him.

The feline stood and walked down Killian's legs to his feet before circling around them and heading for Ariah. Killian didn't want to wake her. She might pull her hand out of his or, worse, leave. He wanted just a few more moments as they were.

Killian shot the cat a hateful glare when it butted its head against her arm. A weird sound, like a boat engine, emanated from the animal. Was that…purring? The feline bonked its head against Ariah a second time. Killian's gaze jerked to her to see a smile curving her lips as she sat up, her eyes closed as she instinctively reached for the animal with her free hand.

He watched how Ariah seemed to know exactly how to pet the cat, which caused its purring to grow even louder. Finally, Ariah opened her eyes and pressed her forehead against the animal's while scratching its neck. The more love she gave the cat, the more it wanted. And the louder it purred.

Killian knew exactly how the animal felt.

Then the cat surprised him by curling up against his hip and laying its chin on him, its blue eyes trained on him once more.

Ariah's gaze briefly moved his way before she did a double-take. Her face slackened with surprise, followed quickly by delight. "You're awake. How do you feel?"

"Fine. Which isn't right. Am I dead?"

"Of course, not." She gripped his hand tighter as a nervous smile flitted across her lips.

"Is this a dream?"

She swallowed and shook her head. "You aren't dead, and this isn't a dream." Her golden-brown eyes filled with tears. "I'm sorry I acted like such an idiot. I should've let you say whatever you needed. You almost…" She paused and blinked rapidly. "I'll listen to whatever you want to talk about."

This had to be a dream. It was the only explanation for her having such an about-face regarding her feelings about him. Though the dream was startlingly clear. It wasn't fuzzy like his others. Even odder was that he seemed to have complete control over his body. The countless times he'd been locked in a dream and needed to fight his way out of something, he'd throw a punch as hard as he could, only to have it to bounce off a wall or face or other object without harm—or never reach his target at all. It was maddening.

Ariah rose to her feet and cupped his face with her hands. "I'm sorry."

They were so close he couldn't stop himself from brushing his fingers across her cheek. Her beautiful eyes were filled with remorse. He dropped his gaze to her mouth, a deep ache tightening his chest. He longed to kiss her and have her taste fill his senses again.

"Killian," she whispered, right before she pressed her lips to his.

The moment their mouths touched, it was like a spark against kindling. He moaned as their tongues tangled in an intimate dance. Desire blazed, the intensity scorching his blood. He wound one arm around her, tangling the other in her hair.

She was in his arms again, something Killian had begun to think would never happen. He deepened the kiss and ran his hand down her back. It was the bump beneath her shirt that pulled him from the haze of passion. He gradually ended the kiss. Ariah lifted her head to look down at him with a soft smile.

He wanted to keep kissing her, to face the questions that plagued him another time. But he couldn't. "Where am I?"

"Carwood Manor. It's a safe place."

The fact that she'd had to add that meant there was something to fear. Killian recalled in vivid detail the pain of the glass in his side. "What happened?"

Her smile slipped, and she straightened to stand beside the bed. "I knew this was coming. I've been dreading it, even as I wished for you to wake."

"Just tell me. Because right now, you're making it worse."

"Once I tell you, everything will change."

Killian reached for her hand, feeling the uncertainty and fear in her words. "I doubt that."

Ariah sank onto the chair once more. "I need you to take everything you think you know about Earth and the timeline of humans and forget it."

"What?" he asked with a startled chuckle.

"I'm serious."

He could see she was. Killian sat up so he reclined against the wooden headboard. He searched Ariah's face and nodded. "All right."

"Humans came from another planet. And Earth was never meant to be ours. It belonged to…others."

Her slight hesitation made him ask, "Who?"

"Dragons." His misgivings must have shown because Ariah hastened to add, "Hear me out. It's a long story, and the best place to start is at the beginning."

"Ariah," he began.

She held up a hand. "I know you'll think this is fantastical and nothing but a story, but I can prove it all."

Killian looked down at his side, which didn't even show a scar. He still wasn't convinced he wasn't dreaming. Dragons, for fek's sake. If they were real, everyone would know. He wanted to refute Ariah's words, but the way her eyes pleaded with him silenced any words. He nodded for her to go on.

Ariah turned her head and stood. She walked to where the cat now stood at the door and opened it a crack to let him out. After quietly closing it, she made her way to the window and placed her hands on the windowsill. Rain pinged against the glass.

"Earth is made of magic. The heart of it is in Scotland. At Dreagan, actually," she said, her back to him.

"Dreagan? As in—?"

"Aye. The whisky." She glanced at him. "Dreagan translates to dragon in Gaelic. The dragons ruled this realm for millions of years before humans were brought here. Those few mortals were plucked from their Druid home world because they didn't have magic."

Killian could only blink as he tried to keep up with everything she said. Dragons and Druids.

"The dragon clans were led by Dragon Kings, those chosen by the magic of the realm. At the arrival of the mortals, they were able to change forms from dragon to human in order to communicate. They welcomed the humans and offered them a place. Things were good for a while, but eventually, they broke down. There was a great war, with the Kings ultimately sending the dragons away and going into hiding."

"At Dreagan," Killian said.

Her shoulders lifted as she took a breath. "Exactly. They made it so no one would want to enter their domain, and much of their estate is still that way. They waited until mortals forgot about dragons, until the mere mention of them was thought to be fantasy and myth. Then they began walking among us."

And made whisky, apparently. It was an unlikely story, but Killian kept his comments to himself.

"Meanwhile," Ariah said, turning to look at him, "some humans began exhibiting magic. They were drawn to Skye, where they set up a community that exists to this day. Of which, I'm a descendant. You were saved by our Healers." She paused, and her gaze lowered to the floor. "Something…wrong has come to the isle. It has been coming after Druids in the past weeks, and I believe Ruby and I were the most recent targets."

Killian waited until she looked his way. "And I just happened to be in the way?"

"Aye. Everything I've told you is the truth."

"I believe you believe what you've told me, but magic isn't real."

She gave him a sad smile. "Oh, but it is. Explain your wound."

He couldn't, and she knew it.

CHAPTER TWENTY

Ariah had expected Killian to say something about not believing in magic. She had even prepared herself for it. But that didn't lessen the sting of his words.

During their summer together, she had almost told him about her Druid roots so many times. There had been instances where she could've demonstrated her magic. It was Killian who held her back. He was a practical man. He devoured law and business books like most people read fiction. He dismissed any kind of entertainment that involved a magical or fantasy element.

Many lived their lives by superstition and lore. But not Killian Flanagan. His thinking was in complete contrast to who Ariah was at her core. And she had been too much in love to want to jeopardize it, so she had kept silent.

Yet she hadn't been able to end their affair. She had loved him too deeply. She certainly wouldn't have been the first Druid in history to keep her magic a secret. That only got tricky if the couple had children. Ariah had convinced herself there was time to slowly bring Killian around. Then things ended between them, and it hadn't mattered.

Now, she found herself right back in that same predicament. Except, this time, she had come clean. Well, not quite. The Dragon Kings and Druid origins were enough for the moment. She could get into Fae, Reapers, and Skye's enemies later. The last thing she wanted was to overwhelm him.

Her gaze lingered on his bare chest. Just a few moments earlier, she had lain nearly on top of him, sharing a ravenous kiss that even now had the power to make her knees weak. She pressed her lips together and tasted him. Killian sat still as a statue, eyeing her as if she were a stranger.

"Carwood Manor is Bronwyn Stewart's home. She and her partner, Elias MacLean, live here. Elias brought some clothes for you to borrow. You'll find them in the bathroom. I'll be downstairs. If you wish to join us, take a left out the door. The hallway will lead you to the stairs."

Killian didn't call her back as she walked to the door. She slipped out, her heart pounding loudly. She closed it and leaned against the wood as tears of disappointment pricked her eyes. But she had already cried enough today. Killian deserved the truth. He had it now. What he did next was out of her hands.

Something brushed her leg. She looked down to find Basher. Theo brought him back and forth from his and Ferne's home and the manor often.

"Hello, my handsome lad," Ariah whispered, lifting the big cat into her arms and pressing her face against his as she scratched the side of his cheek. His purring soothed her.

She carried him downstairs and followed the voices to the library. A fire was lit in the large hearth, making the room cozy in the rain and damp. The talking ceased when she entered, and every eye locked on her, waiting. She walked to one of the empty plush chairs and sat. Basher made himself comfortable on her lap, sensing she needed him.

"Has he woken?" Elias asked.

Ariah looked around the room at the faces staring back at her. Elias sat opposite her, with Bronwyn on the arm of the chair. Elodie, his sister, sat on the sofa with her mate, Scott. Beside Scott was his sister, Willa, and her partner, Jasper. Everyone else was still sorting out who might be responsible. It was where she should be.

She finally nodded. "He has."

"I take it things didna go well," Jasper said.

Ariah concentrated on petting Basher. "They did not. He looked at me as if I was daft. Then he told me he believed that I believed what I told him."

Bronwyn grimaced. "Ouch."

"Oh, it gets better," Ariah replied. "He said magic isn't real. I was getting ready to show him, but I couldn't after that."

Scott exchanged a look with the others. "We could."

"It'll likely come to that," Elodie agreed.

Willa shot her a sympathetic look. "Give Killian some time. It's been a traumatic day for both of you. Besides, we were raised with magic. He's just learning. Everything he knows is being upended."

"That's a good point," Bronwyn said.

Elodie asked, "How much did you tell him?"

"The basics. Our origins, the dragons, and who we are," Ariah answered.

Elias grunted and rested a hand on Bronwyn's thigh. "It's probably a good thing you didna give him the entire rundown."

Ariah blew out a breath. "I lied to him."

"About what?" Jasper asked.

She propped her elbow on the arm of the chair and leaned her head against her open palm. "I told him the attack was likely against me or Ruby."

"That may no' be a lie," Scott said.

Willa looked at her brother and nodded. "That's true."

"Killian suspected someone was watching him. He saw something before the glass blew," Ariah argued.

Bronwyn caught her gaze. "Did you ask him?"

"I meant to do that first thing. But he began asking questions. He thought he was dead. Then he thought it was all a dream. I had everything thought through. I knew how to start the conversation, what questions to ask, and how to tell him the truth. But it all went to shite." Ariah smoothed her hand down Basher's fur.

Scott got up and stoked the wood in the fireplace. After he'd replaced the poker, he turned to face her. "It doesna matter how you planned it. It was never going to be easy. He can ask us anything. We'll answer him."

"But should you?" Ariah asked. She looked at each of them. "I knew when we first met nearly a decade ago that he would have a difficult time understanding and accepting me and our community. Things are in upheaval here. Everyone is in danger, and..." She paused, drew in a steadying breath, and said, "It would be best if he forgot about any feelings he has for me. He needs to return to Ireland."

The conversation ended when Filip came through the front door. He shook off the rain and hung up his raincoat. Striding into the library, he stood in front of the fire warming his hands. "Just came from the village. Forensics is wrapping things up. Theo will be here soon."

"Oh!" Willa said and sat forward. "I was supposed to go help Ferne unload more books this morning. I completely forgot."

Jasper took her hand in his. "It's understandable after everything that's happened, love."

"Where is everyone else?" Filip asked as he faced the room.

Elias said, "Sabryn, Carlyle, and Finn are doing their own investigation where Theo can no'. Rhona is with the deputies, informing them so they can alert their sections. Balladyn is likely with her."

"I wish Esther and Nikolai hadn't returned to Dreagan to look for Henry. We might need them," Elodie said.

Ariah thought about the Dragon King and his mate. Esther was the TruthSeeker, and Henry was the JusticeBringer. They were from an ancient line of Druids who regulated the Druids. As a species, the Dragon Kings had the most formidable power. And they were allies and had come to Skye's defense before. They might be returning sooner rather than later if things continued in this vein.

Lights bounced across the window and drew everyone's attention. No one was worried, though. It was no accident that everyone came to Carwood Manor when things went awry. The house was sentient. It had been built with magical materials on land brimming with magic. The manor had kept everyone safe on multiple occasions and knew who to allow entry and who to keep out.

Two car doors closed. A moment later, there was a rap on the door. Before Bronwyn could rise to answer, the house opened it. Ariah craned her head to see through the double library doors to the foyer. Callum and Kirsi rushed inside.

"We're in here," Bronwyn called.

Kirsi had her arms wrapped around herself as she walked into the library. Callum was slower, his steps hesitant despite the times he had been in the manor. Ariah thought about Killian upstairs and the friendship he and Callum had developed.

"We thought this was the best place to come." Kirsi met Ariah's gaze. "And to find out what happened."

Elias nodded. "You were right to come. Both of you are unhurt?"

"Aye," the pair answered in unison.

Callum caught Ariah's gaze. "Was anyone hurt?"

She nodded once. "Killian took the brunt of it."

"Is he okay?" Callum asked, concern deepening his voice.

"He is now." Ariah studied him for a moment. "He was attacked. I believe whatever hit the store came for him."

Elias shook his head. "We doona know that for sure. He isna a Druid."

Ariah ignored him and kept talking to Callum. "Killian saw something out the window. He shouted a warning, but there wasn't time before the all the glass exploded inward. Ruby and I sustained a few injuries, whereas Killian was badly injured. Whatever was there tossed him to the side afterward. It never came for me or Ruby. Just him."

"Bloody hell," Callum muttered and ran a hand down his face. "But he's alive?"

Elodie looked over her shoulder at him and said, "The Healers were able to save him."

"Save him?" Callum's gaze jerked to Ariah, his eyes wide with shock.

She nodded quickly. "Aye. He had questions, and I, ah, I gave them to him. He isn't taking the truth well."

Callum looked up at the ceiling. "I doona imagine he is."

"Maybe you should talk to him."

Callum's amber gaze slid to her. "I'm no' sure I could do better than you."

"He needs a friend. That's what you are," Ariah urged. "He's on the second floor, third room on the right."

Callum exchanged a look with Kirsi before walking away. Ariah hoped that sending Callum didn't make things worse. Once Killian knew how many on the isle were Druids, he might leave and never return. But wasn't that what she wanted to keep him safe?

She didn't want him to be targeted, and that's exactly what was happening. Everyone could put in their opinion, but she had been there. She had witnessed the assault with her own eyes. Something had gone after Killian. If Balladyn hadn't gotten there in time…

She continued to stroke Basher's fur, wishing Moon was with them. One question kept going through her mind. Why Killian? He wasn't a Druid. He was no threat to whatever was happening on Skye. The only connection she had to the Druids was her.

"Could George be responsible for this?" Filip asked, pulling Ariah from her thoughts.

Bronwyn snorted and compressed her lips. "Doubtful. She doesn't have the book. It could be Beth."

"Or something else," Kirsi interjected. She shifted her feet nervously. "The monster in The Grey has…it's been…" She stopped and swallowed, her nervousness clear. "I've seen it and heard it since. Callum kept my secret. I should've told someone, but I was scared."

Ariah hadn't been a part of those who'd gone into The Grey, but she knew the horrors that had occurred in the place between dimensions. She joined the others in reassuring Kirsi that they understood.

Her gaze drifted to the hearth and the flames within as her thoughts returned to Killian. Why him? She and Ruby had been right there. Whatever had attacked could've come for them, but it hadn't. And that was worrying.

CHAPTER TWENTY-ONE

The smile had yet to leave Edie's face. The Ancients had told her to be at the Tea Talker that morning. She had been unable to look away from the shadow that had attacked the shop, going straight for Killian. She still didn't know if the Ancients had created it like they had the mist, but they would tell her when they wanted her to know.

Edie wanted to celebrate the display of power she had witnessed. The way the glass had imploded had been epic. Killian had seen her. Not that it mattered. There was no way he could survive all the glass that'd struck him.

Before she left, she had seen someone moving about. She had quickly hidden so as not to be seen, so she hadn't been sure if it was Ariah or Ruby. She had no issue with either of them, but if the Ancients tapped them for death, so be it. The Ancients knew who belonged in the new age of the Druids.

Edie turned the wheel and headed toward her husband's work. They had been going through a rough patch the last few months.

Mainly because she had been angry and bitter about her siblings' return and their continued secrets. It had caused a strain in her marriage and with her children.

Edie had decided to put aside her resentment for Elias and Elodie and focus on her family. The change had been exactly what she needed to save her marriage. Trevor had noticed immediately and began acting more like his old self.

It wasn't so long ago that she would often stop by his work just to say hello. Maybe bring him his favorite coffee or a snack. But as the children got older, she had stopped doing it. Edie diverted down a side street and doubled back to get Trevor a coffee and revive some of the old things she used to do. It was a day for celebration, after all.

With everyone crowded around the Tea Talker, Edie was in and out of the coffee bar in record time. She sang along to the radio as she continued her drive to Trevor. Maybe she could convince him to take half a day, and they could spend it in bed. They'd have the house all to themselves before the kids got out of school. The more Edie thought about it, the more she liked the idea.

She pulled into the car park, her gaze immediately going to Trevor's parking space. But it was empty. She pulled into a spot, put the SUV in park, and dialed her husband's mobile.

"Hey," he answered happily as if her call was exactly what he needed.

Her smile grew. "Hey, love."

"Did you hear about the Tea Talker?"

"I did."

"It's terrible," Trevor murmured. "I have no' heard if anyone was injured. Have you?"

"Not yet." But she had seen the damage. She knew someone was more than injured. "What are your plans for the day?"

He chuckled. "Work."

She looked at his empty spot. "Want to skip out?"

"If only. We're swamped. A new client just landed on my desk. I'll be in meetings all afternoon. They're waiting for me now, actually."

Her stomach roiled with unease, and her mind immediately went to the picture of Trevor kissing another woman Kerry had given her. She hadn't pressed him about it for fear of losing him. She had been the one to nearly ruin her family. But now…*now* her gut was telling her something wasn't right.

"How about I stop in for lunch? I could bring your favorite sandwiches."

"That sounds lovely, darling, but today is the worst. Let's try for tomorrow."

She couldn't tear her gaze away from his empty parking spot. Anger began to slowly boil. "If all of you will be in meetings, why don't I pick up lunch for everyone. I'll drop it off, say a quick hello, and leave. I just want to make sure you're eating."

"Have I told you what an amazing wife you are?" he said, a smile in his voice. "I would love that, but one of the assistants has already taken care of lunch. Oh. William just walked into my office. I need to go. Call you later. Love you."

The line went dead before she could reply. For long minutes, Edie stared at the place her husband's vehicle should be. He was lying. Again. Was he at one of their many rentals? She could drive all over the isle in search of him. Again. But she didn't need to. She knew what the outcome would be.

Her eyes slid to her mobile. All the rentals had cameras. She could pull up the feed and look for him. The last time she'd found him at one of their homes, he had been with a female colleague who claimed she was searching for a home on Skye. Trevor had offered to show her the different areas.

Edie had told herself the explanation was plausible, but at the time, when she'd walked in and found them, she had been sure the two were there for a rendezvous. It had taken her weeks to get past that. Now, she was mired in it all over again. Her good mood was gone, evaporating like a snap of fingers.

"What do I do?" she asked aloud, hoping the Ancients would answer.

They remained silent.

She turned off the engine, grabbed the coffee she had gotten for Trevor, and strode to the office door. There was an easy smile on her face despite the hammering of her heart and the pit in her stomach.

The receptionist's smile froze, her eyes widening in distress at the sight of her. And that told Edie everything she needed to know.

"Hey, Sarah," Edie said as she walked past. "I'm just going to drop this off in Trevor's office."

No one stopped her. No one dared. She kept her head up and a smile on her lips, even as others stared at her, a ripple of surprise traveling through the office. Everyone knew. She was furious that no one had dared to tell her about Trevor's affair. Or was it affairs? Did it matter? The fact was, he had strayed.

Edie turned the corner and headed toward his office. The door was open. William, one of the firm's partners, stood outside of his office, talking to his assistant. Edie nodded, waved, and somehow kept walking. Her heart thudded painfully as despair and anguish threatened to choke her. She had a mission, though. And right now, in front of everyone in the office, she would keep her head held high and pretend to be the unaware wife just going about her day.

"Edie. Hi," Rebecca, a pretty twenty-something with large breasts, on-point eyeliner, and amazing hair said as she came around her desk in an attempt to stop her.

"I'm just going to set this on Trevor's desk." Edie breezed past Rebecca into an empty office.

She had known he wouldn't be here, but seeing it was like someone had a fist around her heart, squeezing out all the love and happiness until she was an empty vessel. Only to replace the desolation with wrath. Her hand shook as she set the coffee in the middle of Trevor's messy desk.

"You just missed him," Rebecca said from behind her. "He's going to be away through lunch. He had…"

Blood rushed in Edie's ears, preventing her from hearing the lie. The urge to spin around and flay the skin off Rebecca's beautiful face was so overwhelming that it shook Edie to her core. How many times had she lied for Trevor? How many times had he lied *to* Edie?

Edie had to push away the magic at the ready and calmly turn to face Trevor's assistant. Gripping her hands together to keep from giving into the rage that now consumed her, she said, "I know. I was just on a call with him."

"I just didn't want his coffee getting cold," Rebecca said, chuckling nervously.

How many times had Trevor slept with her? Many, Edie imagined. She glanced out the office door to find that work had halted as everyone watched. How many of the women had fucked her husband? Edie seethed with indignation. She could kill every one of them with barely a thought. They wouldn't dare look at her with pity or amusement if they knew what she could do.

What she wanted to do to every single person in the office.

"*You will have your payback. But not today,*" the Ancients whispered in her mind.

"I bet you know how to heat it up." Edie raised a questioning brow at Rebecca. "Was there anything else you needed?"

"Ah. No. Not at all." Rebecca turned and walked away.

The smile didn't drop from Edie's face until she was in her vehicle. She didn't go home. Instead, she drove to Wild Point. The last time she had been there with Kerry, her eyes had been opened. Kerry had been working with the Ancients, but now she had disappeared. Yet no one seemed concerned about that.

Edie walked out to the point. She didn't realize she had brought her mobile with her until she looked at her hand. She felt detached, as if she were peering down at herself as she logged into the security system and went through each of their rental's video feeds. With each one that came up either empty or occupied solely by those who had leased it, the knot in her gut tightened.

She had found Trevor at one of them before. He wouldn't make that mistake again. If he was on the isle, his liaison was somewhere else. But there was another way to find him.

Edie quickly went to the app that listed their family so they could track the kids, and the kids could find them if needed. However, Trevor's name was grayed out. She tried to press on it, but nothing happened. Edie knew what that meant. He had turned off the app so no one could track him.

All the proof she needed was in front of her. She squeezed her eyes closed as she thought about the picture of him kissing the woman. She had *forgiven* him for that indiscretion. He had blamed her for the widening gulf between them. She had believed she was the cause of everything, including that kiss. It was why she hadn't confronted him about the picture.

She dropped to her haunches and ducked her head to her knees. A roar of fury choked her, begging to be let loose. Edie was afraid to release it, scared of what she might do.

Of who she might become.

"Don't be scared. We've always known what you're capable of."

The Ancients' voice was clear and calm, a balm to her wounded and tattered soul. "Then direct me to someone so I can release this…thing inside me."

"You already know your next target."

Edie slowly straightened. That odd calm took her once more, banking the wrath but not extinguishing it. "Aye."

CHAPTER TWENTY-TWO

The bathroom mirror was still fogged from his long, steamy shower when Killian inspected his bare torso. He shifted to the left and a better angle and spotted the jagged, faint pink line that ran from under his armpit to his last rib. He had seen the tip of the glass sticking out from under his arm after it impaled him. He vividly remembered the shock.

The pain.

That hadn't been the only glass that'd found its mark on his body. His hands had also taken the brunt of the skylights falling from above. He held out his hands, palms down, and barely discerned any sign that there had been an injury at all. If he hadn't seen where the glass had struck him, he wouldn't think anything had occurred. But he had. A closer inspection showed the very faint lines as evidence. Some glass had even fallen out of his hair in the shower.

And if his hands had been struck, then so, too, had his back. Killian spun around and peered over his shoulder into the mirror.

He twisted his arms and felt around on his back, but he couldn't get a good view. But if his side and hands were healed, his back would also be.

There was no getting around the fact that he had been fatally injured. He'd known he was dying and had fought against it because of his need to protect Ariah. He faced the sink and glanced out the partially opened door to the bedroom. He should be in a hospital. Or a morgue. Yet he stood in someone's home, having been healed by Druids, if Ariah could be believed.

Her story about Dragons and Druids was impossibly outlandish. He met his gaze in the mirror. Then again, his being alive also bordered on the incredible and unimaginable. But not just alive. He was entirely healed as if there had never been any wounds.

How was that even possible?

Magic. Druids. It seemed outrageous, incomprehensible. If Ariah was right…if everything she had told him was true… He squeezed his eyes shut, his mind unable to accept or acknowledge it. He shoved it aside to consider again later and turned to something he could sort out—who had attacked the shop.

And why.

He had made his share of enemies. It was part of the job when he sat on one side of a conference table against powerful companies. Some could set aside emotions, knowing it was all business. But others couldn't—and didn't bother trying.

There could be an argument that it was his father or the firm. His family *was* the firm, so he supposed there wasn't any kind of differentiation. Brian was pissed that Killian had walked away. And his father was capable of a lot of things. But Killian didn't think he would attempt to kill his own son. Force him back, manipulate, and even blackmail him, sure, but never kill.

Killian ruled his father out, and no one else in the family or firm would go against Brian. That left other enemies. Which meant plenty of people could have come after him.

There was something else he had to consider. This wasn't his first time on Skye. Someone might be angry that he had returned after hurting Ariah years before. But why would they go after him with Ariah in the building? That didn't make sense.

He absently tugged on the jeans and black jumper. Could the target have been Ruby? He didn't know if she was injured, but he had seen her under the table. Maybe she had been healed like him. He thought back to the bandages on Ariah and frowned. Why hadn't her wounds been healed? Killian blew out a frustrated sigh, closed the lid on the toilet, and sat to put on his socks and boots.

"There is something…wrong on the isle. It has come after Druids in the past weeks, and I think Ruby and I were the most recent targets."

Ariah's words drifted back to him. She seemed sure of who the attack had been aimed at, but he wasn't. The more he thought about things, the more he was sure *he* had been the one whoever it was had been after. He leaned his forearms on the tops of his thighs, a memory just out of reach. But even without reliving it, terror pervaded him, turning his blood to ice.

A short rap on the door yanked him from attempting to pull up the memory. Killian hesitated. He couldn't decide if he wanted it to be Ariah or not. He hadn't made sense of any of her words yet, and he wanted to do that before they spoke again.

He touched his lips, the memory of their passionate kiss returning with a vengeance. For the first time in years, everything had felt right. True. Genuine. He loved Ariah. Had always loved her.

Killian stood and walked to the door. A jolt of surprise went through him when he opened it and found Callum standing there. "What are you doing here?"

"I heard what happened and came to check on you."

In that instant, Killian knew. His new mate considered himself a Druid.

"I understand if you'd rather be alone," Callum said and shrugged. "Then again, you might need a friend now more than ever."

Killian stepped back to let him in. The other man was right. He did need a friend. He stuck his hands in the front pockets of his jeans after shutting the door behind Callum.

His friend walked to the same window Ariah had stood at earlier and looked out the glass dotted with water droplets, causing the outside world to appear fuzzy and distorted. "I can no' imagine what it's like to discover there is more to the world you thought you knew. The majority of people believe what they're taught from history books and think it is all facts and truth." Callum turned to face him. "I find that hilarious when everyone knows the victor writes those books. Or governments decide what they want their country to know. None of it is true. It's always skewed to make those who conquered look righteous and moral for the slaughter of innocents and the claiming of land that was never theirs."

"I'm not sure we can apply that to the story Ariah told me about dragons and magic."

"You're leaving out Druids."

Killian shrugged one shoulder. "Dragons, Druids, and magic. Better?"

"No' really. You doona know everything. Ariah only shared a piece of the puzzle. She didna tell you about the Fae, Reapers, or the Warriors."

Killian shook his head as confusion and doubts rose. He waited for Callum to laugh and say he was jesting, but there was no smile on his face.

"The truth is, there is a vast and terrible history to our world verra few are privy to. Believe me, I've raged at the fact that I'm part of those who know, because I want to be normal. I'm no', and ignoring that only harms me."

Killian's brain felt as if it were overloaded.

"Is it so bad that magic is real?" Callum asked.

Killian leaned against the door and considered his question logically as he did everything. "It can't be real. If people had it, they would show it off."

"They do. All the time. Fae walk among us. Ireland is the home they chose after coming to Earth."

"That doesn't make me feel better."

"I wasna trying to make you feel better." Callum ran a hand down his face. "Look, like with anything, there is always good and bad. For Druids, the *mies* are those on the side of good. *Droughs* are the ones who chose the other option. But there are *mies* who do bad things, and *droughs* who do good."

"*Mies* good. *Droughs* bad," Killian stated.

Callum nodded once. "Ariah is *mie*. So am I. There are *droughs* who call Skye home, but Rhona monitors them closely. The moment they step out of line, they're kicked off the isle. Becoming *drough* is a choice."

Killian felt as if he should be taking notes. How would he ever remember all of this? "How can I tell a Druid from someone who isn't?"

"You willna be able to unless you see them using magic."

Killian grunted. "Great."

"It's a lot, I know. All you really need to know is that Druid magic is special. It also varies in strength by person. Some can talk to trees, rocks, or the wind. There are those who can commune with animals. Some Druids are Healers while others are Seers. And some can only do minimal magic."

"What can you do?"

"I understand metal. It's why it's easy for me to fix things. I can see how things are supposed to work, what has gone wrong, and how to fix it."

Killian blew out a breath. "Fek."

"Druids use spells. Our magic flows through words and movement."

"Show me."

Callum motioned for him to draw closer. "Hit me." When he hesitated, Callum grinned. "Trust me."

Killian walked to him and faked a right jab before coming around with a left hook. His fist never made it to Callum's face. Something stopped him. Killian couldn't see anything, but he felt something. He glanced down to see both of Callum's hands raised as if to ward him off.

"It's a shield. Something every Druid learns when they're young."

"Hmm."

Callum's brow furrowed. "You still doona believe."

"I'm taking all of it in. It's a bit difficult to accept."

"From what I was told, you were badly injured."

Killian nodded. "Aye."

"You're healed now, though."

Killian's gaze dropped to the floor, his hand going to his left side. "As if nothing happened."

"But it did."

His gaze met Callum's. "It did."

"Magic was used. You're walking proof that it's real."

That was one argument Killian couldn't refute.

Callum shoved his hair out of his face with a quick movement. "You've been around Druids for days without knowing it. You spent a summer with Ariah. You know she's a good person."

Killian scratched at the whiskers on his jaw. "She is. So are you. If I hadn't been injured, would either of you have told me?"

"Sometimes, it's better no' to tell than to peel back the curtain and show just how unstable our realm really is."

"That makes me feel better," Killian stated sarcastically and shot Callum a dry look.

He shrugged. "I deal in truths. It's easier that way."

Killian couldn't deny that. Something nagged at him that he was finally able to pull into focus now that his mind had somewhat cleared. "Did a Druid attack the shop?"

"That's still being determined. Theo should be here soon with some answers."

The DI. Of course, he was also a Druid. Killian was beginning to think everyone on Skye had magic. "Ariah said something on Skye is hurting Druids. She thinks what happened was meant for her and Ruby."

"You doona?"

That memory and fear from before rose again, teasing Killian with the truth. He tried to grasp it, but it moved just out of reach again. "Nay, I don't. Who wants to hurt Druids?"

"Are you sure you're ready to know all of this?"

"In for a penny," Killian replied.

"Fair enough." Callum took a deep breath and then released it. "We doona know. It began some weeks back. Strange things that didna make sense. Small things. No' anything to notice unless you saw it as a bigger picture. Maybe if we had, we would've been able to prepare."

"Is Ariah in danger?" Killian demanded. The thought of something being after her chilled his blood. "The nightmares and sleepwalking. Is that part of it?"

Callum shrugged. "Maybe. I doona know. We had mist killing Druids. Some Druids on Skye are even losing their magic. Something's out there." He hesitated, his brows drawing together.

Killian could see him debating whether to say more. "I want to know everything. Don't hold back now."

"I felt it," Callum said in a low voice. "Heard it."

"Heard what?"

"The monster might be what's causing all of this."

Killian thought about the attack earlier. "Where is this monster? Why has no one gone after it?"

"We tried. It nearly killed Ferne, and it's after Kirsi. As for where, it isna a place you can get to easily."

"I can try."

"No, you can no'."

Killian stood his ground. "Tell me."

"It's a place between dimensions, and it isna anywhere you want to go. We almost didna get out alive the last time. I doona ever want to go back."

Killian raked a hand through his damp hair and looked away. What had he expected? That Callum would point him to a house, and they would go in and slay the monster as if they were some mythological heroes? The absurdity of it all wasn't lost on him. But there was one thing he couldn't stop thinking about.

"Why didn't Ariah tell me that summer? I believed we didn't have any secrets," he asked, more to himself than to actually get an answer. But he got one anyway.

"Fear."

Killian swung his head to Callum. "Fear?"

"Of you rejecting her because she had magic. Of you thinking she was daft when she told you the truth."

Killian inwardly winced. Then it hit him why Ariah hadn't wanted to leave Skye. Her people, her community, as she had called them, were here. She wasn't different here as she would be elsewhere. He had pushed and pushed to get her to change her mind, and she had known from the beginning she never would.

"You can walk away. No one will stop you," Callum said and headed toward the door. He paused when he reached it, his hand on the knob. "You came to win Ariah back. Doona forget that."

CHAPTER TWENTY-THREE

SKYE DRUIDS

The library was filled with conversation. Scott and Willa Ryan spoke about their still-missing father and the lengths they were going to in order to find him. Ariah heard them, but she wasn't paying attention. Her thoughts were directed at the floor above and the man she had assumed she would never see again.

She had been beside herself with fear and worry when she saw Killian lying there, broken and bleeding. Dying. He was healed now. Balladyn had gotten him to the Healers, who did their job and erased nearly all evidence that he had even been injured. She could stop worrying. If only she could get the picture of him and all that blood out of her mind.

The walls she had erected to protect her heart were nothing but dust now. They had never stood very solidly when it came to him. Time hadn't dimmed her feelings. Her love had remained nestled in her chest, waiting. Wishing.

Yearning.

Despite attempts to move on and forget Killian, the shadow of him had remained. It was no wonder no one had ever measured up. She compared prospective dates to a man no one would ever be able to match, much less beat. She'd even convinced herself that she was destined to be alone in life. Accepted it. Embraced it.

Then Killian waltzed back into her life.

The sight of him had brought back all the heartache, ripping open old wounds. But other memories had also accompanied those. The ones that brought a smile, the ones that made her long to be locked in his arms again.

There had also been a spark of hope in those recollections. She had tried to stamp it out and shove it away, but it hadn't dimmed. Merely waited. As if it had known all along that she couldn't keep Killian at arm's length.

It had taken him nearly dying for Ariah to have it all laid out clearly in front of her. Killian had the ability to tear her heart to shreds, but she loved him. With all her heart. And everything she was. She couldn't deny him or her feelings. And she was ready to risk more hurt to have another moment in the sun with him.

This time might be different. And that was the allure she couldn't ignore.

The manor door flew open. A second later, Ferne came rushing in, and a few steps behind her was Theo, who shrugged out of his trench coat and hung it up with the other outerwear as the door softly shut on its own. The two quickly kissed hello, their eyes sharing an unspoken message between lovers.

"Sorry I'm late," Theo said.

Basher jumped from Ariah's lap and raced to the couple. He wound around Ferne's legs until she bent and stroked a hand along his arched back. Then he went to Theo and stretched his front paws up onto Theo's legs. Theo lifted the large feline into his arms for a cuddle while Basher rubbed his head on the DI's face.

It made Ariah think of Moon being alone at the cottage. She looked around the library at the growing crowd. Soon, Rhona and Balladyn would arrive. Eventually, Sabryn, Carlyle, and Finn would show up. She cared for each of them, but right now, she needed time to herself to think. She needed the forest and her cat.

Ariah rose from the chair and slipped into the foyer unnoticed. She spotted Kirsi also making a silent retreat. Callum came up behind her as she backed away from the library, gently stopping her with his hands.

"Easy," he said in a low voice.

Ariah closed the distance between them and asked Kirsi, "What is it?"

Kirsi wore a deep frown as she picked at a frayed hem on her right sleeve. "How do you know when it's time to share something?"

Ariah looked at Callum, but his gaze was locked on Kirsi. "Trust your instincts."

Kirsi nodded absently. "It could be nothing."

"It could be something. Trust me. I know," Ariah told her.

As if just now seeing him, Kirsi looked over her shoulder at Callum. "I don't want any of this. I don't want to be a part of it. I don't want to be responsible."

"We doona get to decide such things," he said.

The sadness in his voice struck Ariah. There wasn't a person who lived on Skye who didn't know the Kilmuir history. Ariah liked Callum, but she couldn't deny that she feared he would follow in his family's footsteps.

She put a hand on Kirsi's arm. "Go in there and say whatever it is you need to say. No matter if it is or isn't something to be concerned about. No matter who it involves. No matter what it involves. Share it so everyone knows."

"I suppose," Kirsi said. "It might make some angry."

Callum shrugged. "So?"

"Ariah. Just who I was looking for," Theo said as he walked to her from the library. "Elias said you spoke to Killian. Did you ask him about the attack?"

She shook her head slowly. "We were discussing other things."

"Good. Good. I want to talk to both of you separately." He gave her a gentle pat on the shoulder before striding to the stairs and taking them two at a time.

Kirsi started toward the library. Callum lingered for a moment, pulling his gaze from Kirsi long enough to say, "Killian is getting there. Give him some time."

Then he hurried after Kirsi. Ariah should've asked to borrow their keys. She walked to the door and tried the handle, but it wouldn't budge. She placed her other hand on the wood and rested her forehead on the door.

"Please. I won't be gone long. I want my cat and some air," she begged the house.

It often kept people out, but it seemed intent on keeping her inside. She hoped her words satisfied the sentient house, but when she tried the handle a second time, it remained locked.

"Even the house knows you shouldn't leave," Balladyn said behind her.

Ariah turned to face the Reaper, who had his arms crossed over his chest. She looked into his red-ringed silver eyes. "I'm not running away."

He lifted a black brow. "Aren't you?"

"I need time to think. Away from—" She motioned toward the noise of the library.

"The manor is quite large. I'm sure a room could be found away from everyone."

"I need to feed my cat."

Balladyn dropped his arms to his sides. "Then I'll take you."

It defeated her wanting to be by herself, but it was the only way she could get away from the manor for a short time. And right now, she needed that more than being alone. "All right."

He held out his hand. Ariah placed hers inside it, and in a heartbeat, she stood in her kitchen. Moon let out a startled meow from the counter. Ariah immediately went to the feline and petted her. She purred loudly in response.

"Thank you for getting Killian help in time." She glanced at Balladyn to find him studying one of the books Ferne had brought her.

He slowly set it on the table and met her gaze. "Of course. Killian isn't taking his introduction into our world well, I take it?"

"You could say that."

"He needs time."

Ariah fed Moon and then looked out the window at the forest. "I need to walk in the woods."

"Now isn't a good time. We don't yet know what brought on the attack."

Or who was responsible. Ariah tore her gaze from the forest and filled her kettle with water before putting it on the stove to boil. Balladyn could force her back to the manor with just a touch, but she hoped he didn't. She heard the scrape of the heavy wooden chair as he pulled it out.

"Tell me about this morning," he said.

She took down two cups and placed them on the table, then went through everything again. Balladyn didn't interrupt or ask questions. He simply listened. The kettle screamed by the time she finished. Balladyn remained silent as she chose her tea and filled a steeper with a calming mixture. She quirked a brow at Balladyn to see if he wanted anything.

"Surprise me," he said.

She surveyed her cabinet and chose a black tea aged in a wet whisky barrel from Dreagan with notes of brandied cherries, ginger, and a hint of cacao. Once both steepers were full and resting in their cups with the boiling water, Ariah sat across from the Reaper.

Balladyn rested his arms on the table. "How are your feet?"

"I've not thought about them." Now that she did, she realized they were throbbing. She had been on them too long today.

"You should see the Healers."

Ariah waved away his words. "I'm more concerned about who is responsible for this morning. And who the target was."

"That's what we're trying to sort out. I keep coming back to you and Killian."

She leaned back in the chair. "He isn't a Druid, and all the strikes before were aimed at us. He has nothing to do with what's going on here."

"Maybe."

The timer went off. Ariah removed the steepers and brought over some honey and milk.

He sipped the tea and grinned. "This is very good. How have I not had this one before?"

"It's new."

Balladyn took another drink. "Is that...whisky I taste?"

"It is. I asked Nikolai when he was here if I could buy a barrel or two from Dreagan. He brought me five. I'll be sure and add some to Rhona's next order."

For several moments, they sat in silence, drinking their tea while Moon meticulously cleaned her face at Ariah's feet.

"What do you think Killian saw that would make him tell you to run?" Balladyn asked.

Ariah shrugged. "I wish I knew. When I close my eyes, I can still see the terror on his face. Whatever it was frightened him."

"Which means he knew something was about to happen."

"Maybe." She didn't want Killian involved with Skye's issues, but it was out of her hands now.

The Reaper's unusual eyes focused on her. "Are you sure you didn't see anything when you got out of your car?"

"As I told you, I felt something wasn't right, but that's all."

"You didn't see anything out of place, you mean."

Ariah frowned. He had a point. "There were people, as usual. I didn't see anyone staring my way."

"They could have been hiding."

"They waited until I was inside the store to attack. So, I'm the target."

Balladyn lowered his cup after another drink. "We need to know who or what Killian saw before we determine who the attack was directed toward."

Indeed, they did. Ariah finished her tea and rose. She rinsed both cups and turned around.

"Best pack a bag," Balladyn said. "Just in case."

She grabbed a few items as well as Moon's food and put it in a bag. Then she gathered the cat in her arms. Balladyn jumped them to the manor. Ariah intended to take Moon to her room to get acclimated to her new surroundings, but as soon as Moon saw Basher, she leapt out of Ariah's arms and chased Basher up the stairs.

Ariah took a step toward them when, from the library, she heard Elias's clipped tone say, "We already cleared Edie of anything."

"I know what I saw," Kirsi replied in an even tone.

Ariah glanced after the cats. They would have to wait. She walked with Balladyn to the doorway of the library to see what was going on. Elias's face was set in hard lines, his lips pinched as he glowered at Kirsi.

Elodie reached across the space and touched her brother's arm. "I didn't get a chance to tell you, but I was with Edie at the Tea Talker yesterday. She acted…off."

"Off?" Elias asked, his frown deepening.

Elodie lifted one shoulder. "There's no harm in checking her out again. We need to be sure, and what Kirsi saw makes me uneasy."

The tension in the room rose as Elias and Elodie stared at each other. Finally, Elias nodded, his shoulders drooping. "All right."

CHAPTER TWENTY-FOUR

Where was Ariah? Killian stared at the door, wondering why she hadn't returned. But he knew the answer. Even if he didn't want to admit it.

There were many things he could have said, *should* have said when she told him her secret. Instead, he had mucked things up again. Was she angry? Upset? Had she left? Surely, they wouldn't let her leave the manor. Maybe he should go check. As soon as he knew she was there and safe, he could answer the questions.

Questions. *Fuck*.

Killian swung his head around, his gaze meeting Theo's dark eyes as the DI sat across from him in a chair. "Sorry. What was the question?"

"Ariah is fine. She's downstairs with the others."

That was supposed to make Killian feel better, but it didn't. His actions and words had sent her from his room when all he wanted to do was lay her down and make love to her for hours. "All right."

Theo crossed one ankle over his opposite knee. His gaze was

steady, his face devoid of any expression, but there was no denying the mounting annoyance. "I know this can no' be easy. You no' only went through a traumatic attack, but you also learned the truth about Ariah. The truth about Skye."

"Druids." The word felt stilted on Killian's tongue. Was it because it was one he couldn't remember ever speaking? Or was it because he couldn't wrap his head around what it signified?

Theo bowed his head in acknowledgment. "Do we scare you?"

"If I'm being honest, aye. You have magic. I don't. Makes for a big difference."

"I could argue that having a weapon is the same. Having magic doesna mean I'll use it on you or anyone else."

Killian licked his lips. "True enough."

"You know Ariah. Probably better than most of us."

"I don't think I do. She never told me she was a Druid."

Theo's gaze dropped to the floor for a heartbeat. "Do you still care about her?"

"Aye."

"Do you still want to be with her? That is why you returned to the isle, is it no'?"

Killian knew what Theo was doing, but he went along with it anyway. "It is."

"Maybe focus on that right now." Theo tapped the end of his pencil on his notebook. "Tell me about this morning. Every detail. No matter how irrelevant you think it is."

"I woke up before the alarm. Wait," Killian said as he recalled *how* he had woken.

"Every detail, remember?"

Killian scrubbed a hand over his jaw. "I had one of those

dreams where I thought I heard something, a sound that seems real but isn't."

"Hypnopompic hallucinations. They happen somewhere between us dreaming and being fully awake."

"Aye, those. It yanked me from sleep, and I got the sense that someone was in the room with me. But when I looked, there was no one but me."

"Where did you think it was? Could you sense it somewhere specific in the room?"

"I was on my side and thought it was behind me."

"But you saw nothing?"

Killian shook his head.

Theo jotted something down and then looked up. "Callum shared that you've felt as if someone has been watching you. Was that what you felt when you woke?"

"It was. One moment, I was asleep. And the next, awake. But I would've bet money that someone was there."

"What happened then?"

"I turned off my alarm and saw the text from Callum telling me where he had left my keys. I readied for the day and left the B&B to drive to the shop. I arrived at the same time Ruby did. She let us in, and we were in the middle of morning prep when Ariah walked in." Killian hadn't been sure what to do when he saw her slackened jaw at finding him there.

"Mm-hmm. What next?" Theo asked.

Killian shrugged and looked away to pull up those memories. "I froze as I came out of the back. Ruby hadn't told Ariah I was helping, and I didn't want her to know."

"Why?"

"Ariah made it clear she didn't want to talk to me."

Theo raised a brow. "But you worked in her stead?"

"Just trying to help out after her injury."

More notations went down in the notebook. Theo motioned for him to continue with his hand.

"We were all frozen. No one said anything. I felt Ruby looking between us. I wasn't sure if I should leave or not. Ariah took a step forward."

"Did you see anything outside?"

Something pulled at Killian's mind. He concentrated on the moment after Ariah had entered the building. Her disbelief, his surprise. He relived the memories in slow motion, moving with it instead of trying to force it. The recollection that had stayed out of reach unfurled. "The hairs on the back of my neck rose." Killian closed his eyes to delve deeper into the memory. He looked through the glass to the outside of the shop, but it was fuzzy. He tried again with little change. On the third attempt, the windows cleared. There had been movement outside. Something had drawn his attention. He saw out into the car park. His eyes flew open, and he looked at Theo. "Aye. I saw someone. A woman with blond hair cut very short."

"What was she doing?"

"Staring at me."

Theo's stopped writing. "That's it?"

"Aye."

"Then why did you tell Ariah and Ruby to get out?"

Chills raced over Killian's body. He jumped to his feet, needing to move against the onslaught of restlessness and panic. Against the fear that raged so loudly and fiercely within him that he thought he might break apart at the seams.

"Killian? Did she say something? Do something?"

He kept moving about the room, but the terror wouldn't loosen its hold. He shook out his arms. Why wouldn't the feeling dissipate? "I don't know."

"You do."

"If I knew, I'd say," he snapped, unsure where the anger had come from.

Theo set his pencil inside the notebook and closed it. "You know. You just don't want to say."

"I don't know!" he yelled, still unable to stop moving.

Theo stood and blocked his path. Their gazes clashed. "You know what you saw. It scared you because it was something that could hurt others, something that could hurt Ariah. That's why you called out to her. As soon as you accept the truth, you'll remember."

"I accept it," Killian said, throwing up his hands and moving around the DI. "Annnnd nothing. So, you're wrong. I don't remember anything. Maybe it was just a feeling."

"All right. Then what was the feeling?" Theo asked, turning to watch Killian pace.

Fuck. The DI was like a dog with a bone. Killian felt as if something was crawling beneath his skin. "I don't know."

"You do."

He whirled on the detective inspector. "I don't!"

Theo kept talking. "What did you see? A cloud? Mist? A hand?"

In an instant, Killian was transported to the Tea Talker, staring at his beloved Ariah.

The sight of her was a balm to his soul. He would grovel for the rest of his days if it meant they could be together again. But after what he had done, she might never be able to forgive him.

He thought about the letter in his coat pocket. Killian had decided to leave it at the shop at the end of his shift. He waited for her to demand that he leave. He didn't see anger on her face, though. Just surprise.

His neck prickled, and the hairs stood on end. Instinctively, he reached back to rub his neck. As he did, something caught his attention. He looked out the windows to a woman staring at him. They looked at each other for a heartbeat before he saw a shadow rise from the pavement to form some kind of creature. It smiled at him, a malicious grin full of evil.

Killian looked at Ariah. She had to get out. Now. He called a warning as he felt the air shift. The sound of shattering glass deafened him.

"Sit," Theo urged and dragged him to a chair. "Breathe."

Killian looked at Theo, his stomach roiling sickeningly. "Something was there."

"What?"

"I don't know what it was, but after I saw the woman, it was..." He paused, shrugging. "The only word I can use is shadows. They gathered and rose outside the store to form some kind of monster or creature thing." Killian swallowed as Theo went down on his haunches before him. "It smiled at me. A cold smile. A killer's smile."

There was no laughter or doubt in Theo's gaze as he listened. "Is that what blew in the glass?"

"Aye. At least, I think so. I didn't see it. I shouted to Ariah and Ruby, even though I knew there wasn't time for any of us to get out." Killian briefly closed his eyes as he recalled every cut and stab the glass made along his arms, in his side, and on his back. Even his neck and over his head.

"Is that all?" Theo asked softly.

Killian wanted the memory to stop, but it wouldn't. He had to see it through. "I was hurt. There was so much pain. But I had to know if Ariah was okay. I sensed the shadow thing near. When I lifted my head to search for her, it laughed. Something kicked me across the floor. Then Ariah was next to me."

"Did you see the creature leave? Or did it remain?"

"I don't remember."

Theo nodded and straightened. He ran a hand down his face while he stared at the far wall. Killian watched him, wondering what was going through the DI's mind. Killian had just told him about some shadow monster, and Theo hadn't even blinked. Just what kind of shite went on around the isle?

Killian realized he could breathe easier now. He no longer felt as if he were about to shatter like the glass had. His mind hadn't been able to make sense of what he had seen, so it must have tried to make him forget. But he hadn't been able to. Not completely.

Would he have been able to go through the memories if he hadn't known about the Druids and magic? Had Ariah opening up about her culture allowed him to process everything?

"Do you think it was coming for you?" Theo asked. "Or were you just in the way?"

Killian sat back and rubbed his hands down his thighs. "I think I was the target. I thought that before Ariah told me about the Druids. I thought it after. I'm sure of it now. It could've gone for her or Ruby."

"But it didna." Theo nodded distractedly. "That's where things get weird. Of all the madness on Skye, it has been directed solely at Druids until now."

"What does that mean?"

"I wish I knew."

"What happens to me?"

Theo scratched the side of his head behind his ear. "Did Ariah tell you about the manor?"

"She said it was a safe place."

"It is. It's also the safest place on the isle. No one can get in that it doesna want. I'd like for you to remain here. There are plenty of rooms, and Bronwyn has already told the house that you are a guest."

Killian wasn't sure what that meant. "You make it sound as if the house is a person."

"I hate to add to your already overwhelming day, but the manor is sentient."

"Sentient?" Killian repeated.

Theo grinned and walked to the door, pausing there. "I need to talk to Ariah. I'll introduce you to everyone if you want to come down with me. You can ask them all about the manor."

Killian was tired of being in the room. And he wanted to lay his eyes on Ariah, at the very least. He rose from the chair with a nod. The two of them left the room and turned to walk down a hallway. Some pictures filled the spaces, but there were bare spots, shadows indicating where paintings had once been.

"Bronwyn is slowly bringing the house back to its original form. A lot was sold off in prior years," Theo explained.

Killian liked the dark wood stain along the bottom half of the walls and on the flooring. The runner had a classic floral design in a deep burgundy that accentuated the wood and dampened their footsteps. It led to a set of wide, switchback stairs in the same dark wood. He spotted more artwork, as well as a table with some timeless antiques. It was the kind of old money that piqued his father's interest.

"Whoa," Theo said.

Killian barely had time to jump out of the way as the cat from earlier ran up the stairs, followed by a second one. He turned to follow their ascent up another set of stairs above them.

"There's a third floor," Theo said. "As well as an attic. And many more rooms on the main floor. Everyone was in the library when I left. The kitchen is another favorite space. You'll find everyone in there when Carlyle cooks."

Killian moved his gaze about in an attempt to take everything in. Then they were on the main floor and headed toward the front door. As they neared a set of open double doors, the sound of voices grew louder. Killian stood in the library doorway and searched the room until he found Ariah standing against the wall.

Their gazes met, held. He wanted to go to her, to draw her into his arms. Instead, it felt as if a gap separated them—one he would need to traverse alone while navigating this new reality—and its dangers.

CHAPTER TWENTY-FIVE

London

Devon stepped out onto the stoop of the posh townhome into night air heavy with fog. She slipped off her white gloves and tucked them into her jacket pockets as she made her way down the steps. A quick buttoning of her coat ensured no one saw the tuxedo jacket beneath. The black cigarette pants wouldn't draw any attention.

The heels of her black Jimmy Choo stilettos clicked on the sidewalk. She didn't hurry. The point was to blend in. Her car was two blocks away. The week before, she had mapped out her course, studying every street and alley to find the right one.

Just before she reached the corner, she heard the scream coming from the home she had just departed. She never slowed, never quickened her steps. Devon made her turn and continued on her way as the sounds of sirens wailed in the distance, coming closer with every second.

A dark sedan rolled up alongside her. The soft whir of a window being rolled down drew her to a halt. She turned her head to look at the vehicle. The man behind the wheel simply held out a red folder. She didn't know his name, but she knew the reserved look on his face. It was the same one she wore. Devon closed the short distance between them and took the file.

"You don't have much time," the man said before driving away.

"No rest for the wicked, eh?" Devon muttered as she watched the sedan for a moment.

The sirens were upon her now. She swiveled her head to see them speeding past the opening of the street she was on before disappearing. She continued to the black convertible Mercedes with the folder tucked beneath her arm. After tossing the folder onto the passenger seat, she drove to the other side of the city.

She went to a crowded car park and slipped into a spot next to two other Mercedes. Only then did she look at the folder. Normally, she had downtime between assignments. It was never a good thing when she was immediately sent on another. That meant someone had screwed up, and she was meant to clean up the mess.

Devon rubbed her hands together to warm them. She briefly considered starting up the engine again. Instead, she reached for the red folder and opened it. Her eyes landed on the photo at the top of the left page. She recognized him immediately. The stormy gray eyes, the impeccably cut dark hair, the brown skin. Though Devon knew most of the details, she read over them anyway—name, date of birth, addresses, profession, family. And his current location.

Her eyes shifted to the opposite page and the particulars of her assignment. She read it twice and then slowly closed the folder. Devon sat in the car for another few moments, mulling it over before backing out of the spot. She headed toward one of the safe houses nearest her. She had clothes stashed in all of them.

With the clock ticking, Devon quickly yanked off the wig and brushed out her hair. She then changed and filled a Louis Vuitton suitcase with an assortment of clothes, shoes, and jewelry. She kept a bag of makeup and toiletries with her at all times. Within fifteen minutes, she was back in her car and headed north.

There wasn't much to see at night along the highway. She flew past other cars, unconcerned about any cameras catching her speeding. They had a person dedicated to ensuring those went away. Devon used the time to get caught up on her favorite podcast—*Old Gods of Appalachia*. The horror show was set in the Appalachian Mountains, one of her bucket list places to visit.

She had just settled into the episode when her mobile chimed. The screen in the middle of the dashboard flickered with a message.

Target elimination confirmed.

They never took her word for it. Devon rolled her eyes. Paranoid old men.

They weren't words she would *ever* dare say out loud. Some things just weren't done within the London Druids—things each member found out quickly.

She adjusted her hands on the wheel and pressed the accelerator while turning up the volume on the podcast. Devon wove in and out of the cars around her, enjoying the stretches where no one was in her way. Eventually, she found her exit. The high speeds she enjoyed were shoved aside as she drove along the narrow roads.

Streetlights were gone, leaving only the moon and her headlights to light the countryside. Groves of trees gave way to open fields. Devon didn't bother looking. She kept her gaze on the road as her high beams bounced along the winding, undulating asphalt.

The second episode finished by the time she crested a hill. She ended the podcast when she spotted the lights of the impressive manor house in the distance through some trees. Devon didn't slow until she came to the estate's gated grand entrance. She rolled down her window to press the button on the metal box sticking out of the ground. The screen stayed black, but the speaker had a brief crackle.

A loud click sounded from the gates. She grinned when she saw them opening. Devon settled back in her seat and rolled the window up. Once the gates were open, she drove under the enormous stone arch. A glance in her rearview mirror confirmed the gates closing behind her.

The drive was lined with several-hundred-year-old trees, their giant arms reaching out to each other and the heavens. Soft spotlights were positioned at the base of the trunks, shining upward to show the impressive size of the trees.

The Earl of Brannelly was proud of his family estate, as all the previous earls before him. It showed in the care given to every inch, from the gate to the formidable structure they called home—and most likely beyond. Money always had a way of glossing over the dirty, ugly things. Be they dead flowers, broken tree limbs, or people.

Devon parked near the entrance. The house was lit from within. As she stepped out of the car, she caught a glimpse inside the nearby windows. Many noble families barely clung to their family seats as money dried up year after year. But not this one. They had been lucky.

But that luck had dried up.

If not, she wouldn't be here.

The front door opened to reveal a tall, severe man dressed in a suit. The lights around him showed his neatly trimmed brown hair with gray at the temples. He bowed his head slightly. "Good evening, ma'am. I'm afraid the earl isn't home at the moment."

Devon grinned and popped the trunk with her key fob. The dossier had given her a wealth of information on the household staff. "Good evening, Billings. I thought I might beat Mason back. I told him I'd win."

There was a brief flash of uncertainty on the butler's face. "It seems you have."

"How rude of me," Devon said, making her way up the steps. "I'm Devon Carmichael. Mason invited me to his lovely home and simply wouldn't take no for an answer. Who could refuse such a gorgeous man?" she asked with a wink.

"I'm sure the earl will be here shortly. Do you have bags?"

"In the trunk."

"I shall send someone to fetch them. Come," Billings said and led the way. "We'll wait for Lord Brannelly in the study. Would you care for some tea?"

The grandeur and beauty of the manor was everywhere, and it was tastefully done—nothing too ostentatious. Which surprised her with a house this size and the power the Crawford family had retained. "That would be lovely. Are there snacks, as well?"

"I'll see what I can find."

Billings led her into the study, then left her with a brisk nod. Devon sank onto one of the chairs and closed her eyes for just a second. Then she took out her mobile and sent a text.

I'm in.

CHAPTER TWENTY-SIX

The house lights were dimmed with flames dancing in the fireplace. Trevor hated the fire on unless it was freezing or below. Edie grinned and took another drink of his eighty-year-old Dreagan whisky. It was only for special occasions.

Well, this certainly was one.

For her, at least.

There would be no dinner cooking tonight. No takeout on the table. Edie always cooked. And if she didn't, she picked something up for everyone. Every. Single. Day. Not doing so was just one of the changes about to happen.

She sat in the living room, purposefully choosing Trevor's favorite chair. Cello music drifted softly through the house speakers—something else Trevor hated and she always made sure to turn off before her husband returned home.

Edie had thought he might call her this afternoon. She was sure Rebecca had gotten in touch with him the moment Edie walked out of the office. Trevor knew she had been there. He knew that she knew he had lied. He had always been a charmer when he wanted something. Add in the fact that he had a way of smooth-talking his way out of things, and he was used to getting what he wanted. Long ago, one of her friends had said he was manipulative. Edie had been outraged on Trevor's behalf.

She hadn't seen it then. But she did now. She had for some time but hadn't wanted to admit it.

The house security alerted her that a car approached. She tapped the iPad next to her and woke the screen. Trevor's vehicle came into view as he pulled in beside her SUV. Edie had imagined this moment since she'd left Wild Point. She was the calmest she had ever been, though the anger was there, just beneath the surface. She hoped for his benefit that he didn't unleash it.

The front door opened and then softly closed. She imagined him looking at the empty table, the cold stove, and the dimmed lights throughout the house.

"Hello? Edie? Kids?" Trevor called.

She didn't turn in his direction. "In here," she answered.

His shoes struck the tile as he made his way to her. Edie didn't hide her smile when he paused. She almost turned up the music but refrained, leaving it to softly fill the background. Finally, he entered the room and came around the sofa, headed toward the fireplace. He was tall and trim, working out regularly to stay in shape. The wind had blown his thinning light-brown hair about, showing the balding spot on the back of his head.

"Don't," Edie stated when he bent to turn off the gas.

Trevor froze, a hint of surprise in his hazel eyes when he looked at her. "Excuse me?"

"You heard me. I want the fire on."

"You know how I feel about the waste of money. It isna that cold."

"I don't care. I want it on." She held his gaze, daring him to push the issue.

He straightened, a muscle jumping in his jaw. "Where are the kids?"

"Staying the night with friends."

"It's a school night. You never allow that."

Edie shrugged and poured more whisky into her glass.

Trevor stuffed his hands into his pants pockets. "You're angry."

"I was. I still am, to a degree. But really, Trevor, I'm just done."

His brow furrowed. "Done? What does that mean?"

"It means exactly what you think. I'm done. With you. With the lies. With this sham of a family."

"You can no' mean that."

Edie was surprised to see that he looked dismayed—apprehensive, even. It didn't matter whether it was an act or the real thing. Discovering the truth had flipped a switch inside her. Whatever love or kindness she had toward the man she'd fallen in love with had withered and died earlier today. She was supposed to be celebrating. Instead, she was deep-cleaning her life.

And it started with Trevor.

"I most certainly mean it." Edie set aside the glass of whisky. "The only thing I want from you is the keys. The house is mine. Choose one of the rentals to live in. We'll divide the rest between us. I will also have sole custody of the children."

"Divorce?" He barked a laugh. "I doona think so, sweetheart."

Edie looked into his eyes. She had once thought him the handsomest man she had ever laid eyes on. Now, she saw him for who he really was. A chronic adulterer who could never be happy with one woman because he kept trying to fill a void that couldn't be filled. He no longer seemed even remotely handsome. An air of desperation replaced his usual confidence and rolled off him. "I *do* think so."

"I refuse. We're meant to be together."

She raised a brow. "Are we? Then why can't you keep your pants zipped?"

"You and the kids are my life." He stepped toward her, his eyes imploring. "You three are everything to me."

"Perhaps you should've thought of that before you cheated."

"I'll stop."

Edie looked down at her lap and chuckled. She reached for the dram of whisky on the table next to her and lifted it to her lips. After inhaling the fragrance, she let it linger on her tongue before swallowing.

"I mean it," Trevor said. "I've been an utter fool, but I'll do anything to keep you."

The warmth of the whisky slid down her throat and landed in her belly, spreading. She regarded him stonily. "Now, you want to change because you've been caught? Why not before? Why start at all?"

"I doona know," he muttered and looked away.

"I was sent a picture of you kissing a woman."

His gaze snapped back to her. "Who sent it?"

"Instead of confronting you with it, I let you convince me I was the reason our marriage was falling apart. You gaslighted me into believing everything was fine."

"You were no' acting normally."

Edie shrugged indifferently. "I was going through something. As my husband, as my *partner*, the one who professed to love me until you died, you should've been there for me, trying to figure out what was wrong. Not blaming me. And me,"—she snorted and shook her head—"I let you."

"Sweetheart," he began.

She held up a hand and shot him a warning look. "Whatever was between us is over. There is no coming back from this. There's nothing you can say, nothing you can do. You shattered my trust forever."

"I willna give you the divorce."

There was no mistaking the threat in his voice.

"*There's another way,*" the Ancients whispered in her mind.

"I willna," Trevor repeated and then huffed as he looked around. "Everything we have, we built together. As a family. I'm no' letting you go. I'll drag the divorce out for as long as I can because I'm no' letting you go."

"*You know what to do.*"

Edie thought back over their years together. How happy they had been. Once. Trevor had been her world. She had forgotten who she was. She had given up her identity to be his wife and the mother of his children. She dressed as he wanted, took the role of stay-at-home mum as he wished. She decorated the house as he desired, prepared the meals he preferred, listened to music he approved of, and drove the vehicle he had picked out for her— color and all. Not once had he asked for her opinion on any of those things, and if she gave it, it was ignored.

She hadn't had a say in the naming of their children. She hadn't had a say in much of anything. But she hadn't cared. It had mattered to Trevor. She accepted that and granted him those victories because she loved him, never realizing that, while doing it, he had slowly been chipping away at her individuality.

"I spent the afternoon packing your things. You'll find the boxes in the garage. Take them and go," she said.

"You're angry. Hurt. You're no' seeing things clearly. I realize that now." He put his hands on his hips and gave her a fierce stare. "You need time to calm down. You need me. You've always needed me. You'll see that."

The longer Edie looked at him, the more repulsed she became. How had she ever thought he was her soulmate? He should've been supporting her as much as she supported him over the years. That was what a partnership was. All this time, she believed she had found a good man. Trevor hadn't physically struck her like her father had her mum. She couldn't really even say he verbally abused her.

Instead, his psychological manipulation had rendered her incapable of seeing him in his true form. But that veil had been lifted.

"*It'll be easy,*" the Ancients urged.

"Whatever hold over me you thought you had is gone" Edie held his stare, refusing to back down. "You've lost. Don't push me, or I'll make sure you never see the kids again."

It wasn't anger that contorted his face, but sadness and fear. "Please, Edie. I'm sorry. Doona do this."

CHAPTER TWENTY-SEVEN

Carwood Manor

The fire had long since died out. Ariah could've reignited it with her magic, but she was content staring at the fading embers. Basher was curled up on one side of her while Moon took the other. The two had spent hours chasing each other playfully through the manor while Theo took her statements—one for him, and the *official* one for the report he would turn in to his boss.

He had made her go through everything multiple times. Ultimately, Rhona had joined them, and Ariah had to tell it all again. She was drained by the time they finished and yearned to walk in her forest more than ever. But the house still wouldn't let her leave.

Ariah was so out of sorts she hadn't gone down to dinner. Bronwyn had brought up some takeout someone had picked up. There seemed to be a pall over the manor—or maybe it was just how she felt.

There had been no sign of Killian. He hadn't ventured up to her room, and she hadn't sought him out. She wanted to. She wanted to be near him, to touch him. To kiss him.

Ariah had spent hours trying to sleep, but she couldn't quiet her mind. She had attempted to meditate without success. Pacing the room hadn't helped. Neither had looking out her window to the woods beyond that seemed to beckon her. She didn't mind that it had begun to rain again. All she wanted was to be in the forest.

That was what brought her downstairs. She tried the front and side doors, but the house wouldn't let her pass, no matter how much she begged. Ariah had wandered the main floor until she ended up in the library with all the lights off except the lamp beside her. The report Theo had told her about earlier sat on the coffee table. It was the one he would submit so she could start the insurance claim.

Ariah leaned forward and grabbed it to read. She let out a sigh when she finished. Movement to the side drew her gaze. She looked up to find Killian's face half in shadow.

"Can't sleep?" he asked.

Her stomach fluttered at his deep, sexy voice. She shook her head. "You either?"

"Nay. Mind if I join you?"

"Not at all."

He chose the chair Elias and Bronwyn had used earlier. His gaze was directed at the few embers in the ashes. His blond waves were ruffled from the pillow, his hands, or both. "What are you reading?" he asked without looking her way.

"Theo's report."

"Will he actually tell his superiors what happened?"

Ariah tossed the report onto the table. It startled both cats, so they raised their heads, blinked lazily, and then resumed their sleep. "There isn't much truth in that. It's a lot of coverup to make it seem like vandalism. There is no mention of you at all."

Killian finally looked at her. "You sound upset."

"I don't like lies, and that's what this is."

"I gather it's necessary. For you as much as the other Druids."

At least, he hadn't hesitated over the word this time. That was progress, she supposed. "You're right, of course. Theo—and his father before him—has always protected our community. There used to be more of us with the police, but now, it's just him. I might understand why he has to submit that report, but that doesn't mean I'll use it."

"You're talking about for the insurance to cover the repair costs. Why wouldn't you use it? You were attacked."

She shrugged. "It just seems wrong. I should have enough to cover things myself."

"How bad is the damage?"

"I've seen pictures, but it isn't the same as being there. I'd like to go look at it myself. I know all the windows and the ceiling will need to be replaced. Most of my jars were ruined. I noticed two tables and a few chairs had damage. I might be able to salvage those, though."

The leather creaked when Killian sat forward and put his forearms on his knees. "I'm glad I found you down here. I looked for you at dinner."

"I needed some time."

"Because of me. Because of how I handled things. Again."

Ariah searched his shadow-covered eyes. "Because of all of it. You almost died, and I..." She stopped, her throat clogging with emotion.

"What?" he urged, his voice low and insistent. "You what?"

Her heart began pounding nervously. "I wouldn't have been able to bear it. We might not have been together, but at least I knew you were alive."

Their gazes held, the air between them crackling with awareness.

They reached for each other at the same time.

CHAPTER TWENTY-EIGHT

Thunder rumbled as Killian held Ariah too tightly. But he couldn't loosen his hold. He feared if he did, she might slip away again. Their lips met in a feverish kiss, each frantic for more. So much more.

The kiss was a raging inferno that matched the need pounding through his veins. He remembered the fire, the fervor that she had always stirred. He cradled her soft curves against him as blood shot straight to his cock. And through it all, was a sigh that began in the depths of his soul. He was where he was supposed to be.

Killian cupped her face with his hands and grudgingly ended the kiss. He stared into her golden-brown eyes. He hadn't only been given a second chance. He had been given a third. And he wouldn't muck it up. He released her and turned away.

"Wait," Ariah said hurriedly. "Where are you going?"

He threw her a grin over his shoulder and softly closed the double doors. "I don't want to be interrupted."

"Oh."

Killian couldn't take his eyes off her. She held his gaze and whispered something. Behind her, flames erupted in the hearth. He halted and stared at the fire for several beats. Then he swung his gaze to her. "You?"

"Me," she replied.

"Do it again."

Her lips curved into a smile as she took a throw and spread it on the floor before the fireplace. She kicked off her shoes and stood on the blanket. "Is that what you really want me to do right now?"

"Nay." He clicked off the lamp.

Blood rushed in his ears as Ariah tugged her shirt over her head and let it drop. Her hands wound behind her to lower the zipper of her skirt. It then fell in a pool of material around her feet. She lifted it with her toe and set it aside. The light of the fire showed goose pimples had risen on her flesh.

"I held you in my arms every night in my dreams." He moved to her. "Every. Single. Night."

"I'm not a dream now."

His hand shook when he trailed the backs of his fingers across her cheek. There was so much to be said, so much that *needed* to be said. But not now. His fingers slid into the cool, dark strands of her hair and then dropped to her waist to tug their bodies together.

Her palms flattened on his chest. He could feel her heat through his tee. Years of ignoring—or outright denying—his love for Ariah was over. It coursed through him with such force he was dizzy with it. How could he have ever let her go? It was a mistake he wouldn't make again. This was a new beginning.

He slowly lowered his mouth to hers. Their lips lingered together for a moment. He kissed her again and felt her tongue slide along the seam of his lips. A groan rumbled through him as he captured her mouth in a scorching kiss.

Ariah tasted the desperation in Killian's kiss. It was the same thing she felt. She needed him closer. As if the only way to feel whole was for their bodies to be merged. Her hands moved over his thick shoulders to wind around his neck as the flames of desire swelled.

His hands were all over her—tangled in her hair, skimming along her back, cupping her arms. His arousal pressed into her stomach, making her sex throb. Her body was his instrument to play, and Killian was an expert.

She tugged at his shirt, needing it gone to feel him, skin to skin. Killian broke the kiss long enough to yank at his tee. There was a ripping noise as he removed it, but neither paid any attention to it. Then their lips were together again, their tongues tangled.

Ariah glided her hands over his heated flesh, feeling the strength of his muscles, the power of him. His hardness to her softness. He was the only one who had ever made her lose control. It was only with Killian that she'd felt safe enough to completely give herself over.

His large hand was splayed on her back, careful not to get too near her bandage. Then the straps of her bra loosened. Light fingers caressed to her shoulders and tenderly peeled the straps down her arms. She shifted so the lingerie fell away without breaking the kiss. Her nipples pebbled against him, aching for his touch. He pressed their bodies close once more.

"Ariah," he whispered, his hot breath brushing her ear.

His hand was in her hair again, gently but firmly tugging her head back. She forced her eyes open to look at him. His were hooded, his gaze burning a path over her face and down her neck. Her lips were swollen and tingling from his kisses. Both were breathing hard, desire hanging heavily in the air.

Their gazes locked. Chills swept over her at the love she saw in his olive-green depths. How had she ever believed it was better to guard her heart against him? This gorgeous, amazing man knew her as no one else ever could. Or ever would.

She nodded and slipped her hands into his hair, winding her fingers in the golden locks before tugging his head down. This kiss was slower but somehow contained more… Longing. Need.

Hope.

And her heart answered in kind.

Killian lowered them to the floor. A light flashed through the window, followed by thunder. He kneeled between Ariah's legs and let his gaze leisurely run over her body. The loose, flowy clothes she preferred hid a form that could bring a man to his knees. Because that's what she had done to him.

Her breasts were full, her dusky nipples hard and waiting. There was a smattering of freckles on her chest and shoulders that matched those along her nose and cheeks. Her curves made his mouth water. His eyes followed the indent of her waist before lingering on her hips. Dark pink lace wound around them while a tiny piece of floral material hid her from him.

He hooked his fingers into the lace and tugged. Her hips lifted as he peeled off her underwear. She then raised her legs, putting her knees together in order for him to remove them completely. He then put a hand on each ankle and skimmed his hands up her legs to her knees, then along her thighs. All the while, she watched him.

Killian glanced at her mouth and moaned at the sight of those swollen lips parted while the pulse in her throat beat erratically. She parted her legs, moving them to either side of him. He looked down to her core, to the small triangle of dark curls. Unable to hold back any longer, he caressed a finger along the crook of her thigh where it joined her body. Then higher into her curls and back again.

He didn't need to touch her to know she was eager and ready for him. He could see her dampness. His cock jumped in anticipation. Killian was glad he had left his sweats on. That was the only thing keeping him from thrusting into her at that very moment.

Instead, he moved his finger steadily closer to her sex until he skimmed it over her sensitive skin. She hissed in a breath, causing him to glance in her direction. Ariah bit her lower lip, watching. He wouldn't keep either of them waiting a moment longer. With their gazes locked, he slowly slid his finger inside her.

How could she already be this close to climax? Killian's thick finger filled her, twisting slowly before withdrawing. Only to do it all over again. Thoughts ceased as her body thrummed with pleasure that rippled through her, starting at her center and spreading outward.

She moaned when he added a second finger. It felt so good. She rocked her hips, wanting more. Ariah reached for him, longing to feel his body, but he remained out of reach. She peeled open her eyes and found him intently watching his hand moving in and out of her. His arousal bulged from within the sweats. She wanted her hands around his cock, to tease him as he was tormenting her. It had been one of their favorite positions before. She sat up to reach for him when his thumb grazed her clit. Ariah fell back, helpless against the carnal bliss that rendered her powerless.

A cry of surprise fell from her lips when his tongue swirled about the swollen nub of her clit, all while his fingers continued to move within her. She was quickly spiraling toward an orgasm.

Until everything stopped.

She opened her eyes as lightning lit up the library. Killian leaned over her, his arms braced on either side of her. He had removed his pants. His thick arousal jutted forward as if straining toward her. Ariah went to touch it, but he shifted away.

"I want you too desperately. I'll not last." His voice was barely above a whisper, hoarse with need.

"We have all night." She swallowed and placed her hands on his hips. "We have eternity."

His groan was almost feral before he took her lips in a fiercely gentle kiss that went on forever. She sighed when he finally rested his delicious weight atop her.

Eternity. With Ariah. That's what he wanted. It was *all* he wanted. It was only with her that he felt as if he had found a real home. A true home.

She rolled him onto his back and straddled his hips as her hair fell in a curtain on either side of them, shielding them from the outside world and creating one of their own. She rocked back, rubbing her wet sex along his aching cock. He lifted his hips in response. Then she dragged her breasts over his chest.

Killian moaned and cupped a large globe in each hand. She ended the kiss but kept their lips pressed together for an extra heartbeat. He circled his thumbs around her pert nipples, making her suck in a quick breath. His lips wrapped around a turgid peak and suckled while he teased the other with his fingers. Her breathing was labored, her hips rocking against his erection in tempo with his tongue.

The way her desire coated his rod was too much. He could no longer hold himself back. Killian flipped them. Ariah was so far gone she didn't seem to notice. He reached between them and guided himself to her entrance. With one thrust, he buried himself in her hot, wet heat.

He clenched his jaw at her moan as her body stretched to accommodate him. They found a steady rhythm, one that sent them closer and closer to ecstasy.

Her hands, soft and insistent, glided up and down his arms that strained as he braced himself. Their eyes locked, held. He saw the future in her gaze. It wasn't the first time he had seen it, but he hadn't been brave enough to reach for it before. He was now.

His thoughts halted when he heard her breath hitch. Killian kept up his tempo, knowing she was close. In the next heartbeat,

Ariah splintered. Her eyes slid closed, and her mouth opened on a soft cry as her body convulsed around him.

Pleasure engulfed him. It consumed him. Submerging him in bliss so powerful it left an eternal mark. One his body knew. One he and Ariah had shared before. He buried himself deep, holding back his shout of release. Her arms held him steady as he shuddered until he had emptied himself.

CHAPTER TWENTY-NINE

Ariah had her eyes closed, the heat from the fire touching one side of her while Killian's heat blanketed her. She ran her fingers through his hair and over his back as he remained still until his breathing evened out. Sleep pulled at her, but she wasn't ready to slip away just yet. She wanted to savor this moment for a little longer.

She cracked open her eyes when he rose on one elbow. They shared a smile. Killian looked different, lighter. Maybe she did, too. The summer they were together, she'd thought they had all the time in the world. Endless days and nights. Until their time ran out. It might be the same again, but she couldn't hold her heart back from this man. She loved him. Always had.

Always would.

Killian traced her lips with his fingers, his eyes following his hand. Lightning flashed, but the thunder was so distant they barely heard it. His gaze slid back up to meet hers. "I'm yours, Ariah. I will always be yours. I was a fool before."

She put her finger over his lips. "We were both fools."

"Nay." He gently pulled her hand away. "You had valid reasons for not wanting to leave your home. I wish you had told me about being a Druid then, but I understand why you didn't. I want to understand the magic and customs. All of it. Will you tell me?"

Ariah studied him, almost afraid to believe his words. But she knew they were true. "I will. I also want you to know that I won't hold it against you if you can't accept me."

His brows shot up. "Accept you? Of course, I do."

"You don't know everything yet."

"I know enough. It won't change my mind." He kissed her softly. "I'm not leaving Skye again. I'm not leaving *you*."

She hadn't wanted to have this conversation now, but perhaps it was better to get it over with. Or at least allow her to have some idea of where she stood. "And your family?"

"I quit the firm. I came for you, and I told my family that. They accept you, or they lose me."

"I don't want that. I know what it is to not have family."

Killian smoothed a lock of hair from her brow. "You have family all around you. I've seen how close you are. Wasn't it you who once told me that family doesn't always have to be blood?"

"I did," she said with a grin. He was right. She *did* have family. "But I don't want you to cut things off with yours because of me."

"I'm doing what I should've done years ago. For *me*," he added. Killian plopped onto his back and sighed. "I'm taking back my life."

Ariah rolled toward him, coming up on her elbow. "I just want you t—"

"Shh," he said and pulled her down onto his chest. "We just

had an incredible moment. I still can't feel my legs. Let's sit with that for a while."

She settled against him, her eyelids already growing heavy, sleep calling.

Killian suddenly jerked. "Bloody hell. We didn't use a condom."

"Shh," she whispered. "There's a spell."

He grunted. "Interesting." There was a long stretch of silence. "I need to tell you about the time we were apart."

Ariah couldn't open her eyes. It was almost as if they were sealed shut. She was so exhausted, but she managed to say, "You had someone. Maybe more than one. I understand."

"I, ah…I was engaged."

Maybe she should've been upset at hearing that, but it made sense. Killian was handsome, successful, and came from a well-known family. Of course, he would be sought after.

"We got on well," he continued. "We were good friends, but I didn't want to spend my life with her. I didn't love her. I loved you."

Ariah draped her arm over his stomach and squeezed. "I'm glad you came back."

"Was there…was there anyone serious for you?"

She attempted to open her eyes at his halting, nervous words, but she couldn't. Her voice was slurred when she finally got the response out. "No one compared to you."

Killian kissed the top of her head. "Sleep. We'll talk later."

That was the last thing Ariah heard as she drifted off. She was warm and comfortable, her body sated and held. There was nothing. No sounds, no movement. She floated in peaceful, undisturbed slumber.

The cries were distant at first, but the moment she noticed them, they seemed everywhere, growing louder and louder until they deafened her. Ariah tried to cover her ears with her hands, but she couldn't move. Something held her. She turned her head, trying to see behind her, but there was nothing but all-consuming darkness.

But she *knew* something was there.

The cries turned to screams. Then a searing light splintered the darkness. Ariah gasped as she watched the forest explode, bursting into flames. The trees swayed, trying to dislodge the fire from their limbs. The screams changed. She heard her name in them now. Someone was calling her. It came from the trees and the ground. And the sky.

"*You're too late,*" whispered a sinister voice in her ear.

Ariah sat up, gasping for air. The dream fell away to reveal the library. Moon meowed as she rose from the sofa to jump onto the table and move toward her, sensing her distress.

"What is it?" Killian asked sleepily.

Ariah didn't answer as she jumped up and hurriedly yanked on her clothes.

"Ariah, you're scaring me. What's going on?" Killian asked more firmly.

"I have to go." The screams still reverberated through her head, and the sound left her cold. It was a warning, but she didn't know what kind. She'd never had anything like this happen before.

Killian stepped in front of her, his hands up, palms out. "Wait. Just wait. Let me get dressed. I'll come with you."

"No time." She darted around him.

"Goddammit," Killian muttered.

Ariah rushed to the front door. The handle wouldn't turn. She put her hands on the wood. "Please. I have to get to the forest," she implored the house.

She tried a second time, but the door still didn't move. Ariah whirled around and raced to the back door, but it didn't budge either. Her frustration got the better of her, and she slammed the side of her fist against the wood. "I have to get out!"

"Ariah, please," Killian said, rushing up. "Talk to me."

She whirled to face him. "I have to get to the woods. Now. But the house won't let me."

Killian looked from her to the door and then around at the house. "Um…did you ask?"

She turned back to the door and put her hands on it, resting her forehead against the slab. She let the terror of the dream fill her and then move into the house, trying to get the manor to understand. "I have to get to the trees," she whispered.

The door clicked open. Ariah wasted no time rushing out. She heard Killian calling her name, his footsteps close behind her as hers hit the wet grass. The estate was large, and the grounds close to the manor had been cleared of trees for gardens long overgrown. But she saw the forest in the distance. It wasn't hers, but it didn't have to be. She needed to get there. She didn't know why, and it didn't matter.

She pushed herself past the stitch in her side and the mud threatening to suck her feet down. Something darted ahead of her, and Ariah realized it was Moon. She followed the feline's trail, which kept her on firm ground and away from holes. Ariah didn't stop until she finally reached the trees.

The moment her hand touched the bark of a pine, her knees gave out. Moon hissed at something behind her. Ariah glanced over her shoulder to see Killian jerking to a halt as he eyed the cat.

"I'm fine. Go back to the house," she told him.

He shook his head. "Not a chance."

Ariah pulled herself to her feet and walked deeper into the forest. The anxiety that had threatened to swallow her began to dissipate. The stitch in her side eventually went away. Water dripped from the leaves above them, hitting the ground without a sound. Moon walked next to her.

The moment she saw a ring of trees, their limbs shielding the area below, she diverted to it. She sat on the damp ground and crossed her legs, uncaring that the moisture seeped into her clothes. Then she closed her eyes. Her focus went to her breath.

Within moments, magic moved over her skin and stirred her hair. She didn't fear it, though. This was Skye's magic. Had it been what'd called to her in the dream?

Forest child. Ariah had been called that for as long as she could remember. It had first come from her great-aunt Bonnie, who had raised her, but others had always said it, too. The woods were where Ariah belonged. She had never feared the animals who called the forest home. She knew each of them, just as she knew all the plants—which ones to use and which caused harm. It had been instinctual.

As if it had been in her DNA from the moment of her birth.

Ariah had once asked her great-aunt if her mother had been like that, but Bonnie always shook her head. It would be years before Ariah discovered that her mother had despised nature of any kind. Her father had been the same. So where had she gotten it from? That question had once mattered, but no longer.

There was a new question now. A more persistent, important one: Who—or what—had been screaming in her dream?

The magic began moving quicker around her. It skimmed her

like a breeze, comforting and supportive. She listened for the Ancients' drums in hopes they might be able to shed some light on what was happening, but once again, they were elusive.

However, one truth became clear. Her place was in the forest. It was where she had to be in the coming war.

CHAPTER THIRTY

The sight of the soft, multicolored lights moving across Ariah's body as if guided by an invisible hand brought Killian up short. The serenity on her face and the tranquility of the woods took away his fear. He stood frozen in wonder and astonishment.

He wasn't the only one. Moon sat before Ariah, watching her.

Soft footfalls sounded behind him. Killian glanced over his shoulder and spotted Rhona and the others. They came up alongside him in silence, all staring at Ariah.

"Is this…normal?" Killian whispered.

Rhona's voice was barely audible when she said, "Not that I've known."

Movement near Ariah caught Killian's attention. He spotted something moving near the ground and headed toward her. He caught a glimpse of a fluffy red tail. A fox. A second appeared. Then, a third. They seemed drawn to Ariah. And they weren't the only ones.

"Holy shit," Sabryn murmured. "Look at all of them."

Rabbits, mice, pine martens, and even some red deer drew close to Ariah. The hoot of an owl broke the silence, followed by two others. Killian couldn't find them in the branches, but he knew they were near. Bats dove in and around the trees, their clicking adding to the music of the night.

"Is it the Ancients?" Elias whispered.

Killian wanted to ask who that was. There was so much he had yet to learn.

"Maybe," Rhona murmured.

Bronwyn made a sound in the back of her throat. "I bet there's something in the book about this."

Killian frowned as he listened to them. Something was happening, something the Druids didn't know how to explain. "Is Ariah in danger?" Someone started moving past him. Killian instinctively shot out his arm to stop them and tore his gaze from Ariah to meet Rhona's. "No one goes near her."

Rhona studied him for a long moment. "Why?"

"I…" Killian frowned and shook his head. "I don't know."

Rhona's face went slack a second before her head whipped around to look at Ariah. "Oh, shite."

Killian's heart squeezed painfully. He tried to see Rhona's face in the darkness to no avail. "What? What do you know?"

Her head swiveled back to him. "I need to make sure first."

She left without another word. Killian watched her run back to the manor for a heartbeat, then returned his attention to Ariah. He looked from her to the animals gathered around. Some predators, others prey. Yet they didn't seem aware of it.

Killian thought back to being yanked from sleep. Thankfully, the house had kept Ariah inside, giving him time to dress and reach her. Not that he had grasped what was going on at the time.

He grimaced when he recalled Ariah's taut, flustered face, her voice threaded with terror as she yelled, demanding the manor let her leave. He had no idea how she had convinced the house to let her go, but she had.

It had taken everything in Killian to keep up with her after Ariah bolted from the house. She had run as if her life depended on it. Maybe it had. All she had told him was that she had to get to the trees. He hadn't known where she'd been headed. All he could think about was finding her walking barefoot in her nightclothes his first night on Skye. He didn't want that to happen again.

There had been a discernible shift in her the instant she entered the woods. All the tension vanished in a heartbeat. Many had called her *forest child*. He'd simply thought it meant she was more in tune with nature. That she was a free spirit. A Bohemian. The words took on new meaning now.

The soft lights began to fade until they disappeared entirely, leaving only the moonlight filtering through the trees. Ariah opened her eyes and leaned forward to pet Moon before gracefully climbing to her feet. Then she turned to him. An effervescent smile curved her lips when she spotted him. His heart swelled with love so deep and pure he was amazed he had been able to ignore it for so many years.

She slowly started toward him. The long strands of her dark hair hung freely, her skirt swinging with her movements. She had never looked more beautiful or ethereal. As she walked, the trees swayed toward her as if they needed to touch her. He understood completely. It was how he felt anytime she was near.

She stopped before him. Killian spotted leaves and sticks in her hair. Offerings from the trees, perhaps? Moon wound herself between their legs, purring loudly. Ariah looped one of her fingers around one of his, and Killian dropped his forehead to hers.

"You stayed," she said.

"Always."

She lifted her head and looked into his eyes. "The forest calms me. And…though it may sound bizarre, it needed me."

"I saw." He glanced over her head at the animals that still watched her. "I'm beginning to understand. You feel a connection, don't you?"

Ariah nodded slowly, a soft smile on her lips. "Aye." Her brow puckered suddenly. "I didn't tell you everything about my nightmares. There was this…" She paused, shrugging as if trying to find the words. "This dark entity that rushed me, only to vanish before it reached me. I saw it in a dream last night, but there was screaming this time. From the trees."

Killian's mind had gone blank the moment she mentioned the being. "Did you say a dark creature? Was it difficult to make out its complete shape? Maybe like it was made of shadows?"

Her face blanched. "You saw it."

"It's what attacked me. I shared that with Theo, but he didn't tell me about yours."

Ferne cleared her throat as she stepped forward. "Sorry to interrupt, but Theo is on call and left a few hours ago. I just want to point out that he was conducting an investigation. He wanted to check everyone's stories before he sat down with all of us and laid it all out."

"He could have let us know we saw the same thing after he spoke with us," Ariah said pointedly. Then she caught Killian's gaze. "I kept things to myself, believing I could handle it. I couldn't. It's time everyone knows."

He listened as Ariah told him about the dreams and how the entity had followed her to the forest, preventing her from meditating. She told him how she had seen it rush her at the store. All before he had arrived. What terrified him more was that it had started after he'd shown up.

"You didn't mention the sleepwalking," Killian said.

Ariah's lips twisted. "I'm not sure it had anything to do with the shadow creature."

Killian nodded and swallowed, then began his tale for her and the others. The moment he mentioned seeing the blonde woman, the atmosphere shifted.

"What else did you notice about her?" Elias asked.

Killian turned his head to him and shrugged. "She stared at me with…well, it wasn't exactly disgust. What shook me was the gleam in her eyes. Almost as if she knew what was coming."

"The shadow creature," Ariah said.

Killian released a breath. "Aye. It came at me from outside the building, rising from the ground. It moved through the walls as if they weren't there." He looked at Ariah. "I tried to warn you, but there wasn't enough time."

The last thing Killian wanted to do was relieve the moments after the glass had broken, but he did it for Ariah. She held his hands as he went through the pain and fear right up until he blacked out.

"Well, fuck," Sabryn said. "It certainly sounds like the same entity, creature, thing. Whatever you want to call it," she replied irritably.

Ariah looked around at everyone. "There's a bigger question here."

Elias cursed under his breath and turned away, shoving his fingers into his dark blond hair.

"There's a way," Elodie said. "I'll grab my mobile and meet you all in the manor."

The rest followed until only Killian and Ariah remained. Then he asked, "What am I missing?"

"The woman you saw might be Elias and Elodie's sister, Edie."

Killian glanced over her shoulder and noticed that the animals had retreated back into the forest. "Bloody hell. No wonder Elias is on edge."

"Is this too much?"

"Which part?" he asked, grinning in an effort to lighten the mood some.

"All of it. I left the manor in a bit of a hurry."

"You scared the hell out of me when you did that."

"I didn't have time to explain."

He nodded. "Aye. I gathered that. To answer your question, none of it is too much. I'm struggling to understand and catch up, but you won't be rid of me that easily," he said with a grin.

"Will you promise to tell me if that changes?"

"You have my word." He wrapped his arms around her. "What did you feel when you were out here?"

"Have you ever meditated?"

"I've never been able to still my mind for long enough."

"That comes with practice. Some days are easier than others, but it is something I struggle with despite years of meditation. It's learning to not let your mind control your thoughts."

He thought about the lights moving over her. "Is that what you were doing?"

"It's part of it. The other part is connecting to nature. When I get up, I'm grounded and peaceful. Every time. No matter what might be going on before I meditate."

"Who taught you?"

A small smile pulled at her lips. "No one. Bonnie said she couldn't find me once when I was three. A search was conducted on the isle. They found me a few hours later in the forest."

Killian thought about how the animals had come to her and how the trees and plants had reached out. Had he convinced Ariah all those years ago to move with him to the city, it would've slowly killed her, eating away at the very thing that made her special. Because he had been too blind to see the truth before him.

Now that his eyes were open to the magic, he saw it everywhere. If only he had seen it before.

They walked back to the manor hand-in-hand. Ariah glanced back once. When she faced forward again, he saw a smile on her lips. Moon bolted ahead and through the back door someone had left open a crack, going where the warmth of the inside lights beckoned.

"You saw them, didn't you?" Ariah asked.

"Saw what?"

"The animals."

He wrapped an arm around her, pulling her closer so their bodies met. Killian kissed the top of her head and tugged a twig from her hair with his other hand. He held it out to her. "I saw much more than the animals. It was breathtaking. Maybe I shouldn't have been there—"

"I'm glad you were."

Killian stopped when they reached the door. "I meant it earlier. I'm not leaving you."

"I know," she whispered and pulled his head down.

Their lips met in a kiss that began soft and slow but quickly deepened as desire blazed anew. Killian bent her back over his arm, running his other hand over her shapely arse to hold her against him. Sounds from inside the house finally broke through the haze of passion.

Killian reluctantly ended the kiss. Neither loosened their hold as they fought to calm their breathing. Her fingers threaded through his hair, her nails skimming his scalp. Finally, he looked at her. They shared a smile before facing the manor and whatever the rest of the night held.

CHAPTER THIRTY-ONE

Killian pushed the door wider, spreading the warm light from within into the evening. Ariah hesitated for only a heartbeat before crossing the threshold. The sounds of the night faded, replaced by a chatter of voices that filtered from deeper within the manor. Ariah lingered in that space for another moment, holding on to her connection with the trees for as long as she could. It was severed when Killian closed the door.

Ariah placed her hand on the wall. "Thank you," she whispered to the house. The wood beneath her palm warmed in response.

She turned to find Killian watching her. He retook her hand, and together they headed toward the voices. They passed the kitchen, where Ariah spotted Sabryn and Carlyle deep in the conversation. The others—minus Rhona and Balladyn—were gathered in the parlor. Multiple conversations were happening at once.

Ariah spotted Elias and Elodie against a far wall, their heads bent together as they talked. Jasper stood at the hearth with Willa and Scott. Bronwyn and Ferne were pouring drinks. Callum stood by himself not far from Kirsi, who sat stiffly on the edge of a chair. Finn and Filip were on either end of the sofa, Finn's gaze shooting toward the doorway every few moments, no doubt looking for his friends in the kitchen.

Killian tugged Ariah's hand and led her to the other couch. He sat in the corner, his arm coming around her shoulders after she lowered herself next to him.

Bronwyn brought two glasses of whisky over. Killian accepted one. "Sabryn and Carlyle are bringing tea," Bronwyn said when Ariah declined the alcohol.

Long minutes passed before Sabryn carried a tray into the parlor, her lips pinched. Ariah rose to pour herself a cup of tea, but Sabryn walked away before she had a chance to talk to her. Ariah wasn't the only one who noticed Carlyle hadn't joined them. Finn's frown deepened the longer he stared at the door, waiting for his friend. He rose and went to Sabryn, who stood off by herself. Ariah couldn't tell what Finn said to her, but his gaze returned to the doorway after Sabryn shook her head. A moment later, Finn walked out.

"Well," Filip said to get everyone's attention after draining the last of his whisky and setting aside the glass. "What now?"

Elodie walked to Killian and held out her mobile with a picture of Edie on the screen. "Is this the woman you saw?"

Killian held Elodie's gaze for a moment, then looked at the phone. There was a long stretch of silence before he said, "Aye. That's who I saw."

Elias squeezed his eyes closed and turned his head away. Bronwyn put her arms around him. Elias fisted his hand in her shirt and held her tightly. Ariah couldn't imagine what the family was going through at the moment.

"All right, then," Elodie said dazedly. Scott was at her side immediately, walking her to a chair. Once she was seated, she took a deep breath. "Edie was outside Ariah's store, and then Kirsi saw her smiling as she left the scene."

Filip shook his head, a frown furrowing his brow. "We already cleared Edie from the list. What did we miss?"

"Something must have changed," Sabryn said.

Jasper grunted. "I think it's fair to say that *everything* is changing."

"Can someone start at the beginning?" Killian asked. "I'm trying to get my footing here, and it might be easier if I knew what happened leading up to all of this."

Elodie cleared her throat and glanced at her brother. "I guess I'll start. I left the isle fifteen years ago, believing I had lost my magic."

"That can happen?" Killian asked.

Ariah nodded. "Oh, aye."

"I didn't want to return," Elodie continued, "but I had nowhere else to go. I stayed in my family's cottage."

Elias said, "She never should've been there. She was never meant to return."

"It wasn't only my magic that was gone. Memories had been taken, as well." Elodie took Scott's hand. "You see, something horrible happened in that house. Something I was responsible for."

Elias shook his head. "It wasna you." He looked at Killian. "Our father was a right bastard. He beat our mother and then began hitting me. Everything changed one morning before school when Mum told him she wanted a divorce. Edie was already outside. I heard Dad hitting Mum." He looked at his sister. "So did Elodie. I tried to stop her from going into their room."

Elodie wiped a tear off her cheek. "Dad was choking Mum. I tried to pull him away."

"He backhanded Elodie," Elias said. "Then came after me in a rage. I'd never seen that look on him before. He was going to hurt one of us. I had no choice but to use magic to get him off me."

Elodie licked her lips. "That set Dad off. He didn't know that Mum was a Druid until that moment. He went after her with a knife. And I...I..."

"Elodie created a portal that sucked our father into it. She acted instinctually to protect herself, but the aftermath was too much for her. Mum sent me out to occupy Edie so she wouldn't see anything while she created a scene to make it look as if she had murdered our father. Then she wiped Elodie of her memories and bound her magic."

"Until I returned to the isle, walked into their bedroom, and remembered everything." Elodie sniffed and looked up at Scott.

Scott picked up the tale, explaining how Georgina Miller had sent him to convince Elodie to join the Edinburgh Druids. Ariah glanced at Killian and found him seemingly enraptured by the stories of the killing mist and the havoc it had caused on the isle.

The story then shifted to how the Knights had followed Elias to the isle to assist him and readily stepped in to help fight the mist. They had remained, adding their numbers and battle skills to the fight against the shadow of evil that hung over Skye. Carlyle had no choice but to keep his location from his father since it was forbidden for any London Druids to visit Skye. Now, Carlyle couldn't get ahold of his father at all.

Once the London Druids were mentioned, Ferne spoke about

how her parents had been high up in the society there before their untimely deaths. Her brother, Mason, had been looking into their suspicious deaths when she came to Skye after having a vision of Kirsi. Then, Ferne's brother suddenly had a change of heart and banished her from the family.

Bronwyn detailed the heartbreaking story of her father's murder by her ex-lover, Sydney, who stole an ancient book and turned his attention to her cousin, Beth. It wasn't until Bronwyn spoke about opening a doorway between dimensions that Killian looked toward Callum and Kirsi. It was difficult for Ariah to listen to how Ferne had been trapped in The Grey with the monster and how everyone came together to free her again.

"Bloody hell," Killian said when he learned that Beth had the book and a connection to George in Edinburgh.

As Jasper and Willa finished the sorted story of George interfering with things in Skye again, along with Beth's use of the ebony wood, Killian wasn't the only one who looked like he could use a drink.

"George was nothing if not determined to get what she wanted, and she was prepared to do it by any means necessary," Jasper said.

Everyone in the room was there to fight the evil, but they also had another cause for concern. For Willa and Scott, it was their father. For Elodie and Elias, it was Edie. Bronwyn had Beth, Ferne had Mason, Carlyle had his father, Kirsi had the monster from The Grey, and Callum had family issues. For Ariah and Killian, it was the shadow entity.

And it had all started with Elodie's arrival on Skye.

Ariah's thoughts skidded to a halt as she slowly sat up straight.

"Ariah?" Killian asked from beside her.

She looked around the room. "We're all connected."

"Without a doubt," Scott said.

"No, you don't understand." Ariah stood and shook her head as it all began falling into place. "George sent Scott, Filip, and Jasper. The Knights fought to bring Druids to justice, which led them to Skye."

"Because Elodie told me she was staying at our old house," Elias interjected with a frown.

Ariah kept talking. "Willa and her father were part of the Edinburgh Druids that George runs. And they saw Beth with the book."

"That connects them to me," Bronwyn stated.

Ariah slid her gaze to Ferne. "Your vision about Kirsi brought you here, where you reconnected with your brother's friend, Carlyle."

"Which links both Carlyle and me to the London Druids," Ferne said.

Ariah nodded, her heart racing as the picture became clearer. She looked at Kirsi and Callum. "Those of us born on the isle fill in the blanks to the others."

"What about me?" Killian asked.

She met his gaze. He was the one that didn't fit. "I'm not sure." Ariah faced the others. "All this time, I thought everything began with Elodie. That's when the mist and the other troubles began. But things started much earlier than that. Right here in the manor."

"With me," Bronwyn murmured. "When I hid Beth and used blood magic."

"Maybe even earlier."

Elias's brows shot up. "What do you mean?"

"You think George is pulling the strings?" Jasper asked hesitantly. "She's determined to get revenge on Elias and take down all the Skye Druids, but I doona think she's that formidable."

Ferne shrugged. "I agree. But there is a group that does have that kind of power. The London Druids. Trust me, they can cause the kind of mayhem that's going on here."

"Beth is the one with the book," Willa pointed out. "It has to be her."

Ariah shook her head. "You're partly right. Beth thinks she's in control, but she isn't. The book is."

"Fuck me," Callum muttered.

Filip went to the sideboard and poured more whisky. "I need another drink."

"It makes sense," Sabryn said after a stretch of silence.

The sound of a roaring engine and flying gravel interrupted them. Tires slid on the rocks as the car came to a stop. A second after a car door slammed, the manor threw open the door. Rhona rushed in carrying a notebook, her hair wild and chest heaving.

"Three," Rhona said breathlessly.

Elodie blinked. "Okay. I'll bite. It's a sacred number for Druids."

"Aye." Rhona walked deeper into the parlor and took one of the empty chairs. "There was something about seeing Ariah in the forest that kept nagging at me as if I had seen it before. Then I realized I hadn't *seen* it, but I *had* heard a story about it. From Corann. I couldn't remember what he had called it, but I thought it might be in the notes I used to take." She held up a spiral notepad with a faded blue cover. "It took me some time, but I found it. He called them elemental pillars."

Surprise flashed across Bronwyn's face. "I remember that. There was a story he told us, wasn't there?" Her brow furrowed. "I can't remember what it is, though."

A shiver raced down Ariah's spine.

"I think we found the *talamh* pillar," Rhona said and looked at Ariah.

CHAPTER THIRTY-TWO

"*Talamh?*" Killian repeated. It had been years since he had taken any Gaelic courses, but he recognized the word. Still, he struggled to put the meaning to it. Then it hit him as he looked at Ariah. "Earth."

Confusion furrowed her brow. Ariah briefly looked at him before returning her attention to Rhona. "You're mistaken.

"I'm not," Rhona replied. "Corann told us a story about the elemental pillars."

"He told us a lot of stories," Ariah argued.

Rhona sank onto a chair. "Sky, earth, water. There are always three pillars to stand against attacks."

Killian thought about the magic he had seen wash over Ariah. No wonder Rhona believed she was a pillar. What he didn't understand was why Ariah seemed against it.

"I remember something about the pillars, but Balladyn is the Warden of Skye. I thought that made him the protector," Bronwyn said.

Rhona set the spiral notebook on her lap. "Balladyn is that, and he does protect the isle, but the pillars are different. Balladyn and I merged our magic to protect ourselves against the Fae Others' assault. We will do so again if we're attacked by any other living beings. The pillars are like,"—she paused and considered her words—"gateways. They protect against forces outside the living."

"I'm not a fighter," Ariah stated. "I'm not a pillar."

Killian swung his head to Ariah. "Based on what Rhona just said, you wouldn't be fighting. You would be protecting."

"It isn't me," she whispered.

Rhona sat back in the chair, her gaze locked on Ariah. "After what I witnessed tonight in the woods, you're not going to change my mind."

"What is it you think you saw?" Ariah demanded. "Some animals drawing near? They've always done that."

Kirsi rose and walked to them, holding out her mobile. "We saw this."

Killian watched Ariah's eyes widen as she viewed the multicolored lights moving around her.

"Wouldn't Corann have told me?" Ariah asked when the video ended.

Filip shrugged from his position near the liquor. "Corann wasn't much on laying out details. It was one of the reasons I hated going to his lessons. Everything was always so cryptic."

"He must have learned it from the Ancients," Elodie said with a grin.

Bronwyn crossed her arms, her gaze pensive. "What if Corann didn't know? What if he knew there were meant to be pillars but little else? I can't imagine him not warning Ariah or anyone else."

"Possibly," Rhona agreed.

Elias twisted his lips. "If Ariah is one, then who are the other two?"

"Good question," Rhona answered with a shrug.

Killian could tell that Ariah wasn't taking the news well. "It's been a long night. Why don't we all sit on this until morning?"

A murmur of agreement went through the room. Killian stood and waited for Ariah to get to her feet, then steered her out of the parlor and up the stairs to his room. She said nothing as they undressed and climbed into bed. A soft meow outside the door had Killian rising to let Moon in. The cat leapt onto the bed and curled up at Ariah's feet.

He slid beneath the covers and reached for Ariah. She scooted close to lay on his chest, one arm across his abdomen. Killian listened to her breathing as he stared at the wooden canopy above.

"It can't be me," she whispered.

"Tell me why not."

"I'm not that person. I've never helped when the others fought. You heard their stories. The killing mist, Kerry, Sydney, the ebony wood, The Grey, and other things we probably don't even know about yet."

Killian rubbed his hand on her back. "Did they ask you to help?"

"Nay."

"If they had, would you have?"

"Of course."

"That isn't the same thing as not doing anything."

She blew out a breath. "I knew things were going on. Every Druid on the isle did. But I didn't seek out Rhona and ask what I could do."

"Because you trusted she would handle it."

"I'm not a fighter."

"No one is asking you to be."

She rose on her forearm to look at him. "That's exactly what they're doing."

"Are you telling me you wouldn't take a stand to protect those on Skye from someone meaning to do them harm?" he asked, tucking some hair behind her ear.

Her mouth parted before closing. She pressed her lips together into a flat line.

"That's what I thought," he said. "You saw the video with the lights moving over you. Have you ever experienced that before?"

"I always feel the magic. It was stronger tonight, but I've never seen it." She paused, pressing her lips together again. "Everything about tonight was different. The dream, the screams. The fear that came with it."

"You have a connection to the forest that no one else does."

"The forest, not the earth."

He thought about that for a moment. "Every plant that grows on this planet is done through the earth. Soil connects everything. Like the Tree of Life."

"All right. Say Rhona's right and I am the *talamh* pillar. What if I fail them?"

"You won't." He tried to smooth the lines of worry from her face with his finger.

"You can't know that."

He looked into her golden-brown eyes. "I can because I'll be beside you."

"The last place you should be is on Skye."

"I never should've left the isle *or* you."

Ariah turned away and slipped out of bed. Moon lifted her

head and watched her pace the room naked. "You heard the stories tonight. How many times did someone nearly lose their life?"

"But they didn't."

"Eventually, someone will."

"We're all going to die someday."

Ariah halted and spun toward him. "Don't! Don't make light of this."

Killian sat up. "That isn't what I'm doing."

"You had a life for yourself. A woman you were going to marry."

"That was a mistake. All of it. You were who I was always meant to be with."

She turned away and began pacing again. "Things are going to get worse here."

Killian didn't like that she wouldn't look at him. He thought about the associations she'd made downstairs before Rhona arrived. "What do you know that you aren't telling me?"

"You came within a hair's breadth of dying. That usually sends people running."

He scooted to the edge of the bed. "I'm not dead, thanks to magic. I admit, learning about Druids took me aback, but it didn't make me stop loving you. Nothing will. I'm here, and I'm staying. Get used to it."

"And if that entity comes for you again? It isn't as if we can remain in the manor for the rest of our lives."

Killian got off the bed and stood before her, gently wrapping his hands around her upper arms. "What if it comes for you? What if it goes after Callum or Kirsi or someone else at the manor? What if it goes after someone we don't know? They're valid questions, but none we can answer. Only one thing's certain."

"What's that?"

"That I'm meant to be by your side. I knew it tonight when I followed you into the woods."

Ariah buried her head against his chest. His arms came around her instantly. They stood holding each other in silence for several moments.

"I don't know what's going on, and that terrifies me," she said.

"Me, too."

Ariah tilted her head back to look at him. "Something I couldn't see attacked us. How can I fight what I can't see?"

"I can see it. I'll tell you where it's at. We'll tackle one problem at a time."

"Maybe Rhona's wrong about me."

He tucked more hair behind her ear. "Do you remember the stories?"

Ariah reluctantly shrugged. "Not really. Not until Rhona mentioned the pillars."

"Tell me what you do recall," he urged.

Her brow furrowed as she looked to the left. "Um…just something about three pillars. I was young and thought Corann actually meant columns or something. Three is significant in our culture. It represents a host of things from the three phases of the moon, the earth, sea, and sky, the triskelion… I locked onto that number because of its importance. Other than that?" She shrugged. "Not much."

Killian had picked up a few skills over the years to help his clients recall events. "Tell me about this school."

"It wasn't like that. Corann passed down history and some spells. It fell mainly to families to teach their children about magic and our ways because some don't like sharing certain spells. That was before technology took off. Now, there are Druid chatrooms where you can find pretty much anything you want."

"Who is Corann?"

Ariah began to relax. "He once governed us as Rhona does now. I always thought he looked the part of a Druid."

"Oh? Why is that?" Killian smiled when her lips turned up at the corners.

"He had long, white hair and a beard. He walked around with a staff. Visitors to the isle thought he was an actor. It was only us Druids who understood that was just Corann." She swallowed and looked at him. "He always took time to form an answer or react. Like he had to consider every word. I remember as kids, we used to ask him how old he was because my great-aunt remembered him looking the same when she was a child."

It was Killian's turn to frown. "Is that possible?"

"No one ever got a straight answer from Corann. He would only grin and shrug. But the fact is, he led the Druids for multiple generations."

"How did he die?"

Ariah shivered and tugged him to the bed. She rested against the headboard while he took a pillow and leaned back against the footboard to see her. She had one leg under the covers and the other stretched out toward him. Killian placed a hand on her chilly foot to warm it and met her gaze.

She drew in a deep breath. "Corann sacrificed himself to save us during a battle between the Dragon Kings and their enemies. The only one surprised that he had chosen Rhona to succeed him was Rhona. She's always had a natural ability to lead." Ariah grinned. "She used to follow Corann everywhere. She would even skip school to spend the day learning from him. And he never sent her away."

"Did you skip school?"

Ariah laughed and rolled her eyes. "The idea of breaking rules makes me sick to my stomach."

Killian grinned. "I never had an issue breaking the rules."

"I'm very aware." They shared a smile. Ariah played with the ends of her hair. "Once a month, Corann gathered kids around the same age. There was never a set date. I don't even know how Bonnie knew when it was. She would just send me off to him. We met in different locations, and there was usually some story he imparted or an important spell he thought every Druid should not only know but master. Corann had a way of turning what was an important lesson into fun so we would remember. Except there was no way we could recall everything."

"Maybe not one person. Each of you remembered something, so that when brought together, you would fill in the whole story."

She considered that. "Maybe. That does sound like something he would think to do."

"Do you recall where you were when he told you the story about the three pillars?"

"I know it was outside."

He gently rubbed her foot. "Was it near water?"

"Nay. Actually, I don't remember."

"What about mountains?"

Ariah shook her head in frustration. "I don't know."

"Was it day or night?"

"I—" She blinked. "Night. It was at night."

He kept going, hoping it might jog more of her memory. "Was it warm or cold?"

"Cold and raining," Ariah said, her gaze off to the side. "We were in a valley. It's an important place. One I'm supposed to remember. But,"—she scrunched up her face—"the name is on the tip of my tongue."

"A valley could mean near a mountain. We can drive around the Cuillins tomorrow. Maybe you'll recognize something."

Ariah sat up, her eyes wide. "It was the Fairy Glen."

CHAPTER THIRTY-THREE

Somewhere in Scotland

Beth ran her hands over the worn leather cover. The book had changed her life. Everyone wanted it, but it was hers.

And she had no intention of giving it up.

Inside the cover was a treasure trove of information from both *mies* and *droughs*. There were spells, recipes, and stories. Then there was the other section. It was her favorite.

She brought the large tome to her chest and wrapped her arms around it. Beth was amazed that the book had stayed hidden for as long as it had. Sydney had never told her how he'd heard about it. Or how he managed to steal it from the old woman. That had been during the time when he and Bronwyn were a thing.

Beth's mood soured at the thought of her cousin. Bronwyn would get her due soon. Everyone on Skye who opposed her would learn.

It had already begun. She had been so close to victory with the ebony wood. Someone had helped Jasper. Someone with power and magic. That was the only reason he had survived the pain of the numerous ebony wood slivers she had thrust into his body. And if he was alive, then he was now aware that he had Fae blood.

Jasper was an issue. It was why she wanted him dead. There were other ways to get what she wanted, though. Beth was nothing if not resourceful. She had the book, after all. It held the answer to every problem.

Reading it was easy. Or it had been. Each time she failed, it became more difficult. And when she was successful, new areas opened to her. Beth had thumbed through the book four times and thought she knew every section. There was no denying the excitement at learning there was more. She just had to prove herself worthy.

A figure filled the doorway. Beth turned her head to look at Madeline. Tall, commanding, cunning. Madeline might not be a conventional beauty with her black hair always slicked into a bun, and stark, almost manly features. But she held another kind of beauty that interested Beth—power. Madeline intimidated most everyone—men and women alike. Few dared to stand against her. Madeline kept her hair as she kept herself and her life. Neat and tidy.

"Sydney has had a minor setback," the guard announced.

Beth tightened her fingers on the book and lowered it to lay flat atop her thighs. "How so?"

"The nurse on duty last night transposed the numbers for the nurse this morning."

It wasn't as if Beth needed Sydney. She was doing fine on her own. But she wanted him with her. They were meant to do this together. Bronwyn had wronged them both. Deeply.

And they would dole out retribution to her cousin.

"And Sydney?" Beth asked tightly.

"He's fine and has been sedated, but it sets us back at least a day."

Beth looked down at the book. It had shown her how to fix Sydney, but the price was too steep. "I assume you've taken care of the nurse?"

"Of course. The new one comes in later."

When Madeline lingered, Beth raised a brow. "Is there something else?"

"I've been reviewing the footage of George's encounter with the Skye Druids."

"And?"

"More than just Druids were there."

That piqued Beth's interest. "I didn't think George had it in her to reach out to anyone. Who did she find? Dark Fae, perhaps?"

"I wasn't talking about George's allies."

Beth set aside the book and propped her elbows on the desk. "We know Rhona is mated to someone powerful. Everyone calls him the Warden of Skye. That's likely who you saw."

Madeline glanced at the floor and leaned a shoulder against the doorjamb. "These looked like people. Then, they changed."

"Changed how?"

"Their skin turned a different color. One of them even had wings."

Beth's gaze briefly slid to the book. It would know who the Skye Druids' new friends were, but what would it ask of her in return for that information? There was always a trade. The book gave nothing for free.

"There's more," Madeline said. "Something helped George. She got out through an upper window when she should've been trapped."

"Did you see who came to her aid?"

Madeline's lips flattened. "That's just it. I didn't *see* anything. But something was there. She couldn't have gotten down on her own."

"Interesting. I thought George was nearly done serving her purpose. Seems she has more tricks up her sleeve. We need to find out who she aligned with recently."

"And the others helping those from Skye?"

Beth was surprised to find her hand was on the book. She didn't remember moving her arm. "Put out some feelers. Someone will know about the winged one for sure."

"On it," Madeline said and turned on her heel, the door closing softly behind her.

Beth sat back in her chair, her thoughts turning to Georgina Miller. Beth had used her, though George had known about it. George would've done the same had their positions been reversed. They both wanted power. That was where their similarities ended, though.

George wanted it because she believed she was the only one who could lead the Druids to become who they should've always been. It was a load of shite, a lie George told herself. The truth was, George craved power. The more people who followed her, the more the need grew, feeding the feral beast within her that George had yet to acknowledge.

And it would end up taking George's life.

On the other hand, Beth wanted the power simply to have it. She recognized the monster inside her. It gave her clarity and dominance over those like George. Beth would've had that even without the book, but it added another dimension to things.

George would forever crave what was just out of reach. While Beth would bask in all she wanted very, very soon.

Her hand flattened on the book. The answers were there, waiting.

The buzz of the plane engine filled Carlyle's ears. He looked out the window into the night from his first-class seat. He focused on his reflection. The man staring back at him looked lost. And frightened. He had thought such things far behind him after his mother's death. Yet those emotions were happy to take center stage again.

"Here."

He pulled his gaze from the window to look at Finn, who held out a glass of whisky. Carlyle downed it. The liquid left a fiery trail down his throat. He pulled back his lips and set the empty glass on the tray table he hadn't remembered lowering.

"Aye, I know," Finn said conversationally. "It isn't Dreagan, but it'll do in a pinch. I got extras from one of the attendants."

No doubt Finn had flashed his famous smile. That seemed to make women do just about anything. Carlyle looked at his mobile to see the time.

"We'll touch down in London soon, and then we'll find your dad. The townhouse first. If he isn't there, we'll head to the country estate. You left your car at the townhome, didn't you?"

"Why did you come?" Carlyle asked, looking at his friend.

Finn turned his head to him, his deep brown eyes filled with anger. "Fuck you."

"It's an honest question."

"The hell it is. We're mates. This is what we do."

"They're going to need you on Skye."

Finn ran a hand through his dark brown hair. "There was no way I was letting you come alone. You need backup. If for nothing else than because you aren't thinking clearly."

"I am."

"Really? I hate to tell you this, mate, but you nearly got on the wrong plane. You'd be headed to Switzerland now if it wasn't for me."

Carlyle dropped his head back and looked at the ceiling of the plane. Fuck. How had things gone to hell so quickly? "I spent months dodging my father's calls because he wanted me to return and get married. I lied to him about everything. What I was doing, who I was with, and, of course, that I was on Skye. If he found out, he'd have no choice but to banish me."

"Your father is a good man. All you have is each other. I've talked to him plenty of times. There's no way he would cut you out of his life. Nothing and no one could force him to do that."

"Then something happened to him." Carlyle rolled his head to look at Finn. His voice lowered to a soft whisper as fury laced every syllable. "If I find out the London Druids had anything—"

"I'm way ahead of you," Finn said over him.

Carlyle nodded and looked out the window again. "I should've gone home sooner. I should've answered more of his calls."

"Don't do that. What's done is done. There's no need to think about what you believe you should have done when there's no way to alter it. We'll find him. It's what we do, remember?"

The flight was an hour and twenty-five minutes. It would take another thirty to get from the airport to the townhouse. Carlyle looked at his mobile again. They were fifty minutes into the flight. That left him thirty-five to devise a plan.

He took the napkin and flipped it to the clean backside. Then, he began drawing a diagram of the townhome.

"About fucking time," Finn said as he leaned in to watch.

"Okay," Carlyle said after he'd finished. "The Xs are entry points. I think we should split up. You take that one." He pointed. "I'll go this way."

CHAPTER THIRTY-FOUR

A pink and yellow sky proclaimed a new day. Ariah stood at the window with a blanket wrapped around her as she stared at the sky above the trees. She and Killian had talked for hours until he dozed off a short time ago. She looked back at him sprawled half on his stomach, his beautiful body on full display as he breathed the slow, deep inhales and exhales of sleep.

She didn't know what to think of…any of what was happening. The idea that she might be one of the three pillars was disturbing. More so because she wasn't even sure what the position meant or what she might have to do.

Moon jumped onto the windowsill and yawned, turning her yellow gaze out the glass. The dawn was chasing away the night and sending shadows scurrying. A low growl came from the feline. Ariah followed the cat's gaze. She frantically searched the wooded area. It was far from the manor, and the sunrise made things hazy and difficult to see. Then she spotted it. A hulking shadow the rays of the sun couldn't penetrate.

That was likely as close to the manor as it could get, and Ariah wasn't about to go outside while there was a chance Killian would wake and come after her. A small part of her worried about what had changed to allow her to see the shape, but seeing it gave her an advantage now. One she gladly took. It no longer mattered who the shadow was after. Her, Killian, or someone else. She would end it.

She had told Killian that she wasn't a fighter, and that had been true until she watched him being attacked. And she hadn't even realized she intended to take a stand until that very moment.

Ariah turned away from the window and walked to the bed. She dropped the blanket and put her knee on the mattress as she climbed up. Her hand flattened on the base of Killian's back before she skimmed a finger up the indent of his spine. She stretched out beside him and pressed a kiss to his shoulder.

He drew in a breath and rolled over, looking at her sleepily. His arm came up and around to hold her. She kissed his chest and moved between his legs. Ariah glanced up to find his eyes glued to her as she continued kissing down his stomach. His cock hardened against her. She wrapped her fingers around his arousal and began slowly moving her hand up and down his length while her lips roamed across his stomach to the trail of hair that led downward.

"Ariah," he groaned breathlessly.

She kissed down one thigh and then up the other. He fisted his hands in the blanket so tightly his knuckles turned white. Her sex clenched when a drop of liquid beaded on the head of his erection. She leisurely licked it away.

A low moan rumbled from his chest. Ariah smiled inwardly, knowing she could bring him such tormented pleasure. She wrapped her lips around his cock and took him into her mouth.

He whispered her name, the sound half-groan, half-strangled cry. Ariah took him deep, using her hand and tongue to ruthlessly arouse, mercilessly excite.

The suction had him moaning. It wasn't long before every muscle was taut. She didn't relent, intending to drive him to the edge and beyond, just as he had done with her hours earlier. Every time a groan fell from his lips, she clenched her legs together, fighting the need to feel him inside her again. Then, she gave up the battle.

Ariah lifted her head and crawled up his body. His olive gaze held hers as she straddled him and sat up. His large hands ran up her body and cupped her breasts, massaging them. She dropped her head back, rubbing her sex along his arousal. Her nipples strained, aching for his touch.

He lightly circled one with the tip of his finger and thumbed the other. She gripped his wrists. He sat up and pulled her fingers away with his lips. Then she was on her stomach with Killian behind her. He lifted her hips. Ariah stilled when she felt the blunt head of his arousal at her entrance. She waited for him to push inside. Instead, he skimmed his finger down her back, between her butt cheeks, and over her swollen sex. She pushed back against him and was rewarded with his finger sliding inside her. Ariah moaned at the pleasure. He replaced his finger with his cock, and this time, he filled her with one hard thrust.

She climaxed instantly.

He gripped her hips tightly, holding her as he drove into her again and again. Pleasure surged through her. Killian's tempo gradually increased as their bodies slapped together. He leaned over her, his chest molding to her back. She turned her head, and their lips met. His fingers flexed into her flesh before he tore his mouth away from hers and moaned long and low as his seed filled her.

They fell to the side together, his cock still inside her. Ariah's eyes grew heavy. Killian kissed her shoulder, his stubble scraping her chin. He pulled out of her and rolled her onto her back.

"Please, wake me like that any time," he said with a smile.

She smiled up at him. "Be assured I will."

"How are you?"

She knew what he was asking. "I don't know."

"I thought we might take a trip to the Fairy Glen. Maybe it'll bring back some memories."

"I need to stop by the store and take in the damage. I'm not going to turn in the report Theo gave me to my insurance."

Killian leaned on his forearm, the sun's rays coming in through the window and giving his golden hair a magical look. "You didn't cause the damage. If you could tell the truth, you would. In a perfect world, they would accept the truth, and you'd get paid. Right?"

"I suppose."

"It isn't a perfect world. You didn't cause the damage, and you can't tell them the truth. Theo is giving you a way to get what you need."

"I have money saved up."

He blew out a breath. "Keep saving it. You aren't doing anything illegal."

"It feels like it."

"Only because you hide who you are."

She held his gaze. "Most people hide something."

"True. I hid a lot from my family." He snorted. "I hid my true self." Killian shook his head sadly. "Fuck."

She pushed him onto his back and leaned over him. "Let's not travel that road."

"I won't if you turn in the report to your insurance."

"Fine," she relented with a roll of her eyes. "I still don't feel good about it."

He smiled and gave her a quick kiss. "It'll be fine." He kissed her again. "I'm starving. We should get moving unless you want to stay in bed."

That sounded heavenly, but they needed to address too many things. She rolled out of bed.

"Food, it is," Killian said as he followed her into the bathroom.

After quick showers, they dressed and headed downstairs. Ariah was surprised that anyone was up after such a late night. She and Killian headed into the kitchen, where Ferne and Elodie were making breakfast.

Theo walked in a moment later, yawning over a cup of coffee. He gave Ferne a kiss and took a seat at the table. Killian grabbed some coffee while Ariah chose tea. It was always a little thrilling and a bit odd to see her tea in someone's house. After Ariah grabbed one of the green tea blends, she took a seat beside Killian.

"We should've gone with them," Elias said.

Ariah glanced around the room. "Gone with who?"

"Carlyle and Finn headed to London to search for his father," Sabryn said.

Theo set his mug on the table and sat up straight. "When was this?"

"Last night," Elias answered.

Bronwyn moved to stand beside Elias and put her hand on his shoulder. "Carlyle waited for as long as he could. You would've done the same."

Scott blew out a breath. "We had help looking for our dad. I thought Carlyle had some as well."

"Saber was doing what he could. Just not quickly enough," Sabryn said.

Elodie turned from the stove. "Saber is only one person. It isn't as if he has a team at his disposal."

"Carlyle couldn't ignore the urge to get to London." Sabryn shrugged. "He would've stayed had I asked it of him, but I couldn't. Nor did I want him going by himself. Besides, nothing could keep Finn from going."

Elias scrubbed a hand down his face. "It isn't as if we haven't split up before, but I don't like this."

"None of us does," Ferne said.

Ariah exchanged a look with Killian and then said, "We're going to head to the Fairy Glen today. I remembered last night that was where Corann told us the story about the pillars. I still don't remember it, but maybe being there will jog some memories."

"I read over Rhona's notes last night, but none of it sounded familiar," Elodie said.

Bronwyn passed out plates. "I'm not sure any of us should be alone until we can figure out this shadow thing."

"Then we should all go," Killian said.

CHAPTER THIRTY-FIVE

Killian stepped out of the manor to get some air and try to sort his thoughts while others finished breakfast. He had expected the house to keep him inside as it had Ariah the night before, but he was able to freely turn the handle.

Or maybe the house knew he wasn't in danger.

He briefly closed his eyes. The moment he did, a memory of the shadow rushing him flashed in his mind. He snapped open his eyes, but it was too late. The creature was now front and center in his head. Along with a healthy dose of fear. The entity's rage had been palpable. Its intent clear.

Killian held out a hand and saw it shake. He fisted it. How did he fight the shadow without magic? He didn't want to be a liability, someone who held others back. Nor did he want to put Ariah in additional danger. More than that, he hated how helpless he felt.

How exposed.

Defenseless.

That would have to change. Killian didn't know how yet, but

he would find a way. Not just for himself but also for Ariah's peace of mind. Her attention needed to be on other things, not worrying about him. He could hold his own in a fistfight, but this was far from that. The one thing he knew was that he wasn't leaving. No matter the danger.

Killian blew out a breath and looked around. His gaze caught on Callum standing off by himself near the far side of the manor. He made his way toward his friend. When he neared, Callum glanced his way.

"Quite a night, aye?" Killian said.

Callum grunted. "It was tame compared to some of the others I've witnessed."

"You mean you've been a part of."

"I doona consider myself part of anything."

That made Killian frown. "Why not? From what I've seen, they all think you're one of them. Based on one of the stories, it was you who saved everyone."

"Only by chance."

"Don't minimize what you've done."

Callum lowered his gaze to the ground, his thumbs hooked in the front pockets of his jeans. "I see The Grey everywhere I look now. It comes out of nowhere sometimes. Awake or dreaming, the dim lighting, the low-hanging mist, and that bloody awful silence. I doona even know what I was doing there."

"Aye, you do. Kirsi." When he didn't reply, Killian asked, "What's bothering you? Is it just The Grey? Or is there something else?"

Finally, Callum looked at him. "It's all of it. It's every-fucking-thing. I can no' be who they want me to be."

"I didn't hear anyone asking you to be anything but who you are."

"I'll fail them."

Now, they were coming to the root of the problem. It was something Killian was intimately familiar with. "It's easy to let other's words affect your thinking. Especially family. You aren't your father, mate."

Callum snorted louder this time as he shook his head and looked away. "You doona know my dad."

"I may not know him, but I know men like him. Be your own man. Ignore your father. Ignore the ignorant arseholes who run their mouths. Forget the fucking curse. Trust in your friends. Trust in yourself."

"Easier said than done."

"You're here. I say that's taking the first step."

Callum glanced at the manor. "Being here makes me forget my reality sometimes. Then I go home, and it's like a sucker punch."

"The answer is easy. Don't go back."

"That isna an option. If I doona return and continue working, we'll lose everything."

Killian shrugged. "That isn't your burden. It's your father's. Start your own company. The way I hear it, you won't have any problems earning money."

"I've thought about that."

"If it's money, I'll happily put up the capital to get you started."

Callum briefly met his gaze and shook his head. "Money has nothing to do with it."

"If you won't leave, then stand up to him. Fight back."

"I can no'."

"I know it won't be easy, but once you do it the first time, your father will understand that he can't push you around anymore."

A muscle jumped in Callum's jaw when he faced him and enunciated each word. "I can no'."

There was more to the story, a secret Killian didn't think anyone knew. Something Callum didn't intend to share. He held Callum's gaze and nodded. "All right. But remember that you aren't alone. I'm your friend. So is everyone in the manor."

"Thanks," Callum said, his discomfort obvious as he looked away. He cleared his throat. "Tell Kirsi I'll see her later."

"Where are you going?"

"Work."

Killian was glad Theo had had an officer drive the Audi to the manor yesterday. He dug the keys out of his pocket. "Hey," he called. When Callum turned around, he held out the keys. "Take mine."

Callum hesitated but accepted them with a nod.

Killian watched him walk to the vehicle and drive away. Shoes crunched on the gravel behind him. He turned to find Ariah walking to him, her long, dark floral skirt swirling about her legs.

"Everything all right?" she asked.

He wrapped an arm around her. "I don't know. Callum is heading to work."

"I wish he'd stay. Bronwyn has offered him a permanent place, but he won't accept. I think his life would be easier if he got away from his father. Joe Kilmuir isn't a good man."

"Nay, he isn't."

Ariah moved to stand in front of him and searched his face. She glanced over her shoulder to the drive. "Is Callum in danger? I mean, more than Druids already are?"

Killian knew he was walking the boundary of what he could divulge and what would be breaking his promise to his friend. But he wouldn't stand by and do nothing again. He had a chance to save a life, and he intended to take it.

"I see," Ariah said softly. "Then we must do something."

"Like what?"

Ariah shrugged and rested her hands on his waist. "I don't know. The isle has ignored the Kilmuir problem for generations. Perhaps it's time to shine some light on it."

"Maybe."

"His father used to get into fights all the time. So did his grandfather. It seemed to run in the Kilmuir genes like drinking." She paused, staring at his chest with a furrowed brow. Her gaze lifted to his. "But I've never seen Callum drink or get into a fight. I've not heard anyone talk about witnessing such an altercation either." Her face paled. "The bruises and wounds. Oh, God. Callum isn't fighting, is he?"

Killian realized that not replying would be the same as answering. Finally, he shook his head. "Nay, love, he isn't."

She swallowed hard a few times. "I think I'm going to be sick. We have to *do* something. I wish he could've told one of us, but I'm glad he shared it with you."

"He didn't tell me. I guessed. He was mortified and ashamed. He can't know that you know."

"But I can't let something like that go." She drew in a deep breath, distress tightening her face. "He's an adult. Why doesn't he fight back?"

"I just asked that. His reaction was quite unexpected. He made it clear that he can't."

Ariah's eyes narrowed. "Can't? Not won't?"

"His exact words were: *I cannot*."

"I don't like this."

He pulled her to him, resting his chin atop her head. "Neither do I. And as much as I'd like to put all our focus on it, we have a bigger issue at hand."

"Speaking of that, there's something I have to tell you."

Dread knotted his stomach. "What?"

"I saw the shadow creature in the woods."

"Last night? When you were there?" he demanded urgently. She could've been attacked. She could have been—

Ariah hurriedly said, "Nay. At dawn. I couldn't sleep and went to the window. It was there, watching the manor."

"Then what the fuck are we doing outside?" he asked and began hauling her toward the house.

She dug in her heels and yanked her arm from his grasp. Her jaw was set when he faced her. "I told you last night that we couldn't hide in there forever."

"That doesn't mean we should just stand out here waiting for it to come for us," he argued. "The manor is safe. That's where you need to be."

"Me?" She jerked back as if slapped. "Me! You're worried about me?"

"Obviously."

She threw up her hands and turned away before spinning back to him. "You're the one who was nearly killed. You're the one who needs to stay in the manor."

"Not bloody likely. Unless you agree to remain inside with me."

"I can't. I must go to the Fairy Glen, remember?"

He fought to rein in his temper, but the idea that she was

afraid for him and not herself made him irrationally angry. "I'm the one who suggested it. And I'll be right beside you."

"Killian," she began.

He quirked a brow but didn't back down. "Ariah."

A pained expression flashed over her features before she closed her eyes and took in a fortifying breath. Then she looked at him. "I can't lose you."

"Ditto, darlin'."

She held up a hand to stop him from talking. "Nay. Yesterday morning I saw you bloodied and broken and straining for breath. If Balladyn hadn't… If…"

Killian dragged her into his arms and buried his face in the crook of her neck as he held her. "I know," he whispered. They stood silently for a moment. Then he said, "The problem is we don't know who the shadow wants."

"You're safe here."

"So are you."

"But I can't stay."

"And neither can I."

Ariah let out a loud sigh. "You're being irrational."

"I could say the same." He kissed her temple, then her cheek, then her lips. Killian stared into her eyes. "I came back for you. To win your love once more so we can have a life together. I want to spend every day with you."

"I never stopped loving you. I tried, but I couldn't."

He enveloped her in his arms again. "Let's compromise on who stays where by being together until this is over."

"I'm not sure that's a compromise," she said with a chuckle.

"We'll get through this." He willed his words to be the truth.

"There you two are," Bronwyn said from the doorway. "Ready to go?"

Ariah pulled back and faced her. "We are."

Bronwyn, Elias, Elodie, Scott, and Rhona joined him and Ariah. Rhona sat in the front passenger seat with Killian in the back as Ariah drove. The other four piled into Bronwyn's SUV. They hadn't been driving long when Rhona began talking about her meeting with her deputies. It was the first time Killian had heard of them.

"Sorry to interrupt," he said. "But who are the deputies?"

Ariah glanced at him through the rearview mirror. "If every Druid came to the leader with their problems, whoever was in charge wouldn't get anything done. It was decided long ago when Skye started to fill with our people that the isle would be divided into five segments, and within each is a deputy."

"Each leader chooses deputies carefully because they are the ones everyone goes to. The deputies decide if it's something they can handle or if I need to be involved," Rhona explained. "A lot falls to the deputies, so they have to be people I can trust."

"Kerry once held that position," Ariah interjected.

Shock ran through Killian. "Really? Did she control the mist as a way of revenge?"

"She did that while she was a deputy," Rhona said.

Killian whistled. "That must have been difficult."

Rhona looked out the window. "More than you know. She can't hurt anyone anymore, though."

CHAPTER THIRTY-SIX

"I'll pay," Rhona said as she got out of the vehicle after they found a space to park. Ariah stared at the sign that declared *£2 for 2 hours and £3 for 4 hours,* no doubt the pressure to remember Corann's story weighing heavily on her.

"We don't have to do this," Killian said from the back seat, his hand on her shoulder.

"Aye, we do. We need to remember the story."

He climbed out of the back and opened her door. He had one arm on the roof and the other along the top of car door as he peered inside. "That doesn't mean it has to happen today."

"If there was time, I would take it, but there isn't." She looked at him and nodded to punctuate her words. "We need to be prepared. *I* have to be prepared."

"Aye." He held out his hand to her.

She grasped it, and he pulled her from the vehicle. Killian took the opportunity to inspect the area. The car park was filling up quickly—no surprise since the Fairy Glen was a big tourist draw. Rhona was with the others as if she knew Ariah needed a moment.

Killian hadn't taken much time to think about Rhona's position. He'd been too overwhelmed by nearly dying, the shadow creature, and learning that magic was real. He tried to imagine being in Rhona's shoes. Not just a Druid but leading an entire isle of Druids who kept their magic secret and fought against powerful enemies.

How could any of them handle it? He'd probably freak out later. Right now, he had to concentrate on the matter at hand, which kept his emotions in check. But that would only happen for so long. Did anyone else go mental? Maybe they had been dealing with this for too long to be affected. Or maybe they did it in private.

Yet, for Rhona, there likely wasn't such a time. She had to be ready with an answer or a response at a moment's notice. Granted, she didn't have to carry the load alone. She had Balladyn, which gave her an advantage. Rhona also surrounded herself with people she trusted. That would probably be key to their survival as well as their victory.

The words rang in his head like a bell. A reminder that they weren't up against some large corporation that could take away their company. They would be fighting a being with intent to kill. There wasn't any type of schooling, boardrooms, or courtrooms that could prepare someone for such an encounter.

"We should get going," Ariah said, reaching for his hand, her gaze locked on the path.

Killian noted the people already walking the one-mile loop. He and Ariah took the lead and the rest of the group fell into step behind them. Ariah had brought him here that long-ago summer.

He had been too interested in her to pay attention to much else, even such stunning scenery. They followed the trail beside the road where hundreds of thousands of others had tread and came to the area at the bottom.

When he spotted the small loch, he said, "I don't remember the lochan when we came."

Ariah grinned at him. "You were too busy kissing me."

Killian winked, recalling how they hadn't been able to keep their hands off each other. The small path then took them toward an overlook of Glen Conon. Ariah continued on, so there was no time to take in the beauty.

"The Torridonian sandstone was sculpted by post-glacier landslides," Ariah told him. "It created all of this."

Killian gazed at the craggy, cone-shaped hillocks and random boulders, then took another look at the lochan.

Rhona said, "The gnarled rowan trees were always my favorite part of this area."

"Me, too," Elodie said.

Bronwyn's voice held a note of wonder when she said, "*Bail nan cnoc.*"

"Village in the hills," Elias translated.

Killian knew all of it was for his benefit and appreciated it. Ariah took him to the turning area at the bottom, where he saw the striking view across the glen. A series of spectacular waterfalls plunged down the other side of the valley.

"And back up we go," Elodie murmured.

Killian would've liked to remain for a moment longer, but he was reminded that their visit wasn't for sightseeing. He and Ariah exchanged a look as they retraced their steps. Elodie and Scott were in the lead now, and they headed straight for a steep mound that looked remarkably like a castle.

"I remember that," Killian said at what appeared to be a crumbling medieval fortress.

She grinned at the structure. "Castle Ewen."

It wasn't a real castle, of course, but a natural landmark. He and Ariah had climbed the precipitous path of moss-covered stones surrounded by ancient, weathered rowan trees. They'd had to scramble to get to the top, which led to one of the most breathtaking views Killian had ever beheld. He wanted to traverse it again, and he could look out over the Fairy Glen with new eyes.

But it would have to wait for another time.

The group continued around the lochan and came to the large spiral cut into the grass with small stones sticking out of the ground. The seven of them clumped together to stare at the spiral.

"Well?" Scott asked into the silence. "Anyone remember anything?"

Elodie shook her blond head. "We came a few times. I recall that."

"Aye. And one time was during the night." Rhona's lips twisted. "It was raining."

Bronwyn wrinkled her nose. "That's right. It was also freezing. I was so miserable."

"That's when he told the story about the pillars," Ariah said.

Killian swung his head to her, waiting for her to continue.

"I have a memory of huddling under my raincoat, cold and wet, while Corann stood in the downpour without a jacket." Ariah blinked at the stones. "He walked the spiral from the outside in."

Elodie nodded slowly, "And then back the other way."

"That's right. He did," Rhona murmured. She pointed to the left. "He put us there."

There was a stretch of silence as everyone stared at the spiral. Then Bronwyn said, "I can hear his deep voice in my head. It seemed to resonate all around us, even over the rain."

"It was one of the times he didn't look at us as he spoke," Rhona stated.

Ariah jerked her head around, surprise slackening her features. "He didn't. He kept his gaze on the ground as he followed the coil one way and then the other, over and over again."

"Any of you remember the story?" Elias asked.

Killian jerked his chin to him. "You weren't there?"

"I was older and with another group."

Elodie looked at her brother. "But you still would've been taught the story."

"Without a doubt. I've tried to remember it, but I can no'. Filip either."

Killian glanced at the stones. "Would it help if you walked it?"

Ariah loosened her grip on his hand and made her way to the spiral. Killian and Scott stayed behind while the rest joined her. The many tourists made everyone aware of the need to watch what they said. One by one, the others returned until only Ariah was left in the spiral. When she reached the center for the third time, she paused and turned toward Castle Ewen. Then she hurried over to them.

Ariah parted her lips to speak but paused until a group walked past. "The location for one of the pillars is the top of Castle Ewen."

Everyone looked toward the formation.

"How do we know which pillar it is?" Elodie asked.

Rhona turned back around. "Air, earth, and water. We know

this isn't for the water pillar, which means it has to either be for air or earth."

"You remember it," Bronwyn said to Ariah. "Does that mean this is for earth?"

Ariah shrugged and stared past the others at the *castle*. "I'm not sure."

"If they need to be on top, then that gives them height. I would think it's for the air pillar," Killian said.

Scott glanced at him and nodded. "I agree."

"That does make sense," Elias added.

Rhona smoothed hair away from her face. "All right. For the sake of argument, let's say this is for the air pillar. Where are the others? Are all three meant to be together?"

"Nay," Elodie answered. When everyone looked her way, she shrugged a shoulder. "Don't ask me to explain. It was a gut response."

Scott flashed her a grin. "That means you remember something, even subconsciously."

"Elodie's right. There are three locations. I remember that now that she mentioned it," Bronwyn said.

Rhona's brow smoothed as she grinned. "This is good. Anything else?"

Ariah sidled closer and linked her hand with Killian's. He looked around, wondering if the shadow was near and listening, waiting for an opportunity to attack. "Is this considered sacred ground to Druids?"

"You could say that. Why?" Rhona asked.

Killian said, "I think the pillars would need to be places where it's difficult for enemies to get to them. Somewhere that would protect them. Where else is sacred?"

"The Fairy Pools," Elias said.

A smile curved Rhona's mouth. "That could be the location of the water pillar."

"Then where is Ariah's?" Bronwyn asked.

But Killian knew. It was something they all should've guessed. "The forest."

"Of course," Rhona said with a chuckle. "That one is obvious."

Ariah didn't look convinced. "But where in the forest? It isn't as if I can just walk anywhere. The air pillar has an exact location. It means all three most likely have one."

"That is something to consider," Rhona said when they grew quiet in contemplation. "But that's for another time. We're here to try to remember details of the story. Does anyone have anything else?"

They stood in silence for a few minutes before it became apparent that no one could recall anything else. The trek back to the car park was quiet, everyone lost in thought.

The others returned to the manor, but Killian, Rhona, and Ariah headed to the Tea Talker. The drive there was just as hushed as the walk to the cars had been.

Ariah parked on the street and stared at what was left of her business. Then she got out and walked around the outside of the building. He hung back near the car and was surprised when Rhona stayed with him. She leaned against the vehicle and crossed her arms over her chest as she watched Ariah.

"You seem to be taking things in stride," Rhona said.

Killian shrugged as he, too, leaned against the car. "I'm still processing everything, but it isn't as if there's been a lot of time to sort through it all."

"But you need to. Otherwise, you're just pushing it aside."

He looked at the Druid leader. "I accept Ariah for who she is. I always have. I wish I would've known before."

"Would it have changed anything?" She stared back at him, her green eyes seeming to see right to his soul.

"I wasn't ready to let it then. I am now. I walked away from my old life for her."

Rhona's gaze briefly slid past him. "Have you?"

"You doubt me?" he demanded.

Her lips twisted as she jerked her chin. "Seems we're about to find out."

Killian turned to see what she meant and found himself staring into the face of Brian Flanagan.

CHAPTER THIRTY-SEVEN

London

"How long do you intend to wait?" Finn asked over the phone.

Carlyle stared at the townhome that had been in their family for generations. It was meant to be his someday. A day he had never been able to see.

"Mate?"

"I'm here," Carlyle said.

Finn's sigh reached him through the connection. "We've been watching the house since we arrived this morning. There's been no movement."

"Something isn't right. I can feel it."

"As you've said a dozen times," Finn retorted. "But we won't know what that is unless we see for ourselves."

Carlyle was well aware of that fact, but he had been trying to understand what had made him draw up short before he even reached the townhome. He still couldn't name it. Yet the feeling hadn't dissipated. "I know."

"I'll go in," Finn offered.

"You'll bloody well stay right where you are." Carlyle hadn't meant to snap, but he wouldn't put Finn's life in jeopardy.

Silence stretched across the line. Finally, Finn said, "We risk our lives every day, every time we go up against some evil tosser. You came for a reason."

"I know," Carlyle bit out. He wasn't irritated at Finn. He was furious with himself for waiting so long to look for his father. What kind of son did that? What kind of son put the lives of others above his own family?

Finn sighed loudly. "You're doing that thing again. Stop it."

"What thing?"

"Where you blame yourself."

Carlyle scrubbed a hand down his face. "I am to blame."

"Nay, you aren't. You know exactly who's fault this is."

The London Druids. Everything pointed back to the controlling, power-hungry faction that somehow managed to continue pulling Druids into their organization. No one realized what they had gotten into until it was too late. Then there was no way out. The problem was that many families, like Carlyle's, had been involved with the London sect for generations.

It went back to the time when the Skye Druids had kicked many members off the isle. Instead of remaining in Scotland, those Druids made their way across England to London. There, they began their campaign of hatred against any Druid on Skye.

"We can't fight them," Carlyle said, careful not to call out the London Druids. They had their fingers in everything, everywhere. Including listening in on phone calls. "They're too powerful."

Finn snorted. "The fek we can't. We won't be able to take them head-on, but we have our ways. We just need to finish things… elsewhere first."

Saber made the Knights change mobiles often in case anyone was listening, but they had spent years being cautious and weren't about to stop now. "All right."

"I have your back no matter what."

Carlyle stared at the white townhouse along the row of them. Black wrought iron fenced the front and back, leading to the doors. Finn was right. It was time to have a look. Putting off discovering his father's dead body wouldn't be any easier. Because that's what Carlyle fully expected to find.

It was a message the London Druids would love to send. Carlyle had known he could only hide his location for so long. His father hadn't pressed, but then Thomas had always accepted Carlyle's word for everything. He'd lied to his dad so often that it was easier to tally the times he had spoken the truth than to count the moments of deceit. Yet he had done it all to protect Thomas from any repercussions.

Only, he'd failed.

There was only one reason his father wouldn't return his calls. And that was if he couldn't. So, either he was dead, or the London Druids had him, intending to use him as leverage to force Carlyle to stop working with the Knights.

He would do it, too.

Sabryn had left the States and whatever friends and family she had behind after her father, a US Senator, died in a car wreck. It wasn't that the London Druids couldn't use her family, but Carlyle wasn't sure Sabryn would care.

Finn didn't have family. He grew up on the streets, which

meant there wasn't anyone they could use to control him.

Saber was a ghost. No one knew who he—or she—really was, not even the Knights. It would be pointless for anyone to even attempt to get leverage on him. Even if they used any of the Knights.

As for Elias, his family had once been scattered, but returning to Skye had strengthened their bond. And there was no way the London Druids could get to anyone on Skye. So, that left him, the only one they *could* get to.

"You still there?" Finn asked.

Carlyle pushed away from the building he had been leaning against and moved to the mouth of the alley. "It's time for the pub." He said the code words for them to enter the townhome.

"About fucking time. I'm parched."

Carlyle ended the call and put the mobile in the inside pocket of his jacket. He took one more look around and headed to the back door of the ground floor. He and Finn each had a key. It slid easily into the lock. Carlyle paused for a heartbeat and looked behind him. No one was there. He waited a second more and then turned the key. Relief surged through him when the lock disengaged.

The moment he was inside the dark house, he moved to the left where the alarm panel hung. His finger hovered over the numbers as he stared at the screen that told him the alarm was already disengaged. He gave his eyes time to adjust to the darkness. Beams of light stretched through the windows from outside like ghostly fingers pointing the way.

The townhome was over ten thousand square feet, and several staff members lived here on a permanent basis. Lights should be on, and there should be a hum of movement. Yet the house felt empty. He took the stairs to the lower level and stealthily walked through the kitchen, the staff kitchen, the bathrooms, and all six staff bedrooms. He checked the gym, the utility room, the wine cellar, and the garage.

Every bit of it was devoid of life.

He sent Finn a quick text to let him know. Finn responded immediately.

SAME WITH THE GROUND FLOOR.

Carlyle grimaced and took the stairs up. Finn stood waiting. Carlyle glanced through an open doorway to the conservatory on one side and the dining room on the other. Neither said a word as they silently walked toward the foyer to the grand staircase. The house had seven floors in total, with the very top an outdoor garden area.

The first floor took them no time since it was mostly comprised of a double reception room and a small study in the back. The second floor held the principal bedroom, bath, and dressing room. Carlyle expected to find some evidence of his father in there, but there was nothing.

They quickly went through the two third-floor bedrooms. Carlyle took the lead up the stairs to the fourth floor. Finn went to the left to the front two bedrooms while he went right to check out the other room and his father's study.

Just as he was about to enter the bedroom, he spotted light coming from beneath the study door. Still, Carlyle took the time to check the bedroom first. By the time he came back out into the hall, Finn was with him. They looked at each other before creeping silently to the study door. He had thought it was closed, but it was only pulled shut. Carlyle called to his magic, letting it fill his hands as he pushed the door open with his foot.

The green glass banker's lamp was on, casting its warm glow across the desk. A woman sat in the office chair with her feet on the desktop, ankles crossed.

"Took you long enough," she stated as she set aside his father's favorite pearl Montblanc pen and lowered her feet to the floor. "I've been waiting all day for you to finally decide to come inside."

He noted her luminous gold skin, willowy limbs, and aristocratic British accent. Thick, coal-black hair was smoothed away from her face and gathered into a long ponytail. Small gold hoops dangled from her earlobes with slightly larger hoops in the second piercing. She wore a wide-legged cream pantsuit with matching stilettos. Dark eyes moved from him and Finn.

Magic swirled in Carlyle's hands. "Where is my father?"

"Seems you believed the rules didn't apply to you," she said instead of answering.

"I swear to God, I will kill you," he threatened.

Beside him, Finn lifted his hands, ready to send out magic.

She arched a black brow and gracefully stood. "Two against one. I'm shivering in my Jimmy Choos."

"Tell me where my father is," Carlyle demanded again.

"I don't actually have that information."

Finn asked, "Then what the fuck are you doing here?"

"I came to speak with both of you, of course," she said.

Carlyle walked toward her until only the desk separated them. His anger had swelled so high that he wasn't sure he could hold it back. Or if he wanted to. Someone would pay for hurting his father, and he didn't much care who it was. "About?"

"You haven't been discreet," she told them. "The council knows you've been on Skye, and they are…displeased."

Finn snorted. "I'm not one of your Druids to control. I don't give a rat's ass about your so-called rules, darling."

Her attention slid to him. The intruder said nothing, simply stared at Finn, her dark gaze slowly raking over him as if really looking at him for the first time.

Carlyle fisted his hands as resentment churned within him. "You aren't leaving this house until you tell me where my father is."

She shot him a look of annoyance. "Must we do this ridiculous dance? I just explained that I don't know."

"And you expect me to believe you?"

"I've no reason to lie to you."

He sneered, his hatred for the sect that had governed his and his family's lives consuming him. "You're a London Druid. All you do is lie."

"Your father is one of us. Does that make him a liar?"

She didn't back down despite being outnumbered. Either she was a fool, or she knew she had the upper hand. Carlyle wanted a fight, he needed one to help dispel the fear that had latched onto him. "My father has nothing to do with this."

"He has everything to do with this." The woman came around the desk and stopped next to Carlyle, their gazes meeting. "Your enemies are closer than you know."

Her words caught him off guard, but he recovered quickly, the last of his patience evaporating. "Is that what you came to tell me?"

"I was to deliver only one message."

Finn hadn't moved from the door. "And what is that?"

The woman held Carlyle's gaze. "Stay away from Skye."

"And if he doesn't?" Finn asked.

But Carlyle knew. "They'll kill Dad." If they hadn't already.

The woman shot him a grin. "You can torture me, but it won't do you any good. You could kill me. You have me outnumbered, but I'm only the messenger. You'd be taking the life of an innocent."

"You're hardly innocent," Carlyle replied. And she had known that he and Finn would be here. If she was worried about repercussions, she didn't show it.

Her smile widened. "That's true of all of us, is it not?"

She walked past him. Carlyle turned to follow her progress, trying to decide if he should let her go or not. Finn blocked the doorway, halting her. He looked at Carlyle, waiting for him to come to a decision. Everything she'd said was likely true. The council wouldn't give her details about what they had done with his father. Hurting her wouldn't lead to Thomas's return, unfortunately. Carlyle motioned for Finn to let her go.

"It's too bad you aren't on our team," she said seductively to Finn as she came even with him. She ran a finger down the middle of his chest. "We could have had fun."

Neither Carlyle nor Finn moved until the front door opened and closed behind her.

Finn let out a low whistle. "I think I'm in love. Did you see her? Shite, she's gorgeous."

"She's also a London Druid. She'd eat you alive."

"Could be fun." When Carlyle didn't smile, Finn became serious. "What do you want to do now?"

Carlyle leaned his hip on the corner of the desk. "I suspected they would use Dad as leverage to keep me away from Skye."

"No one will blame you if you remain here. He's your father."

Carlyle looked at the neat desk. "He's the only family I have left."

Finn clapped him on the back. "We can handle things on Skye."

Without him. That meant Carlyle would have to set aside all his convictions because the London Druids deemed the problems happening on Skye unworthy. Honestly, he wouldn't put it past them to be mixed up in it.

CHAPTER THIRTY-EIGHT

Green eyes, blond hair trimmed short with gray at his temples, meticulous beard, handmade Italian suit, and thousand-dollar shoes. Brian looked as rigid and stern as ever. Killian should've known his father would eventually find him, but he hadn't expected it quite so soon.

"Hello, son."

"Dad."

Brian looked toward the water. "Can we talk? I don't like the way we left things."

"Not if you're going to try to convince me to return. I'm where I'm supposed to be."

His father released a long breath and looked at him. "I just want to have a conversation."

"You mean you'll state your ultimatum and expect me to listen."

"I'd like us both to talk and listen."

"That isn't your strong suit when it comes to me."

A muscle in Brian's jaw jumped. "Son, I'm trying here. Please. Can we talk?"

"That's what we're doing."

"Can we go somewhere? I'd like to be alone."

Before walking away, Rhona said, "I'll keep an eye on things."

Killian met her gaze and nodded, then looked at his father. "There's a pub down the road."

"Perhaps somewhere neither of us can get away from the other." He attempted a smile.

The thought that Brian Flanagan might actually listen to what Killian had to say was an opportunity he couldn't pass up. He didn't want to cut his family out of his life, but he would if they couldn't accept the life he wanted with Ariah.

"I'm talking about a drive, that's all," his father said.

"I'll do the driving." Killian turned to look for the Audi, only to realize he had lent it to Callum. He glanced at Ariah's car but didn't want to leave her without transportation. He held his hand out to his father. "Keys."

Brian didn't hesitate to hand them over and point to the silver Range Rover parked nearby. They walked to it without a word. Killian remained quiet as he drove away from town along the winding road next to the water.

"Skye is quite beautiful," Brian said after several tense minutes of silence.

"Aye."

"Why didn't you answer any of my calls or texts?"

Killian adjusted his hands on the steering wheel. "We said everything that needed to be said. At least, you did. You made it clear there is only one option for me. I didn't feel the need to keep rehashing things."

"I'm your father. You should always answer my calls. At the very least, your mother's. She's very upset."

The long-burning resentment and bitterness roared to life. The first opportunity he got, Killian pulled off onto the side of the road and slammed the SUV into park. He sat there for a moment, trying to get his raging emotions under control. But the more he tried, the worse it became. Finally, he threw open his door, slamming it behind him as he got out. He was breathing hard, his hands clenching and unclenching as he paced. He heard the passenger door open and close softly.

"Son," Brian said.

Killian whirled on his father. "Why do you do that? It's always about you or mum. You've always tried to make me feel responsible for *everything*." Once he started, he couldn't stop. "I tried for years to tell you I was unhappy, but you refused to hear it, to even fucking consider it. Because I didn't matter. The family image was more important. The power our family held had to be maintained at all costs. No one even thought to ask what I wanted. Not when my life had already been planned and expectations laid out."

Brian's gaze was steady and clear, his jaw set. "You've not spoken about Skye or that woman in almost a decade."

"That woman?" Killian repeated, anger simmering.

"Aye. *That woman.* She turned your head when you were young, but she's not what you need."

"How the fek do you know what I need?" Killian bellowed.

His father's nostrils flared in anger. "I know you. You think you'll be happy here? You'll tire of this place within a year."

"You don't know me. You never took the time to even try. You tried to make me into some messed-up image you had, and you nearly fekking did it. I've done everything you ever wanted."

Brian snorted. "If that were the case, you wouldn't be here."

"This. This, right here, is why I didn't respond to you or Mum," Killian said tightly. "I told you what I wanted and what I'm doing. You accept it and Ariah, or you don't. That choice is yours."

"You can't be serious."

Killian took a deep breath. "More than I have ever been in my life."

"What about the firm?"

"That's really your question right now?"

Brian looked away and ran a hand down his face.

"You haven't even met Ariah. You might like her," Killian said.

His father turned his head to him but looked past him.

Killian snorted and threw up his hands, letting them fall against his legs. "I don't know why I even bother."

"Son," Brian said slowly. "I need you to come to me. Right now."

"Forget it. I'm not leaving Skye. I'm not leaving Ariah ever again. I love her. Do you even understand what that word means?"

Brian finally met his gaze. "Killian. *Please.*"

Something in his father's voice broke through Killian's haze of rage. He noticed his father's pale face and the stark fear in his green eyes. The hair on the back of Killian's neck rose. He knew without turning around what was there.

"Run!" he yelled.

Darkness enveloped him, cutting off his voice.

Glass crunched under Ariah's feet. Everything was wet from the recent rain. She looked around at the shop that had been whole a few days before. Now, everything was scattered and broken. She looked at one of the shelving units. Well, not everything. One of the painted teapots and a single saucer were intact.

She passed one of the plants and touched the leaves. All of them needed to have glass removed from the soil, and a few would need new pots altogether. So, not everything was ruined. She stored reserves of tea elsewhere, but it would take her some time to rebuild her stock.

Ariah walked to the cash register and pushed a button. The drawer popped open. Other than needing a good cleaning, it worked. She turned and looked at what had once been the wall of jars. Nearly all of them lay broken on the floor.

"Things won't look so bad once it's clean."

Ariah turned at the sound of Rhona's voice. She forced a smile. "I know."

"There isn't anything that can't be replaced."

She shrugged as she faced her friend. "Seeing the damage is like a gut punch, but I'm keenly aware that we all survived." She grimaced. "Shite. I need to check on Ruby. I should've done that before."

Rhona shook her head. "Ruby is fine. I've checked on her. She knows what's going on. Besides, a lot has been going on for you."

Ariah looked for Killian. Did he not want to come in? It might hold too many memories for him.

"His father arrived."

Her gaze swung to Rhona, and her stomach dropped to her feet. "What?"

"Killian's expression wasn't too different from yours when he saw Brian. They left together to talk."

"Left?" Ariah barely got the word out.

"They aren't leaving the isle."

But they could. Brian Flanagan would do anything to have his son returned.

"Killian won't leave you," Rhona said.

"He shouldn't have to choose."

"You aren't the one asking him to. His family is."

Ariah knew she was right, but it didn't make knowing that Brian was on Skye any easier. She walked to the back of the shop to see what damage was there. There was little glass in that area—even the ceiling was wood—so she hoped the magical teas, cups, and machines were in working order. She passed through the doorway and scanned from left to right, only to freeze at the words scratched into the wall.

YOU HAVE A DAY TO DESTROY IT OR HE DIES.

Ariah read the words, but they didn't compute. Destroy what? Who had written this, and who did they have? But she knew.

"Killian." Ariah spun around and ran into Rhona, who had come up behind her. She bounced off and slid on the broken glass while trying to get outside to find Killian.

She fell twice before making it out of the building. Ariah turned in a circle, searching for the sight of Killian's blond waves.

"Ariah," Rhona said as she approached.

She ignored Rhona and raced to her car, yanking open the door to get her mobile. She shook so badly the phone fell from her hands. She picked it up and finally got her finger still enough to press Killian's name. She brought the mobile up to her ear as ringing filled the silence. Ariah closed her eyes and whispered, "Pick up. Pick up. Pick up."

A hand wrapped around hers. "Ariah."

She pulled away and turned her back on Rhona. When the call went to voicemail, she tried again.

"Ariah." Rhona walked around to stand in front of her.

She looked into Rhona's eyes and saw the sorrow there. The regret. Ariah shook her head. "Don't say it."

Rhona glanced away. "We need to go."

Killian's voice filled the phone. But it was only his voicemail message. Rhona gently took the mobile and ended the call.

"He isn't going to answer."

Blood rushed in Ariah's ears. Her mind couldn't comprehend Rhona's words. It simply refused to believe that anything had happened to Killian. If only he had stayed at the manor like she wanted. He would've been safe. They could've been together. Happy and in love.

Arms guided her down the street. Voices sounded far away. Killian had been with her. Right here. They had just gotten out of the car. How could anything have happened? Why hadn't she stayed near him? She had known he was a target. She had known and done nothing.

"...shadow. Are you sure?" Rhona asked.

"Verra," replied a male voice.

Ariah blinked and focused to discover she stood in the back of the co-op with Kirsi's parents, Nora and Matt.

"Drink this," Matt urged and put something in her hand.

Ariah looked down to find a tumbler with a finger of whisky. She tried to push it away, but Matt gently nudged her again.

"It'll help," he insisted.

She downed the liquor, coughing with the back of her hand against her mouth as it burned down her throat. She handed him the glass as more of the room came into focus. Rhona was on the phone. Scott and Filip were there, both visibly shaken. Kirsi stood at the register and glanced through the back doorway to them.

It was Scott who had answered Rhona. Ariah turned to him. She felt everyone's eyes on her. "You saw what happened." When he didn't reply, she shifted her gaze to Filip. "Tell me."

Filip turned away.

Scott dropped his chin to his chest and shook his head. Then he met her gaze. "We saw…" He cleared his throat and tried again. "Killian was on the side of the road talking to another man."

"His father," Ariah supplied.

Filip winced and muttered, "Bloody hell."

Ariah stood straighter, bracing herself, and waited for Scott to continue.

"We were driving." Scott couldn't look at her for more than a second at a time. "The shadow came up from the ground and swallowed Killian. Then it…it tossed his father and the vehicle down the side of the hill."

Black edged her vision. Ariah fought to stay on her feet and not give in to the gut-wrenching fear that crept into her veins and turned her blood to ice. "Where is Killian?"

Scott shot her a pained expression. "We can no' find him."

"Destroy it, or he dies," Ariah said, recalling the message left for her.

"What?" Scott asked with a frown.

Rhona hung up the phone. "It was a message scrawled on the back wall of the Tea Talker."

"Then Killian is still alive," Nora said.

Filip's face creased. "But what is Ariah supposed to destroy?"

"My location as the pillar," Ariah answered.

There was a beat of silence before everyone began speaking at once.

"You can't."

"What's a pillar?"

"Can we trust anything?"

"She can't let Killian die."

Images of Killian flashed in her head. His olive-green eyes, his sexy smile, the way he held her. His laugh, the comfort of his hand interlaced with hers. She had managed to pick up the pieces after losing him once, she wouldn't be able to do it a second time. Nor would she be responsible for his death. But how could she choose to save one person over an entire isle? If she destroyed the location where she stood as a pillar, it would render the other two obsolete.

She walked out of the co-op, her heart twisting painfully. Violence only begot violence. Peace was the only way. Yet she understood why Rhona and the others had taken a stand. They had defended themselves and others. That wasn't an option for her. She had to choose between the man she loved and everyone else.

And no matter what she decided, she lost.

CHAPTER THIRTY-NINE

Edie slowly exited the vehicle, her eyes locked on the secluded, white-washed cottage, the backdrop a distant mountain with mist clinging dramatically to the gently sloping sides. The sun was a hazy ball of light behind wispy gray clouds. Edie could see for miles in every direction. Sheep were scattered, munching on grass. A golden eagle cried above her. There was a soft whistle of wind as it moved down the mountain to brush across the land and against her. Water bubbled in the left back corner of the yard where a brook cut across the property.

It was a stunning setting. Edie fell in love with it the first time she saw it when she was twelve. She'd longed for the house for years. She even took a picture of it and put it on her dream board. Trevor had given it to her as their wedding gift.

The first years of their marriage had been shared here in the cozy, two-bedroom abode. They had spent hours sharing dreams of their future and making plans—both of them ambitious, their wishes aligning. Trevor had been the perfect husband.

But she wasn't the same woman he had carried over the threshold with her heart bursting with love and happiness. Her blinders had been ripped away. She wasn't even sure when she had begun to wear them. Maybe it happened to everyone in relationships. After so long together, it was easy to miss what was right in front of a person. Perhaps they ignored it, like she had, pretending everything was great for the sake of the family—and herself. Hiding the heartache and hurt because the thought of a divorce that separated her from the kids and the life she had created was incomprehensible. So, she'd overlooked, disregarded, and ignored—like millions of other women.

Until she was pushed too far.

When she finally gave in to Trevor's pursuit, she had only been concerned with that moment. As their relationship grew and they fell in love, a measure of trust was formed and shared. That faith and belief were forged into an expectation when they exchanged vows.

Her marriage had never been perfect. It had its ups and downs like everyone's. But she'd believed with utter conviction that she and Trevor were both fully in the relationship, committed to working wholeheartedly to make their marriage last.

Only to discover he had been lying.

The trust and conviction that had fortified their love was agonizingly torn away, cleaved with one strike. The anguish was unbearable. Everything she had created and nurtured in her life, the hours spent…they meant nothing. Were worth nothing.

Her wound had been cauterized, though, ending her suffering and clearing her thoughts. It returned her to the woman she had once been. Before Trevor. Before the lies and deceit.

Edie squared her shoulders and lifted her face to the wind. The

Ancients had urged her to come here. She wasn't sure why, but it didn't matter. She would do whatever they asked of her.

"We know."

She walked to the dark red door. The windows on the front and back were small, but the three large dormers permitted light on the second floor. She put the key in the lock and turned it before stepping inside. The front entry was tiny, barely an entrance at all. A place only large enough to stack wellies and hang coats. To the left was the kitchen with its big stone fireplace. To the right was the living area with a matching fireplace.

Edie walked around, turning on the lights in the darkened cottage. Her eyes scanned the kitchen they had remodeled and furnished with modern appliances. The house was one of their most leased rentals. Everyone fell in love with its location, just as she had all those years ago.

The door slowly swung open. Her head turned in that direction as she leaned to the side to get a better look at the entry.

"Don't be afraid."

She didn't move a muscle as a dark, shadowy shape entered. It had to duck because of its size. Inside, it seemed to shove against the low ceiling as if it didn't like being constrained.

The shadow was enormous, both tall and wide. She discerned two legs and arms. It lumbered a few paces, hunched over, before it turned to her. It wasn't *a* shadow but dozens of them. Perhaps hundreds. When they moved, she caught a glimpse of a jean-clad leg encased within them.

The shadow turned its head to her. Did it have a name? A spike of fear slid through her veins when it tilted its head as if regarding her.

"Show it to the root cellar," the Ancients bade her.

Edie swallowed her fear. "This way," she called to the shadow and slipped by it.

There were no sounds of footsteps behind her, but she felt its presence all the same. Edie went to a small storeroom in the back of the house. She kicked aside the rug, leaned over, and hooked her finger on the round metal handle before hauling it open. There was nowhere for her to move when the shadow filled the room, leaving her no choice but to back up until she was pressed against the wall. Even then, it wasn't enough.

Edie's heart raced, her breath locking in her lungs as its shadowy arm brushed her. The moving darkness felt like a malevolent whisper, leaving a chill in the wake of its touch. It abruptly dropped something into the cellar and then stepped back.

She inhaled, filling her lungs with much-needed air when some space between them opened. Then she leaned over to look down. Killian Flanagan lay still as death on his side, the arm he laid on twisted behind him, and the other lying next to his head. The rise and fall of his chest told her he wasn't dead.

"Lock it."

Edie started at the Ancients' voice. She shut the door, letting it bang closed. The creature held out its hand, showing a lock on its palm. She didn't want to touch the shadows again, but she didn't have a choice. Edie forced her arm to lift and made her hand reach out. She snatched the lock away and could have sworn the being chuckled.

She decided to ignore it as she dropped down to snap the lock into place. Then, she covered the door with the rug once more. When she looked up, the shadow was melting into the floor. No one was getting to Killian. She smiled as she turned off the lights and walked out, not bothering to lock the front door. If anyone was foolish enough to go inside, they deserved their fate.

She drove to the village. Today was the first day of her new life. Edie glanced at the brightly colored cupcakes on the seat next to her and smiled. One of her favorite songs came on the radio, so she turned up the music and sped down the road, singing at the top of her lungs.

After she treated each of her kids' classes to cupcakes, she intended to do some shopping. A new life deserved new clothes. There would be no work today. One of the first things she planned to do was get rid of some of the things in the house she had never liked but had compromised on for Trevor. She didn't intend to live there. She would only remain long enough for the children to come to grips with the changes. It would be difficult for them, but she would be there in whatever capacity they needed.

Her steps were light when she carried the cupcakes into the school. Her smile came easier, and she had a confidence boost she hadn't felt in years. It was astonishing what someone could become when they shed constraints and discarded limitations imposed by someone else.

Edie would find all her favorites again. She didn't know how she had conformed to embody all that Trevor had liked, but she had. She had completely set aside her wants for his. But she had believed that was what someone did when they were in love. Wouldn't Trevor have done the same for her if that were true?

Was that what happened to women? Did they conform and follow what their partners wanted? Trevor hadn't been demanding or cruel. Things had happened gradually over the years without Edie even realizing it. But she wouldn't allow that to happen to her daughter. Edie would educate her. She would also teach her son the correct way to be in a relationship.

The surprised smile on her kids' faces when they saw her only made the day better. She wanted them to be happy because they would soon struggle to find that joy once they learned about their new future.

Once back in her SUV, Edie let out a sigh of contentment. She drove through the village, wondering what it would look like when the Ancients were finished reshaping the Druids. How had the Druids lost their way? Probably much the same way she had. Slowly.

She was now on the right track. Soon, the Druids would be, as well.

CHAPTER FORTY

Hours of endless discussions, debates, and a few shouting matches had driven Ariah to her room. She refused to return to the manor. She needed her home, her space. Only she'd expected to have it to herself. Instead, the entire group had shown up.

Her small home made their voices sound louder than at Carwood Manor. Her head pounded, and the atmosphere became uncomfortable. She couldn't blame her friends. They were here to offer support.

Their voices penetrated the closed door. She couldn't get comfortable. Not standing, not lying on the bed or sitting on the floor. She felt confined, restrained.

No one had come up with a viable solution to their problem. She didn't know where to find Killian. He might not even be on the isle. And there wasn't time to look for him *and* the location she was meant to destroy.

One man's life in exchange for thousands. Killian would never want others to die for him, but she couldn't sacrifice him either. It was a vicious cycle that went round and round in her mind until it felt as if her head might explode.

She needed quiet and some time to think. Ariah stood at the window and saw the forest. It called to her. There, she would find the silence she needed. The threat of the shadow no longer worried her. If it had wanted her, it would've come for her, not Killian. Just as she had feared, Killian had been its target all along.

Ariah opened her window and climbed out. She headed toward the woods as the voices from within her home faded until there was finally silence. An uncomfortable weight rested on her shoulders. One person shouldn't have the ability to save or destroy thousands. Certainly not her. She was the wrong person to be in this position. How could she let the man she loved die? On the other hand, she couldn't doom those on Skye either.

She walked into the comfort of the forest. Where it had once brought peace, she could only find shelter now. It wasn't the trees' fault. That lay with her. Her mind was consumed with uncertainty and fear, her heart aching for the outcome that would destroy her, no matter her choice.

"I knew you would eventually find your way here," came a voice to her right.

Ariah turned to find Callum leaning against a tree, his hands in his coat pockets. "Why didn't you go inside with the others?"

"The same reason you escaped through your window to come here."

She nodded in understanding. "I should've called and told you about…" She couldn't even finish the sentence.

"Kirsi rang me. I went by the manor to check on Moon and Basher."

Ariah wrapped her arms around herself. "Thank you."

"I'll leave you to it, then."

"Stay. I'm going to wander."

He bowed his head in acknowledgment.

Ariah walked among the trees, longing for the solace she usually found. Tears she could no longer hold back flowed down her face. If she only knew who controlled the shadow, she and the others might be able to stop them as they had Kerry. What did she know about battles, though? She had stayed in the background instead of standing beside the others.

Her thoughts turned to who might be pulling the strings in this latest threat. Who had something to gain? Beth, of course. George, too. The London Druids hated Skye enough that they could be part of it. Ariah paused next to a pine and pressed her palm against its rough bark. Who had the power to take the souls of dead Druids, turn them into a mist, and command them to kill others? It wasn't Kerry. Someone had used her, someone powerful enough to keep her silent despite being locked away.

And where were the Ancients? They had never failed the Druids before.

Some said they had been silenced. Druids were losing their magic on Skye. That was a fact no one could ignore any longer. Was it outside forces? Surely it had to be because no Skye Druid would turn against their own. Then again, Kerry had gleefully killed in their community. What did that say about her?

What did that say about Skye?

Ariah watched a squirrel as it sat on a limb, turning a nut over and over in its paws as it nibbled at it. There were other strikes against Skye and the Druids. Ferne had gone into great detail about how she had seen the threat looming over the isle. And Kirsi was meant to stop it. Ariah had taken Ferne's words literally and expected to be able to look at someone and know they were the cause. But what if that wasn't true? What if the threat came from elsewhere?

What if it wasn't even of this world?

Ferne's soul had been caught between realms. The monster from The Grey had tried to kill her. Kirsi had been the only one able to bring Ferne's soul back, and it had been Callum who mended the tear in their dimension before the creature could get through.

Out of nowhere, Corann's face filled her mind's eye.

"It's there. It's always there. No' everyone can see it." Corann looked straight at her. *"Some are destined to locate it."*

Ariah dropped to her knees as her mind raced. She squeezed her eyes shut, trying to remember what he had been talking about. The memory began slipping away. She drew in a long breath and then slowly released it, urging her body to relax. Corann's face started to return. It was fuzzy, his voice distorted at first until it cleared completely.

"Where is your place, Ariah?" he asked.

She answered without hesitation. "The forest."

"That's where the answers will be. Never forget that."

She leaned forward and plunged her fingers into layers of decaying leaves and then into the damp soil. It sank under her nails, the cool dirt beckoning her. Ariah shoved her hands down more. She sensed her connection to the trees through their roots. Her fingers touched the intricate root organism that spawned miles and miles of mushrooms. There were ferns, wild thyme, heather, purple saxifrage, and so many others that she could never name them all. She was part of them. And they, her.

"*The answers are there, Ariah. Look,*" Corann's voice whispered in her mind.

She pushed her hands deeper until she was in the soil up to her elbows. In an instant, she was transported back years. She didn't see the memory. She was *in* it.

The rain turned into a fine mist. Ariah huddled beneath her coat, pressed against the others as they all sought warmth. Corann stood on the start of the spiral at the Fairy Glen. His long robes were soaked, his white hair plastered to his head. He linked his hands behind his back, and without looking at them, began to follow the spiral inward.

The moon followed. Ariah frowned. Nay, it wasn't the moon, it was a small light. Corann's own wee spotlight. She was so cold. All she wanted was to return to her bed and slip beneath the covers to get warm.

"Skye will always have enemies," Corann stated. "There's no getting around that. Where there is power, there will be those who seek to destroy it or take it for themselves. Sometimes, it will be our verra own who turn on us."

Ariah didn't care about any of that. Such things were for the adults.

"It falls to all of us. Every age."

She looked up to find Corann's gaze on her. His look was penetrating. He always seemed to know what she was thinking.

He continued walking the spiral. "Most of Skye's foes will be easily discernible. But..." He paused, the word hanging in the air and making all of them tense with anticipation. "Others, we willna be able to see." He reached the center of the spiral.

His head was bent, making it difficult to see his face because of the spotlight, but he turned, and Ariah saw his apprehension. The stark fear. Her heart skipped a beat. She didn't want to know this. It was too much. They were too young. Why was Corann telling them? If she left now, she wouldn't hear the ending, and then she wouldn't be responsible.

"There's no running from this," Corann stated. He lifted his head and looked at each of them. "The onus falls on the Skye Druids. Each and every one of us. I willna lie. The burden is a heavy one. Nothing may happen, and your generation may no' have to face it."

Standing two people down from Ariah, Rhona asked, "But if we do?"

"Then you must be prepared." Corann's lips flattened. "Magic created this realm. Magic is in every living thing, whether they can wield power or no'. From the darkest depths of the ocean, to the verra ends of the Earth, to where the sky touches space, magic is there. We're privileged enough to know what it feels like. To use it. The verra idea that we have that puts us in the crosshairs of something terrifying."

Ariah took a step back. She didn't care about body heat anymore. Fear had turned her blood to ice. She had to get away.

Come, the forest beckoned.

She spun around and started running.

Suddenly, Corann stood before her. He squatted in front of her, holding her shoulders gently as he looked at her with piercing brown eyes. "I know it's scary, my wee girl. I wish I didna have to tell you any of this, but I must."

"Why?" she demanded. "I don't want to know."

"Because I must. Where is your place, Ariah?" he asked.

She answered without hesitation. "The forest."

"That's where all the answers will be. Never forget that."

"What if I can't get to it?"

"You are a child of the forest. You will always be able to get there."

He stood. "You must hear this, just as I must tell it. Even if I doona wish to."

She reluctantly returned with him to the others. She felt the pull of the forest, even as she stood with the group again. It waited for her, patient and calm.

Corann took his place at the center of the spiral and scanned the children's faces. "Magic bleeds through everything. It seeps from one dimension into another." Corann looked at someone.

Ariah leaned forward to see who it was and spotted Bronwyn shifting uneasily under his gaze.

"Walls separate our world from other dimensions, but those barriers sometimes thin. Especially if something is determined to get through. And if they do, it will be up to the pillars to keep the isle safe. It'll happen in the still of the night. A night like this."

Ariah gasped as the memory unexpectedly ended. She hung her head, Corann's voice still ringing in her ears as if he were right there. She had to swallow twice to wet her dry mouth. Then, she pulled her arms from the ground and climbed to her feet. Just like when she was a girl, she wanted to turn and run from what was happening. But she couldn't. Corann had known. She was sure of it. He had known and desperately wanted to prepare them. He had given them all the information he had. Would it be enough?

She stumbled through the woods back to her house. Callum jerked away from the tree at the sight of her.

"I'm fine," she told him.

Her voice sounded strained, stretched. Much like she felt. Callum fell into step beside her, and they walked in silence to the cottage. He opened the door and waited for her to enter first. Everyone had crowded into the living room and spilled out into the hallway and kitchen. The deafening conversation halted the moment they noticed her.

It was everything Ariah could do to stay on her feet. With the return of the memories came a crushing weight that she was about to share with those in the room. Was that how Corann had felt that night? She suspected it was. And he had handed it to children. But why? There was a reason. He wouldn't have done so otherwise. He protected. Always.

Rhona stood from the sofa. Her expression was guarded as if she somehow knew that what was coming was grave. "What happened?"

"I remember," Ariah told them. "All of it. That night, the story, Corann."

Someone handed her a towel. She took it, noticing the soil clinging to her arms for the first time. The house was so silent she could hear herself breathing.

"Tell us," Bronwyn urged in a tight voice.

Ariah looked at her hands again, remembering how Corann had gently taken her hand in his and given it a squeeze before walking her back to the group. There had been sadness in his eyes. "Corann took us to the Fairy Glen on that cold and rainy night. He told us how our realm was made of magic and that it extended everywhere. He said Skye would always have enemies. Some that would originate here on the isle. Then he began talking about walls that separated our dimension from others."

Bronwyn's face lost all color. Elias took her hand in his.

"He looked at you when he said it," Ariah told Bronwyn. "Corann said those walls could become thin if something was intent on getting through. That the pillars would be what kept the isle safe. That it would happen in—"

"The still of the night," Elodie, Rhona, and Bronwyn said in unison.

Ariah nodded. "The pillars are meant to keep what's trying to get through to our dimension back. Or in. Whatever you want to call it."

"Bloody hell," Rhona said and sank back onto the cushion. "How did we forget something so important?"

Elodie leaned against Scott, who had his arm around her. "Maybe something caused us to forget."

"I doona remember such a story," Elias said.

Filip shook his head. "Neither do I."

"It doesn't matter. The girls do. And we know what the pillars are now," Jasper said.

Theo's dark eyes met Ariah's. "That means we know what has to happen."

"Hold on," Ferne hurriedly urged. "Whatever is trying to get through is the threat I felt. This is what brought me to the isle."

Sabryn said, "You mean The Grey monster."

"Maybe. Maybe not," Ferne replied.

Rhona held up her hands. "We're trying to connect things that might not be connected."

"They are," Ariah stated. "Like the roots of mushrooms, this extends much farther and is bigger than we know. Maybe it involves everything we've been going up against. Maybe it doesn't, but we know it's big."

Filip shrugged. "But does that change anything? All three pillars have to be found and used to keep whatever this is back, no matter what it's connected to."

"It didna target Ariah or any of us. It targeted Killian. That means it'll use anything it can to keep us from succeeding," Callum added.

Ariah turned her head to look at him. Then she slowly scanned the faces around her. "I tried to run from this as a child. Corann stopped me then. I want nothing more than to run now, but I can't. I won't. I'm not going to sacrifice the man I love." She continued when others began arguing. "Nor will I give this adversary what it wants."

"Then what *are* you going to do?" Rhona asked.

Ariah smiled. "I'm going to fight."

CHAPTER FORTY-ONE

Ariah wasn't surprised at the shocked silence that followed her declaration. Maybe she had always known she would come to this conclusion and simply fought against it. Or maybe something had changed to shift her view. The *why* didn't matter. Corann had known all those years ago. He had known and tried to tell her, but she hadn't wanted to listen. Her child's mind hadn't been able to comprehend the magnitude of everything.

"*It's too much,*" she had told Corann that night. "*It's too big.*"

"*I know, my wee girl.*"

Rhona glanced around the room before saying, "Tell us how we can help."

Tears burned Ariah's eyes. She had hoped she wouldn't have to do this alone but assumed she might have to. "I don't know."

"Then we'll figure it out," Bronwyn stated.

Elodie rubbed her hands on her thighs, nodding. "Should we return to the Fairy Glen? It could hold more importance than just being the place of the sky pillar."

"We may not have to. Who all was there?" Jasper asked. "It might be one of those with you all that night."

Elias exchanged a look with Filip. "Except Corann took all Druid children there."

"He did, but I doona recall him saying anything about the pillars," Filip said.

Scott pointed out, "No one recalled anything until Ariah."

"Then how are we supposed to locate the other two?" Willa asked. "They probably don't even know they *are* pillars."

Theo shrugged. "The same way we discovered that Ariah was one."

"That will take time we don't have," Rhona said.

Ariah watched bits of soil fall to the floor as she continued to wipe the towel down her arm. "Whatever is doing this attacked Killian instead of me. That's what I keep coming back to. Why him? Why not me?"

"It didn't just attack Killian. It tried to kill him," Ferne pointed out.

Callum asked, "What if it didna mean to?"

Ariah thought back to the violence at her business. "I think it wanted Killian dead."

"Callum might be onto something," Rhona said. "Neither you nor Ruby was seriously hurt."

An image of Killian gasping for breath, the large shard of glass in his side, filled Ariah's mind. "Besides being impaled by glass, it kicked him across the room."

"What if it went after Killian because it can't get to Druids?" Kirsi asked from the back of the room.

Jasper nodded slowly. "That could explain why it targeted Killian."

Ariah wadded up the towel in her hands. "I don't care if it can come after us yet. I wish it would. We're prepared to fight it. Killian was nearly killed before. Now, he's missing. And his father..." She trailed off as she realized she hadn't asked about Brian. She swung her gaze to Theo. "How is he?"

Theo shook his head.

Ariah might not have cared for Killian's family, but she had never wished them harm.

"All right," Bronwyn said. "Let's just say for the sake of argument that Killian was meant to die during the attack at the shop. Did it take Brian's life because he happened to be near Killian? Or for some other reason? That brings me to the biggest question. If it wanted Killian dead before, how do we know he isn't now?"

That thought had gone through Ariah's mind, as well. "It isn't as if I can ask for proof of life."

"What if you could?" Scott asked.

Theo scratched his jaw. "That's a good point. If they have..." He paused and met Ariah's gaze. "Then there's no reason for you to destroy the sacred spot."

"Who am I going to ask for proof of life?" Ariah asked.

Elias let out a weary sigh. "Edie."

Elodie's eyes grew wide as he looked at her brother. "Do you really think—?"

"Aye, I do," he said over her.

Filip crossed his arms over his chest. "Then we should pay her a visit instead of ringing her."

"I second that," Jasper said.

Rhona gathered her hair behind her head and wound a tie around it to keep it in place. She looked at Elias and then Elodie.

"Are you sure you want to confront your sister? This is your family. We don't know for sure that she's involved. If she isn't, then this could severe any bonds between you."

"Elodie was right. Edie hasna been acting herself. I didna want to see it." Elias's face was pinched as Bronwyn wrapped her arms around his waist. "A man's life is at stake. If we're wrong, then Edie should understand once we explain. And if we're right, then we have a chance to save Killian."

Ferne cleared her throat. "What if there was another way to see if Killian is alive? I might be able to reach him. That would prevent any family issues in case Edie *isn't* a part of it. If she is, then it gives us an edge without letting anyone else know."

"Killian isn't a Druid," Ariah reminded her. "You were able to communicate telepathically with Kirsi and Theo because they have magic."

Ferne shrugged a shoulder. "But we're on Skye. Corann said magic is everywhere. If the walls separating dimensions are thinning, that might mean Killian could be receptive to magic."

"It's a long shot, but what do we have to lose?" Rhona asked.

Theo looked at his mate. "I'll be right beside you the entire time."

"Bronwyn," Ariah said to get her attention. "You might want to return to the manor. That creature from The Grey tried to get through once. It could again."

Bronwyn twisted her face into a grimace. "It also might be the very thing manipulating all of this. I'll head there now."

"No' without me," Elias said.

Sabryn walked to the couple. "Or me."

"I'll get the word out to the deputies about the danger. They'll let the rest of the Druids know," Rhona stated as she texted something on her mobile.

It took all of Ariah's patience not to scream at Ferne to reach Killian immediately. It felt like forever, but it was only a few moments before Ferne got comfortable in a chair.

She closed her eyes and then opened them. "This might seem like a stupid question, but has anyone tried to call Killian's mobile again?"

It had never dawned on Ariah. She fumbled for her phone and quickly dialed Killian. Hope tightened painfully in her chest when the line connected and began ringing. She hadn't thought to try after not being able to reach him once he was taken. She had assumed that line of communication was gone. With every ring that went unanswered, hope began to shrivel, then vanished completely when Killian's voicemail answered.

Ariah ended the call and lowered the mobile.

"I've got this," Ferne said with a smile and closed her eyes again.

Ariah couldn't tear her gaze from Ferne, letting hope once more swell in her heart. It was a long shot, she knew, but Ariah needed to know if Killian was alive. It could be a trick. It likely was. The attack at her place of business had meant to take Killian's life. It didn't make sense that whoever had him now would allow him to live.

Yet her mind refused to believe that Killian was dead.

The house was as silent as a tomb. Ferne stayed relaxed for a long period of time before her forehead furrowed. Blood slowly ran from her nose.

"Fuck," Theo murmured anxiously as he watched.

Ferne's face became tense with effort. Ariah had to look away.

She couldn't stand the waiting and hoping. The suspense was slowly killing her. The forest called to Ariah, but she couldn't leave without knowing if Killian was alive.

There was a loud gasp. Ariah swung her head around to see Theo handing Ferne a napkin to wipe her nose. Her eyes locked with Ariah's.

"He's alive," Ferne said with a smile.

Emotion overcame Ariah. She hadn't dared to believe. She blinked rapidly to hold back the tears. "Where is he?"

"In the ground," Ferne answered softly.

Chaos erupted as everyone began speculating where Killian could be. Ferne's communication had been severed, preventing her from learning more. But he was alive. It was the bolster Ariah needed.

She backed away, grabbed her coat, and left the house for the forest. Maybe it could give her more. As she came around the corner, she found Rhona leaning against the cottage.

"It doesn't make sense, does it?" Rhona asked.

Ariah shoved her hands into her jacket pockets. "What doesn't?"

"Killian. Do they want him dead or not? I saw him after the attack. It looked as if he was targeted."

"That was my thought."

"And now they decide to kidnap him to force you to do what they want?"

Ariah glanced at the forest, eager to be within it. "That's the conclusion I've drawn."

"What if there's more?"

"Meaning?" she asked, her interest piqued.

"The conversation earlier got me thinking. What if the shadow can't touch us? Not in our world, at least." Rhona turned to face her. "What if they don't know who the other two pillars are?"

Ariah shifted her weight to her other foot. "Then how do they know about me?"

"I've been thinking about that, too. If they know about you, why wouldn't they know about the others? I mean, we just remembered the pillars."

Unease slithered down Ariah's spine. "What if they found out like we did?"

Rhona stiffened and slowly straightened. "I trust everyone in this group. We've fought together. Bled together. I don't believe any of them would turn against us."

"I don't either. But what if they didn't realize it was happening?"

"Fuck," Rhona murmured as she flattened her back against the cottage. She blew out an exasperated sigh. "We don't know who we're up against or how to fight them."

Ariah grinned and kicked a pebble. "We do it as Corann used to tell us."

Rhona's head turned to her, and her lips curved into a smile.

In unison they said, "One battle at a time."

"All right, then. Looks like the next one falls to you." Rhona searched Ariah's face.

She swallowed. "I tried to run away that night with Corann. His words terrified me. I knew then how menacing and frightening this would be and didn't want any part of it. I thought if I ran home, I wouldn't be involved. There was fear in Corann's eyes. That's what scared me the most. I'd never seen that look on his face before. He stopped me, but only from physically leaving. From that moment on, I pulled away from anything that seemed even remotely like the story he told us. I even forgot it."

"We all did," Rhona said.

"I'm not running anymore. It's time for me to take my place among you. I think Corann knew this would come to pass with us."

Rhona released a long breath. "He probably did. I wished he had prepared us."

"He did. He taught us the stories. We're the ones who are supposed to remember." She nodded at the woods. "That is where I belong. He told me to go there for answers. In the forest is where I will stand against the shadow. Alone."

CHAPTER FORTY-TWO

Pain greeted Killian first. His head throbbed in time with his heartbeat as he opened his eyes. There was a second of panic when only darkness met his gaze. Almost at the same moment, he realized something was wrong with his body.

He attempted to move, only to discover that one of his arms was caught beneath him and numb. Stretching out his legs proved impossible. His hip ached from something poking into it. Killian managed to lift his hips up so he could slide his arm free.

When he pulled his arms against him and began rubbing each of them as best he could to help with the circulation, prickles of feeling ran up and down both. He blinked, trying to let his eyes adjust so he could hopefully make out something, but it remained dark. And silent.

The scent of damp earth filled his nostrils. That and the slight chill gave him pause. He patted around until he touched soil and rock. His heart lurched as he realized he was underground. Had he been buried alive?

"Dad," he murmured, remembering he had been with his father when the shadow struck.

Killian swallowed heavily. Maybe his father was with him. He reached out in hopes of contacting a body, but he hit a wall instead. He rolled halfway onto his back, only for his knees to strike something solid. He raised his arms and hesitantly felt around. His fingers brushed a wooden board. He flattened his hands on it and shoved. The board lifted, giving him a brief jolt of exhilaration, but it was fleeting as the boards held, the distinct sound of metal against metal noisy in the quiet.

He dropped his arms to his chest and rolled his head in the other direction. There was no way to tell if there was another wall there or if it extended beyond what he could see.

"Dad?" he whispered.

Killian held his breath, waiting to hear anything that would let him know he wasn't alone. Eventually, he had to accept that his father wasn't with him, or Brian was unconscious. Killian tried not to think about the flash of terror in his father's eyes when he saw the shadow.

Ariah. Killian's heart sank when he thought of her. Had the being gone after her, too? Someone else? Had anyone seen him being taken? Did they know he was missing? Ariah would look for him, Killian was sure of it.

He felt behind his head, hoping it was open so he could stretch out his legs that were beginning to twinge from being in the same position. His movement was too quick, causing him to jam his hand into a rock.

"Fuck," he bit out.

There would be no straightening out or turning over. He was stuck in the position on his side until someone found him. But why had they taken him? Especially after trying to kill him before. He had been sure Ariah was the intended target. He never should've left her. He had been so sure Rhona would keep her safe. If only Killian had remained in the village. If he had, none of this would have happened.

He had never been claustrophobic, but the longer he lay in the small space, the more it felt as if the walls were closing in on him. He hadn't been buried alive. Not yet, anyway. There was some kind of locked opening preventing him from getting out. Since his arms and legs hadn't been tied, then whoever had put him here didn't expect him to find a way out.

That was their loss, because he would get out and find his way back to Ariah and his dad.

Killian startled as he realized he might have the answer. He felt around in his back pocket and grinned when his fingers closed over his mobile. He pulled it out and lifted it to his face. The screen brightened, bathing him in blue light. A laugh bubbled up when he saw his battery still had half its juice. Plenty left to make a call.

He tried Ariah first, shaking his head at the foolishness of his kidnappers. They should've taken the mobile from him immediately. But as he waited for the line to connect, his elation dampened and curdled to dread. He tried a second time. Then a third. Killian dialed Callum, his father, his mother, but none of the calls connected.

Despair tried to take hold, but he shook it off. He tapped the torch app on his mobile and shined it around his prison. The hole was as short and narrow as he had mentally pictured, and the space didn't extend out behind him like he had hoped. Also, he was alone.

Killian turned off the light and tucked the mobile back into his pocket so he wouldn't waste the battery. He would try to call them again. He shoved against the boards overhead. If he could find where the lock held it down, he might be able to use enough force to break it. Or at the very least, reach it. He didn't know what he would do then, but he had to focus on something.

He used his knees and hands to push against the wood with everything he had, but the lock held. He kept trying, refusing to give up.

"Killian?"

He stilled, listening. There had been a voice. It was soft, barely a whisper, but he was sure he had heard something. Unless he was going daft.

"Killian? Can you hear me?"

It was a female with a British accent. A voice he recognized. Was that…? "Ferne?"

"Killian?"

"Ferne, I'm here. Where are you?"

"Killian, can you hear me?"

"Aye," he replied. "I hear you. Can you hear me?"

"Killian?"

He paused. He heard her, but not through his ears. He heard her in his head. Could it really be Ferne?

"Killian! You can hear me. Thank God!"

He blinked in confusion.

"I've been trying to reach you for some time. It's very hard to keep this connection, so I'll be brief. Can you tell me where you are?"

In the bloody ground, that's where he was.

"The ground?"

Did she hear his thoughts?

"Yes. I'll explain when we get you free. What do you mean in the ground?"

Killian grunted and thought of the small space he was in. Locked away in, actually. But that was all he knew since he had been unconscious after the shadow seized him.

"Can you hear anything?"

There was nothing but silence outside of his attempts to get the latch open.

"Is there...?"

He held his breath as Ferne's voice became so faint he couldn't hear her anymore.

"...Killi—"

Ferne? He waited for her to answer, but she didn't return.

He slammed his fist into the wood in frustration.

CHAPTER FORTY-THREE

The night was alive with sounds. Ariah walked the woods of central Skye, every step purposeful. She didn't need a light to show her the way. The forest led her.

A pair of bats twirled around each other and dove in front of her before soaring back up into the tree limbs. A fox screamed in the distance while another padded close to her on the right. She had never feared what was in the woods, whether it was day or night and she didn't now, either.

Even though she would soon face something that didn't belong.

She still didn't know what she intended. It had made its purpose clear. It wanted the place she would stand to protect Skye destroyed. Of course, she needed to find it first. She hadn't asked the forest for its location yet.

The woods sat between the Fairy Glen and the Fairy Pools, and that wasn't a coincidence. The line stretched from north to south. Three locations. Three pillars. Three Druids who would work to keep out the wickedness attempting to break through. It would take more than the pillars to win the war, however.

Ariah wasn't the only one who had put that together. Rhona had, too. Ariah wasn't sure Kirsi comprehended how crucial her role was yet, but she would before long. Because war had been waged on Skye before. The Druids had been victorious, but they hadn't been able to end the conflict for good. It was why Corann had passed on the story. Because it was inevitable that it would all play out again.

And here they were.

As she passed a fern, its long stems brushed against her leg with force. A warning. The second came as an owl hooted behind her. The shadow was here. It wasn't a surprise since she had been expecting it.

From the moment Ariah had stepped into the forest, she had warned every living thing about what would come. The woods and its occupants were as prepared as she was—they were probably more equipped for battle. For most of her life, she had claimed to be a pacifist who worked for peace because she believed that's what the forest meant.

When, in fact, nature, in and of itself, was violent. Brutal.

Ferocious.

Her eyes were open to the truth now. She had stood back in fear of the very thing that had come for Killian and her home. Giving in and standing aside would only mean death and destruction to everything she held dear. Corann had done his best to warn her, but she hadn't been old enough to fully understand the implications at the time.

Ariah sensed the shadow gaining ground behind her. The night grew still and silent. The time had come, just as Corann had predicted. Ariah stopped and turned to face the creature. It hid in the obscurity of nightfall, away from the moonlight filtering through the trees. But she didn't need to see it. The forest and its occupants let her know exactly where it was.

She followed a ray of moonlight that cut across the ground and came to a point at the base of the creature. A quiver of icy fear spread across her chest. She recognized it as the same emotion that had caused her to run from Corann, but she wasn't that scared little girl anymore. She was a Druid, a child of the forest, one who knew exactly who she was and where she belonged.

And what she needed to do.

Apprehension gave way to rage. Ariah didn't let it consume her because she would be no better than those she stood against if she did. The forest held its breath, the plants and animals waiting for her.

She let herself think about Killian. *Hold on,* she silently bade him.

Ariah let the magic of the forest flow up from the ground and into her body. It hummed through her, gaining momentum until she had to fight to remain still. "I've been wondering why you haven't come after me or other Druids."

The shadow moved from behind a tree and stretched taller to tower over her.

"You want to hurt us, though, don't you? It would've been better if you had."

It took a menacing step forward.

Ariah didn't back down. "You aren't the one in charge. You're a puppet, an expendable pawn sent to create havoc. Who's your master? The beast in The Grey?" When there was no response, she grinned. "Ah. Someone else, then. We'll sort that out eventually. Though you won't be here to see it."

The shadow took another step.

Ariah lifted her chin. "You answer to another, and you can't come after the ones you hate the most. What is it you want? Our world, or the magic? Both?"

The shadow now stood in moonlight and tilted its head, appearing as if its mouth were open in a snarl.

"You took the man I love."

The snarl turned into a smirk.

Her heart thudded with a mixture of rage and terror. She channeled it into her magic. "Your master should know that love always triumphs. You dared to invade our home, attack innocents, and threaten us. You attempted to bend me to your will. It just proves that you have no idea who you're going up against. Let me show you."

The shadow made to move. Ariah dropped to one knee, her palm on the earth. Roots shot up from the ground and wrapped around the shadow, trapping it. The entity struggled violently and managed to sever one root, but more sprang up to hold it.

The intensity of the power surging through Ariah was euphoric, exhilarating. She stood and walked around the creature, watching it flail about helplessly. She halted when she stood before it once more.

"All the answers are in the forest," Ariah said. "That's what my teacher told me once. He was right. Everything I need to know is here, waiting to tell me. All I had to do was ask." She jerked her chin at the roots. "Take those, for example. Did you know that roots extend around our globe. They connect everything, some going so deep they come out the other side of the world. That isn't the only thing they link. Take the dimensions, for instance. Some of our mightiest, tallest trees have roots that move from one dimension to the next. Others use their roots to create walls—the very ones that prevent our world from melding into another. I wouldn't be able to trap you. Just like you can't touch me. But the roots can. And they are eager to help."

She leaned her head to the side. "It's been easy for you, hasn't it? Moving about freely, listening to our conversations. You even found your way into my dreams."

It smiled.

"Had fun with that, did you? You tried to take control of me that one night when I was sleepwalking, but you didn't have enough power. The forest took over and sent me to the one person it knew I wanted." Killian. If only she had discovered that sooner.

The creature yanked against the confines of the roots, throwing its head back and forth.

"You slunk around, learning about us and what we knew. And discovering yourself. You had to adapt to our world where your enemies were just out of reach. But you had access to those without magic. Tell me, did you lose your temper? Is that why you attacked Killian? Because things weren't going according to plan?"

A wave of pure rage slammed into her.

Ariah caught herself before it could shove her back. "That's it, isn't it? You're like a petulant child who acts out without thinking. I wonder if your master knows how close you came to killing Killian before you got me to destroy the location of my pillar."

The shadow stilled.

The way it watched her sent ice down Ariah's spine. If it could kill, she would be dead. "You had all the information at your disposal until we gathered in the manor. It wouldn't let you near us, which meant you had no idea what we had learned or decided."

Ariah thought the entity smiled. She took a step closer. "I wanted to be the one to tell you that you failed. I won't be destroying anything. We've kept our worlds apart before, and we'll do it again. You're done here, but I imagine your master would like a few words."

The roots squeezed the creature. Shadows bulged between the stalks as if trying to escape, but there was nowhere for them to go. The roots continued contracting until the shadows burst and floated to the ground like dead leaves.

Balladyn dropped his veil, revealing himself behind where the creature had been. He walked to stand beside Ariah as she stared at what was left of the shadow monster. She should be thrilled at the victory, but she wasn't.

"What is it?" the Reaper asked.

Ariah swung her head to him. "That was too easy."

"I don't think I'd call what you just did *easy*."

"That thing isn't working alone. I stopped it, but we need to find Killian." She didn't bother to say the rest.

Balladyn nodded. "Tell me where to take you."

And that was the problem. It was the one thing the forest hadn't told her. Ariah dropped down and curled her fingers into the soil. Why weren't the trees telling her Killian's location? Everything was connected. They should know where he was.

The only answer the forest gave her was flashes of darkness. It confirmed that Killian was somewhere dark, but it didn't know where. Or even if he was still on Skye. Ariah refused to consider that she might lose him.

"I need Roy," Ariah said and straightened.

Balladyn touched her arm. In the next breath, she stood outside the deputy's home. Ariah pounded on the door. It swung open to reveal Roy, dark hair fastened in a man bun, pale blue eyes, clean-shaven. He preferred to be alone but was powerful enough that Corann had made him a deputy. A mottled blue cardigan with tattered cuffs from too much wear covered a navy tee. Roy's light blue gaze moved from her to Balladyn and then back again.

He set aside the book he held and removed his reading glasses. "What happened?"

"Can you ask the stones where Killian is?" Ariah asked.

Roy walked outside without hesitation. They followed him around the back of the house to a carefully stacked two-foot-tall mound of rocks. He placed his hands atop them and closed his eyes.

"Hold on," she whispered to Killian.

CHAPTER FORTY-FOUR

SKYE DRUIDS

There was oxygen, so he could breathe. That should've eased some of Killian's fears, but it only heightened them. The shadow had already tried to kill him. Did it want an isolated location so no one could find him? That made sense, but if that was the case, where was it? Why wasn't he already dead?

Something more was going on. That could also be why he hadn't been buried alive. Instead, they'd stuck him in a hole in the ground with a latch keeping him in place. He stared up at the darkness above him where the door was. It wasn't a secure spot. Isolated, maybe, but not all that fortified from what he could tell.

Maybe that was the point. They'd put him somewhere Ariah and the others couldn't find him. Of all the ways he'd thought he might die, starvation hadn't been one of them. He swallowed, suddenly parched.

"Ariah." He closed his eyes, regret swelling in his chest.

He could've shared all these years with her. Instead, he had ignored the love in his heart and bent to his family's wishes. And for what? To never see Ariah again. To never have the future they both wanted.

The Druids fought for their home. They put themselves in danger over and over again to protect Skye and their community. He might not have magic, but he loved someone who did. If the Skye Druids could take a stand, so could he. And he wouldn't go down easily.

"Come on, you fucker, whoever you are. You wanted me. Now, you have me. What are you going to do, eh?"

Roy turned to the side, his hands braced on his thighs as he fought for breath. Ariah started to go to him, but he held out a hand to stop her. He then held up a finger, asking for a moment. It was time she didn't have. She impatiently shifted her weight from foot to foot. The only thing stirring on Balladyn was his long, black-and-silver hair drifting in the breeze.

Finally, Roy straightened. His lips were pinched, and his brow was furrowed. "Something's stopping me from seeing the exact location."

"Nay." Ariah fisted her hands. The panic she had kept at bay took a firm hold now, the cold press of it spreading around her heart and squeezing painfully.

Balladyn swung his red-ringed white gaze to Roy. "Can you see anything?"

"I see him in a small area." Roy paused, his face wrinkled as he searched for the word. "Almost like a root cellar. It's dark, and I can sense him there, but I can no' get more than that. Again, something is preventing me from seeing the exact location." He caught Ariah's gaze. "But I saw something. Marsco Peak."

Ariah's knees nearly gave out. Her eyes blurred with tears as she turned her head to Balladyn. Before she could thank Roy, Balladyn jumped them away. To her dismay, he didn't take her to the mountain but Rhona's. Ariah was still reeling from the fact that she wasn't any closer to finding Killian when she noticed Roy with them. Within moments, Rhona had notified everyone to head to Marsco Peak. There was no warning from Balladyn when he teleported them to the mountain in the Red Hills.

"The area is too big," Rhona said, looking out.

Ariah scanned the barren landscape devoid of trees, only broken up by the sight of a white cottage rising from the rocky grassland. "He could be anywhere."

"Let me try again," Roy said.

He squatted down and rested his hand on a stone protruding from the ground. His eyes weren't closed this time. Instead, they looked slowly from one side to the other. He removed his hand and met her gaze, regret tightening his face.

"We need to try the other side of the mountain," Ariah said. She wouldn't give up easily.

Killian tried to get comfortable in a place that would never be comfortable. He thought he heard something. He stilled and held his breath, the strange quiet stretching. Something tickled his cheek. He rubbed his shoulder against it to stop the itching. Then it happened on his other cheek. Then his hand.

Foreboding saturated the air.

He shoved at the hatch, using all his strength.

Ariah shook her head as she moved away from Balladyn, Rhona, and Roy. An urgency that hadn't been there before pushed her to *do something*. She turned in a circle, searching for anything that would lead her to Killian.

"Bloody hell," Roy ground out as he struggled to use his ability in the new location.

Ariah swung around to him. Without thought, she closed the distance between them and curled her fingers into the soil next to the rock. It wasn't the forest, but with Roy's magic alongside hers, she could use the roots of the grass and other fauna to help.

Please, she beseeched them.

She felt a response from the nearest set of trees and then softly behind it, that of the grass.

"Doona stop," Roy told her.

Ariah pushed more of her magic into the ground, seeking the connection she knew was there, the link the forest had shown her. Finding it while away from the woods took so much more effort. But she was the *talamh* pillar. That should give her some flexibility.

"I got it," Roy called.

The bugs were crawling over his face and body. Killian couldn't knock them off fast enough. Each time he did, more were there. The sound of their legs scraping together made him want to scream, but he didn't open his mouth for fear one of them might fall in.

He had to keep blowing air out of his nose to keep them away. His eyes were squeezed shut, and he had to continually move his head from side to side so his shoulders could scrape his ears to keep the bugs out. They were piling up around him, filling the space.

Starvation wouldn't kill him. The bugs were going to suffocate him.

The wind whipped savagely across the barren, moonlight-soaked countryside, tangling her hair and skirts, but Ariah barely noticed. She stood in the drive, her gaze locked on the empty space where a home was supposed to stand. But nothing was there.

"Killian is here," Roy said with conviction.

Rhona walked across the grass with measured steps as if she might run into an invisible wall. Ariah half-hoped she did because then they would at least know magic was at work. Balladyn squatted down, his head tilted, staring silently at the vacant spot. The wild winds seemed to move around the Reaper as if he were a force they chose not to go up against.

Ariah's gut twisted painfully, the knot of uncertainty heavy in her stomach. She was ready to fight, but that wasn't easy when she had no one to go up against. They were being toyed with.

Car engines roared behind them. Ariah looked over her

shoulder as headlights from three vehicles traveling close together at high speed bounced along the rutted road toward them. Ariah was glad her friends had arrived because she needed all the help she could get.

She turned back to look at the void. The driveway was the only one for some distance. That made the location a perfect place to hide someone. Car doors slammed, drawing her attention as the rest of the group walked up.

"I know this place," Elias said.

Ariah moved to see him better. "How?"

He glanced at Elodie before quickly shaking his head as if he didn't want to say. "This is the location of Edie and Trevor's first home."

"But where *is* the house?" Scott asked.

Balladyn straightened. "Hidden."

"Really?" Rhona stood in the middle of what was supposed to be the cottage. "How?"

Elias joined Rhona in moving about the area. "Good question."

"Killian is here," Ariah announced.

Sabryn turned in a circle. "Where?"

"There," Roy said, pointing to the plot they were standing on. "Right where the house should be."

Jasper's face tightened with dread. "That...could prove problematic."

"We have to start somewhere," Elodie said. "We can split up and begin searching."

Theo nodded in agreement. "A grid pattern."

The cold, calloused fingers of terror clamped around Ariah.

They didn't have time for this. She knew it in the deepest recesses of her soul. Yet what else could they do?

Tires squealed in the distance, followed by the roar of an engine as a vehicle headed in their direction. They turned as a group to face the new arrival—be they friend or foe. The vehicle slid to a stop behind the others. A moment later, a single person got out. Theo flicked on a torch and moved the light to the stranger.

An audible sigh of relief went through the group at the sight of Callum. Ariah noticed that half of his hair had fallen from the queue at the back of his neck. There was blood coming from his nose and lip. His left eye was beginning to swell, the dark splotches of a bruise showing signs of forming.

Callum wiped his mouth with the sleeve of his jumper and walked straight to her. The seams along the top of the sweater's right shoulder were ripped so it hung to reveal the black tee underneath. Ariah looked into Callum's eyes. Any thoughts of asking if he was okay vanished at the sight of his resolve.

"Where is Killian?" Callum asked.

Ariah shrugged. "He's here, but we're not sure where."

"We're about to spread out to start looking," Theo explained.

Callum's brows snapped together as he motioned toward the location of the house. "Why are we no' starting there?"

"You can see it?" Ariah was so surprised she could barely get the words out fast enough.

Callum's frown deepened as he glanced around him. "You can no'?"

"Nay," they said in unison.

Everyone spoke, Ariah realized, except for Kirsi. She was staring at the area of the house as if lost in thought. A flare of anger shot through Ariah. She didn't want to think that Kirsi had seen it this entire time and not said anything, but now wasn't the time to ask. Not when they needed to locate Killian.

Callum shrugged. "All right, then. I'll go look."

"Not alone, you won't," Ariah replied.

Callum held her gaze for a heartbeat before bowing his head. She followed him toward the house she couldn't see.

"Wait a moment. I'm all for finding Killian, but how? Elias and I are standing in the middle of what should be a cottage, and nothing is here," Rhona said. She moved her arms about as if to make her point.

Callum drew in a breath and slowly released it. "I doona know what to say other than I can see it fine. I'm about to walk through the door."

"Let's go," Ariah said, the urgency to find Killian quickly pushing her onward.

Without a word, Callum took a step forward. And vanished.

"Callum!" Ariah shouted.

He returned. "What?"

"I lost you."

He looked over his shoulder. Then he held out his hand. "Let's try this."

"Hold up," Jasper said as he hurried to them. "I'll stay here. Hopefully, we'll be able to communicate."

Elias strode to them. "The root cellar will be toward the back on the right side. It's a small room. You can no' miss it."

Ariah tightened her fingers around Callum's hand. He looked her way. She nodded, and they walked through the door to find Killian.

CHAPTER FORTY-FIVE

The moment Ariah went through the door with Callum, she could see the cottage and everything within. She blinked repeatedly to try to clear her vision because everything was blurry. Like a pane of glass when rain struck it. The dim, hazy light only made it worse. Clumps of mist moved lethargically across the floor, leaving a distinctly eerie feeling. As if she were in a house of horrors on Halloween night.

It was exactly how her friends had described The Grey.

Ariah chanced a look at Callum, who was slightly ahead of her. She only saw his profile, but the muscle tightening in his jaw said everything. At first, he walked with purposeful steps, but his strides began to slow. She wanted to shove him to move faster, but his crushing grip on her hand kept her silent.

"Fuck," Callum bit out.

She moved to come even with him. "Talk to me. What is it?"

"It's just like the bloody fucking Grey." He shook his head once. "I had trouble walking there. It's happening here, too."

Ariah looked around, wondering what could be affecting him. "Why you and not me?"

"I doona know."

"What if I push you?"

Callum hesitated before he shrugged. "Maybe."

"Let's try."

Ariah kept a hold of his hand and stood behind him. She leaned into his back with her shoulder and shoved. That let them make some headway, but she realized that the more she pushed, the more it felt as if something was pushing back. As if something sought to keep Callum in one spot. She couldn't imagine how frightening that must be for him. He said nothing, just kept shuffling one foot in front of the other. They weren't making much headway, but some was better than nothing.

Soon, they were both breathless from the exertion. Ariah glanced back to see that they had only gone a few feet. She was so close to Killian, yet so far away. Frustration choked her. It would be easy to give in, but she couldn't. Killian was counting on her. Her friends were counting on her. Skye was counting on her.

And she wouldn't let them down.

"It wants me here. Just as it wanted me the last time," Callum said between gulps of air.

She leaned more into his back, pressing her feet into the floor as she propelled him forward a couple of inches. "That isn't going to happen."

He glanced back at her. Ariah met his gaze and nodded. He gritted his teeth and trudged on, the top portion of his body inclined forward as he grunted with the effort. She stayed behind him, shoving and pushing with everything she had while never losing her hold on him. She wasn't sure what would happen to her if she did, and she didn't want to find out.

Perspiration trickled down the side of her face. Callum grunted as he strained onward. They were both exhausted, but neither quit. Tears ran down her face, along with sweat, and all the while, she prayed Killian was alive.

Callum abruptly sagged against a door. Ariah was unprepared for his sudden stop, and her foot slipped out from under her. Callum half-turned to pull her up by her hand. They shared a look, and then Callum motioned with his head. She looked around him into a small room. It had to be where the root cellar was.

"Beneath the rug," Callum wheezed.

Ariah walked around him to enter the room first and then tugged him with her. She thought it would be easier than pushing but regretted it immediately since it proved more difficult. Yet she got them inside. Her lungs ached, and her body begged for a moment of rest, but she sucked in large mouthfuls of air and kicked away the rug. And there before her was a hatch. Two hinges lined the opposite side while the handle and lock were at her feet.

She squatted to jiggle the lock. "I don't see a key, do you?"

"Nay."

"We'll have to use magic to open it.

"Wait," Callum stopped her. "It took power we can no' even begin to fathom to hide the cottage from even a Reaper. We doona know what we'll face when that opens."

She looked up at him. "I'm going to find Killian. No matter how long it takes, no matter where I have to go or who I have to face. I'm going to find the man I love."

Callum shot her a crooked grin. "Then let's open it."

Ariah straightened and tightened her hand on his. She was glad she wasn't alone. Within the confines of the forest, she'd been ready to face anything. But it was a different story here in this gloomy place.

"Be ready for anything," Callum warned.

A shiver raced over Ariah. She gathered magic in her palm and propelled it out, imagining the lock falling open. The magic bounced off the lock and hit her in the left shoulder. Callum's fingers tightened as the impact tugged her hand from his. He not only kept hold of her, he also kept her on her feet.

"Bloody hell," she muttered from the surprise hit and the pain radiating from her shoulder.

Callum tugged her down so they squatted next to the lock. "I have an idea. Try that again, but this time, we'll both use magic."

The moment their magic touched the lock, it swung back to them. Ariah managed to pull them away before it struck either of them.

"Guys? Are you okay?"

Ariah glanced out the door at the sound of Jasper's voice coming from far away. "We're at the root cellar," she yelled back.

She and Callum got to their feet. The more she looked at the lock, the more she thought about how useless it appeared. That's when realization hit.

"Forget the lock," she told Callum. "Bust the wood."

His frown gave way to a grin. "Aye. Of course. Ready?"

"Ready."

They sent a surge of magic into the wood. It broke in half with a loud snap. Callum flung the boards away, and Ariah gasped at the sight of Killian on his side, too still and unmoving.

"We need to get him out," Callum said.

Ariah tried to get into the root cellar with Killian, but Callum held her back. He forced her to look at him.

"I'm going to need both hands. It'll be up to you to keep a hold of me. Do you understand?" Callum asked.

She glanced at Killian and nodded.

Callum moved her hand to his belt loop. "Doona let go."

"I won't," she promised.

Callum stepped down into the hole and almost immediately jumped back.

"What? What is it?" Ariah demanded.

"Fucking bugs," he muttered.

She wasn't sure she'd heard him right, but before she could ask him to repeat it, he bent over. Ariah had to watch her footing as she shifted forward so she didn't lose hold of Callum's belt loop. She waited impatiently, her nerves stretched to the breaking point as Callum, already weakened from whatever had happened before he arrived and then his walk through the cottage, attempted to wrestle Killian across his shoulders in a fireman's carry.

Ariah wanted to help. She needed to help. She was just about to drop into the cellar beside Callum when she felt him tip to the side. He swore at the same time Jasper shouted something. She pulled her lips back over her teeth in a grimace and used herself and magic to right Callum.

Finally, he stood firmly again.

"Thanks," he told her.

She patted his back. "It's going to take both of us to get Killian up and both of you out of the cellar."

"Sadly, you're right."

Ariah used both hands to keep Callum steady while wrapping her magic around him to give him strength. She glanced at the dirt in the cellar and almost kicked off her shoe to sink her foot into it to find the connection to the roots again. Then she remembered where they were and decided not to take the chance. She concentrated on magic, feeling it rush through her body and outward around Callum.

They needed the Ancients. Why hadn't they reached out to someone? Why were they silent?

The murky surroundings were a reminder that they didn't know this enemy or what it could do. Could this foe prevent the Ancients from getting through? It had taken Killian, hidden an entire house, and gathered the souls of dead Druids while forcing them to kill. It might very well be able to silence the Ancients.

Callum grunted as he heaved Killian across his shoulders. "I got him," he replied breathlessly. "I got Killian."

Her muscles screamed for relief. If she hurt, she could only imagine how much worse Callum felt. Yet he said nothing. Ariah swallowed to try to ease her dry mouth. "Now, we go out the way we came in."

"Sounds simple enough."

They both knew it would be anything but.

It took Callum three tries before he was able to climb out of the cellar. Ariah continued to keep him steady, which took more effort since he also carried Killian. She kept to Callum's back, both hands now on his belt loops as they trudged from the room. Killian was right there. Near enough to touch. She so badly wanted to put her hands on him, but they had to get out of the cottage first. Ariah planted her feet and shoved Callum forward.

He fought for every inch, his body shaking as he battled against whatever tried to hold him. Ariah wasn't sure what was happening, but the sooner she got Callum out of the cottage, the better.

"Ariah? Callum?" Jasper shouted.

She leaned around Callum and looked toward the open door. They were only feet away, but Jasper sounded much, much farther. She could see him waiting outside, his gaze searching. "We're here," she yelled.

"Hurry! We're under attack!"

Callum gritted his teeth and let out a shout as he endeavored to move his legs faster. Both of them were doing everything they could to move, but they weren't getting anywhere.

Suddenly, Kirsi was inside. She stood before Callum, her face ashen. Then she passed Ariah, her eyes widening in fear.

"Doona look behind you, Ariah!" Callum shouted.

It was all she could do not to turn around. Would she be able to get a glimpse of what it was that had tried to end Killian's life?

"Doona do it," Callum said as if knowing what she was thinking. Then he shouted Kirsi's name.

It seemed to snap her out of her shock. She grabbed Callum's arm with both hands, leaned back, and pulled. Her eyes never left whatever was behind them.

Something let out a breath behind Ariah. It was so close to her that it stirred her hair.

"Ariah, doona let go of me!"

Her gaze locked on Killian as Callum shouted. Something wrapped around her waist from behind and hauled her back.

"Nay!" Callum roared.

Ariah watched as Kirsi tugged him out the door, even as her hold on Callum's belt loops loosened precariously. She couldn't hold on. Whatever had her wasn't letting go. Her gaze moved to Killian's back. She wanted to see his face one more time.

The chuckle behind her made her blood ice over. Her strength was waning. She couldn't keep a hold of Callum any longer. Whatever held her yanked again. One hand slipped loose. This was it. This was the last time she would see Killian or any of her friends. A tear fell down her face for all that would be lost.

Callum spun around rapidly while maintaining his hold on Killian, latching onto her arm just as her other fingers slid away.

His gaze locked with hers. "I've got you."

She gripped his arm as tightly as possible, but she was still slipping.

"Jasper!" Callum shouted.

Someone took Killian from Callum's shoulders, and then he used both hands to grab Ariah. Callum looked over her head with a glare and bared his teeth. He braced his feet on either side of the doorway and leaned back as he heaved her forward.

Ariah felt like she was being torn in two. Whatever had her wasn't letting go. It wanted one of them, and she was the last one in the cottage. Callum fought to keep hold of her, but it was futile. If he didn't let go, he would be pulled in with her. That couldn't happen. Kirsi needed him. So would Killian when he woke. Because Ariah refused to believe he wouldn't.

She tried to yank her arm away from Callum. His eyes widened as he stared at her.

"What are you doing?" Callum demanded.

"Let go."

He shook his head. "I willna."

"You have to."

He gripped her tighter in response. The arm around her waist yanked hard, pushing the breath from Ariah.

Then Kirsi was there. She reached through the door, wrapped her hands around Ariah's arm, and pulled. Now, both she and Callum might be caught along with Ariah. She parted her lips to beg the two of them to let her go, but then she caught sight of Killian lying on the ground. All the love and hope for the future she had swelled in her chest.

She had ventured into whatever lair this was to rescue Killian. She had fought against the shadow to protect her home. She had taken a stand for Skye—and herself. She wasn't about to have her life snatched from her without fighting back.

Ariah closed her eyes and reached out to the nearby trees. Unfortunately, they were too far away. Pain cut through her arms and shoulders as she felt them being pulled out of their sockets. She opened her eyes for one last look at Killian, and at the same moment, Kirsi released her.

Time slowed to a crawl.

Callum shouted Kirsi's name as she placed a foot inside the door. The hold around Ariah's waist loosened. Callum gave a final yank, and Ariah surged forward. She and Callum grabbed for Kirsi at the same time, both seizing her as the three of them broke free of the cottage.

They fell with a bone-jarring thud onto the ground.

Kirsi wouldn't look at either of them, while Callum couldn't take his eyes off her. Ariah scrambled up and raced to Killian. She didn't get two steps before the sounds of battle drew her up short. She spun and saw her friends in combat with other Druids. Ariah glanced at Killian to find Jasper standing over his unconscious body, protecting him.

The ground next to her exploded as magic hit near her feet. Ariah raised her hands to block another strike and walked up between Bronwyn and Elodie. She dropped to one knee and released a shot of magic toward the opponent. Corann's battle lessons came back to her as she took down foe after foe. At first, she only wanted to maim, but it soon became apparent that it was kill or be killed.

Ariah had no idea how long she fought. Exhaustion weighed heavily on her, but she kept going, fighting side by side with her friends until there was no one left. She stood looking over the field, her hands still raised as she waited for another to pop out of the grass.

"It's over," Elodie said.

The adrenaline that had kept Ariah going sputtered quickly. She dropped her arms to her sides and looked at the bodies of the dead. They had families somewhere who would wonder what'd happened to them.

Bronwyn released a long breath. "It was hard to see them my first time. It's still hard. But war always is. We didn't ask for this. But if we don't stand against them, who will?"

"I'd like to know what it is about us they hate to such a degree they'd come here to kill us," Ariah said.

Elodie shook her head. "I doubt we'll ever know."

"I know something that will make your night better," Bronwyn said.

Ariah met her gaze to find her friend grinning. Bronwyn hooked a thumb over her shoulder. Ariah turned and spotted Killian on his feet. Her breath left her in a rush. Their gazes locked. The tears she had held back streamed down her cheeks as she ran to him. He met her halfway, and they fell into each other's arms.

"Is it really you?" he whispered.

She cried, holding him tighter. "It's really me."

He leaned back and cupped her face in his hands, tenderly wiping away her tears with his thumbs. "I knew you would come for me."

"Always."

"I hate to interrupt such a touching scene, but can we get out of here?" Filip asked and held his injured arm against his body. "This bloody place gives me the creeps."

Rhona straightened from looking at one of the dead. "We have a lot to discuss. Let's get to the manor."

Ariah still had so much she needed to say to Killian, but it would have to wait. Besides, she didn't want to be here any longer either. Whatever was in that house might get through. She slid her hand into Killian's, and they walked to the vehicle Callum had driven. The sun was cresting the horizon when she sat beside Killian in the back seat.

"Do you have any injuries?" she asked.

Killian shook his head, his lips twisting. "I do have a newfound fear of bugs, however."

"I saw them when I was getting you out," Callum said.

"They were all over me."

Ariah felt Killian shiver and couldn't imagine the horrors he had been through.

Killian slapped Callum on the shoulder. "Thanks for coming for me, mate. Thank you both."

Callum nodded. Ariah noticed the two share a look in the

rearview mirror before Killian settled back against the seat. He smiled and brought her against him to kiss her temple. Callum started the engine and drove away.

A long moment passed with Killian's gaze on the rising sun before he said, "I didn't think I was going to see another day. How did you find me?"

Callum shrugged. "Magic and luck."

"Did the shadow say anything to you? Did you see anyone?" Ariah asked.

Killian shook his head. "Nothing and no one. Well, except for the bugs." He shuddered. Then his head swung to her as he looked between her and Callum. "Tell me everything that happened."

Ariah didn't want to share that yet, not so soon after the ordeal, but she did, and as succinctly as possible. When she finished, Killian looked as if he might be ill.

"It almost took you," he said.

Ariah covered the hand that rested on his thigh with hers. "It didn't."

"But it could have." Killian looked at Callum, who hadn't said anything. "What was it? What did you and Kirsi see?"

Callum was silent for a long time. Finally, he said, "Evil."

No one said anything after that. They were the first to arrive at Carwood Manor, but none of them exited the vehicle.

"I owe you both," Killian said.

Ariah smiled. "It's what we do for those we love."

"You're my friend. I doona have many of those." Callum turned in his seat to look at them. "You owe me nothing."

Ariah put her hand on Callum's arm. "I hope you consider me your friend, too." She jerked her chin to the manor. "Everyone in our group. Because we are."

"Aye," Callum said softly. He turned back to look at the house pensively. "We need to watch Kirsi."

"That we do," Ariah said.

Callum swallowed and looked down. He parted his lips as if he were going to say more, then seemed to change his mind. He exited the car as Rhona and the others pulled in. Ariah and Killian watched him.

"He was beat up when he arrived to look for you," Ariah said.

Killian followed Callum with his gaze until he entered the manor. "We'll keep an eye on him, as well."

"Aye. We certainly will."

Killian held out his hand. "I love you."

"I love you, too."

He frowned and put a finger to her lips. "Let me talk."

Ariah nodded and pulled his hand from her mouth to hold it in her lap.

"I had a lot of time to think while I was being held. About you, about us." He paused. "About this war."

She looked away as dread soured her stomach. This was what she had feared; that her world would be too much for him to handle. And she didn't blame him. It was a lot. Even for her, and she had been born into it.

"Your world is dangerous in ways I can't even begin to fathom."

Ariah closed her eyes, waiting for him to say the words that would end their relationship again.

"I can't protect you as a Druid would. I don't have magic." His finger gently nudged her chin up until she met his gaze. "But I will defend you with my dying breath. I'm more sure than ever of what

I want, and that's you. As long as we're together, I have everything I'll ever need."

Ariah was overjoyed at his words. She should just leave things alone, but she couldn't. She needed him to know the realities of what it meant for him to be with her. "We're in the middle of a war. And you were nearly killed."

"As were you."

"It might happen again."

He nodded, his expression serious. "I know. And we'll deal with it if it does."

"What about your family?"

"I've made my choice."

Her gut twisted painfully when she thought about Brian. "There's something I need to tell you about your father."

"Jasper told me."

"I'm so very sorry."

"Me, too." Killian leaned down and softly placed his lips on hers. He lifted his head, his olive-green eyes studying her face. "I came to Skye to beg for your forgiveness for what happened in the past."

"You don't need to do that."

"I do," he insisted. "I'm sorry. I'm sorry for not listening to you and not seeing how important your home was. I'm sorry for thinking only of what I wanted. But mostly, I'm sorry for letting you go. I should've fought for you."

She placed her hand on his chest. "I'm sorry for not telling you who I really was. And for walking away."

"You're forgiven."

"So are you," she said with a smile.

He put his hand over hers. "I came to Skye for something else, too."

"Oh?" she asked, brows raised.

"I came for you."

"You've always had me."

He smiled before taking her lips in a searing kiss.

EPILOGUE

Five days later…

Ariah wiped the new windows clean while Ruby danced around the shop with the broom, using it as a mic as she sang to a song on the radio. Ariah grinned at her friend. Everything had changed, but sometimes, life had to be shaken up in order to give someone what they needed the most. In her case it was Killian.

She would be lying if she said she didn't fear what was headed their way in the war. Despite many attempts by all of them—even Rhona—the only thing they had gotten out of Kirsi and Callum about the being that had grabbed Ariah was that it was evil. She might not have seen it, but she *had* felt it, and evil was an apt word for it. Whatever Callum and Kirsi had seen had changed them profoundly.

Ariah forgot about them when Killian's Audi pulled into the spot next to hers. She tossed aside the towel and hurried outside.

He unfurled from the SUV and wrapped his arms around her in greeting. They shared a lingering kiss.

"You're back sooner than I expected," she said.

He shrugged, smiling. "What can I say? I missed you."

She glanced at the SUV. "I thought you were supposed to pack up your flat."

"I brought the things I wanted. They're in the back. I want to start over with you."

Ariah gave him another kiss before leaning back and asking, "How did the funeral go?"

Killian had wanted her to go to support him at such a trying time, but they'd ultimately decided it would be better if he went alone. He needed to pack up his flat and make sure his mother knew that he wouldn't be returning to work in the firm in Ireland. They hadn't been keen on letting him go, but they had offered him the option of having an office on Skye.

"As good as can be expected. The talk with Mum was much harder."

Ariah inwardly winced. "I can imagine."

"It started badly but ended on a good note. She wants to visit soon to meet you."

"I'd love that."

Killian pulled her against him and faced the store. "I was hoping you'd say that. She's planning on coming next month. She's in love with the teas you sent."

"I'll send her whatever she wants whenever she wants."

"Get ready to start shipping more than that because she shared some with her friends. They're lined up and ready to place orders as soon as your store opens again." He looked at the windows. "How soon will that be?"

"Sooner than expected, actually. The windows got here two weeks early. You wouldn't know anything about that, would you?" she asked, her brows raised.

Killian grinned. "Actually, I do."

"I knew it was you."

"It wasn't."

Ariah frowned. "What do you mean?"

"When I told Mum she'd have to wait on the teas because of the damage to the shop, she made a few calls."

"What?" Ariah asked, stunned.

He shrugged, his smile widening. "I also made a few on your behalf, acting as your attorney. The insurance will get its payout to you within the week."

"I don't know what to say."

His smile dropped. "Did I overstep?"

"Nay. I'm just used to doing things on my own. Thank you. I never would've thought to ask for your assistance. And I need to repay your mum."

"She won't accept it. She can be pretty stubborn." Killian faced her. "Mum apologized for her part in the past. Our talk was good, and I think, going forward, we can have the kind of relationship we both need."

Ariah put her hands in his. "That's what love does."

"What?"

"It conquers all."

"Then no one stands a chance against us," he said with a grin.

Ariah let out a startled cry when he swung her up into his arms and carried her into the shop as Ruby held open the door. There were new beginnings everywhere. And to think she had almost refused to hear anything Killian said.

She brought his head down for a kiss. "Here's to us," she whispered.

"To us," Killian replied with a sexy smile. "And our life together."

Elias closed the car door and looked at the house. Elodie met him at the front of the car.

"We don't have to do this," she said.

Elias glanced at her. "We do."

"All right, then," she said with a sigh.

They walked up and rang the bell. A few moments later, Edie opened the door. Elias watched her carefully. She wore a smile, but it wasn't reflected in her eyes. It was more just polite, the kind a homeowner gave strangers at the door.

"Do you have time to talk?" Elodie asked their sister.

Edie glanced between them before opening the door wider so they could enter. Elias noticed the difference immediately. Some furniture was missing, and a few walls were bare. What furnishings remained had been moved around.

"It was time for a change," Edie said.

Elias met her gaze, searching for the sister he knew. But he realized he didn't know Edie. He had been absent for years from both his sisters' lives. He had gotten to know Elodie, but he had made the mistake of believing that Edie was the same as she had always been. No one stayed the same.

"What is it you want to talk about?" Edie asked.

Elodie put her hands into her back pockets. "We wanted to see how you were. We've all neglected to spend quality time with each other. You made a point the other day over tea that we weren't close anymore. You were right." Elodie glanced at Elias. "I realized I missed the bond the three of us had when we were kids. We all have significant others, and you also have the kids, but—"

"Nay, I don't."

Elias frowned and exchanged a look with Elodie.

"Um…you don't what?" Elodie asked.

Edie walked around the island in the kitchen and took out a bottle of white from the fridge. She poured herself a glass and leaned her hip against the island. "I don't have a significant other. Trevor and I are done."

"What did he do?" Elias demanded. Even though he feared Edie might be caught up on the wrong side of the war, she was still his sister. He knew how much she loved Trevor, and if they were over, then it had to be Trevor's fault.

Edie took a sip. "He couldn't keep it in his pants."

"I'm so sorry," Elodie told her.

Edie shrugged. "Oh, don't worry about me. I'm fine. The kids are taking it pretty hard, though."

Elias frowned as he took another look at the house. "Where is Trevor? I'd like to have a word with him."

"I packed his stuff and told him to get out. I don't know where he is."

It sounded like what anyone would say in that situation. Why then didn't Elias believe her?

Balladyn was working a crossword puzzle when the car pulled up. He tucked the pen into the book and closed it, setting it aside as he got to his feet. "We've got company," he called out.

A cabinet slammed at the back of the house. Rhona had needed to focus her energies on something and had decided organizing every room was the way to do it. It was better than seeing her pace, her anxiety rising with each passing day that they still didn't have any answers to what had happened at the cottage.

She walked around the corner, twisting her red hair into a bun atop her head. "Who is it?"

No sooner had she asked than she opened the door. Balladyn came up behind her and grinned when he saw Esther and Henry. The siblings were the last of an ancient line who policed the Druids. The TruthSeeker and the JusticeBringer, respectively.

"We heard about the latest and thought we'd offer our assistance," Esther said.

Henry added, "If you want it."

"Oh, we want it," Rhona said. "Please, come in."

Behind the siblings were two others. Balladyn wasn't surprised to see Nikolai. The Dragon King was mated to Esther. It was the sight of the Dragon Queen, Melisse, that brought him up short.

"Don't worry, Reaper, I'll leave some of the bad guys for you," Melisse said with a grin.

Henry chuckled and wrapped his arm around her. "At least, we'll try."

"About time the two of you worked things out," Balladyn said.

Esther turned to Rhona. "Speaking of working things out. Where can we help?"

"London," Rhona said.

"Bloody hell." Finn gaped at the sprawling mansion as they walked up the steps.

Carlyle wasn't sure what he was doing here. He had searched his family's country estate three times in hopes of finding something about his father. Then, he'd gone back to London and done the same there to no avail.

"Are you sure about this?" Finn asked.

Carlyle banged the knocker. "Nope."

"Well, then. That makes me feel so much better."

Carlyle ignored Finn's sarcastic words. He hadn't been able to sleep or eat. He knew without a doubt that his father was in grave danger, and he was at his wits' end. Mason was his last hope before he did something stupid like going after the elders.

"Lord Oliver," Billings greeted when he opened the door. "It has been years. It's nice to see you. Please, do come in."

Carlyle walked into the house with Finn on his heels. Everything looked the same, but Mason wasn't. That much was clear by his about-face when it came to his sister, Ferne. Carlyle didn't know if the London Druids had gotten to him or if it was something else.

"I was hoping to see Mason," Carlyle told the butler.

Billings nodded. "Follow me."

The sound of their footsteps echoed in the massive foyer. Billings took them to the left where Mason's office was. The estate looked the same, but it *felt* different. Cold. Silent. So very different from the times he had spent here with Mason, Ferne, and their parents. There had always been music playing. And laughter. So much laughter.

His thoughts returned to the present when Billings opened the door and announced them. Mason stood behind his desk, his gaze locked on Carlyle. Carlyle's steps faltered when his gaze landed on the woman standing beside his old friend. It was the same female who had been waiting for him and Finn in his father's study.

"That'll be all, Billings," Mason stated, glaring daggers at Carlyle.

Finn stepped up behind him and whispered, "I really think this is a bad idea."

Carlyle walked into the office. "Tell me where my father is."

"You're not welcome here." Mason took a step forward, but the woman put a hand on his chest to stop him.

She looked at Carlyle and said, "Just a second, darling."

"What the fuck?" Finn said behind him.

Mason's gaze moved over Carlyle's shoulder to Finn, but to his surprise, Mason didn't move an inch.

"He doesn't know where your father is," the woman said.

Mason moved her hand from his chest but kept a hold of it. "Devon, don't bother."

"Definitely bother." Carlyle was done playing games. "This is my fucking family we're talking about. I want to know where my father is, and I demand to know now."

Mason walked around his desk. "You dare to talk of family!? You took Ferne from me."

"You lost her all on your own," Carlyle retorted.

The anger surged, and the two went after each other. Mason got in a punch, but so did Carlyle. Then they were dragged apart.

Finn had him by the arms, holding him back while Devon stood between him and Mason.

"Get out," Mason stated as he wiped his bloodied lip. "And never come back."

Carlyle jerked his arms from Finn and smoothed down his shirt. Then he turned on his heel to walk away.

"I don't know where your father is, but whatever happens to him, it's your fault!" Mason yelled.

Glasgow

Kurt lifted his final rep and racked the bar on the weight bench. His muscles screamed in protest as he sat up and wiped the sweat from his face with a towel before taking a long drink of water.

The warehouse had been a good find three years earlier, and he'd worked to get it set up perfectly. He'd situated the area where he lived and worked in the back corner of the top floor. There were tens of thousands of pounds worth of computers along the wall, as well as software for the many and various things his teammates needed of him.

He stood up from the bench and walked to a picture of him and Sabryn with their arms around each other. It was during a fall carnival. That was when things had been good. Before he'd fucked it all up. As far as she was concerned, she had cut him out of her life. Neither she nor any of the other Knights had any clue as to his true identity.

And he never intended to tell her.

He had skills the Knights needed. At least, it had started that way. But it had quickly changed. He wanted to be a part of those changing things for the better. If he came clean and told Sabryn the truth, she would… Actually, he wasn't sure what she would do, but whatever it was, it wouldn't be good.

So, he kept quiet. And year after year, it became harder and harder to tell her.

The colored LED lights strung along the top of the wall suddenly changed to orange in warning that the warehouse perimeter had been breached. He looked at the monitors wired into the cameras at the doors and saw individuals coming through both. Kurt zoomed in for a better look at their faces.

"Fuck," he muttered when he recognized a London Druid along with two from Edinburgh.

He flipped the switch that would wipe the computers and blow up the warehouse before running toward the exit crafted for just such a hasty escape. He scaled up to the roof and then slid down a hidden pipe. The moment his feet hit the pavement, he spun and ran to where a sentry stood on lookout. Kurt thrust magic into the guard's back, which propelled him forward and slammed his head into the concrete, killing him instantly.

Kurt was two blocks away when the warehouse exploded.

He didn't stop running until he came to the go bag he had stashed. He slung it over his shoulder and sent a text to a buddy that would trigger new mobiles to be sent to the Knights. They had been compromised, and he needed to figure out how.

Thank you for reading **STILL OF THE NIGHT**. I hope you enjoyed the story! I love the Skye Druid world, and it's always so much fun to return to it.

If you want more Skye Druid stories, than be sure and grab the next book in the series, **BLOOD SKYE**.

BUY BLOOD SKYE NOW
at www.DonnaGrant.com

* * *

To find out when new books release
SIGN UP FOR MY NEWSLETTER today at
https://www.tinyurl.com/DonnaGrantNews

Join my Facebook group, Donna Grant Groupies, for exclusive giveaways and sneak peeks of future books.
https://www.facebook.com/groups/DGGroupies

* * *

Keep reading for a peek of BLOOD SKYE…

EXCERPT OF THE NEXT SKYE DRUID BOOK

BLOOD SKYE, SKYE DRUIDS SERIES, BOOK 6

New York Times and *USA Today* bestselling author Donna Grant returns with another seductive novel in the magical and dangerous world of the Skye Druids.

Keep reading for an excerpt of BLOOD SKYE…

BLOOD SKYE EXCERPT

Light rain pelted Carlyle's oilskin jacket. His breath puffed from his lips as he watched the side entrance to the estate from behind bushes.

"Are you sure about this?"

Carlyle looked to the Irishman beside him. He and Finn had been through a lot together. All of the Knights had. But this was his mission. Not the Knights. And not Finn's. "I told you to return to Skye."

"When do I ever do what you want?" Finn asked with a grin, his deep brown eyes sparking with amusement. "Besides, someone needs to watch your arse. You certainly aren't doing it."

They had been over this argument a dozen times in the last twenty-four hours. Carlyle should've known Finn wouldn't leave. And he was glad of it. Something was dreadfully wrong at the estate. Not just the manor. There was Mason. His long-time friend wasn't himself. Mason had even cut off his sister, Ferne, after she went to the Isle of Skye.

"There may be better ways of getting to Devon," Finn said.

Just thinking about her made Carlyle see red. She was behind his father's disappearance. Add that to the fact she had embroiled herself in Mason's life, and it confirmed his suspicions that the London Druids were pulling the strings.

Carlyle glanced at the manor. "She's here. That means we have an opportunity."

Headlights bounced across the land as an old Range Rover pulled into the drive of the cottage. A man exited the vehicle and made his way to the door before entering.

"Come on," Carlyle said as he bolted from the bushes, keeping low.

He moved around the side of the cottage and stood at the back door. A light was flipped on inside, spilling its glow out into the night and illuminating him. His gaze met those of the man inside.

The door was unlocked and hastily swung open. "Quick. Inside," Billings ordered.

Carlyle entered the kitchen with Finn behind him. Water dripped from them onto the floor while the estate's butler checked outside before closing and locking the door.

"Did anyone see you?" Billings asked.

Carlyle studied the aging servant from his impeccable stature and dress to his neatly trimmed brown hair with gray at the temples. Billings wasn't just the butler. He was more of a second father to both Ferne and Mason when their parents died in a plane crash. "No," he finally answered.

"Took you long enough to get here."

Finn looked between them. "Excuse me?"

"I suspected Carlyle would want my help," Billings said.

Finn snorted. "I'm not sure we should accept it. After all, you didn't let Ferne talk to her brother."

"I know." The butler sighed, his shoulders stooping. It made him look decades older than he was. "It was Lord Mason's orders. I tried to dissuade him, but he wouldn't listen to reason. If I had gone against him, he threatened to let me go."

"Which wouldn't give us a way to him," Carlyle said.

Billings nodded. "Exactly. He kept a lot from Lady Ferne. She had no idea how deep he had dug into their parents' death."

"She knew some of it," Carlyle said. "Both her and Mason believe they were murdered."

Billings motioned to the table. "Sit. I'll make us some tea. And you are?"

"Finn," the Irishman answered at the question. "Friend to both Carlyle and Ferne."

"It is a pleasure then," Billings replied.

Finn wasted no time in shedding his coat and sinking into a chair. Carlyle moved slower, letting his gaze skim over the kitchen and Billings.

"Lord Mason told his sister just enough to satisfy her. He had been cautious while she was in the country for fear of what might happen to her." Billings put water in the kettle and set it on the stove

"As he should have been," Carlyle stated.

Billings pulled three cups and saucers from the cupboard and put them on the table along with sugar and milk. As he did, he said, "Yes, well. Be that as it may, things fell into place when London demanded Lady Ferne leave the city. The moment she mentioned Skye, he knew that was the answer."

"What right do the London Druids even have in telling someone if they can live there or not?" Finn asked.

Carlyle ran a hand over his jaw. "That's the power they wield." He looked at Billings. "Ferne going to Skye went against everything both her and Mason were taught."

"But she was safe. As formidable as London might be, they don't hold a candle to Skye," Billings stated. "Yet."

Finn shook his head. "Bloody hell."

"The moment Lady Ferne was gone, Lord Mason went full throttle into the investigation," Billings said.

Carlyle sat up and put his forearms on the table. "I gather that took him back to London."

"It did, indeed."

"And after?"

Billings' dark eyes dropped to the floor. "He returned as you've seen him. He's not the same man I've watched grow up since birth. I've served the Crawfords since I was eleven. Fifty-five years of my life I've spent here. They are my family. The plane crash devastated Mason and Ferne, but at least they had each other."

"And the woman? Devon?" Carlyle asked.

Billings went to the kettle when it began to whistle. He poured the boiling water into a teapot. "She showed up alone before Lord Mason returned from his most recent trip to London. At first, I didn't think he knew her, but she said something to him. From then on, they've been inseparable."

"Are they sharing the same bed?" Finn asked.

Billings shrugged as he brought the teapot to the table and poured into their cups. "She has a room connected to his. I assume they are."

Carlyle looked at Finn. "Why does that matter?"

"Just wondering," the Irishman said with a shrug.

BUY BLOOD SKYE NOW
at www.DonnaGrant.com

ABOUT THE AUTHOR

New York Times and *USA Today* bestselling author Donna Grant® has been praised for her "totally addictive" and "unique and sensual" stories.

She's written more than one hundred novels spanning multiple genres of romance including the bestselling Dragon Kings® series that features a thrilling combination of Druids, Fae, and immortal Highlanders who are dark, dangerous, and irresistible. She lives in Texas with her dog and a cat.

www.DonnaGrant.com
www.MotherofDragonsBooks.com

facebook.com/AuthorDonnaGrant
instagram.com/dgauthor
bookbub.com/authors/donna-grant
goodreads.com/donna_grant
pinterest.com/donnagrant1